PEPPER WINTERS

FOREVER

NEW YORK BOSTON

This book is a work of fiction. Names, characters, places, and incidents are the product of the author's imagination or are used fictitiously. Any resemblance to actual events, locales, or persons, living or dead, is coincidental.

Forever
Hachette Book Group
1290 Avenue of the Americas
New York, NY 10104

www.HachetteBookGroup.com

Printed in the United States of America

RRD-C

First edition: July 2015
10 9 8 7 6 5 4 3 2 1

Forever is an imprint of Grand Central Publishing.
The Forever name and logo are trademarks of Hachette Book Group, Inc.

Library of Congress Cataloging-in-Publication Data

Winters, Pepper.
Ruin & rule / Pepper Winters. — First edition.
pages cm.
ISBN 978-1-4555-8933-3 (paperback) — ISBN 978-1-4789-0670-4 (audio download) — ISBN 978-1-4555-8934-0 (ebook) I. Single women—fiction. 2. Man-woman relationships—Fiction. I. Title. II. Title: Ruin and rule.
PS3623.I677R86 2015
813'.6—dc23

2015010924

RUIN & RULE

PURE CORRUPTION MC

For those who were with me from the beginning.
You know who you are.

Prologue

We met in a nightmare.

The in-between world where time had no power over rhyme, reason, or connection. We met. We stared. We knew.

There was no distortion from the outside world. No right or wrong. No confusion or battles from hearts and minds.

Just us. In our silent dreamworld.

That nightmare became our home. Planting ghosts, raising fantasies. Entwined together in our happily skewed reality.

We fell in love. We fell hard.

In those fleeting seconds of our nightmare, we lived an eternity.

But then we woke up.

And it was over.

Chapter One

I always believed life would grant rewards to those most worthy. I was fucking naïve. Life doesn't reward—it ruins. It ruins those most deserving and takes everything. It takes everything all while watching any remaining goodness rot to hate.

—*Kill*

Darkness.

That was my world now. Literally and physically.

The back of my skull hurt from being knocked unconscious. My wrists and shoulders ached from lying on my back with my hands tied behind me.

Nothing was broken—at least it didn't feel that way—but everything was bruised. The fuzziness receded wisp by wisp, parting the clouds of sleep, trying to shed light on what'd happened. But there *was* no light. My eyes blinked at the endless darkness from the mask tied around my head. Anxiety twisted my stomach at having such a fundamental gift taken away.

I didn't move, but mentally catalogued my body from the tips of my toes to the last strand of hair on my head. My jaw and tongue ached from the foul rag stuffed in my mouth and my nose permitted a shallow stream of oxygen to enter—just enough to keep me alive.

Fear tried to claw its way through my mind, but I shoved it away. I deliberately suppressed panic in order to assess my predicament rather than lose myself to terror.

Fear never helps, only hinders.

My senses came back, creeping tentatively, as if afraid whoever had stolen me would notice their return.

Sound: the squeak of brakes, the creak of a vehicle settling from motion to stopping.

Touch: the skin on my right forearm stung, throbbing with a mixture of soreness and sharpness. A burn perhaps?

Smell: dank rotting vegetables and the astringent, pungent scent of fear—but it wasn't mine. It was theirs.

It wasn't just me being kidnapped.

My heart flurried, drinking in their terror. It made my breath quicken and legs itch to run. Forcing myself to ignore the outside world, I focused inward. Clutching my inner strength where calmness was a need rather than a luxury.

I refused to lose myself in a fog of tears. Desperation was a curse and I wouldn't succumb, because I had every intention of being prepared for what might happen next.

I hated the sniffles and stifled sobs of others around me. Their bleak sadness tugged at my heartstrings, making me fight with my own preservation, replacing it with concern for theirs.

Get through this, then worry about them.

I didn't think this was a simple opportunistic snatch. Whoever had stolen me planned it. The hunch grew stronger as I searched inside for any liquor remnants or the smell of cigarettes.

Had I been at a party? Nightclub?

Nothing.

I hadn't been stupid or reckless. *I think...*

No hint or clue as to where I'd been or what I'd been doing when they'd come for me.

I wriggled, trying to move away from the stench. My bound wrists protested, stinging as the rope around them gnawed into my flesh like twine-beasts. My ribs bellowed, along with my head. There was no give in my restraints. I stopped trying to move, preserving my energy.

I tried to swallow.

No saliva.

I tried to speak.

No voice.

I tried to remember what happened.

I tried to remember…

Panic.

Nothing.

I can't remember.

"Get up, bitch," a man said. Something jabbed me in the ribs. "Won't tell you again. *Get.*"

I froze as my mind hurtled me from present to past.

I'll miss you so much," she wailed, hugging me tighter.

"I'm not dying, you know." I tried to untangle myself, looking over my shoulder at the FINAL CALL *flashing for my flight. I hated being late for anything. Let alone my one chance at escaping and finding out the truth once and for all.*

"Call me the moment you get there."

"Promise." I drew a cross over my heart—

The memory shattered as my horizontal body suddenly went vertical in one swoop.

Who was that girl? Why did I have no memory of it ever happening?

"I said get up, bitch." The man breathed hard in my ear, sending a waft of reeking breath over me. The blindfold stole my sight, but it left my nose woefully unprotected.

Unfortunately.

My captor shoved me forward. The ground was steady beneath my feet. The sickness plaiting with my confusion faded, leaving me cold.

My legs stumbled in the direction he wanted me to go. I hated shuffling in the darkness, not knowing where I came from or where I was being herded. There were no sounds of comfort or smothered snickers. This wasn't a masquerade.

This was real.

This is real.

My heart thudded harder, fear slipping through my defenses. But full-blown terror remained elusive. Slippery like a silver fish, darting on the outskirts of my mind. It was there but fleeting, keeping me clear-headed and strong.

I was grateful for that. Grateful that I maintained what dignity I had left—remaining strong even in the face of the unknown terrors lurking on the other side of my blindfold.

Moans and whimpers of other women grew in decibels as men ordered them to follow the same path I walked. Either death row or salvation, I had no choice but to inch my way forward, leaving my forgotten past behind.

I willed snippets to come back. I begged the puzzlement of my past to slot into place, so I could make sense of this horrible world I'd awoken in.

But my mind was locked to me. A fortress withholding everything I wished to know.

The pushing stopped. So did I.

Big mistake.

"Move." A cuff to the back of my head sent me wheeling forward. I didn't stop again. My bare feet traversed . . . wood?

Bare feet?

Where are my shoes?

The missing knowledge twisted my stomach.

Where did I come from?

How did I end up here?

What's my name?

It wasn't the terror of the unknown future that stole my false calmness. It was the fear of losing my very self. They'd stolen everything. My triumphs, my trespasses, my accomplishments and failures.

How could I deal with this new world if I didn't know what skills I had to stay alive? How could I hope to defeat my enemy when my mind revolted and locked me out?

Who am I?

To have who I was deleted... It was unthinkable.

"Faster, bitch." Something cold wedged against my spine, pushing me onward. With my hands behind my back, I shuffled faster, negotiating the ground as best I could for dips or trips.

"Step down." The man grabbed my bound wrists, giving me something to lean against as my toes navigated the small steps before me.

"Again."

I obeyed.

"Last one."

I managed the small staircase without falling flat on my face.

My face.

What do I look like?

A loud scraping noise sounded before me. I shied back, bumping against a feminine form. The woman behind me cried out—the first verbal sound of another.

"Move." The pressure on my lower back came again, and I obeyed. Inching forward until the stuffy air of old vegetables and must was replaced by... copper and metallic... *blood*?

Why... why is that so familiar?

I gasped as my mind free-fell into another memory.

"I don't think I can do this." I darted away, throwing up in the rubbish bin in the classroom. The unique stench of blood curdled my stomach.

"Don't overthink it. It's not what you're doing to the animal to make it bleed. It's what you're doing to make it live." My professor shook his head, waiting for me to swill out my mouth and return white-faced and queasy to the operation in progress.

My heart splintered like a broken piece of glass, reflecting the compassion and responsibility I felt for such an innocent creature. This little puppy that'd been dumped in a plastic bag to die after being shot with BB gun pellets. He'd survive only if I mastered the skills to stem his internal bleeding and embrace the vocation I was called to do.

Inhaling the scent of blood, I let it invade my nostrils, scald my throat, and impregnate my soul. I drank its coppery essence. I drenched myself in the smell of the creature's life force until it no longer affected me.

Picking up a scalpel, I said, "I'm ready—"

"Holy fuck!" The man guiding me forward suddenly whacked the base of my spine. The hard pain shoved me forward and I tripped.

"Wire—get me fucking reinforcements. He's started a mother-fucking war!"

Wind and body motion swarmed me as men charged from behind. The darkness I lived in suddenly came alive with sound.

Bullets flew, impaling themselves into the metal sides of the vehicle I'd just stepped from. Pings and ricochets echoed in my ear. Curses bellowed; moans of pain threaded like a breeze.

Someone grabbed my arm, swinging me to the side. "Get down!" The inertia of his throw knocked me off balance. With my wrists bound together, I had nothing to grab with, no way to protect myself from falling.

I fell.

My stomach swooped as I tumbled off a small platform and smashed against the ground.

Dirt, damp grass, and moldy leaves replaced the stench of blood, cutting through the cloying sharpness of spilled metallic. My mouth opened, gasping in pain. Blades of grass tickled my lips as my cheek stuck to wet mud.

My shoulder screamed with agony, but I ignored the new injury. My mind clung to the unlocked memory. The fleeting recollection of my profession.

I'm a vet.

The sense of homecoming and security that one little snippet brought was priceless. My soul snarled for more, suddenly ravenous for missing information.

I skipped straight from fumbling uncertainty into starvation for *more.*

Tell me! Show me. Who am I?

I searched inside for more clues. But it was like trying to grab on to an elusive dream, fading faster and faster the harder I chased.

I couldn't remember anything about medicine or how to heal. All I knew was I'd been trained to embrace the scent of blood. I wasn't afraid of it. I didn't faint or suffer sickness at the sight of it pouring from an open wound.

That tiniest knowledge was enough to settle my prickling nerves and focus on the outside world again.

Battle cries. Men screaming. Men growling. The dense thuds of fists on flesh and the horrible deflection of gunshots.

I couldn't understand. Had I fallen through time and entered an alternate dimension?

Another body landed on top of mine.

I cried out, winded from a sharp poke of an elbow to my ribs.

The figure rolled away, crying softly. Feminine.

Why aren't I crying?

I once again searched for fear. It wasn't natural not to be afraid. I'd woken up alone, stolen, and thrown into the middle of a war, yet I wasn't hyperventilating or panicked.

My calmness was like a drug, oozing over me, muting the sharp starkness of my situation. It was bearable if I embraced courage and the knowledge that I was strong.

My hands balled, grateful for the thought. I didn't know who I was, but it didn't matter, because the person who I was in this moment mattered the most.

I had to remain segmented, so I could get through whatever was about to happen. All I had was gut instinct, quiet strength, and rationality. Everything else had been taken.

"Stop fighting, you fucking idiots!"

The loud growl rumbled like an earthquake, hushing the battle in one fell swoop. Whoever had spoken had power.

Immense power. Colossal power.

A shiver darted over my skin.

"What the fuck happened? Have you lost your goddamn lovin' mind?" a man yelled.

A sound of a short scuffle, then the fresh whiff of tilled dirt graced my nose.

"It's done. Throw down your weapons and bend a fucking knee." The same earthquake rumbled. The weight of his command pushed me harder against the damp ground.

"I'm not bending nothing, you asshole. You aren't my Prez!"

"I am. Have been for the past four years."

"You're not. You're his bitch. Don't think his power is yours."

Another fight—muffled fists and kicks. It ended swiftly with a painful groan.

The earthquake voice came again. "Open your eyes and follow the red fucking river. Your chosen—the one you hand-picked to slaughter me and take over the Club—he's dead. Did you ever stop to think Wallstreet made me Prez for a fucking reason?"

Another moan.

"*I'm* the chosen one. I'm the one who knows the family secrets, absorbed the legacy, and earned his way into power. You don't know shit. *Nobody* does. So bend a fucking knee and respect."

Another tremor ran down my back.

Silence for a time, apart from the squelch of boots and heavy breathing. Then a barely muttered curse. "You'll die. One way or another, we won't put up with a Dagger as a Prez. We're the Corrupts, goddammit. Having a traitor rule us is a fucking joke."

"*I'm* the traitor? The man who obeys your leader? Who guides in his stead? *I'm* the traitor when you try and rally my brothers in a war?" A heavy thud of a fist connected with flesh. "No... I'm not. You are."

My mind raced, sucking up noises and forming wild conclusions of what happened before me. Was this World War Three? Was this the apocalypse of the life I couldn't remember? No matter how I pieced it together, I couldn't make sense of anything.

The air was thick with anticipation. I didn't know how many men stood before me. I didn't know how many corpses littered the ground, or how such violence could be permitted in the world I used to know. But I did know the cease-fire was fragile and any moment it would explode.

A single threat slithered through the grass like a snake. "I'll kill you, motherfucker. Mark my words. The true Corrupts are just waiting to take you out."

The gentle foot-thuds of someone large vibrated through the ground. "The Corrupts haven't existed for four fucking years. The moment I took the seat, it's been Pure Corruption all the way. And you're not fucking pure enough for this Club. You're done."

I flinched as the sulfuric boom of a gun ripped through the stagnant air.

A crash as a body fell lifeless to the grass. A soft puff of a soul escaping.

Murder.

Murder was committed right before me.

The inherent need to nurture and heal—the part of me that was as steadfast as the beat of my heart—wept with regret.

Death was something I'd fought against on a daily basis, but now I was weaponless.

I hated that a life had been stolen right before me. That I hadn't been able to stop it.

I'm a witness.

And yet, I'd witnessed nothing.

I'd been privy to a battle but seen nothing. Knew no one. I would never be able to tell who shot whom, or who was right and who was wrong.

My hands shook, even though I managed to stay eerily calm. *Am I in shock?* And if I was, how did I cure myself?

The woman beside me curled into a ball, her knees digging into my side. My first reaction was to repel away from the touch. I didn't know who was friend or foe. But a second reaction came quickly; the urge to share my calmness—to let her know that no matter what happened, she wasn't alone. We faced the same future—no matter how grim.

Voices cascaded over us, whispers mainly, quickly spoken orders. Every sound was heightened. Being robbed of sight made my body seek other ways in which to find clues.

"Get rid of the bodies before daybreak."

"We'll go back and make sure we're still covered."

"Send out the word. It's over. The Prez won—no anarchy today."

Each voice was distinct but my ears twitched only for one: the earthquake rumble that set my skin quivering like quicksand.

He hadn't spoken since he'd condemned someone to death and pulled the trigger. Every second of not hearing him made my heart trip faster. I wasn't afraid. I should be. I should be immobile with fear. But he invoked something in me—something primal. Just like I knew I was female and a vet, I knew his voice meant something. Every inch of me tensed, waiting for him to speak. It was wrong to crave the voice of a killer, but it was the only thing I wanted.

Needed.

I need to know who he is.

Wet mud sucked loudly against boots as they came closer.

The woman whimpered, but I angled my chin toward the sound, wishing my eyes were uncovered.

I wanted to see. I wanted to witness the carnage before me. Because it was carnage. The stench of death confirmed it. It was morbid to want to see such destruction, but without my sight all of this seemed like a terrible nightmare. Nothing was grounded—completely nonsensical and far too strange.

I needed proof that this was real.

I needed concrete evidence that I wasn't mad. That my body was intact, even if my mind was not.

I sucked in a breath as warm fingers touched my cheek, angling my face upward and out of the mud. Strong hands caressed the back of my skull, fumbling with my blindfold.

The anticipation of finally getting my wish to see made me stay still and cooperative in his hold.

I didn't say a word or move. I just waited. And breathed. And listened.

The man's breath was heavy and low, interspersed with a quick catch of pain. His fingers were swift and sure, but unable to hide the small fumble of agony.

He's hurt.

The pressure of the blindfold suddenly released, trading opaque darkness for a new kind of gloom.

Night sky. Moonshine. Stars above.

Anchors of a world I knew, but no recognition of the dark-shrouded industrial estate where blood gleamed silver-black and corpses dotted the field.

I'm alive.

I can see.

The joy at having my eyes freed came and went as blazing as a comet.

Then my life ended as our gazes connected.

Green to green.

I have green eyes.

Down and down I spiraled, deeper and deeper into his clutches.

My life—past, present, and future—lost all purpose the second I stared into his soul.

The fear I'd been missing slammed into my heart.

I quivered. I quaked.

Something howled deep inside with age-old knowledge.

Every part of me arched toward him, then shied away in terror.

Him.

A nightmare come to life.

A nightmare I wanted to *live.*

If life was a tapestry, already threaded and steadfast, then he was the scissors that cut me free. He tore me out, stole me away, changed the whole prophecy of who I was meant to be.

Jaw-length dark hair, tangled and sweaty, framed a square jaw, straight nose, and full lips. His five-o'clock stubble held remnants of war, streaked with dirt and blood. But it was his eyes that shot a quivering arrow into my heart, spreading his emerald anger.

He froze, his body curving toward mine. Blistering hope flickered across his features. His mouth fell open and love so achingly deep glowed in his gaze. "What—" A leg gave out, making him kneel beside me. His hands shook as he cupped my face, his fingers digging painfully into my cheekbones. "It's not—"

My heart raced. *Yes.*

"You know me," I breathed.

The moment my voice webbed around us, storm clouds rolled over the sunshine in his face, blackening the hope and replacing it with pure hatred.

He changed from watching me like I was his angel to glowering as if I were a despicable devil.

I shivered at the change—at the iciness and hardness. He breathed hard, his chest rising and falling. His lips parted, a rumbling command falling from his mouth to my ears. "Stand up. You're mine now."

When I didn't move, his hand landed on my side. His touch was blocked by clothing but I felt it *everywhere*. He stroked my soul, tickled my heart, and caressed every cell with fingers that despised me.

I couldn't suck in a proper breath.

With a vicious push, he rolled me over, and with a sharp blade sliced my bindings. With effortless power, so thrilling and terrifying, he hauled me to my feet.

I didn't sway. I didn't cry. Only pulled the disgusting gag from my mouth and stared in silence.

I stared up, up, up into his bright green eyes, understanding something I shouldn't understand.

This was him.

My nightmare.

Chapter Two

I couldn't fucking believe it. I *wouldn't* fucking believe it. It was a lie. A horrible, terrible lie to undermine everything I'd done since they'd ruined me. The moment she'd looked into my eyes, I'd wanted so much to give in. To believe in the impossible.

But that naïveté had been beaten out of me.

I wouldn't fall for it again.

—Kill

"Get them in here. Don't have all night."

The roller door on the back of the truck opened again. I blinked, thankful my eyes weren't covered this time and everything was visible.

With steadfast determination, I focused on the next stage of my unknown life. The new destination wasn't a field or grotty industrial estate. It was a large parking garage with low-hanging halogens and rows of motorcycles. A few muscle cars rested toward the back of the cavernous room, but there were more bikes than I could count.

My mind skipped back to the ride here. It hadn't taken long.

After the green-eyed man who'd devoured my soul had unleashed my wrists, he'd picked me up and placed me back on the platform of the truck. He'd grunted in pain, his black shirt torn and soaking with copper, glistening in the night. The scent of blood hovered around him, pumping warm and sickly from whatever wound he tried to hide. He did well keeping his agony hidden. I'd tried to find where the wound originated, but it was impossible in the gloom of the truck's interior.

He also hid his previous reaction to me. His eyes were shuttered, watching me like a perfect stranger. Whatever had happened between us was gone.

But it *had* happened. I wasn't sure of anything else, but that one glimpse between us was deeper, truer, more real than anything I'd experienced.

The knowledge was a constant drumbeat in my bones, a never-ceasing rhythm demanding I find out more.

He knew me.

I knew him.

Of that I was absolute.

I need him alone. I need to know.

The moment I was reloaded into the van, the other women who'd been tossed to the ground were ferried on board, too—their blindfolds off, wrists freed.

I didn't bother looking at or assessing my companions. Everything inside me turned inward—focusing on my own predicament, my lack of memory, and my unswerving knowledge that I had something to do with the ringleader of this mess. As selfish as it was, I had no time for others.

Not yet.

The man with green eyes didn't join us. Instead, he'd growled orders at the three men hovering around us like dogs with a herd of sheep, and threw down the door with an almighty clang.

Darkness.

My heart wedged itself in my throat at once again losing my sight.

No light, or seats, or in-travel refreshments. The women were quiet, even though we had the power to talk once again. Clusters formed, shuffling closer in the blackness. One tried to take my hand, offering consolation in numbers.

I shook her off, preferring to stand alone, holding on to the side of the vehicle and paying attention to the sway of the cumbersome truck. I counted the corners we took. I drew a map inside my head. Not that it made any difference. I would never find my way home.

Where is home?

Exactly.

Even if I did get free, I had no idea where to run to, who to turn to for help. I was a damn mystery, and for now, I was in a place where none of that mattered.

Blinking, I forced myself back to the present and the garage full of motorbikes and muscle cars.

"Move, bitches." A new man with a goatee appeared, chewing a piece of gum loudly.

The women shuffled forward into the light, cringing away from the offered hand of the man in the brown leather jacket.

Five.

Five women I counted as they all descended from the vehicle and into the new world of whatever existence we were in.

"You." The man pointed in my direction. "You deaf?" He held out his hand, raising an eyebrow. "Come here."

I narrowed my eyes, moving forward and placing my hand resolutely in his. "No, I'm not deaf." Jumping down the small distance, I untangled my fingers from his the moment I touched the concrete.

The sound of my voice startled me. *I have an accent.* I hadn't noticed before in the field.

The men around me spoke with an American looseness. Short, to the point, with a slight drawl. I spoke with a subtle difference... sounding vaguely posh with clipped consonants and drawn-out vowels.

"Get them inside. We've got a shitload of work still to do. This damn shipment wasn't due until tomorrow, and I want them locked up tight before other shit hits the fucking fan."

The voice came from another man in an identical brown leather jacket. He had black hair, cut short into a slight mohawk. The large emblem stitched onto the back of his jacket depicted an old-fashioned abacus with a skull burning with fire and a waterfall of coins spewing from its mouth. The motto PURE IN THOUGHTS AND VENGEANCE. CORRUPT IN ALL THINGS THAT MATTER. encircled the image.

A motorcycle club.

Sweat trickled between my shoulder blades, slipping down my spine like a glacial melt. The fear I'd been missing sprang into being like wintery needles. A headache pressed on my temples as I tried to understand my sudden horror. Why did terror affect me now, but not when I'd woken to being kidnapped?

What could be worse than being stolen and trafficked?

They can.

I waited for a memory—for another snippet of truth. But nothing came.

I shivered, wrapping my arms around my waist. I scanned the garage, searching for him—the green-eyed earthquake who sent my blood rushing and heart to flush.

Something inside me recognized him. *He* recognized *me*. Either fiction or reality, I needed to see him again. I needed to question him while staring into his eyes, searching for the truth.

But he was nowhere to be seen.

Three men surrounded us, penning the other women closer together. "Move, bitches. Time for your welcome party." With narrowed gazes, they herded us forward.

Questions ran through my head.

Who were they?

What were we doing here?

What did they plan to do?

Curiosity burned, but I didn't voice my questions. I remained silent.

"Silence is ammunition, darlin'. Don't give it up before you're sure of the facts and know you can win."

The fleeting memory gave no hint as to who told me that, who they were, and where I'd come from. I felt as if I were still blindfolded—lost to everything, even though my eyes were unhindered.

Leaving the parking garage, I followed the trail of girls through a thick door and down a narrow grey corridor. The men didn't touch us; they didn't draw weapons or raise their fists.

There was a calmness about them that transferred to us as their victims. The women trembled, an occasional hitch in their breath as they cried quietly, but no one screamed or did anything to shatter the brittle truce.

The corridor twisted, leading into a large room with a few scattered couches, a large red rug, huge pictures showing an eclectic mix of enlarged magazine covers, and shelving ringing the walls with every liquor and spirit bottle imaginable. The bare floor was worn, satiny wood, with the occasional pockmark from... *bullets*?

The stylish room was nothing like I envisioned. I thought an MC Club would be strewn with litter, discarded reading material, and other gang-related messiness.

The hygiene of the place was impeccable.

Who are *these people?*

Two of the men turned to face us, cocking their heads. "Stand in a line."

The women shuffled, standing behind one another quickly.

"Not like that. Goddammit, a *line*!" The older of the two with sandy-blond hair grabbed the second woman, hauling her level with the first. Repeating the same with the third and fourth, he arranged the five women until they all stood shoulder to shoulder.

I didn't wait to be manhandled; I moved to position without being told. But instead of heading to the bottom of the sad little lineup, I squeezed myself into the center.

Straightening my spine, I kept my face blank as the black-haired man raised an eyebrow. "Fine. Good enough, I suppose."

A chill darted down my spine. The hair on the back of my neck stood up and I just *knew*.

He's here.

Awareness was a woodpecker knocking tiny holes into my soul as I tilted my head, looking over my shoulder.

Walking tall—taller than most of his entourage—he moved with dangerous grace. A mesmerizing war between a fighter's bulk and a dancer's elegance.

His black jeans and T-shirt hid the puddle of blood well. He'd zipped up his dark brown jacket, further hiding whatever injury he'd sustained in battle.

Planting himself in front of us, he glowered at each woman. The other men faded behind him, his army of leather-jacketed warriors all beaten up, bruised, bloodied, and war-weary.

What had they been fighting over? What was this place?

The man never looked at me, skipping my awareness as if I were invisible.

My mind was more intrigued by my predicament than the most important question I continued to ignore. I didn't want it to form because the moment it did, it would itch my brain until it drove me mad.

Why can't I remember anything?

The question blurted loud and fierce—cutting through my wavering ignorance.

What happened to make me like this?

Or maybe not *what* but *who*?

My left hand cupped the singed skin of my right forearm. I winced in pain from the moderate burn.

What happened to me?

Green-eyed man froze as his gaze landed unwillingly on mine. His attention dropped to where I cupped my arm. His feral energy seemed to reach between us, drawing me deeper into his spell.

I tingled with a desire so powerful, it overrode my current situation and the fear dancing on the outskirts of my brain.

Who are you?

Almost as if he heard my question, his eyes locked onto my mine once again, glowing with pent-up emotion. Recognition flickered, love smoldered, and a heartbreaking sorrow only those who have loved and lost can know etched his eyes.

He clenched his jaw, shoulders seizing with tension the longer we stared. Regardless of what happened, or what would become of me, I knew he was a clue.

A vital clue.

The linchpin that would be the catalyst to my undoing.

My heart pumped and tricked beneath his careful scrutiny. My lips parted as fingers of magnetic awareness drew us tighter and tighter and *tighter* together.

His nostrils flared as if he tasted the air—unraveling my secrets by scent alone.

I waited for him to speak. I willed him to touch me again—to hold my face and dive into my locked thoughts. But he stayed frozen, bristling with rage and hate.

Please, let him have answers.

Even if he did, he'd probably never tell me. I might not suffer a debilitating level of terror, but I wasn't an idiot. I didn't need to know my history to guess the likely scenario of my new future wouldn't end well.

I'll find a way to run before that happens.

My mind raced, eyes locked with his. A silent duel ensued, each wielding sharp-edged questions, trying to decipher the other without a spoken word. He was as remote as the peak of Everest with his height and unreadable icy gaze.

The shock and passion he'd shown when we first met was absent. Gone. Never existed.

The longer I stared, the more the sense of familiarity stuttered, pushed further inside as the green fire in his eyes scorched my thoughts. There was no denying he was handsome, scary, and throbbing with power—despite his injury—but there was something else there... something he hid so well... *too* well.

The way he so effortlessly cut me out, left me floundering with fear worse than any I'd felt up till now. The severance of any connection made me throb as if he'd cut out a piece of me.

My hands fisted.

To be denied the tiny piece of home I'd found in him reinforced my conviction that I would do anything—absolutely *anything*—to get the answers I desired.

I didn't care what I had to do.

I didn't care who I had to tolerate.

I would find out the truth.

I will.

The men behind him shuffled uncomfortably. Black Mohawk cleared his throat. "Eh, Prez?"

Earthquake Man stiffened, balling his hands. Instead of looking away, our connection lashed tighter—tentacles crisscrossing the space until we'd somehow knitted an intense cognizance.

It grew deeper, firmer—more demanding than ever.

The chill down my back evolved to a tremor, an aftershock rippling down my spine to my legs.

Something threaded blistering hot between us. A dangerous combination of competition, attraction, and threats.

You know me.

He gritted his jaw, almost as if he'd heard my thought.

I didn't know if I should be overjoyed at the unswerving intuition that we were linked, or petrified that someone from my past could treat me like this.

Tell me.

Are you my lover?

My brother?

My nemesis or friend?

I hated wallowing in nothingness, where even reality wasn't believable without the documentation of a past I could no longer recall.

The connection reached a fever pitch, turning the burn on my arm into an inferno.

Then...he blinked.

Smashing the awareness into smithereens and tearing his gaze from mine, he broke the web. Whatever I thought I felt or knew disappeared in a flash. The tremor left, dissolving into the ground, leaving me empty and more alone than before.

Any remembrance or realization in his gaze vanished, replaced with livid anger.

He was no longer intrigued or enticed by me but furious and hate-filled.

What changed?

How had he cut me out so successfully?

And how had he done it so completely that he made me doubt I'd even seen the hint of something deeper?

Is it all in my head?

Running a large hand through his hair, he paced in front of the lineup. His bloody and bruised hand opened and closed by his thighs, violence wisping around him like an aura.

Slamming to a halt facing us, he sniffed loudly. "Suppose it's now my job to welcome you." He kicked at nothing, grinding his large black boot into the floorboards. "Excuse the disorganization. And ignore the fight you saw." His eyes landed on each of us, pinning us to the concrete. "My name is Arthur Killian, but you and everyone else, address me as Kill. You're a transaction—nothing more, nothing less."

My eyes widened. His name...I waited for it to jog a memory.

Nothing.

An influx of men, five or six, appeared from the corridor, moving to lean against the button-leather couches. They looked as if they belonged in a lawyer's office—the couches, not the men; the men looked as if they were born riding Harleys with cigarettes in their mouths and their minds in the gutter.

The women beside me shuddered, sneaking glances at the new arrivals. They were just as bloody; some with torn clothes, others with cut lips and bruised cheekbones. They all had an edge—wiry, unpredictable.

I stayed locked in place, watching, drinking information, and trying to stay as unnoticeable as possible.

Arthur Killian, whom I'd placed into the center of my new world for lack of a better anchor, spun to face them. "You gonna behave, or do I have to kick your sorry asses again?"

The men smirked, crossing their arms. "We get it. You're still the Prez."

Kill growled, "You get it, but you don't feel it. Too bad. It's done. Been done for four fucking years and I won fair and fucking square. You obey *my* rules. You don't, you're dead."

A man in his early thirties with a stringy moustache nodded. "Know your reasons. Can't say I'm pissed but I'm on board with what you've been saying. Wallstreet vouched for you many times. Gonna trust his judgment, regardless if you're a shit-eating Dagger."

"Hey. Club business. Visitors." Black Mohawk cocked a chin at us.

Kill scowled, reining in his anger. "You're right. Shut the fuck up. The lot of you."

"You're telling us to shut up? You've been demanding us to pledge fealty for years, and now that we're about to, you want us to shut the fuck up?"

Kill gritted his jaw, a vein pumping in the cords of his neck. "Fine! But let's get one thing straight, I'm not a Dagger. Not anymore. I'll be the first to take them out—so stop this in-house fighting and have my fucking back for a change."

The guys shifted but they nodded. One muttered, "That's what I'm trying to do. You got my weapon."

"Good." The Prez—I guessed short for president—nodded. "We're no longer sloppy one-percenters. We're done with that shit. Haven't I already proven that if you follow me, Wallstreet's vision comes true and no one else has to die?"

A man with a short crop of dark hair and a skull shaved into the strands snapped, "That's all fine and fucking dandy to say, but you're hardly here! A Prez is meant to be seen with his army—"

"Enough!" Kill roared. "What I do in the name of this Club is none of your goddamn business." He moved forward, his head cocked threateningly. "You're grown men. I'm not your fucking babysitter." Shoving a finger in Stringy Moustache's face, he muttered, "You don't like the money I've made you? Fine, give it back."

Stringy Moustache gritted his jaw. "We earned it."

Kill laughed darkly. "Exactly. Just like I earned your fucking obedience."

Shaved Skull growled, "You think you've won? You'll never win."

"Funny. I just did." Kill held up his bloodstained hands. "Karma, boys. I'm giving you until tomorrow morning to pack up your shit and leave if you want out." His body tightened, terrible anger rippling over his muscles. "But if you stay, everything that happened tonight is over. Done."

"Enough Club talk," Black Mohawk snapped. "Time and place, gentlemen."

My eyes ping-ponged between the scary looking men in identical jackets, to the blood-drenched president breathing hard through his nose. To the uneducated, he looked furious. In control, strong, and vital. To the ones knowledgeable on pain, the glow in his eyes wasn't from anger but agony—the tension in his back wasn't from ferocity but whatever caused him to bleed profusely.

How I knew the nuances of pain and body language, I didn't know. It wasn't explainable to have my entire life wiped out and only parts of my past just there... to be used unthinkingly.

But it was.

The men's eyes trailed to us. A line up of despairing females waiting to hear our fate.

One cocked his head, sneering, "What about them? Unwilling women would be a damn sight more fun than the Club whores lurking around this joint. Wouldn't mind me some live skin."

Skin?

The women on either side of me whimpered, slapping shaking hands over their mouths.

Kill glared at us, before looking back to his men. "Five are already spoken for. You know the trades will happen tomorrow."

"Okay, the sixth can be ours. Give her to us and we'll forget about tonight." Shaved Skull grinned.

Kill moved, charging into motion from a standstill. His face shot white as pain laced his system, but he didn't hesitate.

His fist collided loud and hard with the man's face. He went down like a heavy piano, complete with a bone-rattling crash.

"Get. Out," Kill whispered. "I'm done with your shit. You're cut."

The man glowered up, his nose gushing blood. "You can't banish me. I took the oath, motherfucker!"

"Can and just did. My Club. *My* rules. Tear off your patch."

The man snarled, "You're a fucking dead man, Killian."

"Like I haven't heard that before." Kill snapped his fingers. Black Mohawk and Sandy-Blond charged to his side. "Strip his patch. Get rid of him."

"With pleasure." The men scooped the bleeding man from the floor, shoving him toward the exit.

"You're dead. The lot of you—you hear me?" Shaved Skull waved his fist, uncaring that his nose rivered crimson.

"Yeah, yeah. Look at us—we're fucking petrified," Black Mohawk said, pushing him hard.

The other men stopped lounging against the wall, standing tall.

Stringy Moustache stomped forward, grabbing his bleeding comrade. "We've got him." His eyes fell on Kill. "You look like the reaper's ridin' you, Kill. Get this done"—he pointed at us as if we were melting groceries needing a home in the fridge—"we'll catch up at the meetin' in a few days."

Killian huffed, his chest rising and falling with a mixture of testosterone and adrenaline. He finally nodded. "Fine. Hopper, Mo, stay here. Need your help with the women. Keep them safe. The trade is for unsullied, unmarked stock. Don't need any refunds being demanded."

My back went rigid. He made us sound like animals.

We weren't items to sell or be used.

Fear slowly crept thicker through my veins.

My eyes narrowed, searching for the shred of truth beneath his tone. He wasn't like the men who slinked back to the garage. Yes, he was rough, tall, angry, dangerous, and entirely in bed with criminals, but there was a shrewd intelligence and rational mind hiding in his green, green eyes.

He was a walking contradiction.

Same as me.

Kill didn't say a word, only nodded as the arrivals became deportees, and we were left in an eerily silent bubble of eight. Five women, three men.

If I knew who I was—what skills I possessed other than veterinary—I might've been tempted to negotiate for freedom or help grant a way out of this for the women crying beside me.

I pursed my lips, searching for the overwhelming need to run, to hide—but it was still missing. The trickle of fear was my only hint of being alive. And that was directed at the man with the green eyes, rather than the horrific situation I faced.

I'm broken.

My fight or flight reflex had been torn out along with my memories.

We're to be sold.

Kill ran both hands through his hair, centering himself. He winced, hissing between his teeth, and dropped his right arm immediately. Swallowing hard, he growled, "You're lucky to overhear Club business. No one outside our oaths is privy to inner workings. But it's probably best you saw that. You can take my word for it when I say things aren't...stable. I'm the only one keeping you intact, so show some respect and believe me when I say, you do *not* want to piss me off."

His voice increased in volume, the timbre echoing from gruff to gravel. "Forget what you heard. You can't bargain with it. You aren't lucky to know it. You're damned. Forget about your old life because you're never seeing it again."

The coldness in his tone sent icicles shimmering in the air.

Another ooze of fear slithered through my blood.

A girl clamped a hand over her ears, a small scream erupting from her mouth.

Kill scowled, flinching as another wave of agony assaulted him. "You're probably wondering *why* you're here, who we are—what we want. If you're smart, you'll have figured it out, but I'm going to lay it out in black and fucking white."

His eyes latched onto mine, drowning me in green grass, moss, and emerald. "You are mine. Ours. The Club's. We own you—every inch. I'm in power, which means your welcome is a shitload better than it would've been four years ago, but my temper is short."

His voice lowered to a decibel that echoed in my heart. "The only thing you need to remember—to make your stay with us seem like the fucking Ritz rather than a prison sentence—is to obey me. If I ask you to do something, you follow immediately and explicitly. You don't, and my courtesy will end. And when that courtesy ends—it's gone for fucking good."

A shadow crossed over his features. Pain speckled his brow with sweat. Gritting his teeth, he swallowed before ordering, "Strip. The lot of you. I have to make sure you're not hurt. Your new owners are expecting perfection—don't want to disappoint them."

My heart stopped.

"No, please," a girl with long blonde hair begged. "Let us go."

Kill held up his hand—it came up sword-fast and just as sharp. "What did I *just* say? Immediately and explicitly."

"Do it, bitch." Black Mohawk came forward, his hands curling by his side. Violence reentered the room, gusting into being with his uttered threat.

The girls twitched and fidgeted, looking to each other for help.

Strange, they didn't look to me—didn't seek out my sisterhood or squeeze closer for comfort.

The longer we stood in the line, the more obvious my exclusion was from the tearstained, terrified women.

As much as I wanted answers, perhaps it was a blessing not to know who I was. To not remember my family, marital situation, or who I might never see again.

I was set apart from them. I couldn't determine if it made me stronger or more vulnerable to be cast out from the group. A small lance of pain pricked my heart. I truly belonged nowhere—even this horrible life into which I'd been thrown.

Kill dragged a hand over his face, smearing a cut from his forehead and drawing the dark red down his cheek. "I gave an order. Don't test me so soon. Not tonight."

His gaze zeroed on mine. This time there was nothing there—no pull or whisper of knowing. He was in charge and I was nothing more than *skin*.

His lips pressed together as he dropped his vision to my breasts. A not-so-subtle command to obey.

Strip.

Looking down my body, I plucked at the faded blue jeans and white T-shirt with a large, intricate rose on the front. Both smelled of smoke but weren't burned like my arm. I had no shoes, no jacket.

I didn't remember buying the items, or where I'd showered and dressed this morning. In a way, it made no difference to me either being clothed or naked. They didn't offer protection. They weren't armor against evil happening.

They were useless. Just like tears were useless and terror was useless. I had no need for any of it.

I don't know what I look like naked.

My heart kicked into a curious beat. I had no idea if I had freckles, or moles, or scars. I lived in the mind and body of a stranger. Maybe if I looked, I might know? Might figure out my conundrum?

I looked up again into the green eyes of my nightmare incarnate. He'd never looked away, his jaw locked as my fingertips traced the delicate rose on my T-shirt.

I sucked in a breath, my skin prickling. I couldn't deny he stole everything from me with just one stare. But he also gifted a piece of himself in return. I read him clearly—or maybe I only thought I did.

His legs were spread, the stance threatening as well as for balance to combat the pain he lived with. He looked menacing, but something deep in my soul wanted to believe he wouldn't hurt me.

Don't be stupid.

I tilted my chin. I wasn't. I was going out of my way to be rational and collected. Being stupid would be ignoring my instincts and running.

He means to sell you. Turn you into a whore.

I knew that. But my gut said he wasn't a vicious man. He was a killer, undoubtedly. He'd lived a life of crime for a long time. But he was also hiding something that deep inside me *knew*. I couldn't explain how I knew but I *had* met him.

Once upon a time, I'd loved him in a nightmare so much worse than this one. I'd grown wet for him in another reality, all while he worshipped me, adored me.

It wasn't my fault I couldn't separate fact from fiction, truth from fable.

Raising an eyebrow, he waited.

I waited.

We both waited to see who would break.

I did.

Not for him—but for me. I wanted to know who I was beneath my clothes. I wanted to shed the lingering past and had no reason to cling to things I couldn't recollect.

Grabbing the hem, I tugged the T-shirt over my head.

The girls beside me froze, watching with moon-size eyes. My skin scattered with goosebumps as Kill sucked in a breath.

His inhale sent a clench fluttering through my core. Power. He'd granted me power over him with that tiny noise of appreciation.

Thick hair fell over my shoulder, dangling in my line of sight.

My hair.

Hair I didn't remember.

I fingered it, running a soft wave through my fingertips. Whether it was natural or real, it was a beautiful shade of auburn and cherry. A rich pigment that spoke of passion and rippled like blood.

I'm a redhead.

My eyes traveled down my front.

I gasped.

"I know how much you've always wanted one. I wanted to be the one to pay for it. So you'll always remember me." He pulled a drawing I'd been working on for years from his back pocket. "I know how much this means to you."

I leapt into his arms, hugging him.

"Thank you. So, so much."

I turned to the artist, pulling my T-shirt over my head. Taking the drawing, I pressed it into his hands, then splayed my palms on my naked stomach and chest. "Here. Ink me here."

The memory ended.

The first pressure of tears itched my eyes. The tattoo spanned my entire side, up my rib cage, engulfed my left breast entirely, and teased with the final design by my collarbone. The tattoo disappeared into my jeans below. My arms weren't inked, and I couldn't comprehend the amount of hours such a piece would've taken.

I was braless. I guessed my cup size was a full C.

Even my nipple was tattooed.

My heart bucked as a body I didn't remember taunted me with such vibrancy—such experience and clues. Who was I to do such a thing?

The tattoo encapsulated something tugging deep and painful in my heart. It meant something. It meant *everything.* But I couldn't remember *what.*

The design was a world within a world within a looking glass within a perfect mirrored pond. To the interloper I'd become, I appreciated the artisan lines of the feathering and shadows. The detailing was superb as well as entirely eye-catching.

But it was more than that. So, so much more.

The throb in my soul knew what it was, but nothing burst forth or let me guess.

To me, the perfect stranger, it was nothing more than a beautiful feather with cobalt-blue forget-me-nots, words intertwined with vines, and interlocking images so perfectly synced, I couldn't tell them apart.

But it was my right side that made my heart pound in horror.

Burns.

Mottled tight and shiny skin graced my entire right side, almost a mirror image of the gorgeous tattoo on my left. Where beauty was inked, ugliness was stretched.

I waited for some memory of being in a fire. After all, the scars hinted at a terribly traumatic event in my past. But nothing. Not a lick of a flame or the scent of smoke.

My lungs worked hard, dealing with the amazement of my strange form. I expected a visceral reaction—or at the very least a minor freak-out over the bizarreness of my body. But the damn calmness never left, keeping me levelheaded and clear.

I didn't know who I was, but soon...soon I hoped the story on my skin would make sense.

The new burn on my arm flared bright with pain. Old burns and new.

Is there significance in that, or am I clutching at straws?

I was a coin with two sides: scars and stars. Skin grafts and tattoos. Stunning and hideous.

Rustling occurred to my left and right—the other women stopped gawking at my uniqueness, rushing to follow suit and obey. My attention faded from my scars, back to my tattoo, drinking it in.

"What does it feel like?"

I tensed, grasping his fingers until sweat and heat erupted into a bonfire between our locked palms. "Like flames. Endless tiny teeth of hell."

"Can you stand it? To have it all done?"

A tear squeezed from my eye as the needle skittered over a bony rib. The pain was indescribable. Awful and tear-inducing but…addictive, too. A peculiar kind of agony that soothed my shattered soul.

I willed the pain to do what other things had failed to.

Looking first at my scars that carried the weight of my sins, I then looked at my virgin skin and murmured, "Yes. I can stand it. Because I've withstood so much more."

The memory flickered luminescent like a lightning bolt, only to fade just as quickly.

No!

Who *was* I? What had I lived through to warrant such an incredible piece of body art all in the remembrance of… what?

I was so caught up in the tattoo, I didn't notice the women undressed before me.

A slap to my cheek sent my eyes soaring upward, locking onto my green-eyed nightmare. "And the rest. You're not done."

My heart raced having him so close. He reeked of sweat and blood. I inhaled hard, drugging myself on him. Did I know him from another time and place or was that entirely false? How could I describe the overwhelming sensation of *recognizing* him?

How do I feel as if I've loved you and hated you and ruined you in another time?

When I didn't move or speak, his large fingers went to my waistband. Never taking his eyes from mine, he undid the button, then the zipper, before placing his hands on my hips and tugging the denim away.

My skin ignited beneath his touch, zigging and zagging with flames.

His jaw remained locked, face tight. He gave no hint of being affected by my presence or touching me. I hated the lie he projected.

I wanted the man who'd dropped his guard in the battlefield. The man who'd looked at me like I was priceless and scarcely believed I'd been found.

His eyes caressed my body, his nostrils flaring as the jeans puddled to my ankles, displaying the rest of my tattoo. I was wrong to think it finished on my hipbone; it continued down the left side of my buttock and thigh, all the way down my leg to trace around my ankle and finish on my pinky toe. The ink followed a similar path to the scars trailing down my right leg to my foot. I looked as if I'd stepped from fire and straight into a waterfall of color, stained by both—forever changed.

I stood naked before him, my chest rising and falling. My skin alive and tingling beneath his inspection.

It seemed whoever I was, I had an aversion to underwear. Just as I was braless, I was panty-less, too.

He didn't move. I *couldn't* move.

His hands rested on my hips, fingers digging hard into my flesh as he devoured me with his gaze. The connection between us hummed, dulling the room and inhabitants, placing us in a tight bubble of crackling lust.

I do *know you.*

How do I know you?

My heart flurried the longer we stared. Vulnerability spread warm between us, smothered by confusion.

His breathing turned shallow, his body once again curving toward mine—as if invisible threads bound us together.

"Kill." The voice was faraway. "Kill! For fuck's sake, Prez!"

The man holding me blinked, snapping the link between us. The warmth in his gaze turned to snow, shutting me out completely.

Stepping back, he cleared his throat. "Shit." He swayed a little on his feet.

I liked to think it was because of whatever existed between us, but a trail of red droplets decorated the bare wood below. His blood splashed darkly on his large combat boots, looking like rusty tears.

Increasing his distance from me, he crossed his arms, flinching. His eyes tightened with agony but he was good at hiding it. "Take their clothes away, Grasshopper."

The man with the mohawk did as he was told, scooping the mismatch of skirts, trousers, and dresses, wadding them into a ball and shoving them into a black rubbish bag.

Keeping his eyes from mine, Kill muttered, "You'll be given new attire once you've been washed and inspected."

More tears and whimpers.

But not from me.

I was steadfast in my concentration. Locked to the floor with the knowledge the man before me may seem invincible, but he wasn't. He bled. Same as any other. He hurt. Same as the men he'd overthrown. He needed help, and soon.

"Once you've been inspected, you'll be fed, given a room to sleep, and permitted a night of rest before your true fate is determined. I don't care what your names are. I don't care where you've come from. To me, you are nothing more than skin. Skin to sell, skin to trade. Tears won't save you; screams will only hurt you. So fucking listen, keep quiet, and look at your stay with us as a small holiday before your new reality."

The woman with the long blonde hair whispered, "Please… This can't be happening. What do you want?"

Kill bared his teeth, wrapping his arms tighter around his middle. It projected as aggression but I saw the whiteness of blood loss creeping up his jaw.

"Told you; not my fault if you didn't listen. And you won't see me again after tonight." Straightening his shoulders, he growled, "Mo, Grasshopper, get them bunkered for the night. I trust you'll ship them out to their destinations tomorrow? I don't have time to go over it with you."

You don't have time because you're bleeding out.

The sandy-blond-haired man nodded. "Got the deets. Don't worry about a thing."

"Good." Kill sighed.

A couple of women sniffed, tears trailing their cheeks. I quickly scanned our sad group. One pretty Asian girl, two blondes, one redhead, and one brunette. We were all similar in height, build, and curves.

We'd been chosen.

Hand-picked for whatever they meant to do with us.

A flutter of fear cut through my steadfastness.

Green eyes landed on mine.

The feeling of history, connection, and rebellion came again, thick and fast in our locked gaze. He suddenly stumbled to the left, shaking his head, eyes wide with amazement that his body disobeyed his order to stand.

I wasn't amazed. I was stupefied he was still upright, let alone leading and possessing the respect of the men behind him.

Snapping his fingers, Kill growled, "I'm leaving. I'll take the sixth trade with me until I can find a buyer. Don't trust the brothers after what happened tonight."

Mo, the sandy-blond-haired man, frowned. "Is that wise? I mean—"

"It's very fucking wise." Stalking forward, Kill beelined for me.

I took a step backward, but it didn't do me any good. Grabbing my elbow, he snarled over his shoulder. "Give me something to dress her in."

Immediately, a large black T-shirt with the words VENGEANCE IS SWEET across the front sailed from the bag in Grasshopper's—the black-mohawked biker—hand.

"Put this on." Kill balled it up, wedging it into my stomach.

With shaking hands, I shook the T-shirt till it faced the right way and pulled it over my head. It fit me like a dress, skimming my thighs.

Kill nodded. "It's not perfect, but it'll do."

Grabbing my wrist, he jerked me toward the corridor. "I'll call you guys tomorrow. Deal with this shit."

Without another word, he yanked me to the garage and an awaiting black Triumph. Throwing his leg over the side, he tugged me close. "Get on."

"I don't like motorcycles."

The thought came from nowhere. *Why don't I like motorcycles? Same reason I don't like motorcycle clubs...the men who exist in this world.*

It didn't make sense. If I'd had anything to do with clubs and violence, I would remember—surely? After all, I remembered my profession. I wouldn't have gone into healing animals if I'd come from an environment where women were subservient and more stay-at-home types.

Something about that thought didn't sit right.

The itch in my brain wouldn't give up, switching from a gentle annoyance to a full-on scratch-fest.

"This isn't a negotiation. Get the fuck on." Kill twisted and hoisted me onto his bike. His hands were large, encasing my waist easily. Once again the cognizant awareness and intensity shot through my blood.

The moment I sat behind him, he let me go, hissing in pain.

"You're hurt," I muttered.

He shook his head. "Superficial. Don't think I'm gonna die and you'll be free—you'll be waiting a long time for that to happen."

My stomach grappled with my heart at the thought of him dying. If he died, answers died with him. *But if he dies, you're free.*

The thought of freedom didn't excite me nearly as much as figuring out the riddle of my amnesiac brain.

"You need to see a doctor."

You need to stay alive long enough for me to get the truth.

His leather jacket creaked softly as the muscles in his back tensed. "Mind your own business."

Our connection is my business.

Grabbing the handlebars, he pressed a button that opened a small section of the large garage roller door. Freshness from the night outside flurried in, obscuring the scent of leather and gasoline.

"If you want to stay on, you better grab hold."

The metaphor of his words didn't escape me.

If I wanted to move forward in this strange, scary existence, I had to put my faith in the man who held my life in his roguish hands. And if I didn't, I'd fall.

I have nothing left to lose.

With a sure heart, I wrapped my arms around his considerable bulk.

His muscles bunched beneath my hold and once again awareness and twisted desire sprang into perception.

We didn't say a word.

We didn't have to.

Our bodies hummed with more depth than words ever could.

With a shiver and wrench of his wrist, my nightmare and kidnapper fed fuel to his mechanical beast, and we shot forward into the crisp silence of early morning.

Chapter Three

ain.

I'd known all facets. Endured physical, emotional, and spiritual agony. The wound in my shoulder throbbed like hellfire, but it was nothing to the confusion inside. What the fuck was I doing bringing this liar back to my home?

And why did my heart ache in the worst pain imaginable?

—*Kill*

The third journey in just a few hours stopped abruptly as Arthur Killian eased on the throttle, coming to a rest in front of huge black gates. Straddling the bike, his large legs kept us from tipping over as he reached into a fake rock and punched in a code.

Instantly the gate split in two, rolling into the thick undergrowth ringing the large stone wall. To have a property like this right on the coastline must cost a fortune.

Gripping his leather cut, I asked, "Where are we?"

"My home."

Not quite the detailed answer I was hoping for.

Where are we in the *world*?

Why couldn't I remember my nationality or where I lived until a few hours ago?

Why did I know that the flowers in my tattoo were forget-me-nots, but not my name? I wasn't completely clueless—I knew how to talk and interact—I remembered the basics of human life, but my brain was selective, hiding everything that I wanted to know.

Kill teased the acceleration, gliding us from street to stone driveway. He drove to the right of the whitewashed and pillared mansion.

Uplights cast the property in a warm glow, masking the sterile white and making it seem like a cozy cream. There were immaculate flower beds set like regimented soldiers beneath the many windowsills, and the front portico soared upward, keeping the double front door dry from temperamental weather.

Another garage door rolled up. Automatic lighting switched on as we drove with a loud rumble into the large space. Scanning the area, I quickly noted it didn't look lived-in. There were no overflowing cupboards of personal belongings or Ping-Pong tables or even old exercise equipment. The only thing that the garage housed was a black sports car and now the black Triumph we'd arrived on.

My ears rang as Kill cut the thundering engine and kicked down the stand. He looked over his shoulder. "Get off."

I tugged his jacket harder. "I don't want to. Tell me why you brought me here."

Tell me how I know you.

"I'm not telling you jack shit unless you obey. What part of what I said at the compound didn't you understand?"

"Most of it."

He sucked in a breath, an arm lassoing around his bleeding chest. "You're either the stupidest person I've ever met, or you're broken in some way."

I gasped. "Broken? What makes you say that?"

I thought the same thing. Where was the fear? The shock? The horror?

"You're looking right into my eyes. You're refusing to get off my bike, and you don't seem to understand what's going on here."

I no longer wanted to be washed away by circumstances I didn't understand. It was time to push—to dig for clues.

"What *is* going on? Why did you seem to know me... back there?"

His body went rock hard with rage. "Don't."

"Don't what?" I knew what he meant, but something inside made me rebel. I couldn't get a grip on how drastically my life had changed—or at least I thought it'd changed...

I hated being in the dark. I hated having memories taunting me while staring into the eyes of a killer. I wanted to *know*.

He growled under his breath, swiping his free hand over his face. The sheen of pain hadn't diminished; if anything it'd become worse.

"Get. Off. My. Bike," he whispered. The sharp control in his tone sent a smattering of warning down my back.

Carefully, I obeyed. Swinging my leg over, I hated how naked I was beneath the black T-shirt, and backed away the moment my feet touched concrete. At least it wasn't cold tonight. The mugginess of humidity lived in the porous floor, warming my toes.

Kill climbed off his motorcycle, grunting in pain. He stood up, his features blanching in agony. Spinning to face me, he growled, "Get inside. I don't have patience for nonsense."

I eyed him, then glanced at the already closed garage door.

He chuckled. "You run and I'll put a bullet in your head so fast, you'll wake up in heaven without ever remembering what happened."

I already have that problem. However, I'd woken up in hell with no reflex fear of the devil.

"Why did you bring me here?" *Why me and none of the other girls?*

He sighed heavily, pinching the brow of his nose. The tips of his fingers left another streak of blood across his face. It glistened in the bright lights of the garage. "Don't make me repeat myself." With a fast move, he reached behind and pulled a gun free from his waistband.

I knew it was there. I'd seen it glinting like black death while he bent over the gas tank of his bike and drove us here. Every mile we'd traveled, I'd toyed with the idea of grabbing it and holding it to his temple.

But every scenario of threatening a man who was the only link between keeping me from being roadkill ended badly. I preferred being alive to spread on the road. And I definitely preferred the element of surprise.

Act docile. Then he would never expect the mayhem building inside me.

I squared my shoulders. "You won't shoot me."

"Why not?"

Because you do know me. No matter how vehemently you deny it.

"Because you said it yourself—I'm to be sold. What happens to you when the buyer doesn't get what he paid for?"

It was a gamble, but I decided to use shock value to get a reaction from him. I wanted to scream that there was something between us. To force him to acknowledge it, but at the same time, I had no proof. I needed to see evidence from him, before I fully believed it myself.

He cocked his head. "You're seriously gonna make me believe you care about what happens when a trafficker doesn't deliver skin to his buyer?"

I swallowed. "No. But I do care about getting answers. Answers I'm willing to risk my life to gain."

He grinned, motioning with the gun for me to head toward the door leading presumably into the house. "You think I'll answer your questions?"

I nodded, padding toward the door and pulling it open. A waft of air-conditioning greeted me. "You will because you'll owe me."

My eyes fell to the spreading bloodstain on his chest. His deterioration had been gradual but not unnoticed. I could sense his wooziness, the lack of strength ebbing like a tide. I couldn't explain it—yet another hint at who I'd been before this nightmare.

He laughed softly. "*I'll* owe *you*?"

Turning in the doorway, I pointed at the soppiness of his shirt dripping from beneath his brown leather jacket. "You're bleeding profusely. If you don't stop moving and lie down, you'll pass out." Lowering my voice, I added, "I can help you."

He stalked forward. "Do I look like I'm fucking weak?"

I gritted my teeth, battling against the flush of fear with him storming so close. He brought the reek of blood and metal and the power of a pissed-off male. His jaw was strong and square, his nose neither too big nor too long. Everything about him was symmetrically in proportion, making him the handsomest criminal I'd ever met.

You think *you've ever met.*

My brain hurt.

"All I know is you're hurt, and if you don't sit down soon, you'll pass out and I'll just leave you there and escape."

To where?

You're mostly naked with no identity, no money—how far could you run with nothing?

But none of that mattered because there was one thing keeping me alive. One thing driving me forward, giving me strength, making me fight and not give into the horror of my situation.

Answers.

I needed them more than I needed air. I needed truth more than I needed safety, freedom, or rescuing.

Answers were my driving force because I currently lived in a worse prison than any Arthur Killian could trap me in.

I was nothing. Nobody. Lost. Alone. Orphaned from all thoughts.

Answers were the key and this man had them.

"Escape!" he snorted. "Fuck, the cops won't save you. They're worse than us."

The police will *help. You've done nothing wrong.*

I would flee if there wasn't some horrible niggle poking my brain every time I thought of screaming for help and running. There was no doubt in my mind I could run fast enough to make my capturer chase me, cause his heart to pump harder, and for him to pass out. His eyes were hazy and pain-filled already. It wouldn't take much to make him topple.

Then why didn't I do it?

Because the thought of entering a world where I have no idea where I belong scares the bejesus out of me.

Baby steps. My world had shrunk to this man, his house, and fixing an injury I had the skills—hopefully—to heal. Everything else... It held no allure. A kindly spoken police officer couldn't help me. A shrink couldn't help me.

But this man could.

Kill waved his gun. "Stop talking and get in the house."

I didn't back down. I didn't flinch from his anger or smug power.

When I didn't move, he muttered, "The police are just as corrupt as us. The minute they caught you, you'd be living an entirely different nightmare."

Shoving the gun back into his waistband, he suddenly shoved me forward into his house. "You're like a one-woman comedy show. Just shut up and do as you're told."

I didn't retaliate. Instead, I let him push me down the corridor that spilled us out into a rotund two-story entrance hall. The architecture of curved wall, domed glass roof, and wooden circular stairs would've been spectacular if it wasn't for the dangerous man hissing in pain behind me.

I whispered, "You need to sit down. I'd guess you only have a few more minutes before you pass out."

"Shut up."

My heart did a weird skip-shuffle. Part of me willed him to fall unconscious. Escape and freedom would come gift-wrapped and easy if he was no longer an issue. But it went back to the one thing I desperately craved.

Answers to my voidless world.

The stronger part of me had no intention of letting this man pass out, leaving me with nothing.

He stalked to the stairs, breathing harder with every movement. He paused with a foot on the bottom rung. He looked up to the landing, a flicker of rage shadowing his features.

"You can't climb up there. You'll pass out. Who knows if you'll break a bone or two when you fall."

He shot me a hate-filled glare, gripping the banister. His entire body looked as if he wanted to dismantle his house and burn the staircase.

He took another step, hauling himself up with the aid of the curved handrail. His leather jacket creaked as he breathed hard.

I prepared for him to pass out. I didn't know if I should stand close by to try and catch him, or avoid him to let him crash on his own.

I couldn't decide, so I just watched. And waited.

He paused, then sighed angrily. Throwing a quick glance at me, he stomped back in his large boots and grabbed my wrist. "Don't think you're smarter than me," he grunted.

Dragging me silently to another door, he kicked it open to reveal a huge sterile room with soft pewter on the walls and massive frames hanging in perfect symmetry.

The lights in the house were hidden, so it seemed to light up as if by magic with no discernable lightbulb. Kill didn't give me time to study the picture frames, dragging me over the bare, white-tiled floor to the huge kidney-shaped desk with four large computer screens all linked together with two keyboards in front of them.

The soft hum of machinery and glare of the screens were the only liveliness in the entire mansion.

"Where is everybody?" I asked as he threw me into an office chair, sending the coaster wheels sliding a little with my weight.

There was an emptiness about the house—a silence that wasn't possible if there were other people dwelling within.

Kill grabbed the only other chair, sitting heavily. His jaw was tight, eyes narrowed against the immense pain he must be feeling.

"I live alone." Grabbing his gun, he placed it loudly and pointedly on the desk. "Doesn't mean you're not in danger. Believe me when I say that makes it more dangerous than ever for you."

I nodded, looking briefly at the picture frame towering over him. Equations. Billons of mathematical equations, all scribbled and transcribed in a mismatch of cursive, print, and handwriting. No color. Just black and white.

At first glance, it looked like an image might exist in the bold equations but it was only an optical illusion.

Kill grunted, "Stop looking over my shoulder and pay attention."

I obeyed, looking into his vibrant green eyes, feeling once again that link of remembrance...connection...*love.*

Love?

I slapped away the thought. I didn't know the meaning of it. I'd forgotten people I once loved. I'd forgotten my parents, any lovers, or siblings, or friends. How could I forget them, yet feel as if I loved this horrible, bleeding man who'd kidnapped and meant to sell me?

I am *broken.*

I wanted to rattle myself and see if the shards of my soul tinkled like chipped china. I needed to find a way to put myself back together again, and fast.

Kill sucked in a deep breath as a fresh wave of pain made his fists clench. "You said you can help. Why?"

I rested my hands on my naked thighs, wishing the T-shirt covered me more. "I'm a vet. Or at least I *was* a vet, or training to be one... Regardless, I know how to stem bleeding."

I hope.

No, I knew. Something inside throbbed with the knowledge of how to heal, how to stitch and tend.

He raised an eyebrow. "How old are you? You look too young to have that qualification." His head cocked, belying the eagerness behind his innocent question. Was that to figure out how he knew me or purely disbelieving about my skills?

I don't know.

I waved my hand. "Do you really need to know? I thought you said you didn't care who we were or what our names are. Tell me where your first aid kit is, and I'll help you."

I wanted answers but I didn't want to show my weakness by asking. If I didn't prompt, how much extra could I learn by his error and slipups?

He locked his jaw, deliberation glowing in his eyes. Finally, he sat up and with a pained groan slipped his bloodstained jacket off his shoulders.

I gasped, rolling forward on my chair. "Oh my God." The sight of blood didn't faze me but the knowledge that he hurt cut me in a way I couldn't describe.

He gritted his teeth, looking down at his shredded T-shirt. "Aw, shit. Hoped it wouldn't be that bad."

So much blood.

He swayed a little, his head bowing, before he muttered, "Bathroom to the right. Under the sink."

"I—I think... you need to go to the hospital." The amount of blood made the wound look unsurvivable. Stomping around, driving motorbikes in the dead of morning, and keeping me hostage certainly hadn't helped the situation.

He looked up, gaze blazing green. "No fucking doctors. Go get the—"

His eyes rolled back, his jaw went slack, and he slumped forward.

I shot to my feet as he tumbled from the chair, face-planting to the white tile below. I rushed forward, grabbing his cold bicep, hoping I could stop him from damaging himself further. But it didn't do any good. He collapsed into a pile of black clothing and blood, his jaw-length hair sticking to his five-o'clock shadow.

Those beautiful eyes that lived in my soul—those eyes that haunted me—closed.

The hum of the computers carried on but the rest of the world went silent. Without his green eyes teasing my heart, I breathed hard, trying to unscramble everything inside. Was this a cruel joke? Being held hostage by a man who held the eyes of someone who possessed my love and soul?

Why couldn't I remember?

My stomach ached with pain... with grief—to have lost something I couldn't recall. It hurt worse than anything that'd happened since I woke.

Kill's breathing was shallow but he was alive. His arm lay outstretched, cheek pressed against the hard floor, body twisted at a painful angle.

My heart lurched, staring at his unconscious form.

I live alone.

My head snapped up, gaze locking onto the exit. Here was my chance. The only one I would get before my life turned from nightmare to horror show.

Run.

I stood there, locked in place as scenarios and horrible conclusions filled my brain.

If I ran, I would be at the mercy of doctors, tests, and interviews. If I ran I would be running from one unknown to so many others.

If I didn't run, I would be destined to a world where I wouldn't be human but a toy. I'd be abused and raped and treated like dirt.

Sold.

I couldn't let that happen.

Biting my lip, I prodded Kill with my foot. I needed to make sure he was out cold before I made my escape. He didn't groan or twitch. Completely unconscious.

The sinister gun glinted beneath the glare of the computer screens. I picked it off the desk, shocked and slightly horrified at the weight. I didn't know what model it was, how many rounds it held, or even how to shoot the damn thing, but I cupped the handle, resting my finger on the oh so dangerous trigger.

Arthur Killian didn't move.

I should've felt powerful—safer with the loaded weapon in my hands, but I didn't. I felt exposed and a fake.

Just go.

I tiptoed toward the exit, looking over my shoulder, fearing he'd wake up. I stopped at the door frame, breathing hard.

He still hadn't moved.

My heart thundered in my ears. This was my chance to bolt—to be free. But the thought of leaving him to bleed out on his floor—to die all alone—I...

The connection I suffered fisted my heart. *What if you let the only person who might be able to grant you answers die?*

I swiped a hand through my hair, hating the confusion inside.

I couldn't let him die.

I stiffened.

But he wasn't a nice man—by his own admission.

Spinning to face him, I leveled the gun at his head. Could I heal him, then walk away? I was the one with the gun—he would do what I demanded.

But where would I go?

I still had the impossibility of being homeless, clothesless, and nameless.

Perhaps, I should take myself to the hospital?

But if I did that, then I would only come back—driven by the itch to know—and be in the same predicament I was currently in with no bargaining power. Kill groaned, struggling to wake up. His outstretched arm tensed to push himself upright. He cried out, throwing himself onto his back.

My heart beat harder.

His eyes opened, confusion bright, even from the distance between us. Then recollection slammed into him, and he angled his head toward the door.

He froze when our eyes connected, the muzzle of the gun aimed at his skull.

It felt like an eternity that we stared. The challenge in his eyes. The threat. It danced between us, lacing with my rebellion and need for freedom—not just from him but this blank reality I'd awoken in.

I wanted to remember.

Ask him. Demand.

Kill laughed, his mirth echoing with pain. "You're a good little liar, I'll give you that."

"Excuse me?"

"All that talk of healing me? What were you going to do? Grab the medical kit and find a way to stick a needle in my eye?" He writhed on the floor, slapping a hand over the injury in his pectoral. "I'm such a fucking idiot. Should've kept you at the compound. Let them deal with you."

I inched forward, despite myself. "Why didn't you?"

He glowered. "Why didn't I what?"

"Why didn't you leave me there? You left all the other girls there."

Was it because you're as intrigued with me as I am with you?

He growled, "You think you're in a position to ask questions?"

The gun was warm and friendly in my hands, rather than an enemy. I dashed forward, standing just outside of grabbing distance but definitely in range to shoot, even as inexperienced as I was. "I think I'm in a perfect position to ask questions."

Kill smirked. "Only until you screw up. Then I'll take back my fucking gun and you'll wish you'd squeezed the trigger when you had the chance."

I ignored that.

Leveling the weapon at his forehead, I said, "A new deal. I'll help heal you if you answer some of my questions. If I like your answers, I'll stay. I won't put up a fight, and I'll give you back your gun."

He frowned. "Why would you stay? You know what will happen to you."

Because I prefer to deal with the devil I know rather than the one I don't.

"I don't have to answer that. It's not me with a gun pointed at their head."

"No, but it soon will be," he muttered under his breath.

I skirted around him, careful to stay out of reaching distance. His green eyes followed me, never letting go. My skin prickled; my heart raced. When he looked at me like that—as if I were the only thing of importance in this world—the bond inside stretched and strengthened.

Who *was* he?

He played havoc with my willpower—my common sense. Everything I knew I should do seemed out of the question until I found out if we knew each other.

It couldn't all be in my mind. Could it?

You're willing to give up freedom—a long and happy life—all because you need reassuring that you somehow know him?

I shook my head. The questions were drowning me. I couldn't focus on what I was giving up, only on what I hoped to gain.

"Will you take my deal or not?"

He scowled. "Doesn't look like I have a fucking choice, does it?"

I shook my head again, my arm starting to ache with the weight of the pistol, revolver, whatever I held. "No. Not unless you want to bleed out all over your office floor."

He chuckled breathlessly. "That would give the cleaning lady something to talk about."

"I thought you said you live alone?" Nervousness attacked my legs, making me inch toward the door again.

He rolled his eyes, wincing. "I do. She comes twice a week."

"And there's no one else who might interrupt us?"

"Unless you mean the business meeting I have in a few days, then no. Nothing. You're safe to fucking murder me and make your getaway before the sun's up."

I ignored that and moved to sit in one of the office chairs. Resting the gun on my knee, I said, "Okay, first question. Where are we?"

He groaned. "Seriously? What do you want? A map? Coordinates? We're at my home. I told you."

I bounced the gun on my leg. "No. I understood that part. Where *are* we? What town? What country?"

The room went deathly silent. His head rose from the tiles, his skin white as a ghost. "What?"

I swallowed. I hadn't realized that by asking such basic questions, it would show my weakness in return.

What can he do? So what you lost your memory? He doesn't want to know about you anyway. It doesn't make you any more vulnerable or easier prey.

I might even be stronger because my secrets were safe—no matter how much I wished to know them.

I leaned forward in the chair, letting my red hair cascade over my shoulder. The waves were thick—the ends a little straggly.

"Answer me. The longer this takes, the less your chances are of me actually being able to heal you without a doctor."

Kill clenched his jaw. Finally, he said, "The Florida Keys." Rolling his eyes, he added, "You know. *America?*"

I froze. America? *So I'm an American?* My accent didn't sound like it. Maybe they'd stolen me from another country and brought me here?

"And where did your men kidnap me from?"

"No fucking clue. I don't micromanage. They had orders for five girls—they came back with six." He shrugged, flinching. "I don't ask for a report. I trust my guys—even if they can't count."

"What will happen to the other girls?"

He narrowed his eyes. "Don't turn all tenderhearted on me. You're in charge right now. The minute you start making demands of me to let them go or have fucking mercy, that's where it all ends. Their fates were sealed months ago, before they even knew we were coming. Pretend you never saw them, because that's the best you can do for your little conscience."

I clasped the gun harder, my finger stroking the trigger. "Fine. We'll come back to that. How long do I have before you find a buyer for me?"

His nostrils flared. "You ask the weirdest fucking questions. How about where's your phone? What's the number to dial the local police station?" He struggled to sit up, his legs splayed in front of him, blood blazing bright on the white floor from where he'd been lying. "Don't you care you're mine? Don't you care that I'm about to *sell* you? What the fuck are you still doing here asking me questions that have no fucking point?"

He pointed behind him. "Stop waving a gun in my face, and leave. You'll have a pretty good head start before I can get off my sorry ass and chase you."

My eyes flew to the door. The temptation fired my blood, sending adrenaline into my legs. I stood up, pointing the muzzle at his chest.

He smiled coldly. "There you go—a normal reaction. Run from me, sweetheart. This is your one and only chance."

I inched toward the door, my fear growing thick and fast the closer I got to the exit.

It wasn't fear at leaving or running half-naked through streets, or even calling the police to come and find me, it was the thought of leaving with yet more mysteries strewn behind me.

Planting my feet on the tile, I gathered my scattered courage.

Ask him. The one question you want answering.

My heart tripped over itself. I desperately wanted to know but desperately didn't at the same time. Either answer threatened to ruin me, just in different ways.

Kill glared. "What the hell are you still doing here?" He pointed at the door. "Go, goddammit."

I stormed forward, lost in my need to know, consumed by the urge to look into his eyes when I asked him.

Standing over him, I snarled, "Tell me one thing, and then I'll decide what to do with you. Save your life or kill you."

He smirked. "Oh, better make it a good one, then, seeing as my life hangs in the balance."

Leveling the gun at his forehead, I whispered, "I know you. I know it deeper and stronger than I know myself. Tell me the truth. *How do we know each other?*"

Something flickered in his emerald gaze. Something I would've given my life to decipher, then the ground swooped from beneath me and painful tile crashed against my spine.

The boom of the gun ricocheted around us as it spat its deadly bullet into the wall. The black weapon skittered away, hiding beneath the desk and out of reach.

Kill wedged me beneath his blood-soaked body, breathing hard and reeking of copper.

In my need to understand I'd gone too close.

Now I was trapped.

Now I was doomed.

Kill bared his teeth, looking wild, unpredictable, and almost insane. "I'll tell you how we know each other." His head bent, pressing his lips against my ear. "I'm your worst fucking nightmare and now I've got all the power."

I gasped.

I knew it.

My nightmare.

He said it himself.

Chapter Four

Who was this woman? This trickster and fraud? I wanted to wring her neck for making me hurt this way, but at the same time, I wanted to tear through her lies and see. See the impossible. Believe in the improbable.

She made me want things I'd sworn never to want.

She made me weak.

She made me hate.

—*Kill*

"Let me up."

"What, so you can threaten me with the gun again? You almost spread my brains all over my home." His grip moved from my hip to my throat. "No fucking chance."

I glared into his eyes. There was no hint of whatever he'd thought before he tackled me to the ground.

His body was unmovable, his touch warming me as well as searing my skin with proximity.

My heart deflated. It wouldn't be possible to keep such knowledge from his eyes. There was no way he could hide what he felt when we first met—not when we were glued together. Not when our hearts thundered against each other.

Sadness crippled me.

"You're bleeding all over me," I muttered, shoving unsuccessfully against his large, strong chest.

He chuckled. "Gonna do a lot more than that before this is over."

My heart lodged itself in my throat. "Excuse me?"

He ducked his head, nuzzling into my neck. "I haven't met anyone like you before. You had the chance to run, but you didn't. You ask the weirdest fucking questions, and I can't deny you turn me the hell on."

Haven't met anyone like you before...

He was either a brilliant con artist or a master at deception.

He reared back. "Why should I sell you when I want to sample you myself? After all, the order was for five girls, not six." A cold grin spread his lips. "It's almost like you were destined to be mine. It must be right—it's my birthday in a few weeks—you're my present for dealing with all the shit in my life."

My world screeched to a stop.

"Your birthday?"

He smirked. "The first of October."

The world began to spin—only this time in the wrong direction. "You're a Libra?" I barely breathed.

He froze.

Every muscle in his body locked down. His eyes became weapons as he dove past my gaze and into my very soul. I felt him—deep inside—searching, tearing through my unremembered memories—laying havoc to my existence.

"You're a Libra. I looked up what that means—it was rather interesting." I smiled over at the boy who held my heart.

He grinned. "Let me guess. I'm a badass, have a raging temper, and intelligent as fuck."

I giggled, my red hair glinting in the moonlight. "No, you're diplomatic."

"Yeah...sure." He chuckled. "You sure about that with my track record?"

I rolled to face him, tracing his face with my fingers. "You're graceful."

He huffed. "On my bike, maybe, but nowhere else."

"Peaceful."

He laughed. "Um, biggest lie yet."

I shook my head, seriousness layering my voice. "You are peaceful. You fight for what you believe in. You fight to protect what's yours, but in your heart... you're kind and gentle and not a part of this world." My voice dropped to a whisper. "Same as me."

He stiffened. The words "I love you" danced in his eyes. We hadn't said it yet. But I wanted to. Shit, how I wanted to.

My lips twisted into a smile. "You're also an idealist."

He nodded, pulling himself back from love and unspoken truths. "Okay, kind of agree with that one." He nuzzled my neck. "Those all sound pretty good. Any bad traits I should watch out for?"

I sighed, my eyes latching onto his lips. I wanted him to kiss me. So much. "Superficial and vain."

He huffed dramatically. "Ah, so the perfection ends." Pressing his body against mine, he murmured, "Pity I agree with them the most."

The flashback ended, hurling me against the cold tile floor below and the furious man above. I couldn't see the boy from my past. He'd been obscured—like a hazy lens or faulty photograph.

What was real? What could I believe?

"Why the fuck are you mentioning astrology?" Kill demanded. His fingers wrapped around my throat.

My skin prickled with heat. Every inch he touched set off a bonfire beneath my skin.

"You're fucking with me. If you think I'll let you play with my thoughts—" His anger welded with... Was that terror?

The lost look in his eyes came and went, like a dying firefly.

"You're nothing to me—got it? You don't know me. You don't have any power over me. And you certainly can't mind-fuck me with whatever bullshit you're trying to pull." He lowered his lips to my ear, breathing harsh. "Why the fuck would you say that?"

I couldn't answer. My racing heart stole all capability of speech.

"Answer me, goddammit," he roared. "Now!"

Everything he said—it was a lie. He felt something when I mentioned his birthday. He reacted to something hidden in his past. His anger was a front—a terrible wall around the intense historic pain blazing in his eyes.

"I'm not playing you," I whispered. "Please, tell me what you know."

He reared back, his face bloodless and savage. "I'll never tell you anything, because you aren't *her*, goddammit. It's a fucking trick. A cruel, vicious trick."

My heart cracked open, spilling its life force. I would've given up ten years of my life just to see what he hid from me.

Suddenly, his fire burned out and he slouched on top of me. His fingers unraveled from around my throat, and I sucked in a greedy breath.

He passed out, the barest whisper on his lips. "You're not her. You're not my Sagittarius."

I froze, willing his breathless confession to awake something inside me. I squeezed my eyes, letting his unconscious bulk press me harder against the tiles.

Please, remember.

My brain ached; my eyes bruised.

Sagittarius and Libra.

Nothing.

Pain leeched through me. The fireflies of truth I'd seen in his eyes fluttered around us, dispersing faster and faster with every uneven breath.

Kill's hips pressed against mine—a large belt buckle digging against my tender flesh. Despite being almost unconscious and full of pain, his masculine form woke the dormant femininity inside me.

I couldn't ignore the maleness between my legs. Or the scent of him—of midnight winds and ocean—beneath the leather and blood. My senses were alive and sparking—drinking him in.

I twisted and wriggled, trying to get free. I had to heal, had to fix, before he disappeared forever. Because one thing was for sure, I wasn't going anywhere. The flashback had cemented my decision. Regardless of my future.

His love for someone—for *her*—only strengthened my resolve to hammer him with questions until I got answers.

Kill's eyes popped open, glassy and heavy. His hips spasmed, rubbing against mine.

I bit my lip, hating how the small action sent electricity lighting up my bloodstream.

He raised his head slowly, blinking and looking drugged. The haze of his injury was thick; I worried the next time he passed out, he wouldn't wake.

"I'll make you a deal," I whispered. Hating how my voice had become soft and malleable. Every inch of him turned me from victim to seductress against my will. My fingers ached to run through his thick, long hair. My nipples tightened to feel his chest pressed firmly against mine.

I shouldn't be thinking of sex. But it was all I could focus on with how close we were.

His eyes tore wide, drenching me in green moss. "You're not in a position to—to bargain." He winced, his teeth snapping together in agony.

Keeping my voice low, I murmured, "I'm in a perfect position to bargain. If you don't let me stitch you up and get you into bed, you'll pass out again, and I'll be long gone by the time you wake up."

I'm not leaving until I understand.

His eyebrow quirked, even as pain laced his features. "You should leave. It's obvious I won't be able to stop you." He sighed, dropping the pretense of angry biker. "Why are you still here?"

"You know why," I breathed. *Please, tell me why.*

He shook his head. "You..." He stopped, changing his mind and muttering, "Hang on, you said you want to get me into bed?" His hips flexed, testing me.

I knew I should act repulsed, horrified, and rage against him taking advantage of me—but I... couldn't.

I wouldn't play games. I had too much to lose and everything to gain by being everything that I was. I wouldn't hide the fact I found him intensely attractive. I wouldn't try and pretend that I didn't want him—all of him—including every memory he kept hidden.

My world had shrunk from family and friends and a career I didn't recall, to him. Just him and me. Here and now.

Truth was the only way forward.

I never took my eyes from his. "You're focusing on the wrong part of that conversation. If you don't let me help you, you'll die."

"And that would work in your favor, so why do you care?"

"I told you. I care because I have questions, so many questions, and you're the only one around to answer them."

He grinned, but his face lost its energy, going slack once again. "I don't have the answers you need."

"I think you do."

"And if I do, but choose never to tell you—what then?"

I paused, confidence settling into my bones. "I'll make you." I smiled softly. "I can be very persuasive."

I think.

A heartbreaking shadow of despair filled his eyes, only to fade a second later. "Someone once told me I was extremely stubborn."

"Obviously. Otherwise you would've let me up by now and I'd be healing you."

He didn't smile, tension knotting his muscles. "Who *are* you?"

Sadness crept from nowhere. "I'm hoping you'll tell me."

He looked away, anger granting him energy. He rolled off me as if he couldn't stand to be close anymore. Staring at the ceiling, he growled, "Fine, fix me."

I sat up, pressing a palm against my aching back.

Kill added, "I give you my word that I'll lie here and let you poke me with a goddamn needle. I'll even permit you to wave the gun in my face if it makes you feel safer, but I want something in return."

My eyebrows rose. "You want more than your life? That's a bit greedy, don't you think?"

His head turned, his green eyes latching onto mine. "I want to know everything about you. The scars. The tattoos. All of it. I don't care how long it takes. I don't care what I have to do to make you remember." The air shimmered as his temper grew. "But I'll tell you this—if you lie to me, I'll kill you. Fair and fucking simple. I don't know if you're bullshitting me or if this is real, but regardless—one lie, and you're done."

He held up a finger, pointing rudely in my face. "You *never* lie to me. The moment you do, your life is over and this"—he waved between us—"whatever is going on with us—this ridiculous cease-fire—it's over. I'll sell you and never think of you again. I'm through being manipulated, sweetheart, and you do *not* want to make me your enemy."

He slapped a hand over his wound, his body bowing off the tiles. "You agree to those terms?"

I trembled with hope. The connection—the inexplicable bond throbbed. "I do. But only if you promise never to lie to me in return."

He closed his eyes, his forehead furrowing with grief. "Sometimes lies are the only thing keeping us sane. I won't give you that promise." His words were final. Absolute.

I hated that he asked so much from me, but I might never get what I needed in return. "And if I can't tell you the story. If I never remember?"

He shrugged awkwardly, his jaw clenching. "Then you'll just have to stay in the dark and I'll get rid of you. Don't make me regret every fucking thing I've ever done."

My hands clenched. "What do you regret?" *Was it something to do with... us?* "Please... do you know me or not?" Anxiousness made my heart thrum with pain. "Please..."

He coughed. "Go get the medical kit. I'm not feeling—" His face went slack.

Dammit.

Scuttling to my feet, I left the office and its multitude of computer screens, and dashed into the foyer. I tried two doors—one to a sitting room and another to a TV den, before finding the bathroom.

It felt strange to be running around barefoot and without underwear in the home of a man who'd stolen me from my life and who ran a motorcycle gang.

All thoughts of leaving were gone.

The front door didn't tease, nor did the phone on the cradle by the staircase.

Nothing could give me what I needed.

Only the surly man bleeding on the floor.

What if he refuses to tell you?

What if he gets tired and sells you?

My thoughts demanded some rational reasoning, but I couldn't give them any. I just knew I couldn't leave. Not yet.

This might be your only chance. You can't trust him.

Trusting him was the price I had to pay. He said he'd keep me until I could tell him the story of my tattoo and scars. It might take me a day to remember, or a year.

He'd keep me.

You hope.

Turning my thoughts off, I entered the bathroom where a glassed shower, toilet, and single vanity welcomed me with white sparkling mosaic tiles. There was no mirror, leaving me to wonder what I looked like.

Another image of mathematical equations hung from the crisp walls.

The computers and frames—was he a genius? An evil mastermind who pulled the strings of the world through the use of code?

Opening the under sink cupboard, I found what I was looking for.

Grabbing the bright red plastic box with the white cross, I made my way back into the office.

Kill lay on his back, an arm thrown over his eyes, his lips parted.

He didn't move as I fell to my knees beside him and unlatched the case. He didn't twitch as I grabbed the sterile scissors and cut his ruined T-shirt away.

I pushed the bloody garment off his shoulders and his arm fell away from his eyes. He was unconscious again.

I hope you stay that way for the next part.

Staring at the medical kit, I selected some antiseptic wipes, ripped open a needle, and threaded medical-grade twine. The kit was well equipped, more so than a normal, everyday one. Why did he have the need for something with its own battery pack and defibrillators?

Do you really need an answer to that?

His lifestyle was obviously dangerous. He held the respect of most of the men back at the compound, but not all. He'd been challenged and hurt. To live in a world where life was an uncertainty would require the use of a medical kit such as this once in a while.

Cleaning his chest of blood, I poured a decent amount of Betadine in his wound to disinfect, then tried to stem the bleeding as best I could with the use of gauze. Holding it down with pressure, I quickly swiped his chest with an alcohol wipe, watching his features carefully to see if he'd wake.

Nothing.

My heart thundered in my ears but my hand was steady. Muscle memory took over mind memory as I rested on my knees beside the naked chest of Arthur Killian and pinched the puckered ends of his wound.

I guessed it was two to three inches. Fairly deep, made by something sharp, like a switchblade or jagged point. I hoped the muscle wasn't ruptured or needed internal stitching because all I could do with the items I had was sew the outer layer.

He's lucky it wasn't over his heart. The wound was on the right side of his chest, about a hand's width from his nipple. My eyes skated over his body, taking in the firm muscles, the deep shadows that formed a six-pack, the hairless chest, and the dark happy trail disappearing into his jeans. He had the most perfectly formed V muscles, taunting me with everything that was male.

The belt buckle that'd jammed into me was the same emblem as the one on his jacket—an abacus and skull with a waterfall of coins from its mouth.

He needed a thorough cleaning. There was mud and dirt all over him, not to mention the dried blood.

Taking a deep breath, I pushed the needle through his flesh, sewing the two sides together.

He didn't flinch. His breathing stayed shallow but regular.

One blessing, I supposed.

I lost track of time as I sewed and tended to the man I should've let bleed out and run far away from. I saved his life, all while mine hung in the balance.

But I was rewarded with some resemblance of peace. *Serenity.* Partly because in doing something I obviously had talent for, I was also saving someone who could save me in return.

I knew that. Completely. He had the answers—I just didn't know if he'd share them with me.

The last few stitches, Kill sucked in a harsh breath, his eyes flaring wide.

"Ah, fuck me, that hurts." He coughed, trying to move away from the inserted needle in his muscle.

I gritted my teeth, keeping a firm pressure on his shoulder. "I'm not done. I have a few more to do. Stay still."

He glowered. "It feels like you're butchering me."

I tugged on the needle, threading it through the second part of his wound. "I'm fixing you. Don't moan."

He chuckled darkly. "Moan? Lady, you're lucky I'm not howling."

I kept sewing as he chewed the inside of his cheek and permitted me to finish. With each puncture he twitched, his muscles tightening and breath catching.

"Do you hurt anywhere else?"

He laughed, then coughed again. "You're joking, right?"

We made eye contact. A small smile graced my lips. "I meant—is there anything broken or other serious cuts that I should know about?"

He paused, staring silently as if he couldn't understand me at all. The softness in his gaze sent a fluttering of butterflies through my belly. "No," he murmured. "Nothing that you can fix."

I sucked in a breath, dying to ask what troubled him. He carried something deep—something that tarnished him, hanging over his head like a thunder cloud.

Dropping my gaze, I tied off the final stitch and sat back on my heels.

His brow dotted with sweat even though his body was ice-cold and too white. He shouldn't be on the cool tile, but I wouldn't be capable of moving him. He would have to stay there until he could move himself.

"Stay here," I ordered, climbing stiffly to my feet.

He closed his eyes, a smile tugging his mouth. "Where the fuck am I gonna go? I can barely see straight."

"I just came to the same conclusion." I dashed from the room and back to the bathroom. Grabbing the face towels from a shell-shaped bowl on the vanity, I filled the bowl with warm water, grabbed all the bath towels from the heated towel rack, and made my way back to the office.

At the last second, I dumped the towels and placed the warm water at the entrance of the room, and tore upstairs.

Was I prying by jogging down the corridor and peering into the multiple bedrooms? Perhaps, but I had one goal, and no ulterior motives.

Coming to the room at the end of the corridor, I paused and entered. It was the only one that looked lived-in. The king-size bed wasn't made, the black-and-white abstract covers bunched to one side. The scent of masculine soap and aftershave mixed with more leather and the salt spray of ocean.

Tiptoeing into Kill's bedroom, I glanced to see if there were photos or personal items. The house was too stark—missing a soul. Grabbing the thick black blanket from the end of the bed, I made my way to leave but something caught my eye on a table where coins and a lighter rested. Tucked against the wall, looking as if it'd been handled many, many times, sat an eraser.

My heart clenched as pain leeched through my blood.

"I don't care what the traits are. You could be any star sign and I'd love you."

He sighed deeply, nuzzling into my neck. "I'll be anyone you want me to be as long as you continue to give me your heart."

I pulled back, drowning in the adoration in his gaze. "Forever."

"For always."

The eraser.

It...*hurt.*

It drove a spike deep into my heart, making me cry in impatience. Unsolved mysteries—I wanted with my every breath to know *now.* That very instant.

With shaking fingers, I picked up the eraser, smoothing the faded shape of the scales of a Libra star sign.

Chapter Five

I drifted in agony, my mind touching memories too swollen with hate and disgust to linger long.

Everything inside me reeked with the need to reap vengeance. It was all I lived, all I ate, all I breathed.

Until her.

Until the imposter with green eyes.

—*Kill*

Kill's gaze opened at the sound of the large bowl clinking onto the tile. A small wave of warm water splashed onto the floor. Placing the towels beside his head, I kept the blanket away for now so it didn't get wet.

He raised an eyebrow. "What exactly are you doing?"

My heart still hurt, my mind desperately trying to unlock the meaning of the eraser. It meant something. The connection—the flashback.

I refused to meet his eyes. "Cleaning you. You're covered in blood. It's unhygienic. Then, if you can move, you need to get into bed to rest; if not, I'll make you a bed here and I'll get you something to eat."

He stared for a long moment, his eyes warring with astonishment and disbelief. "You're going to *clean* me?" He swallowed. "You're going to bathe me, feed me, and stay...even though only hours ago my brothers kidnapped you and you woke in the compound of the Pures?"

Ignoring most of that, I asked, "The Pures?"

He frowned, still unable to figure out if I was insane or just incredibly stupid. "Pure Corruption. My MC. You do understand I'm the president?" His hand swept up, heavy and slightly shaky to press against my temple. "I'm seriously fearing for your mental capacity."

Ignoring that, too, I asked, "How did you become president?"

Keep him talking. Every word from his lips was like a bread crumb leading to a meal I desperately wanted to devour.

He breathed out hard. "None of your damn business."

"Why do you live alone and not with your brothers? Isn't it a requirement to live as one happy family?"

He growled, "Again, none of your damn business. And I'm the fucking president. I can do what I want, so stop asking questions."

I nodded, eyeing his belt buckle. "Okay. Take your trousers off if you don't want to talk."

He half laughed, half groaned. "You are the strangest woman I've ever met." He looked down his shirtless front. Instead of the wry smiles he'd been giving, seriousness glowed in his eyes. He looked younger and older all at the same time—giving me a glimpse of genuineness below the rough exterior. "You want to get me into bed and out of my pants?" The words pretended to be jovial, but the tone... It wasn't.

Something tugged in my stomach, stronger than the tug in my heart. My scalp prickled with intensity and the high ceiling room with its quiet humming computers filled with stagnant awareness.

I swallowed, cursing the skip in my racing heart.

"Would you let me?" I whispered.

Kill sucked in a breath, his stomach rippling. The red, raw stitches on his pectoral looked angry against the whiteness of his flesh. The edge of a tattoo peeked from the sides of his ribs, hinting at a full back piece.

"I'll find out who you are, Forgetful Girl. And when I do, you won't be safe from me." His voice whispered around me—a trap that I doubted I'd get free from.

"I'm counting on it. And when you find out who I am—tell me." I looked into his gaze, transmitting my wish. *Unravel my life.* Then I wouldn't be locked in the dark with an unfathomable connection.

My hand went tentatively for his buckle. Without a word, he

pushed me away, reaching for the belt. He winced, letting his right arm fall to his side. "On second thought, I can't do it one-handed. You'll have to help."

Taking a deep breath, I helped him undo the heavy silver buckle, then locked eyes with him as he popped the top button and moved his hand away from the zipper.

We didn't speak, but something so sharp and in tune hung between us. It spoke in whispered verse, in barely acknowledged lyrics.

Kill cleared his throat.

I didn't move.

Then my fingers fluttered over the most private part of him, grasping his zipper and tugging slowly, oh so slowly down.

He gritted his teeth. His jeans gaped open, showing dark grey boxer-briefs. He arched his hips, giving me space to yank them down.

My eyes flew briefly to the gun resting beneath the desk. I could crawl to it within seconds. I could hold it to his head while I stood and walked away. He wouldn't die—not now that I'd stemmed the bleeding.

I didn't need to ask questions. I'd been given all I needed to know.

But I couldn't.

I just couldn't.

The only sound was the clunk of his heavy jeans as they slipped off his large legs. His hips fell back onto the cold tiles and my eyes latched onto a huge art piece encapsulating his entire left leg. The design was of crashing waves with hidden symbols, equations, and promises hidden in the froth. A girl, whose red hair flowed up with the tide and disappeared into his boxers, smiled sexily, while her green mermaid's tail kissed his knee. The damn Libra sign was in there, too—repeated over and over—yet another reminder of something I'd forgotten.

"You aren't anything like I expected a biker lord to be like."

"You had expectations? That's dangerous."

I tensed, wanting to trace the beautiful colors on his leg. "Regardless, it seems we have something in common," I whispered.

He breathed hard, kicking away the material by his feet. His eyes fell to my T-shirt-covered side, almost as if he could see my tattoo beneath the cloth. "Seems so."

His cryptic reply sent my nipples stiffening. Something undeniable drew me to him. Something I doubted I would ever be able to understand.

I jerked into action.

Grabbing the first fluffy white towel, I tapped his hip. "Up. I'll put this beneath you."

He smirked. "If you're worried about getting the tiles wet, don't bother."

I scowled. "It's for you. You're freezing. Your body has been through enough."

He froze; his eyes searched mine, deeper, harder than anyone before. "Who *are* you?" he breathed again. "Why the fuck do you care if I'm uncomfortable or bleeding to death?"

"Did you have someone to take care of you?" I hated the thought that another woman had been close to him.

I'm jealous.

He never stopped staring. "What does it matter?"

"Why is it such a mystery to be cared for? I can't let you die."

"Any other girl would've pulled that trigger the moment she got her hands on the gun."

I asked, "If I hadn't helped you, who would? You live alone. Those men at the compound seemed like half were on your side and half weren't. You have a first aid kit stocked with things I doubt are legal, yet you're amazed that I'm willing to stop you dying. I think the main question is—who are *you*?"

Tell me.

He didn't respond for a minute, raising his hips again for me to spread the towel beneath him. His boxer-briefs were so tight they didn't hide the very obvious outline of his large but flaccid cock.

His tone dropped to a curse. "No one."

"No one?"

"I'm no one. And no one would've helped me. In my world—you survive or you die. You don't rely on others to make sure you do either one. It's the very first fucking lesson you learn." The pain in his voice notched around my heart, squeezing.

"It doesn't sound like a fun lesson. Who taught you that?" I whispered, crawling to his shoulders and tapping his side to sit up, so I could place another towel below his torso.

He obeyed, never taking his eyes off mine. "I don't know why I'm indulging you, but if you must know, my father."

Father.

"Buttercup, don't go far. I'll only be a second."

I smiled at my dad. My big, strong teddy bear of a dad, who succumbed to my wish and had nicknamed me Buttercup after my favorite movie of all time: The Princess Bride.

The sun was setting, silhouetting his large body with a red-orange hue.

The brief memory faded. My father's voice was loud in my ears as if he'd literally just spoken, but I couldn't remember what he looked like, smelled like, or even if he was still alive.

Homesickness and despair lodged a ball of tears in my throat.

Kill hadn't noticed my trip to the past; his eyes squeezed as a fresh wave of pain cut through him.

Busying my hands, I murmured, "What happened? Why did your father teach you such a brutal lesson?"

His face shut down; any warmth he'd shown disappeared as he growled, "Nothing fucking happened. None of your goddamn business." He lashed out, wrapping his fingers around my wrist.

I froze.

"I never should've fucking mentioned him. Don't ask me any more questions—especially about him. Got it?"

My heart lodged in my throat; I nodded. His fingers squeezed, cutting off my circulation until little heartbeats thrummed in my fingertips, then he let go.

Sighing heavily, he stared broodingly at the ceiling.

I kneeled beside him, afraid, anxious, and most of all, burning with curiosity. It wasn't just me blanking out the past. Kill had done the same thing.

Slowly, I placed my hands into the bowl of warm water, squeezing the flannel free of excess water. "Sorry," I whispered. "I didn't mean to upset you." I shook the cloth out and placed it over the dried blood on his stomach.

His eyes flared at the warmth. He looked up, locking gazes. "You're the strangest girl."

Girl.

Not woman.

Why in that moment did I really want him to think of me as a woman?

He'd seen me naked. He'd been affected. Hadn't he?

His attention flickered between my legs, where the T-shirt did little to hide the nakedness beneath. He groaned quietly, masking it as pain, but something inside reacted. Something primal.

My eyes shot to his groin. The flaccidness had given way to something firmer, his poor blood-deprived body making an attempt to send supplies south.

I shouldn't be so pleased, but a small smile tugged my mouth. "At least we know you'll probably survive."

He looked down, anger in his eyes, then wry amusement replaced it. He half smiled. "Guess it's good news for everyone."

Shyness crept over me, and I bent my head, rubbing the damp cloth over his bruised and dirty torso, slowly cleaning him.

Silence fell between us, but it wasn't awkward. More like restful... *peaceful.*

Minutes passed as I transformed his dirty flesh to pink cleanliness.

Swirling the cloth in the bowl, I wrung it out and washed his left leg, studying his tattoo closely.

Arthur cleared his throat. "You've asked your fair share of questions of me. It's my turn. What's your name?"

My hands stilled on his kneecap.

Name?

I closed my eyes, searching deep within for something. A headache bloomed, shoving me backward, slamming a locked door in my face.

Returning to cleaning, I whispered, "I don't know."

"What do you mean you don't know?"

I shrugged. "I don't remember anything apart from waking up in the van before you tore my blindfold off."

"Nothing?" His voice was part amazement, part incredulousness. "I thought you were making that shit up."

I shook my head, once again cleaning out the cloth. The water was now grey and stained with crimson. "I wish, then I might have the answers I need and understand what I'm still doing here."

Kill clenched his jaw. "Guess I have your crap memory to thank for being alive, then."

Shifting to the other side of his body, I ran the material over his right leg, my eyes never leaving his tattoo. It looked old. Slightly faded in color but the lines were sharp and well drawn.

"What does it mean?"

He sucked in a breath, immediately going on the defensive. "What does yours mean?"

I sat back on my heels. "I just told you, I can't remember anything."

"Well, the price of knowing my ink is telling me the story of yours. And since that seems like a price you can't pay..."

"You're that protective of your design?"

"Aren't you?"

We seethed.

My chest rose and fell beneath the T-shirt. Arthur's muscles stood out, while blood blazed around his wound.

Finally, I bowed my head, resuming my cleaning. "Fine."

"You have an accent. Do you remember if you lived overseas?" he pried, dispelling the animosity between us. It was odd to think that only an hour ago we'd threatened to kill each other. Now he was mostly naked and permitting me to wash him. In some ways, even though he would deny it, he trusted me. And in a way I couldn't deny or explain, I trusted him.

"No," I murmured, cleaning the last of the dirt from his chest. Rinsing the cloth, I hovered over his face. "May I?"

He tensed, then slowly nodded.

With infinitesimal gentleness, I pressed the cloth against his cheek, cleaning away the mud and blood and hints of battle. Small scratches were visible, now the grime had been removed. His cheek was split slightly from a punch to his face, and a small tear in his ear would heal. Apart from the stab wound in his shoulder, he looked surprisingly untouched.

I bit my lip, concentrating as I wiped carefully below his eyes and up to his forehead. His long hair stained the tiles and towel below.

"I need to be able to call you something," he murmured as I ran the cloth ever so delicately along his jaw.

I looked up, entrapped by his grassy gaze. "Give me something. Something you want me to call you."

Buttercup.

I instantly dismissed the idea. That was treasured with my father. If I couldn't remember him, it was the only thing I had. I didn't want a man who seemed caring and normal one minute, then tyrannical and monstrous the next to own it.

I shook my head. "I don't have a suggestion. You choose."

He chuckled. "I'm not exactly imaginative."

I looked away, dropping the dirty face cloth into the water and moving to grab another towel. Arthur suddenly moved, grabbing my waist and pulling me on top of him.

He winced as my body sprawled on his, chest to chest, hips to hips. I felt so delicate and unsubstantial lying over his bulk. His muscles were hard, his skin warming up beneath me.

I squirmed.

He only held me tighter. "You do realize that every move you make flashes me. Seeing glimpses of your body, of places that should be hidden, is driving me fucking insane." He cupped the nape of my neck, bringing me closer. "You're not wearing underwear beneath my T-shirt, I'm concussed and blood-deprived, but it doesn't stop my thoughts from thinking things I shouldn't."

Wait, *his* T-shirt?

I stopped moving. "You're blaming me for making you uncomfortable? You made me strip. Remember?"

He smiled coldly. "I didn't say anything about being uncomfortable." His face hardened. "Having you stand in front of me naked was one thing—having it teased while you care for me is entirely another."

My lungs stuck together.

His arm lashed from my waist to my hips, pressing me firmly against him.

I gasped at the hardness of his erection, digging into my belly. "It seems as though my body is making up lost blood rather rapidly."

I couldn't speak.

"Was this your plan all along? Make me think you cared about me, so I would let you go? Out of what…decency?" He cupped my chin, his eyes boring into mine. "Because if that's your plan, Forgetful Girl, then you don't know me at all." His voice dropped to a deadly whisper. "I don't know the word 'decent.' Life beat that godforsaken word out of me, along with the knowledge of forgiveness, gentleness, and right and wrong."

I shivered at the promise in his tone—it dripped with raw emotion…of *truth*.

Whatever happened in his past had scarred him as surely as my burns.

"I had no plan," I whispered.

He thrust against me, bruising my clit with the rigidness of his cock. "You've won, though, haven't you, Forgetful? I'm almost naked and in a makeshift bed of towels. Isn't that what you wanted?"

My breath caught in my lungs. "My intention was never to sleep with you."

"Bullshit."

"Excuse me?"

"You want me. I saw it in your eyes the moment we met."

Anger siphoned through my veins. "The moment we met, you pulled a blindfold off me in the middle of death and battle. Sex was far from my mind."

He shook his head. "That's not what I mean and you know it."

Despite myself, the memory of his hands on my hips and the intensity between us as he stripped me at the compound came back.

Heat flooded my core.

Fear came thick and fast.

What if I'm married? Or already spoken for? Who would I betray if I allowed this...this angry, damaged stranger to twist my intentions?

I didn't know if I was on protection or my sexual experience.

I know nothing.

Tears prickled again and for some inexplicable reason Kill let me go.

I scurried away, climbing to my feet. I couldn't stop my eyes from locking onto the erection between his thighs.

He smirked but it was sad, hiding something I couldn't understand. "You won't ever hear me say this again, so listen closely."

I paused.

He swallowed as if it physically pained him to voice the two words that should be second nature. "Thank you," he snapped. "Thank you for not killing me and running. Thank you for stitching me up." Taking a deep breath, he pushed upright and climbed unsteadily to his feet. He swayed, grabbing hold of the office chair as he lurched forward.

I moved to catch him. "You shouldn't be standing. Not yet."

He shook his head. "I'm not going to spend the night on the floor of my fucking office."

"I brought you a blanket. I can make you comfortable."

He shook his head, his forehead furrowed. "No chance."

Grabbing me, he draped an arm round my shoulders, using me as a crutch. "Take me to bed, Forgetful Girl. I'm ready to pass out and put this day to fucking rest."

Chapter Six

I'd been spoon-fed lies all my life. I'd become a master at smelling untruths. And the woman currently residing in my home—the woman who'd healed me—smelled terrifyingly toxic. A scent that made me want to run with one heartbeat and then fuck her with the next.

She made me face things I was no longer strong enough to face.

She made me look past her scam and crave.

—*Kill*

"No. Don't!"

" 'No' isn't a word in my vocabulary, little one."

"But you're supposed to be—"

"I'm not supposed to be anything. Especially a fucking babysitter to a traitor."

The smell of smoke crept over my senses like a drug—a horrible, debilitating drug that doused me in white-hot terror. Fear I'd never comprehended squeezed my heart until I couldn't breathe. It clogged my lungs until I gasped for help.

Then the crackle and singe of burning furniture roared into being so loud—so scarily loud.

"Help!"

A cold cackle of laughter was the only help I received. "Burn, baby girl. Burn."

I was wrenched awake by large hands tearing me from sleep,

dumping me into a reality I'd rather not face. A reality that I had no tether to.

"Christ's sake, woman." Kill bowed over me, his green eyes diving into mine. "Stop screaming."

Him.

Green eyes of my lover.

Green eyes of my murderer.

The past clawed at me, dragging me back into smoke and flames and pain.

I screamed. The floodgates of my tears and fears and strain of the past hours faltered, spewing forth everything in a loud wail.

I sobbed.

I cried.

I came utterly apart.

And I did it alone.

I was an oasis of grief as Arthur Killian stood livid beside my bed. Flickers of yesterday came back, fluttering around me like memory snowflakes.

Kidnapped.

The threat of being sold.

Stitching him up.

The relief of finally having a shower and sinking into a soft, warm bed.

"For God's sake, stop." Kill shook his head. "Quit it, or I'll have to fucking gag you."

I stopped instantly. My tears dried up as if they never existed, and the raggedness of my breathing receded.

He sighed heavily. "Much better." His beautiful green eyes were bloodshot and tired but his face had a healthy glow and his jaw-length hair was swept back off his face. His black T-shirt hid my handiwork, but he kept his right arm protectively shielded by his body.

I glanced behind him, taking in the room I'd slept in. The white walls, sheer drapes, and nondescript decorating could've been any hotel in any city around the world.

He locked me in here.

After a torturous climb up the stairs, he'd left me alone in this room, and turned the key. He'd let me care for him then locked me up like a prisoner.

Scooting higher beneath the blankets, I squinted through the warm glare of the sun cascading through the window. "You should really wear a sling until the muscles aren't so sore." I pointed at his stiff arm. "You don't want to rupture the stitches."

He backed away from the bed. "You're not my nurse any longer. Get up. We have business to attend to."

"Business?"

He nodded. "You might've bought yourself some time by making me be...ah yes, that word I hate...*grateful*, but I have people to deal with, things to organize." Grabbing the covers, he tried to yank them off me, but I curled into them and didn't let go.

He scowled.

"Got shit to do, sweetheart, and I'm not leaving you here on your own. I don't fucking trust you. So you're coming with me."

"I saved your life last night, yet you don't trust me?" I wrapped my arms around my legs, hugging the warmth from the blankets.

What happened to the connection we formed last night? The truce?

He smirked. "It's the reasons *why* you saved my life last night that I don't trust you." Moving toward the black-lacquered dresser by the door to the bathroom, he jerked open a drawer and yanked out some clothes. Board shorts and another black T-shirt stating AND REVENGE SHALL BE SWEET.

I eyed him. He looked angry and bitter—no trace of the man I'd glimpsed no matter how briefly last night. There was no denying he had a vendetta against someone.

"Put these on. We'll get some clothes for you this afternoon."

"You're dressing me now?"

"You want to walk around naked?"

"No."

He stormed to the door. "Good, put the fucking clothes on."

He suddenly changed course, stomping back to the bed. He'd already dressed in black trousers, T-shirt, and big biker boots. Grabbing the end of the covers, he tore them off me, leaving me exposed and chilled.

"Hey!" I cried out as he shoved me onto my back, and yanked up the hem of my T-shirt, exposing my nakedness below. His eyes didn't latch onto my pussy or breasts but the tattoo decorating my entire left side. His nostrils flared as he followed the colors down to my hip and the perimeter of my leg.

His face darkened, gaze churning with questions. "Do you really not remember anything about this?" He poked my hipbone where a spray of cobalt blue forget-me-nots danced merrily amongst the black shadow of smoke beneath.

"No."

He poked my ugly, shiny burns. "And this. Tell me you remember something as fucking traumatic as being burned this bad. Who did it? What happened?"

"I don't know how it happened."

Burn, baby girl. Burn.

I shivered. Wrestling the hem out of his large grip, I covered myself. Had he spent the night thinking about *her*? This mysterious girl I seemed to remind him of?

"Are you sure about that?" He stood tall, towering over me. "What if someone tried to kill you all those years ago? Would that be traumatic enough to block it out?" His jaw chewed the words, yet again saying one thing while holding so much back.

Yes. No. I don't know.

Green eyes.

Green eyes held the answers to everything.

"The trauma I experienced was blocked out by being taken by your men." I held up my arm, showing him the minor burn on the underneath of my forearm. "Something happened last night. I was burned again. Maybe it triggered something in my brain, giving me amnesia."

"So you *claim*. Your last chance to tell the truth." He leaned over me, searching my gaze. "Your last chance to admit you're just faking it. I've agreed not to sell you . . . for now. I'll honor that for you helping me last night. Tell me the damn truth." His posture hinted that he fully believed this was all an elaborate act. His strong features were fierce—determined to make me trip.

I shook my head. "I *am* telling the truth. I truly don't remember anything. Don't you think I would prefer to know who the hell I am? To be able to remember my family, my name—my *purpose* in this life?"

He backed away, smirking coldly, no trace of understanding on his face. "So I guess the nickname Forgetful Girl is staying." He raised a hand, pointing at me. "I'll know when you remember, sweetheart. I'll see it in your eyes and when I do, then we'll discuss your future."

I gritted my teeth, hating his smugness, the cold aloofness that had replaced the small connection we'd been able to build last night. I had no reply.

"Get dressed. We're late."

Without another word, he stalked from the room, leaving me to slip into the board shorts and T-shirt he'd left at the end of the bed.

Prison.

I didn't know what I expected when Kill dragged me from his home, plonked me on the back of his bike, and drove along busy roads beneath hot sunshine. Ideas of returning to the compound, or going to see a doctor—which would probably be advised—even the concept of a restaurant to eat at wasn't far-fetched.

But jail?

That never crossed my mind.

Kill parked the bike in a designated parking spot and took back the helmet he'd graciously given me.

He had the manners of a gentleman all wrapped up in the cut-throat harshness of a criminal.

His brown leather jacket hid the well-tailored black blazer he'd slipped over the requisite black T-shirt and trousers. He looked like a bad businessman who'd escaped from the office to play gangster.

But I knew the truth. There was nothing playacting about him.

He smoothed his hands through his long hair, jerking it back so it looked effortlessly styled and sleek with just one motion.

I hated how capable he looked. His skin was a healthy tan, his green eyes bright with intelligence, and his five-o'clock shadow trimmed but not shorn. Until I witnessed the painful way he moved, I would never have guessed he'd almost died from blood loss last night.

"Why are we stopping here?" I tried to shield my eyes from the sunshine.

"I have to go in there."

"Why?"

He scowled. "You really think I have to answer your questions?"

"You want me to answer yours."

He huffed. "Fine. My boss is in there." He looked to the tall, threatening building, then back to me. "Shit, I didn't think this through."

He massaged the back of his neck, eyeing me coldly. "I'm so used to coming here—I didn't think about visitor's passes or what the hell I'd do with you."

My skin crawled at the thought of entering such a place. "I don't want to go with you."

He chuckled. "You and me both. There's no way I'm parading you in front of Wallstreet. Even if I could get you in."

"Wallstreet?"

He smashed his lips together, then snapped, "None of your—"

"Goddamn business," I finished for him, attempting a small smile, even though I felt exposed and entirely too vulnerable to be outside Florida State Penitentiary.

Yesterday I thought having no memory was a blessing—granting me strength where I might've been catatonic with terror. But now... now I felt as if strangers knew more about me than I ever would, that my secrets were floating around unclaimed, drifting further and further out of reach.

Kill rubbed a hand over his jaw, wincing as his injury made itself known. Then his eyes lit up, and he pulled out a cell phone from his back pocket. "I'll call a babysitter. Keep an eye on you."

"I'm not babysitting a fucking traitor."

I jolted at the violence of the sentence. Questions followed swiftly. Who was the traitor? *Me?* Was my dream from my past or just a figment of my imagination?

My fingers tickled my side as I traced the burns below. Is that how it happened? A house fire?

I couldn't stomach being around other people. Kill was my link. The green-eyed answer who I needed to keep close. I didn't want anyone else.

My head snapped up. "Wait! I'll stay. You have my word I won't run."

He paused, his thumb hovering over the screen. "I don't trust you."

"You do. I proved you can last night."

He shook his head. "Last night and today are two entirely different existences, sweetheart."

I climbed off the bike. "I agree. But you could've left me tied to the bed at your place. Why didn't you?"

His jaw worked in anger. "Contrary to what you think of me, I only tie up women who *want* me to." The way his voice dropped, as if that was a lie, sent a small ripple through my stomach. "I didn't know how long I'd be. Couldn't risk it."

"And you think bringing me into public, where I could scream and bring attention, is a better alternative?"

His forehead furrowed, green eyes blazing. "You're saying you would've preferred to be chained to the bed, unable to move, with no food, water, or bathroom facilities for the entire day?"

I blinked. "No."

"There you go, then. You're welcome, by the way." He rolled his eyes. Stepping forward, he crowded me with his large bulk, pressing me against his bike. "Two choices. I'll be the gentleman and let you decide which you want."

My stomach somersaulted with the fierceness of his stare. My skin prickled and my fingers itched to touch him—just to find proof that I knew him in some small, teeny tiny way.

He raised his hand, cupping my cheek. The roughness of his thumb caressed my bottom lip. My skin tingled and begged for more, but his touch wasn't sweet. It was almost vicious with intensity. "Two choices. Number one—you continue to be the odd girl you are and stay right here, don't move a fucking inch, and wait patiently till I come back."

Oxygen played hard to get as his thumb trailed down my throat, pressing on the very delicate and extremely vulnerable spot at the base of my neck. "And option two?" I whispered.

His voice lowered, rasping over my flesh. "Option two only comes into effect if you lose your mind and decide to tell the police what's going on here." He cocked his head. "Are you leaning toward that particular option?"

My eyes refused to move from his lips. Full, curved, way too sensual for a man who still reeked of blood and death. "Not really," I breathed.

And if I was, I wouldn't tell you.

My heart twisted at how blank and scary my future was. How unknown. Each decision came with consequences that I wouldn't know the outcome, or even how I would react, until it came to pass. I strained for another unlocking—begging my mind to be kind. But only empty blackness returned.

The world around us paused, slowing until nothing else mattered but heartbeats and breath. Arthur moved his fingers, stroking my collarbone. "In that case, option two isn't required." He bowed into me, whispering against my ear. "I don't relish the thought of hogtying you, gagging those beautiful lips of yours, and throwing you into a Dumpster to wait for me. Chances are you'd die from either the trash fumes or the heat."

My heart raced. "You wouldn't."

He chuckled. "I admit from the brief interaction we've had, I've given you the wrong impression of me. You've seen me weak." He prodded the tip of his forefinger against my temple. "Made you believe that I'm . . . what was the word . . . *decent*."

I sucked in a breath. "I know you're not weak."

He smiled hard. "Damn right, Forgetful Girl. I'm not. And you'd do well to remember that. You do *not* want me as your enemy." Something in his tone had my skin prickling. Enemy. He spoke from experience.

"How many do you have?"

His eyebrow quirked. "What?"

"How many enemies?"

He let me go, stepping away and withdrawing completely. "Too many for you to understand." Pointing at his bike, he snapped, "Stay. I'm giving you one chance. You run and I promise I will find you. And if you make me find you, I won't go through the trouble of selling you; I'll be the one to make your life a living hell instead."

Without another word, he spun and stormed toward the jail.

I reclined against the bike, wondering what the hell I'd gotten myself into. He disappeared through the visitor's entrance, leaving me free, unhindered, and fully dressed in baggy men's clothes in the noonday Florida sun.

Run.

The urge to leave was strong. My legs shuffled on their own accord, drifting away from his bike.

Wait.

I stopped.

Looking left and right, I brought my hands up to tangle in my red hair. I hadn't tended to my hair in the shower last night, so it needed a wash, my teeth needed a brush, and I needed to remember. A headache pricked against my temples as I strained to recall who I was and where I'd come from.

The sun glowed from above, searing the painful skin from whatever burned me last night.

I groaned slightly with exhaustion. I didn't know what I was doing—the risks and dangers I faced. But I couldn't ignore the one thing I was certain about. The one thing I had to explore, regardless of my safety.

Arthur Killian was the key to finding my memory. I didn't know how I knew. I didn't want to question it. But my heart was the leader while my mind took an unwanted sabbatical.

I sighed, moving back toward the Triumph.

I was staying.

For better or for worse.

Kill appeared like a black stain against the grey-washed building. Even with people milling, and the imposing presence of police, he stood out like a flare lighting up the dark.

I held my breath as he glared toward his bike. A shadow crossed his face; his hands balled by his sides.

His eyes darted around the parking lot, searching for something. Searching for *me*.

He stalked forward, no hint of injury or pain. He moved like a man barely controlling his fury, then reining in his feelings with a scary nonchalance. He was a master at discipline, beating away the unwanted emotions as easily as locking a drawer.

I didn't move from my tiny sliver of shade granted by the white Land Rover I sat against. For an hour, I'd stood under the glare of the sun but as the seconds turned into minutes and the tightness of my nose told me I was burning, I had to move.

The panic bubbling in my blood almost drove me insane as I searched for some semblance of shade. I might not remember what burned me, or how I earned half a body of scars, but my instincts did and it hated the very idea of singeing intentionally.

Kill stalked to his bike, his lips sneering as he muttered a violent, "*Fuck*."

Two hours I'd waited for him, and in that time I'd done nothing but let my mind free. I hadn't thought or forced memories to come. I'd stared at the road and conjured stories for the men and women coming and going from the visitor's entrance of the jail.

It'd been healing in a way—not to force myself. Just to be. To learn how I thought, how I reacted. And I liked what I'd learned. I cared. I didn't roll my eyes at the scantily dressed women obviously going to see their lovers behind bars, or scowl at the sprinkling of young children who screamed and threw tantrums as their mothers dragged them back to the car.

I was glad I didn't have a temper or lack of tolerance for others. I just had to hope I liked the rest of myself as I grew to remember.

Kill spun around, glowering around the parking lot. I wanted to wait to see how irate he'd get—how fast he'd lose his temper—but I didn't want him angry with me. I needed him on my side.

Standing, I stepped from shadows and into sunlight. Immediately, his gaze latched onto mine. The same reaction he'd had when he saw me on the battlefield blazed bright and true. My heart leapt out of my chest, winging to him.

The starkness of truth was a beautiful thing, reinforcing my craziness to stay.

He couldn't hide that fervor for long. It just wasn't possible to swallow something so powerful and real.

His face rearranged into the hard rage I recognized, and he stormed forward. Crossing the small distance in a blink, he grabbed my elbow. "Where the *hell* have you been?"

I pointed at the Land Rover. "Making sure I didn't turn into a charred piece of barbeque while you left me in the hottest time of the day with no sun protection."

His eyes soared up to the sky, the briefest sign of guilt crossing his face. He locked his jaw, looking back down. "You would've seen me leave the prison, but you stayed hidden. Why? Having second thoughts?"

I squirmed in his hold. "I wouldn't be here if I'd had second thoughts, now would I?" I scowled. "I would be long gone, so let me go."

My eyes widened as he obeyed, releasing me with a small shove. He grunted, swiping a hand over his handsome face. "What the hell are you doing to me? First, you make me say two little words that I haven't said to anyone in the last five years, then you make me fucking *apologize*." His eyes narrowed. "Which, for the record, hasn't happened for the last nine years of my life."

I hid my triumphant smile. "You haven't apologized—not yet."

He growled under his breath. "Don't push me, sweetheart."

I nodded. "Okay. Well, do you mind if we get out of this sunshine?" I hugged myself uncomfortably, trying to shield my arms from the glare.

He frowned but nodded. Cocking his head at his bike, he ordered, "Get on. I'll take you somewhere cool."

Chapter Seven

Riding was precious to me. The wind, the open roads, the knowledge I could go where I wanted and never return. It was the exact opposite of the cage I'd lived in for the past few years of my life.

I'd had not only freedom stolen but hope, kindness, and decency.

I no longer knew who I'd been.

I no longer *wanted* to know.

My past was dead and I fucking refused to dig up the horrors I'd endured.

It was just too damn excruciating.

—*Kill*

"You coming?"

Kill swung his leg off his bike and buckled his helmet to the handlebars of his huge Triumph. I looked around the undercover parking lot. It had low ceilings and lots of exposed pipes. "You've brought me to a plaza?"

He turned around, keeping his right arm wedged against his side. "Told you I'd get you some clothes. Plus, I'm starving."

"Probably because your body is busy trying to heal while you're gallivanting around town."

"Gallivanting?" He chuckled. "Interesting word." Stalking forward, he grabbed my hand, tugging me toward the entrance of the mall. "For someone who can't remember, you have a good dictionary inside your broken brain."

My fingers locked with his, tingling hotly. The sensation of him touching me resonated right in my core.

I tottered beside him, feeling too many things at once. My free hand went to my waist, wishing the drawstring on the baggy board shorts tied tighter. I had a feeling I'd lose them and have my pantyless behind exposed.

As we entered the mall, the sounds of eager shoppers, the smells of different cuisines, and the feel of blissful air-conditioning settled around us.

It reminded me of another time and place.

"You need a completely new wardrobe. You can't go overseas to learn how to cut up innocent puppies and be dressed in a sack."

I shook my head. "What happens if I like this 'sack'?" What if it reminds me of the past that I'm walking away from?

"Don't. Don't hurt yourself any more than you need to." Taking my arm, he added, "No more arguing—"

The flashback snuffed out like a butterfly's life span, leaving me wanting.

The crowd parted hesitantly as Kill and I entered the flow, moving with the tide toward the food court.

Kill didn't pay any attention, striding powerfully with his head high and jaw locked. It wasn't the weird wardrobe I wore bringing people's attention, or even the height and physique of the man prowling beside me. It was the leather jacket slung over his shoulders. It was the motto engraved, PURE IN THOUGHTS AND VENGEANCE. CORRUPT IN ALL THINGS THAT MATTER., and the symbolism of what he stood for.

Biker.

Criminal.

Unpredictable.

Tugging on his hand, I whispered, "They're staring. Are you sure we should be in here?"

Kill looked around. "Fuck 'em. I'm proud to wear this patch;

they're just ignorant of our world." His lips twitched. "Probably thinking I kidnapped you."

A small laugh escaped. "They'd be right."

He slowed, a pensive look flickering beneath his scowl. "So much happens beneath our noses. Even if they suspected the truth, no one would call it in. Know why?"

I sucked in a breath, sensing the importance of what he was saying—how close it was to everything I needed to understand. "No."

"Because it's more convenient to believe what they're told, rather than form their own opinions." His eyes clouded as his fingers tightened painfully around mine. "Innocence doesn't matter when ignorance is what people prefer."

There, in the crowded shopping mall holding the hand of a biker president, I glimpsed something I wasn't supposed to see.

Kill carried a weight inside. A betrayal so deep he lived, breathed, almost died with it, all while it rotted away at his happiness.

"I'm sorry," I whispered, breaking his trance, slamming him back to me.

His lips tightened and he glowered, striding faster toward the small restaurants, cafes, and well-known fast-food chains.

He didn't acknowledge me or ask what my apology was for. He knew. He just didn't want to admit that I'd seen through his lies.

Silently, he carted me inside a Wild Wild West–looking establishment, complete with horse heads, spurs, and muskets mounted on the walls. "Sit," he snapped, throwing me into a black vinyl booth.

Turning, he headed to the bar. He ordered quickly, then slid into the booth opposite me without so much as looking into my eyes.

We sat awkwardly, looking anywhere but at each other.

The décor was a good distraction but I couldn't stop my thoughts from bouncing back to Kill with every heartbeat. Last night I'd been so sure I knew him. So blind in my conviction that I'd allowed him to keep me and entered a world where I had no money, no guarantee of safety, and no promise of ever remembering who I truly was.

All for the slim chance that my gut was right.

I have no idea what I'm doing.

I still don't know what I look like.

Who lived like this? Who drifted through life completely blank and didn't tear the world apart trying to find their purpose?

Luckily, the food didn't take long to arrive; the scent of grease and salt made my mouth water.

The waiter placed two large plates with burgers and beer-battered fries on the table. "You guys want some mayo? Sauce?"

Kill shook his head.

"Okay, then. Enjoy." The waiter smiled and left us to eat. Once we were alone, Kill went to pick up his huge, oversize burger but hissed between his teeth as his right arm refused to do what he wanted.

He scowled at his chest, hating his weakness.

"I should check to make sure you don't have an infection."

His eyes darted to mine and I nodded toward his stitches. "You didn't let me see how it looked this morning." I couldn't see anything with his thick jacket in the way, but he could've popped the stitches and be bleeding again for all I knew.

"Don't worry about it," he growled, shoving a few fries into his mouth. "I was able to drive a bike; I damn well don't have an infection."

I pursed my lips. "If you feel faint—"

He lowered his head, glowering at me from beneath his brow.

I held up a hand. "Fine. I'll drop it. But it's on you to make sure you don't die."

Eating another fry, he rolled his eyes. "Thanks for reminding me that I live or die by my own hand."

Temper curled hot in my belly, but I let it go. There was no point to that argument. None at all.

Investigating my food, I couldn't hold off eating any longer and grabbed the sharp knife meant for thick fillets of beef rather than burgers. Stabbing the blade into the middle of the delicious-looking burger, I sliced it down the middle.

Kill still hadn't touched his, even though he'd devoured most of his fries.

I hesitated, glancing at the knife and back to his meal.

What can it hurt?

He needed help, and I couldn't stand by and not give it.

I reached across the table, pierced his burger, and cut it into two easy-to-hold pieces.

He froze.

Relaxing into my seat, I looked away and focused on my food—giving him some space. The look in his green gaze shouted that he wanted to punish me—for no other reason than making him feel weak by caring.

Kill still didn't move, glaring at his food. I wanted to yell at him to eat it—I hadn't poisoned the damn thing—but I kept my lips sealed.

For a moment, I thought he'd throw it away just to prove a point. But finally he picked up a half and brought it to his mouth.

I hid my smile, pretending fascination in my own beef-and-cheese goodness.

His jaw worked, the muscles in his neck making my tummy flip as he swallowed. Everything he did was done with undisputed power. It both scared me and turned me on.

Regardless of my future, I was glad I'd been there when he needed someone. If I hadn't been kidnapped or delivered to him, he would be dead. He wouldn't have sought help. In fact, he looked as if he expected to die sooner rather than later. He had an aura about him that clouded and twisted with too many dark and dangerous things.

I won't let that happen.

Nursing my promise, we ate the rest of our meal in silence.

"What are we doing in here?" I asked, looking at the wide-eyed girls and the female sale clerks eyeing up Kill in his leather cut. Their gaze held interest, fear, and a curiosity that had my tummy curling with possession. I'd seen him hurt and that vulnerability belonged to me.

Not them.

I hated the thought of others thinking they had that right.

"Buying clothes." Kill tapped my head. "You're not getting worse, are you? Short term memory fading, too?"

The high-end department store held clothing that I didn't have to look at the price tags to know I wouldn't be able to afford—even if I'd known how much money I had to my name.

Name.

Funny, I'd like to know that, too.

I waved at a rack of gorgeous skirts. "I don't have any money."

Kill immediately pulled out a silver clip, and flicked off five one-hundred-dollar bills. Holding them out to me, he said, "Take them."

My mouth fell open, eyeing the crisp notes. "You're offering me five hundred *dollars*?" I couldn't stop my face twisting with incredulity. "I can't take that."

His eyebrow quirked. "Why not? I'm not going to put up with you wearing my clothes, and you currently look like a child playing badass dress-up." He whispered, almost as an afterthought, "It looks fucking unsexy and not the way a woman should dress."

Woman.

He'd called me a woman, rather than a girl like last night.

In a fast move, he grabbed my wrist and squeezed my metacarpal bones until my hand had no choice but to flop open.

"Ow!"

He slammed the money into my palm.

Letting go, he went to move away but wasn't fast enough. I closed my fingers over his.

He stopped breathing.

Our eyes locked and the rest of the world disappeared up a vacuum where only silence and anticipation remained.

I trembled as the connection between us slugged me in the heart. His fingers twitched beneath mine; his lips parted as he fought hard against whatever existed.

I couldn't look away. I couldn't do anything but give in to the power sparking and arching and making me feel alive even while I felt completely empty. Empty of thoughts, of memories, of histories that could ruin what I'd found in the most unlikely of places.

His chest rose as deep-seated attraction and animalistic control entered his eyes.

I wanted to be alone with him. I *needed* to be alone with him.

He snatched his fingers from mine, smashing through the tender bridge we'd built.

"Take the damn money." His face whitened, the cuts from last night standing out brightly.

Money?

I struggled to remember what we were talking about.

Swallowing hard, I murmured, "If I take it, I'll pay you back."

I didn't want to owe him—no matter that it was just a simple thing, I had no intention of being in his debt.

He smiled, half cold, half full of pity. "Of course, you will. You'll pay me back when I sell you." Glancing around the store, he towered over me, dropping his voice to a whisper, "Your body will pay me back a thousandfold. Your obedience will pay me back for the small investment I'm making into your appearance."

My heart shattered.

My stomach dropped.

All softness and attraction disappeared.

Sell me.

He'd been deliberately cruel to remind me. Not that I'd forgotten, but I'd hoped that time would grant me mercy—that it would...

What? Make him fall in love with you?

I lowered my head, all happiness at being with him dissolving.

Then anger shot through my veins, granting terrible recklessness. I scrunched up the money and threw it in his face. He jolted in shock as the bills fluttered down his legs, landing on the grey carpet.

His expression locked into that of sheer anger, hands balling by his side. "Pick. That. Up."

I stood my ground. "I'm not buying clothes just so you can parade me around and get a better price for your *investment*." I hated the wobble in my voice—the pain of knowing he only kept me around because he'd ended up with six girls instead of five. I was collateral. A *bonus*.

I didn't want to be there anymore. I wanted to be somewhere quiet, so I could figure out the mess that was my life.

Heaviness settled over my shoulders. "You truly don't know me—do you?"

He tensed, looking around the store again as if people were eavesdropping on priceless information. "I told you the truth."

"You've never seen me before?"

A flicker of something crossed his face. I pounced on it.

"Last night, when you took my blindfold off—you *recognized* me. Tell me that wasn't in my head."

He gritted his jaw. "I don't have to tell you a damn thing."

"Please!" I said, louder than I'd planned. "Please... why did you look at me as if I were..."

A lover you'd lost and found.

He scrubbed a hand over his face, his shoulders bunched. "You really want to know? You're seriously going to push me—here—in a fucking department store?"

My heartbeat thrummed as I tasted the truth. "Yes. I really want to know—more than anything."

His entire demeanor shadowed, looking as if he'd stepped out of darkness itself. "You remind me of *her*. Every time I look at you, I see her. You stab me in the fucking heart every time you look at me with *her* eyes. My gut twists every time the sun catches *her* red hair. But it's a lie. You aren't her. You could *never* be her."

Finally. *Truth.*

My body trembled in my rush to uncover more. "But I could—don't you see? What if I am? I'm drawn to you, Arthur. I'm—"

"*Don't* use my name." His face went black. "And you can't be her. It's impossible."

"Why? Tell me why!"

His control snapped and he thundered, "Because she's *dead*. Okay? I've stood over her tombstone. I've read the death report. You. Aren't. Her. You're just a horrible fucking reminder of what I've lost."

He ruined me, not with his distraught voice or the agony in his eyes, but with sharp brutal reality. Here was a man drowning for a woman he'd loved so fiercely only for her to die.

He was in love with a ghost.

I wrapped my arms around my chest, holding my bleeding heart together. What could I say?

I'm sorry I look like her?

I'm not sorry I look like her?

I'm sorry she's dead?

Let me try and take her place?

Nothing would work when I'd successfully stripped away his darkest secret, the one he held so close and guarded.

"How? How did she die?"

His eyes flared wide. "I'm not telling you shit. You aren't her. You will *never* be her. You talk differently. You're burned and tattooed where she was pure, and when I truly look at you, you're lacking."

The word destroyed my heart.

"Lacking..." My head hung heavy and dejected.

He sucked in a breath, his booted feet shifting in place as if he wanted to disappear. "I told you not to push me."

I nodded. Ignorance...I suddenly wanted it back.

We stood there, breathing harsh, not caring about the milling women and their carts full of items. Finally, after what felt like an eternity, Kill ducked and collected the crumpled money. Standing, he muttered, "Go. Try some shit on. I'll wait for you."

I swallowed, then shook my head. "I—I'm not in the mood. You choose. I just want to leave."

He laughed; it was full of anger. "Me? Choose women's fashion?" He ran a hand through his hair. "Yeah, no fucking way. Not going to happen."

"Then I guess I'll stay in your clothes until you get rid of me."

Just let me go home.

I needed peace and quiet and a mirror. I craved a reflection to look into my eyes and see what was so *lacking* for him to despise me.

"Oh, for Christ's sake." Kill stole my wrist and hauled me past racks and hangers, straight toward the changing rooms.

What the hell—?

People looked up from browsing, their mouths popping wide. But no one stopped us. No one intervened. Kill was right about people staying away—even if they knew something bad was going on beneath their noses.

The second we entered a changing room, he slammed the door, locked it, then shoved me against the wall. His fingers dug into my throat. "Let's get a few things straight, shall we?" His scent of ocean winds and leather drugged me. "Never stand up to me in public. Never think you can order me around. Never think I will give a shit about you."

He breathed hard, sweat beading on his brow. "And *never* pretend I'm anything more than what I am. A man who had every inch of softness inside gutted the day they threw me in prison. The day *she* died. I'm not the man you think I am, sweetheart. Don't ever forget it."

Prison?

My legs gave out; my hands gripped around Kill's wrist. "Please let me go," I gasped. "I can't breathe."

His eyes narrowed, his fingers squeezing tighter. "Oh, and one other thing, *never* ask me about her again. I won't be so nice next time you meddle in my past."

He let go.

I bent over, sucking in huge lungfuls of air.

He backed up, pressing himself against the wall of the changing room. The small box was claustrophobic, with a bench, a chair, and a full-length mirror on the back of the door.

A mirror!

I latched onto the reflection like it would dispel all my problems.

I couldn't move as I drank in the features of the woman my soul dwelled within.

My eyes: they were green and large and luminous.

My cheekbones: they were apple-shaped and flushed.

My lips: they were full and wet and naturally pink.

My figure: feminine with muscle definition and strength.

My hair: cascaded over my shoulders in a riot of cherry and burned orange.

I was *pretty*...

I leaned forward, touching the delicate skin beneath my eyes. No wrinkles apart from a few signs of maturity. I'd say I was midtwenties.

"Recognize yourself?" Arthur never took his eyes off me, his leather jacket creaking softly as he crossed his arms.

I shook my head, my red hair rippling over my shoulders—the stranger in the mirror copied me move for move. "No," I whispered. "No, I don't."

And it hurt so damn much to see myself but feel no love, no history—*nothing* but smoldering anger for a brain so damaged it blocked everything out. Who was the girl in the mirror and why did I hate her?

Because she's lacking.

A knock on the door startled both of us. "Um, excuse me. Only one person at a time in the changing room, please," the voice of a prissy attendant sailed through the cheap veneer.

Kill snapped into action. Shoving me to one side, he wrenched open the door, and tossed a hundred-dollar bill at the woman with oversprayed blonde hair. "Forget the rules. Go and get whatever is the latest style for a girl her size." He opened the door wider, pointing at me as if I were fungus growing on the wall.

Bastard.

Arrogant, egotistical bastard.

I should've run when I had the chance. I should've run from the parking lot at Florida State. Next time, I would run and never look back.

But I didn't and I won't. Because I'm an idiot who craves answers over life span.

The girl narrowed her gaze at my figure. "What cup size are you?" she asked, eyeing my chest.

I slapped an arm over myself.

"Full C," Kill replied. "Least that's my guess." He winked cruelly. "I did get to see them in their glory last night, after all."

Tears speared my eyes, but I balled my hands.

The attendant scowled.

Not caring that the girl hadn't left, Kill slammed the door in her face.

He cracked his knuckles and slipped his jacket off his shoulders. If the action hurt his stitches, he didn't show it—back to being the hard-ass president who treated everyone else like dirt.

Sitting in the velour-covered chair, he spread his legs so I would have to step over him if I wanted to move.

I perched on the bench, crossing my arms.

Ten minutes later, the woman returned, passing me skirts, jeans, T-shirts, and dresses, along with a few gorgeously feminine lingerie sets.

I hung the hangers haphazardly on the hooks.

Kill once again shoved the door rudely in her face with a sharp kick from his chair. Looking at me, he snapped, "Try them on. Then we're getting out of here. I'm done being around society that doesn't have a clue about the real world."

"The real world being the ones with guns and jail sentences and death?" I spun away, not wanting to see a response. Gathering a pretty silver maxi dress off its hanger, I kept my chest to the wall and away from Kill's prying eyes.

Pulling his T-shirt over my head, I quickly shimmied into the dress. Once the dress was on, I bent and pulled off the ridiculously large board shorts, hiding my modesty.

Kill growled under his breath. "Clever."

I faced him, hiding my victorious smirk. He might've seen me naked once, but I had no intention of letting him see me again. He was still in love with *her.* He didn't need to see other women who lacked.

"Does it pass your approval?" My skin burned with anger—it misted from my stomach right through my limbs.

He shifted in his chair, eyes dropping to my chest. "It hides too much."

I ignored that.

It fit me well; the size was perfect and the color set off my milky skin. Turning to face the wall again, I grabbed a pair of skinny jeans and hoisted them up below the dress. Bunching the material—so he could see the jeans—I turned.

Kill's jaw was locked, his legs spread.

No! *Not again.*

I hated this man. I *deplored* him.

So why had the undercurrent of fighting suddenly switched to intensity?

Chemistry's cruel trick—sending pheromones into the air—forcing two people together who wanted nothing to do with each other.

I sucked in a breath as my eyes fell involuntarily to his lap. There was no disguising the rapidly building erection beneath the tightness of his black jeans.

His long dark hair fell over one eye, obscuring the blistering want in his gaze. "Fuck, you drive me crazy with your broken memories and pushiness, but I can't deny you've got a gorgeous ass."

My cheeks pinked as my blood notched up a few degrees.

"Glad you noticed something about me," I muttered sullenly. Dropping the material of the dress, I turned to get a sequined T-shirt with a tropical umbrella on the front. *Ignore him.* Then maybe whatever *this* was would disappear.

Tugging the T-shirt over the front of the maxi, I turned to show him. It bunched over the dress, but at least this way Kill wouldn't see any part of me. "Does this fit your strict criteria?"

He gritted his teeth. "If you're trying to piss me off—it's working."

I tilted my head, gathering my long hair and twisting it into a coil. "I don't know what you mean."

His hips twitched a little. "You know exactly what I mean."

I smoothed the T-shirt. "You claim we don't know each other, Killian, so how would I know what you mean?"

He stayed silent.

Sighing, I asked, "What do you think? Yes or no? You're the one buying it—your call."

His nostrils flared. "You don't want to know what I think."

My stomach twisted. The way he watched me did awful things to my blood pressure. An intolerable ache built between my legs.

I hated him but wanted him at the same time. It seemed my mind was locked to me but my desires weren't. I knew what appealed to me. *Him.* This brooding, temperamental man who loved a dead girl. A man who was going to sell me. Trade me. A man who denied me freedom by hiding answers rather than with chain and key.

Turning away, I jumped as Kill suddenly stood up and grabbed my shoulder. He gathered my hair, fisting it into a ponytail. "Take off the dress." Reaching with his injured arm, he hissed in pain as he plucked the buttercup-yellow bra and panty set off the hook and dangled it in front of my face. "Try this." His hand tugged my hair. "And I expect you to face me while you do it."

I gulped.

He let me go, returning to the chair.

My hands shook. Shakily, I put the underwear back on the hook. I wouldn't—I couldn't expose myself again.

My eyes snapped shut as he murmured, "Don't make me tell you again, Forgetful Girl. I want to see you. I want to see how the clothes I'm buying fit."

He was an ass, but damn if his voice didn't lick through my insides and make me quiver.

"You're not being fair."

His voice throbbed. "*I'm* not being fair? You threw five hundred dollars in my fucking face. You made me talk about things I haven't spoken to *anyone* about. You made me feel things I've tried to forget. All of that means you're completely in my debt. And you said it yourself, these clothes are mine. You're just the convenient hanger that will wear them for the time being."

I spun around, angry tears glassing my eyes. "I'll never be in your debt. Never!" Temper shot up my spine. "You're an asshole."

"I know." Placing an elbow on the chair, he cupped his chin and ran a single finger over his bottom lip. "Now strip."

"I don't owe you anything."

He waved at my body. "Won't ask again."

I backed up until the hooks pressed into my shoulder blades. "I could refuse. You can't make me."

He smiled slowly. "You could refuse. But then you'd get no clothes."

"I could walk around naked. I can imagine that would be rather inconvenient to you—your so-called brothers at the compound wouldn't do too well with double standards. What's it going to be? Letting me have my dignity, or letting your brothers see me naked?"

I didn't care my reasoning was rash and lacking common sense. I was done being cooperative.

His entire body vibrated with tension.

My voice dropped to a husky whisper. "The men who fought against you will want what you have. They'll see me by your side and imagine fucking me. Taking me. Owning me. You'll have to—"

"Shut up!" The seat squeaked as he exploded upright.

"Don't hate me for pointing out facts."

His muscles twitched. "You're taunting me." He scowled. "You really are fearless."

"Not fearless. Just strong enough to know when to fight. You've forgotten that."

"I've forgotten nothing." His green eyes swirled with smoke, full of pain and torture. "I forget nothing."

"Let me go," I murmured. "This was a mistake. Give me the answers

I know you're hiding and let me walk out the door here and now. I won't press charges. You'll never have to see or hear from me again."

Kill shook his head, gaze narrowing in suspicion. "What did you mean about double standards?"

The rules of the Club.

No getting caught.

No using the merchandise.

And, above all else, no going against family.

You broke the last rule. You and him. You were both to blame.

I stumbled forward as the flashback ended.

"Oh my God," I whimpered. How did I know that? I didn't come from this life. *You don't believe that.* I'd hated Kill's bike when I'd seen it because it reminded me of something I couldn't remember. Once upon a time, I'd been immersed in this life. This biker world of hard-edged justice and danger.

Kill didn't move. "What? What did you remember?"

There was no reason to hide it—no point ignoring the power the memory gave me.

I whispered, "Double standards. The rules of a Club. No getting caught. No using the merchandise. And, above all else, no going against family."

He grabbed my shoulders, shaking me with violent fingers. "Where did you hear that?" He vibrated with anger. "Who the *fuck* are you?" he roared.

My head bounced on my shoulders. "I don't know!" I cried. Winds, and the harsh whoosh of flames exploded in my ears, building and building until a cacophony existed inside my head. "I don't *know*!"

Kill spun me around, slamming me against the mirror. The pain made my mouth pop wide.

His lips suddenly crashed down on mine, stealing my pain, muting the loud noises inside my head.

What!?

I froze.

His large hand grabbed my wrists, pinning them above my head. His heavy bulk sandwiched me hard against the mirrored door.

My body shot to life, roaring into bearing as his magic touch awoke every part. Fire—it existed inside, scarring my innards as truly as it'd done on the outside.

What the hell was he doing?

I squirmed, trying to get free. But his fingers were tight around my wrists, keeping me prisoner.

"Quit it," he growled. "Just one taste. Just one—" Then his mouth was on mine again. His heat poured down my throat. His tongue shot into my mouth sending a convulsion of need through my body. His flavor—whoa, his delicious dark flavor made me instantly drunk on him.

My heart splintered.

My core throbbed.

My tummy clenched with heat.

My lips moved under his, unable to fight the attraction—the need.

I gave myself over to the kiss, wanting to grab his hair and hold him tight. I wanted to drink him. I wanted to *bite*. I wanted to feel him driving inside me, pounding at the padlocks of my mind and freeing me from secrets.

"Fuck," he groaned, driving his hips into mine, grinding himself punishingly. There was nowhere to run, no way to hide. I was his in that blissful crazy moment.

"More," I begged.

Something unlocked inside him and the kiss went from wild to feral. I moaned as he bit my bottom lip, licking, kissing, *thrusting* his tongue deep. Our finesse and control deteriorated us into two animals battling for the upper hand.

I arched my back, pressing myself harder and harder. He rocked his hips, his erection a scorching weapon between us.

We punished each other but our bodies craved more, more, *more*.

I melted. I glowed. I begged.

He kissed me so hard the mirror crunched against the back of my head, but I didn't care. All I cared about was getting him to lose the rest of his tightly reined control.

I moaned as he kissed me deeper, drawing blood as my teeth cut into my upper lip.

Metallic blood shadowed the kiss with brutal flavoring, but he didn't stop.

He kissed me as if I were the dead girl he'd lost and he couldn't stop the love blistering in his heart. He kissed me as if I were so endlessly precious and desired.

His body drove me higher and higher until wetness trickled down my thigh and my thoughts became nothing but sex and writhing need.

I scrambled to get closer.

Our heads moved as our kiss grew frantic.

Our legs entwined as we rode each other.

Our moans echoed as we gave ourselves over to pleasure.

I rocked, panting as my core throbbed for the part of him encased in his jeans.

I'd never been devoured this way. I would remember if I had.

In one kiss, Kill obliterated any past lovers I might've had and stamped his absolute mark on my soul. I didn't care about the rest of it. I didn't care about the complications between us. All I cared about was connecting with someone on a visceral level.

Kill pulled back, his pupils black and full of fire. "We're leaving."

I nodded, breathless and bruised.

"I'm going to fuck you."

I swallowed and trembled.

"You're mine."

Chapter Eight

Fuck.

I'd kissed her to see.

To drink her lies and taste the truth.

I'd kissed her hoping to put an end to the blistering pain inside my heart.

To admit to myself that whatever drew me to her was false.

It didn't work.

Her mouth intoxicated me. She made me want her more than anyone.

That was a lie.

There was someone. Someone I couldn't think about without wanting to tear my chest open. Someone I would betray. Someone I was *already* betraying by permitting this woman to warp my mind.

I had to throw this imposter away.

Before it was too late.

—Kill

I'd lived trials I couldn't remember.

I'd learned skills I couldn't recall.

I'd lived a life that no longer existed.

Yet I knew one thing with utmost certainty.

I'd never been more alive than when Kill held my hand and marched me to his bike.

I'd never been more aware as I sat behind him and wrapped my arms around his muscular waist.

I'd never been so willing to throw everything away for more of what he conjured in my core, in my heart, in my *soul.*

The heat.

The throb.

The *need.*

He was an addiction to my painfully deprived mind.

And I was petrified.

Not because of the recklessness in which I pressed my breasts against his back, or the greed with which I took his mouth when he pulled into his garage.

No.

I was terrified that nothing else mattered to me.

Nothing else but the selfish pleasure of want.

And that was a dangerous, *dangerous* place to be.

One tracked. One minded.

Completely vulnerable and open for pain.

I played with my demise.

I ran straight toward my downfall.

Chapter Nine

How the fuck could I stop this?

I couldn't stop this.

I didn't want to stop this.

For the first time in my godforsaken life, I felt…felt *something* instead of the cold hatred of vengeance.

It gave me strength all while making me weak.

I wanted more.

Therefore, I had to stop.

Before she destroyed me—just like all the rest.

—*Kill*

We stared at each other.

Breathing hard and rough, we didn't move to close the distance between us.

The moment we'd entered his bedroom, we'd sprung apart like magnets that went from connection to polar repulsion.

I stood hesitantly in the middle of his bedroom, unable to control my crazy overbeating heart. Kill stood braced against the door, his hands balled by his sides, his face a mask of lust and confusion.

In that second, I was a student.

About to be taught how to please a biker lord.

The bedroom shimmered with everything that sparked between us. Prisms of need bounced with the late-afternoon sunshine, the air thick with unspoken explanations.

I had so many questions.

But we somehow wordlessly agreed not to say anything. One wrong sentence would jeopardize everything that was about to happen.

Kill dragged a hand through his disheveled hair. It gleamed almost black, windswept and sexy from the manic bike ride home. I'd never been so eager to do something so wrong.

Was I about to commit adultery? Would my soul go to hell for being so consumed by one need—one incredibly selfish need?

Kill's green eyes never unlocked from mine, cranking my anxiety until I trembled.

He made a half-distraught, half-throttled noise in the back of his throat as he leaned against the door; his hand gripped the handle as if he couldn't bear to let go.

I tried to guess what was going through his head.

But I'd been lost the moment he'd kissed me in the changing room. This was all him—I wasn't in charge; I didn't *want* to be in charge. I hoped he'd slip and somehow shed light on everything that taunted me.

"Get on the bed," he ordered, his knuckles going white around the doorknob.

I stiffened and inched toward the large mattress.

I felt as if I existed in a booby-trapped battleground. One wrong move and something would snap and kill me. I tried to swallow but had no lubrication in my throat—it had all drained below to throb between my legs.

I'd never been so turned on.

You think.

I shouldn't be doing this!

You won't stop.

"I won't tell you again, sweetheart. Get on the bed." His voice was dark and full of gravel. My eyes dropped to his jeans. He was rock hard—just like he'd been while pushing against me in the store.

God, help me.

What if I'm a virgin, not on the pill, married?

I shoved those thoughts away, moving faster toward the bed. The closer I got, the heavier Kill breathed.

I bit my lip as the bed brushed against my legs. Instantly, Kill pushed off from the door, prowling toward me.

With a powerful shrug, he discarded his leather cut, letting it puddle against the charcoal carpet. In another step, he reached down and tugged off one large boot, then the other.

His jaw twitched as he grabbed the hem of his T-shirt and ripped it over his head, hissing between his teeth as his stitches pulled, but he never stopped closing the distance between us.

A spiral of lust shot through my system as I gawked at his cut muscles, the smoothness of his skin, and the dark happy trail disappearing into his jeans. His freshly stitched scar looked red and puffy. Panic filled me at the thought of infection.

My heart raced to slow down the monstrous wave of animalistic need. "I should really tend to that."

He shook his head, his eyes hooded. "You're tending to something a lot more important." Only a yard separated us, his body heat singeing me even from that distance.

My stomach twisted, sending sparks through my body.

"Take off the dress," he murmured. My fingertips brushed the silver maxi he'd bought me at the store. After our kiss, he'd bundled everything into a pile, dragged me from the changing room, thrown some money at the clerk, and stolen me away on his motorbike.

With fluttering heartbeats, I gathered the material at my shoulders and shimmied out of the soft dress. It pooled around my ankles, leaving me exposed in the buttercup-yellow lingerie.

He tensed, his stomach tightening so every ridge of him stood out with chiseled male perfection.

"Christ, you're beautiful."

A moan built in my chest. He'd barely whispered, only breathed the words, but it made me feel like the most powerful woman alive. He didn't look at my scars. He didn't see the strange mix of inked beauty and burned ugliness. He just saw *me.*

I'm not lacking.

"Yellow suits you." His eyes shadowed with pain.

"Come on... let me call you it, too."

I shook my head, planting my fists on my hips. "Nope. Only he can call me that. You call me Sagittarius. My dad calls me Buttercup—that's how it works."

He pounced on me, wrapping his arms around my waist and plucking me effortlessly from the floor. "But you're my sunshine. You glow in yellow. I want to—"

I squealed as his hands tickled me and the rest of the argument of my nickname dissolved in favor of kisses.

I blinked, dispelling the memory.

"What's another word for yellow?" I breathed, willing, hoping, *praying* I could trip him up. What if the grave of a girl who still had his heart was false? What if she was *me*?

I didn't care I spoke differently or he said the girl in his past wasn't scarred or inked. Things changed. Life took familiarity and often turned it foreign.

There were too many coincidences. Too many pieces slotting together inside my head.

Kill froze, his large hands pausing on his belt buckle. "What?" His nostrils flared and anger—bright and blistering—stole the erotic nature of his glare.

His hands dropped from his belt. "Explain what the fuck you meant by that."

No! I felt him withdrawing, his soul lurching faster and faster out of reach.

I shot away from the bed, darting to his side.

His eyes tightened and every muscle in his body went rigid.

"I didn't mean anything by it. I'm sorry—forget I said anything."

He breathed hard, his chest rising with a heavy inhale. He didn't say a word, searching my eyes.

"Please, Killian. I want you to kiss me again."

Kiss me like you did. Forget the past.

The intensity between us sparked again like smoldering tinder. I flushed. I shivered. My body didn't know if it should be hot or cold, embarrassed or confident.

He didn't touch me.

Only watched.

Finally, never breaking eye contact, he undid his large belt and unzipped his jeans with steady hands. His pectoral muscles twitched as he pushed at his hips and discarded the denim with one shove.

My mouth went bone-dry. I couldn't stop looking at the silver scars from past injuries, or the bright red one that gave him a reason to let me into his very private world. I was under no illusion that I'd been granted an exclusive pass and not one that I wanted to ruin.

"Take off your bra," he whispered. His hand went to his cock, wrapping around the insane hardness visible in his grey boxer-briefs. A damp spot darkened the material from his excitement, and all I wanted was to see what he would give me.

Every inch of me was hyperaware, made worse by him not touching me. By making me strip, he forced me to give him everything I was, all while being exposed and on show.

My hands disappeared behind my back. My fingers fumbled at the clasp. The pretty lace bra unsnapped, sagging off my shoulders. Catching the cups, I held them for a moment against my flesh.

This was worse than stripping at the compound—that had been business. We'd be merchandise, stock—this…everything about this was pure sex. And dominance. And crazy anticipation.

"Drop it," Kill murmured.

I obeyed, letting my arms fall to my sides, watching the bra flutter to the floor.

Suddenly, his fingers pressed against my chin, guiding my eyes up and up, until I drowned in his green gaze. "Never look away from me."

I shook my head, unable to speak.

"Take my boxers off."

My heart ceased to beat as I hesitantly placed my hands on his hips. He shuddered beneath my touch. My tummy somersaulted as he sucked in his bottom lip and bit hard.

I *loved* that I affected him.

Hooking my fingers into the elastic waistband, I tugged slowly.

His head fell back as the large length of his erection sprang free. I couldn't stop looking at it. The huge size seemed to grow in thickness and length beneath my inspection—looking more swordlike than a piece of anatomy.

Oh, wow.

The mermaid's red hair that swept up with the tide in his leg tattoo wrapped around the base of his fully shaved cock. Over the top of his erection, the cascading hair dwindled downward—the barest of strands inked on his balls.

"That must've hurt."

His jaw clenched. "It did."

"Why go so close to something so delicate?"

"Why did you seek the same pain by tattooing your nipple?"

I had no reply for that. "Stop deflecting. What was your reason?"

He opened his mouth, then snapped it closed. Something flashed over his face and he shook his head. "Because she died in agony. I wanted to own that part so she would know she wasn't alone."

The slow burn in my stomach turned to red-hot heat. "Kill—"

His hand shot up. "Stop talking." His green eyes blazed with menace. "Promise me that under no circumstances you'll touch me unless I let you."

"What? Why?"

He grasped my hair, holding me firm. "Because I said so. That's why."

Walking me backward, he pressed a strong hand on my sternum, toppling me onto the bed. Towering over me with his erection sticking proud and strong between his legs, he looked like the god of sex and delirium.

I loved him naked. I loved his effortless power and danger.

"Prop yourself up on your elbows. I want to see you."

My mind stuttered like a faulty television set, flickering with memories of a younger boy with narrower hips and total innocence. I couldn't distinguish between the green-eyed boy I loved and this beast of a man standing naked before me. Were they the same? *Please, let them be the same.*

"Spread your legs," he murmured.

I obeyed, my heart squeezing.

If he was my soul mate from my past—how could I have forgotten him? How could I have ever walked away from a love so all-encompassing? I hated to think I'd hurt him by either breaking up with him or disappearing.

But...I couldn't have left him.

He thought his girl was dead. He had proof. His belief was absolute.

My hope tore into smithereens. I wasn't her. No matter how I tried to force it. I was homesick, lovesick, but most of all mindsick for everything I didn't know.

"Wherever your mind is, stop," he growled, fisting his cock. His colorful tattoo jerked as his quads locked in place.

My entire attention became riveted on his harsh grip.

"I'm here."

"You better be."

I latched eyes with him. "There's nowhere else I would rather be, than here—with you."

He snorted. "So damn strange." His hand moved up and down, leisurely but punishing himself with pressure. He looked as if he would leave at any moment or attack and ruin me for life. He was...elusive. As if *he* was the one not truly here. His body was, but his mind—that was with his true love. The ghost I would never be able to compete with.

The thought made me endlessly sad. There would be no connection building—this was just sex. I had to keep that wrapped around my heart, so he didn't shatter me when it was time for this fantasy to end.

His eyes went to my nipples—one colorful, one natural. His pace increased and his cock went ever harder. "God, I want to crawl inside you." His gaze danced over my skin, taking in my tattoo.

His stomach rippled, tensing as my pants moved the fine hairs on his upper thighs. Bowing over me, he pulled my hips so my feet pressed against the floor then knocked away my elbows so I sprawled flat on my back.

I cried out as his hot, wet mouth captured my nipple, sucking it deep and hard.

My hands instantly flew to his hair, crushing his face against my chest.

He stormed upright, breaking my fragile hold on his long dark hair. "What did I just make you promise?"

I gulped.

Not waiting for my reply, he shook his head and stalked toward his walk-in closet. Coming back a few seconds later, he held out a gold tie. "Give me your hands."

I blinked. A riot of thoughts went through my head, but I snatched onto the strangest one. "You're a president of a biker gang, yet you have a *tie*?"

His lips twisted into a cold smile. "There's so much you don't know about me. Now give me your hands."

"I want to know everything there is to know."

He scowled. "We never get what we want. Learn to live with disappointment."

Then he pounced. Effortlessly, he pinched my wrists together and tied the silky material around me. The second I was imprisoned, he plucked me from the end of the bed, marched me to the side of the mattress, and patted my ass. "Climb into the middle. Get on all fours."

I looked over my shoulder. His face was unreadable, blocking all lust or clues. He wanted me—there was no doubt about that—and I wanted him—the wetness between my legs was a testament to how much I did—but he'd shut down a part of himself that I missed.

The part I'd seen very briefly last night and in the changing room today.

"Next time I tell you to do something—you do it. Immediately, remember?" Spanking me, he grabbed my waist, and practically threw me on the bed. Crawling with bound wrists wasn't easy, but I did as he'd asked and moved to the center of the bed.

There was nothing vulnerable about this man. He was there to take and not give anything in return.

"Spread your legs," Kill ordered.

The bed creaked as he climbed behind me, the heat of his naked thighs warming my backside. I jolted as his fingers dug into my hips, tugging at the yellow G-string.

Slowly, he dragged them down my thighs, letting them imprison my knees on the bedspread. I waited to see if he would tell me to remove them, but he only spanked me again—not hard, but enough to keep me very obedient. The heat on my skin ensured I would jump to his next instruction.

"Wider."

I opened wider, fighting against the tightness of the panties wrapped around my knees. The degradation of not seeing what he was doing and being kept in the dark as to what he planned made my heart gallop like a feral pony.

He leaned to the side of the bed and with long arms pulled out a blue wrapper from his bedside table.

I tensed. He was going to take me so soon?

What happened to the passionate man in the changing room? What happened to his fiery touch and insanely possessive kisses?

My tummy clenched at the thought of being used like this.

Kill placed the condom on the mattress beside my knee. His breathing hitched and my head lolled forward as his touch landed between my legs. He stroked my pussy, going from clit to entrance. There was nothing tentative about his fingers. This wasn't even foreplay—it was a means to an end.

I bit my lip as he stroked me again, dragging his large fingers through my wetness—the wetness he'd conjured when he'd kissed me so damn passionately.

What was this? This impersonal act reeked of self-preservation on his part. He didn't want me to face him, touch him—give any hint that I had feelings for him other than sexual.

He's protecting himself.

"Fuck, you're so ready for me." I didn't know if that was awe or disgust in his voice.

My mind was intrigued with what was happening but my heart was revolted. I didn't sign up to be used like a plaything. I'd agreed to let him *connect* with me.

Every second that connection faded, until we might've been strangers and money was about to exchange hands.

Stop this.

The word echoed in my brain.

You can't.

My hair stuck to my neck as my body flushed. I had to go through with this. I had to break inside his heart if I had any hope at learning more. Maybe sex was the key.

Deciding to take what this was—a release for both of us and nothing more—I murmured, "I was ready for you the moment you kissed me in the changing room."

He made a noise in his chest. "Yes, that was a mistake on my part."

"A mistake?" My voice turned soft. "A kiss can never be a mistake. I loved it."

He growled low. "I don't kiss. I have my reasons why."

The sadness in his tone drove me wild.

Tell me!

He suddenly inserted a finger deep inside me, causing my back to bow and my skin to break out in goose bumps.

Oh God.

There were no butterflies or sparks. His touch was a spear, fast and swift, building need in an instant.

He withdrew, smearing my wetness around my clit, stroking me hard, fast, and with expert precision.

My legs trembled and my arms burned with the awkwardness of staying on all fours. I wanted to collapse from pleasure.

"Have you had sex before?"

I struggled to understand the question while he touched me so exquisitely. I racked my brain, trying hard to remember. Surely, I should remember something like that—something so basic?

You don't even know your age. How could you know if you've had sex when your name and birth date are more important than lovers?

I hung my head. "I don't know."

Kill grunted, moving his fingers from my clit and sliding back inside me. The delicious pressure and rocking of his touch unspooled me. I panted, my hips moving on their own accord.

"God—*please* ... more ..." The words spilled from my mouth.

Obeying, he added another finger, stretching me with delicious dominance. I cried out as he sank deep and wriggled his digits inside, spreading intensity through my pussy.

My legs tried to scissor together, but he pressed on my lower back, keeping my legs spread and at his mercy. "I don't think you're a virgin. You're tight but two fingers shouldn't bring you such pleasure."

I shook my head, gritting my teeth, wishing it didn't feel so good—not when he was analyzing me as a piece of equipment rather than a woman.

"Please…" I murmured again, not even sure what I was begging for. A hug? A kiss? A kind word?

Kill drove his fingers harder, his voice full of sin. "A few things you should know about me, sweetheart."

He expected me to listen? When all I could do was *feel.*

"I'm going to fuck you. I'll fuck you until I come, and I'll be grateful for the release. But I will never kiss you, tongue you, stroke you, or snuggle. I don't want your lips around my cock. I don't want your arms around my neck. And I certainly don't want your love." He brought his fingers up to my clit again, pressing hard and almost cruelly against me.

Sparks erupted; my nipples throbbed.

The pressure was *good.* Too good. The unhurried but fast pace was mind-blowing; the sensation of being hated, all while being turned on, twisted my moral compass until I couldn't understand where I stood in this new world.

"Do you agree to those terms?"

I panted, stars popping behind my eyes. An orgasm built from nowhere and I forced my pussy harder into his hand.

He gasped, rubbing hard and fast, his other hand gripping my hip and rubbing his hard cock against the crack of my ass. "Come, sweetheart. I won't wait for you once I'm inside you. This will be fast—a means to an end. I want to be inside you, but mark my words, this is *not* making love."

His touch turned even more brutal, and I had no choice but to propel myself down the slippery slope and leap into the nether, where fireworks, symphonies, and crashing waves of passion ignited between my legs.

"God, oh God…*shit!*"

My entire body spindled then unraveled in a cataclysmic release. I moaned loudly, collapsing from my elbows and face-planting into the covers.

The vague sound of foil tearing, the angry grunt of Kill as he rolled the condom onto his length, and then the pinching, possessing, *consuming* pressure of being taken smashed through my senses.

His heat smothered me; the long, thick intrusion of his cock stretched me with no softness or shyness. He took me as if I'd always belonged to him.

The instant he sank inside, he hissed, "*Fuck*."

The power of that little word, and the violent reaction he had, set my body aching with the need to release. Again.

Shuddering, his hand squeezed the base of himself as he sank farther and farther. Inch by inch, he sheathed himself until I couldn't move without feeling him everywhere.

With no warning, he pulled out and slammed back inside me. A ragged grunt exploded from his throat as he drove fast and deep.

My heart burst with feeling. There wasn't anything sweet about this, but despite his rules of no touching, looking, or any connection whatsoever, he couldn't stop the sublime way our bodies moved. The perfect synchronicity of pace and pressure.

The second he'd thrust inside, we'd locked together like two out of place beings who found their true home. No words could ever dispel the certainty of that.

I cried out as he drove deeper. "Fuck, you look so good with my cock inside you."

My stomach flipped and I grasped the sheet to propel myself backward to meet his speed. "More," I moaned.

Decorum didn't exist in the room. Civilization and conversation were moot points as Kill lost himself and fucked me.

There was no way to explain the frantic way he clutched my hips—diving into my wet heat as if he was born to take me. He fucked me as if I would disappear. He fucked me as if he couldn't stand himself. Self-hatred oozed from him with every perfectly driven thrust.

"Fuck. Why do you have to feel so fucking good?" The curses dripped from his lips.

I relished in anguish, knowing he must feel something and it was killing him to be unfaithful to the memory of his ghost girl.

But he had to move on.

I'll help you move on.

His fingernails dug into my flesh as he brought me back, slamming against him as he thrust harder and faster.

"Shit," he gasped. "Goddammit, you feel fucking amazing."

"Oh, baby, you feel so amazing."

I smiled with tight lips and stared at the ceiling as I rode out the pain of losing my virginity. I refused to look into his sweet brown eyes.

He pressed butterfly kisses all over my brow. "I'm so happy we're each other's first. So special. I'll always remember you."

I nodded and kissed him back and moved my hips and moaned as he thrust for a few seconds then came.

I stroked his back and kissed his flushed cheeks and lay silently below him.

All the while I screamed inside. I cried with dry eyes for another.

The flashback came and went, so full of emotion and heartache, I choked on a sob. I couldn't contain the pain. The boy who'd taken my innocence had been so tender, so kind, so in love with me.

Yet I'd felt endlessly trapped.

He wasn't *him*.

But here... with a man I didn't know driving into me with reckless uncaring, I felt... free.

Free from a past shrouded deep in my brain. Free from wrong decisions. I was unshackled and taken and *possessed*.

I loved it.

My lips parted as I breathed hard, my knees digging into the covers as Killian rocked viciously. He was the opposite of caring, the polar eclipse of gentle, yet he made my heart spread its atrophied wings and fly.

"Yes," I moaned. "Don't stop."

His hot balls slapped against my clit as he rode me harder and faster than I thought possible.

"Shut up," he growled, slapping an open palm against my ass. The punishment sent my blood arcing to the surface of my skin, making everything blister in intensity.

I wanted more. I wanted to be alive.

"Arthur..." I looked over my shoulder. The image of his tight eyes and pleasure-flushed face sent another clench through my core.

"Shit, you don't learn." His large hand came down, clamping around my neck, forcing my face away and my eyes to focus on the plain wall. "My name is not yours to use. Shut the fuck up while I take you."

Why?

Because you don't like to be reminded that you're human? A man who needs companionship?

He groaned in a mixture of guilt and bliss. My stomach twisted and another orgasm sparked as he drove upward, hitting my G-spot.

Not letting go of my neck, he grunted as he thrust again and *again*. I squirmed beneath his grip to look at him. I wanted to see this animal consuming me.

But his fingers tightened around my nape, pressing my cheek harder into the bed. "Don't look. Don't fucking look at me with *her* eyes."

My heart broke as his voice cracked. The pain inside, the misery—it was all wrapped up in anger and rage. My eyes fluttered as a throb in my core took me completely by surprise. Yes, he was demanding and stripped me of dignity, but at the same time he'd given me himself to pleasure and please.

The fierce, slightly unstable Arthur Killian became a simple-minded creature. He surrendered to me completely as I wriggled my hips and lavished the feeling of being taken. The heat of his flesh scalded my thighs; the rush of his breath tickled my back.

I wanted him to come. I wanted his release. I wanted to have that power.

He panted in time with his thrusts. His hand on my neck pushed harder, forcing me to take more and more. My eyes watered as he took me to heights I'd never explored.

Suddenly, he bent over me, pressing his body along the length of mine.

I barely had time to suck in a breath when he thrust harder from behind, gliding deep and fast. I was so turned on. Soaking for his violence.

His large hand spanned my hip, while the hand on the back of my neck never stopped gripping me. He half throttled me from behind as he fucked me hard, so damn hard. And ruthless, so damn ruthless.

It was the hardest I'd ever taken—at least I thought it was—but he still held something back. Still didn't give me his all. I jerked my hips, encouraging him to go deeper. I wanted to come again. I wanted to own his pleasure.

His cock stroked me until my mind filled with sparks. His fingers tightened around my neck and then he came—spurting inside, fucking me into mind-flipping oblivion.

His body jerked as the waves of his orgasm wracked his frame. He groaned long and low, shuddering as the last ripple drained him dry. The moment he finished, he pulled out and rolled away.

I collapsed onto my stomach, bruised, tingling, and struggling with the mixture of emotions squeezing my heart.

Kill bent over me, undid the tie around my wrists in a quick release, and then climbed off the bed.

Nothing was said. Nothing was mentioned.

Silence was absolute. And we both had no courage to break it.

I lay in artificial darkness with an unbearable throbbing between my legs as Kill strode naked from the room and didn't come back.

Chapter Ten

Happiness was not permitted in my world.

I couldn't afford to think of softness or weakness or want.

I hurt more than any other time I'd been unfaithful to her memory. Worse than any moment of disgusting sexual need.

I cheated on the woman who owned me. I wanted to howl at the moon, curse the gods, and wreak havoc on the earth for what they'd done to us.

I was so damn alone, so fucking broken, so hauntingly lonely.

And I would never find peace until I was with her again.

Death was my one salvation.

But not yet.

I couldn't join my lover until I'd taken care of a few things.

Carnage.

Payback.

Retribution.

—*Kill*

"No, you got it wrong again." He leaned over me and snatched the pencil from my fingers. Turning it upside down, he used the barely there eraser to rub out the equation.

Once my answer had disappeared, he passed me back my pencil. "You need a better eraser. You make more mistakes than anyone I know."

I pouted, brushing off the eraser shavings from my homework. "You could be a little nicer about it."

He scoffed. "Nicer? You asked me to be hard on you. How else will you get the grades you want to be a vet?"

I looked into his green eyes. "You don't have to rub your geniusness in my face, though. I feel stupid next to you."

His cheeks pinked.

Was this our first fight? My heart rabbited and I felt sick, so sick to think we weren't as perfect for each other as I'd hoped.

Then he smiled, pulling me into his embrace. "I might have a brain more adapted to numbers than you, but you... One look from you... and I'm the stupidest boy alive."

I froze. "I make you stupid?"

He kissed me ever so softly. "Crazy stupid. Insanely stupid. Want to know why?"

"Why?" I breathed into his mouth.

"Because when you're around, I never think with my head, I only think with my heart, and it only knows one thing—how much it adores you."

The sunshine stole me from the wonderful dream, shoving aside teenage crushes and depositing me back into a body that burned from sexual overuse.

My muscles creaked and groaned as if I were a derelict house after withstanding a brutal earthquake.

I stretched, wallowing in the sadness of missing a boy I didn't know was real. I still hadn't seen him. The dream had been crisp apart from the deliberate fuzziness around his image. My brain seemed to enjoy teasing me with snippets but never giving me the full clue.

Kill had never returned last night and I'd spent the witching hour full of loathing one minute and victory the next. He'd taken me—in that I had power. But he'd left—so I was nothing more than a body to use.

I needed to find a way to obliterate his protective rage and explore what he kept hidden beneath.

But first, I had to do the same to myself. I refused to be blind in a world with so many secrets. It was time for Operation Smash Through Amnesia.

Staring at the white ceiling, I balled my hands. Breathing deep, I said out loud, "What is your name?"

I paused. Waiting for my brain to search through the mess, unlock doors I had no keys to, and deliver an answer. Buttercup was the only thing that came. Even Sagittarius wasn't strong, as I somehow knew he'd called me Buttercup, too.

"Where do you live?"

I waited.

And waited.

"What's your best friend's name?"

Corrine.

My heart rate spiked.

"Corrine."

Oh my God, I remembered her. Pixie-cut blonde hair, slim, energetic. She'd been studying veterinary science with me at...

I growled in frustration and skipped to my next question. "How old are you?"

You're three and a half years younger than him. He thought it was too much of a difference. That's why he refused to take your virginity.

I slapped a hand over my mouth. I willed more to come. Nothing but blankness returned.

The shrill sound of ringing drifted in through the open door. A doorbell? A phone?

Last night, after I'd come alive beneath the man who held my very existence in his hands, I'd welcomed the dawn in an empty bed.

Kill had gone and I'd battled with the urge to follow. I'd wanted to go after him, but managed to stay in bed—*his* bed. I knew it wouldn't be wise to chase him, not with how complex his emotions were. I had no right to pry into his heart.

But curiosity was an insatiable need.

Sliding from the warm covers, I wrapped a blanket around my nakedness and went in search. Down the long corridor, and ascending the stairs, I found Kill in his office—the same room where he'd very nearly died.

The floor was cleaned and the towels and bloody water had gone.

Did the cleaning lady do that or him?

Sunshine bounced into the room, defying the white blinds, half drawn to stop the glare on the computer screens, and the large mathematical artwork loomed ever higher, as if taunting me from my dream.

He helped you with your homework.

Whoever the boy was who owned my heart, he was smart—just like this brooding president.

Kill sat in the glow of early morning sun, his naked chest gleaming from a recent shower. He hadn't dressed yet, but wore a pair of black boxer-briefs. His tattooed leg was hidden beneath his desk. I leaned against the door frame, watching the planes of his back as the golden light made him seem otherworldly. The large ridges of muscle elongated down his spine, looking both masculine and graceful. The huge tattoo was a stain on his flesh. The skull and coins were there, along with the motto—but it looked clouded. As if it'd been drawn over another design—a design that refused to fade beneath the new ink.

I much preferred the tattoo on his leg. It had stories to tell—good stories, *happy* even. The one on his back was more of a sentence—a lifestyle I didn't fully understand.

My eyes went to the information dancing on the computer screens.

"See that, Buttercup?"

I opened my eyes, turning to face the television. I lay on his lap, drowsy and content after our day in the sun at the beach. "See what?"

He leaned down, running his gentle fingertips through my hair. "The stock market. That's called a pip spread. It's how people make money from trading. And this particular platform is the most lucrative one there is."

I scrunched my nose. I couldn't make sense of the flickering colors and lines jerking down, then up, then down again. "What is it?"

"It's the FX."

"In English, please, brainiac." I pinched him, smiling as he chuckled quietly. No one else got to hear him laugh. That was mine and mine alone.

"It's the foreign currency market and I'm going to use it to make us a fortune."

The flashback ended.

The knowledge was bright—each small glimpse into my past building a picture out of slices of history. I had no idea what the big picture would reveal but I had to trust my brain would work it out—eventually.

He trades.

I stayed silent by the door, taking in Kill's intense concentration as he sat on the high-backed office chair and stared into the four screens as if they held the meaning of life.

Graphs, charts, and pie diagrams covered one computer, while another held candlestick evaluations and world clocks. The other two were black with blinking red and green numbers, changing rapidly on different columns.

His head moved slightly, gathering information from each screen, his fingers tracing over the keyboard, making snap decisions based on the conclusions he came to.

How wealthy is he?

What is he hiding?

I jumped as the harsh sound of a cell phone buzzed beside his mouse.

He snatched it up without looking away from the screens. "Kill."

I couldn't hear the caller, but Kill's back stiffened. He straightened, dragging a hand through his damp hair. "Did stage one go off okay?"

Silence while the caller replied.

"That's good. Tell Wallstreet I'm grateful for his insight. It seemed he was right about that particular issue. I'm just fucking glad it worked." Kill's tone was dark with grim pleasure.

What had been done? What projects was he puppeteering all while babysitting me?

Kill suddenly tensed. "Tell him it's none of his goddamn business."

I smothered my smile. Seemed that was a favorite saying of his.

"No, I don't care. We sold the five. He got whatever he wanted by doing something the Club was against. Why the fuck does he care about the sixth?"

I froze. Icicles formed in my blood. *Me. They're talking about me.*

"How the fuck did he find out?" He bowed forward, resting his elbow on the table, and dragging his fingers overs his face. "No. I'll deal with him. Thanks for the heads-up. I've got the girl here."

The caller spoke; Kill breathed harder.

"Fuck. That's bullshit. I said I'd find a buyer. I don't—"

The caller cut him off. Kill punched the top of his desk. "Goddammit, what the fuck is his problem? When does he want her?"

Silence as the caller answered.

"No, I'm not gonna hand her over; I'll take her myself." Opening the top drawer of his desk, he pulled out a gun. "Wait for me—I'm coming over." He hung up.

Oh God. Was that gun for me? To *threaten* me?

I faded into the corridor, not wanting to be caught, but not willing to let him out of my sight. He *lied* to me.

What did that mean? That the bargain we'd made was broken? I thought he was the *president.* Why was he bowing to others' demands?

My body trembled with the need to run—to get as far away from false promises and complicated bikers as possible, but I paused.

Kill bowed his head, massaging his neck with both hands. He looked weary and carrying the weight of endless grief.

Don't feel sorry for him. Don't you dare *feel sorry for him.*

I inched closer to the stairs, ready to scurry back to my room and plot an escape, but Kill bent to a bottom draw and opened it with a key. Slinking his hand in, he pulled out a small piece of paper. I couldn't see what it was. A photograph? A shopping list?

My skin prickled as he growled, "I will have my vengeance. I will find my peace. I will ruin those motherfuckers and hope to God I will be free."

The words were arrows, raining around me, piercing deep into my soul.

"I will have my vengeance. I will find my peace. I will ruin those motherfuckers and hope to God I will be free."

Every hair follicle stood on end. The words weren't a promise or a prayer. They were an obsession. A consuming, passionate obsession that had kidnapped his entire existence.

I couldn't watch anymore as Kill reverently placed the item back in the drawer and clutched his gun. "It's almost time," he murmured. "Almost time to do to them what they did to me." His tone echoed with revenge and hate.

I turned tail and ran.

Kill found me half-dressed.

Wearing his usual black T-shirt and jeans, he whispered with energy.

I'd bolted and was determined to be fortified and brave when he came for me with a gun drawn and broken promises trailing behind him.

Stalking into the room he'd given me the first night, his eyes locked on my bra and the denim skirt I'd just pulled over my hips. "What are you doing in here? I left you in my room."

I faced away, hating the chill in his eyes and the lies corrupting the air between us. I couldn't look at him without demanding to know how he could fuck me, all while knowing he meant to get rid of me soon.

So much for time. So much for waiting until I could tell him the story of my scars and ink.

"This is the room you locked me in. I'm sorry for taking up your bed all night." Plucking a white T-shirt from the store bag, I muttered,

"You obviously couldn't stand the thought of sleeping beside me, seeing as you never came back."

He strode toward me, planting his large hands on my shoulders, and jerking me to face him. The gun I'd seen in his office had disappeared. "What the hell are you doing?"

I narrowed my eyes. "What am *I* doing? I could ask the same about you!"

His lips opened, then snapped together. Anger rolled off him. "We fucked. There was nothing more to it. As impersonal as—"

"Strangers. Don't worry. I get it." Rolling my shoulders, I broke his hold and moved toward the bathroom. The door had a lock on it and I fully intended to use it. The way my body jittered and tongue wanted to spew obscenities, it was best for both of us to have some distance.

My hand reached for the doorknob but an arm lassoed around my waist, pulling me against hot, strong muscles. "Did I say you could walk away?"

Did I say you could sell me?

I breathed hard through my nose, swallowing my retorts. "Let me go."

"No."

I squirmed, wishing I was stronger. I briefly entertained the idea of spinning around and kneeing him in the groin, but that would only make him furious. I had no way of winning. Letting the fight siphon from my limbs, I said listlessly, "I overheard you."

He froze. "You were spying on me?"

"No. I came to say good morning..." *And to tell you how much I enjoyed last night even though you have issues.*

"Don't act surprised. You knew what your fate entailed. Just because my cock has been inside you doesn't mean you're free." His breathing turned harsh as his fingers brushed away red strands sticking to my neck. "I allowed myself one taste. I've been transparent right from the start. Don't—"

I laughed, twisting quickly in his arms to stare fiercely into his green eyes. "You've been transparent? Shit, I'd hate to see you when you're being obtuse. You fucked me. I get that, and I understand you're hurting for something I can't help with, but you said you wouldn't—"

"*I'm* hurting? What the fuck makes you say that?" His face glowered as his lips thinned.

I rolled my eyes. His ignorance or sheer-minded determination not to acknowledge how heavily he was dictated by his past had surpassed my threshold of limits. "Admit it. You're in love with a ghost, and you can't stomach the thought of ever caring for another woman. You proved it when you stopped me from touching you, from even *watching* you take me. You've got issues, Arthur."

"Don't use my name!" His hands lashed out, gripping my hair and walking me backward until I slammed against the wall. Our lips were so close. All I had to do was stand on my tiptoes and kiss him. Lick him. Tease him. See what his rage tasted like beneath all the guilt he carried.

His chest rose and fell against mine, squashing my bra-covered breasts against his T-shirt. Without a word, his knee nudged mine, spreading my legs and settling between them. Subconsciously, he rocked against me.

My anger twisted into something sparking with red swirling passion.

"What the fuck are you doing to me?" he growled, his eyes piercing mine. My heart flurried like a blizzard, glittering with ice and snow even as it melted and shot hot blood to my core.

I honestly had no answer. "I have the same question," I murmured, transfixed on his mouth. My eyes went heavy at the thought of his tongue slinking with mine.

He stopped breathing as the room turned thick with awareness. The same need sprang vicious and consuming and his hips went from rocking to a blatant thrust. I swallowed my moan as his erection bruised my pussy.

"I have to go," he murmured. "Business."

"To organize the transaction to get rid of me, you mean." I tried so damn hard to keep the fear from my voice but failed.

He bit his lip, almost as if he reacted more to my vulnerability than my strength. "That was the order, yes."

Throwing everything away and using every trick to change his mind, I grabbed his hips, pulling him hard against me. "Don't." Raising myself on my tiptoes, I kissed him.

He sucked in a breath; his hand swooped up to capture my chin and jerk me away from his mouth. His forehead furrowed as we stood staring, not breathing, not talking—just staring.

His pupils dilated as time ticked past. My lips tingled to feel his again and my fingers curled around his hipbones, wanting to pierce his flesh and cause him pain. Cause him to *feel*—to see if I could get him to snap out of the walking anger-armor he wore so well.

His grip never relaxed on my chin. Who would break first? Who would look away or admit defeat? Before I could decide, his head bowed and his lips met mine in a featherlight kiss. His eyes remained open and I didn't blink as he tilted his mouth to press deeper. The kiss changed, dancing with eroticness and the softness he ran from.

Slowly, his eyes hooded and I allowed mine to close. Cutting off my sight but granting every other sense to take over.

With a groan, he held my face immobile, his firm lips demanding me to respond.

So I did.

I threw myself into the kiss. The tip of my tongue sought entry to his mouth and he jerked against me.

He gave up. His body fell forward, crushing me against the wall, and his fingers dropped from my chin to my throat.

I moaned as his lips opened, dragging my taste into his soul, sharing his flavor in return. His breath was hot and crisp with mint, the black desire I'd sensed in the changing room swirling angrily beneath his restraint.

His head twisted, his heart galloping against mine. "Fuck." He poured the curse down my throat. His hips drove against me, pinning me against the wall.

I couldn't stop my hands from sliding up his back, adoring the bunch and strain of his muscles, to tug on the long strands of his hair. I pulled, jerking his neck back, deliberately taking the kiss to a more passionate place.

"Fuck!" he groaned again as my tongue dueled with his and our pace increased to out of control. Our breathing and sanity snapped and the only thing I was aware of was hands, lips, and slippery dances of tongues.

"I want you," he panted.

"I want you," I begged.

"My way. The only fucking way."

I nodded. "Any way. I don't care."

Then I was alone, my nipples slicing through the suddenly cold air and my mouth lonely for his heat.

He disappeared from the room. The only sound was the roar of my heartbeat and harsh breathing. Then he came back, returning with a hard expression and a spreader bar with cuffs. Storming to the bed, he raised an eyebrow. "You want me. You let me do this. I want to plunge inside you. I want to feel you come around my cock. But I don't want anything in return."

I shivered as lust skittered down my spine.

His voice lowered as he waved the bar. "I don't want your hands stroking me, or your eyes watching me. I don't want your lips on my skin, or your body against mine. This is the only way I'll take you a second time. Give me that control, and I'll give you what you want."

Drifting toward the bed, I couldn't take my eyes off the bar. "That isn't what I want."

His eyes flared. A singular cryptic look flickered over his face.

Looking up through my eyelashes, I whispered, "I want to touch you. Everywhere."

"I want you to touch me. Everywhere," he said, pulling his T-shirt

over his head. His chest was well formed, sinewy muscles creating a treasure trove for my eyes. He had a splattering of dark hair that disappeared into his jeans, turning him from boy to man.

My stomach flipped in awe and anticipation.

"Everywhere?" I asked, my fingertips aching to obey.

He smiled softly. "Everywhere. Don't leave a place untouched. I'm all yours."

"No touching," Kill growled, dispelling my memory. He shook the spreader bar. "It's this or nothing."

Fear squeezed my heart. Being restrained couldn't be any worse than not remembering anything. My mind had trapped me well before him. And I wasn't fearful of being captured or hurt—I was already his prisoner; what did a pair of cuffs matter? I doubted I had any true fear unless it was from fire. But I'd yet to test that theory.

I didn't fear him—not in that way. He was a brutal lover but he wasn't a sadist. He had boundaries that I could trust.

Let him.

Let him do this so you can earn another day by his side.

Cocking my chin, I stepped forward with my hands balled. "You can bind me on one condition."

His lips twitched into half a smile. "You're not in a position to make demands."

I reached behind my back and unclasped my bra. Dangling it from my finger, I raised an eyebrow. "You want me as much as I want you. Don't lie and deny it."

His eyes couldn't look anywhere but at my breasts. Ink or natural—he didn't seem to care as he drank in my half-nakedness. "Fine. What's your condition?" His erection pressed against his jeans, and pain and annoyance lit up his gaze.

"Don't sell me. Whoever was on the phone? Don't listen. Keep me here. With you. Like you promised when I saved your life."

He stopped breathing. "You're using your body to barter with me? You have no fucking shame."

That hurt, but I ignored the sting. "I'm asking for more time. I'm asking for what you owe me. The willingness to sleep with you isn't a payment—it's as much for my enjoyment as it is yours."

Unzipping my skirt, I stepped out of it as it slithered to the floor. "I'm only asking you to keep your side of the bargain."

He bit his lip as his erection leapt in his trousers. His stomach tensed as he said, "You're making this sound like an agreed contract. There were no rules. No conditions."

I didn't reply, hooking my fingertips in the top of my G-string and wiggling my hips in invitation. "Do you accept?" My voice had turned to husk and allure, sending a scattering of goose bumps over my skin to realize how sexual I'd become.

Had I always been confident or was this new?

It was so hard to know who I was when faced with a situation such as this. Was it just survival making me lust for my kidnapper, or my mind drip-feeding me tales of a boy who held the same impossible traits as Arthur Killian?

He swallowed hard as I took another step, his throat contracting. He never took his eyes from my lingerie-covered core but his decision blazed true in their depths.

Holding up the bar, he nodded once.

I closed the distance between us, tensing against the heat from his body and the tingling awareness of being so close. "Where do you want me?" I murmured.

"Lie on your back," he ordered.

I did as he asked, unashamed of my seminaked body as I climbed onto the bed and crawled to the center. Somehow my scars and ink gave me sanctuary. They gave me a place to hide even while being so incredibly vulnerable. Rolling onto my back, I tried to control my breathing as Kill hunted after me on all fours.

In the time it'd taken me to get into position, he'd removed his T-shirt and discarded his jeans. His black boxer-briefs failed to hide his massive erection.

Climbing over my body, he straddled me with power.

"Hold out your arm," he whispered.

I did as I was told, placing my wrist into the soft, supple cuff. With a fierce look, he buckled it quickly, sliding the spreader bar through his hands until my arm was outstretched. "Raise them."

I settled back onto the mattress and placed my arms above me. Kill straddled me higher, his hard cock coming within centimeters of my mouth. He looked magnificent—a long-haired rebel with a mermaid smiling her secret smile on his leg.

My breathing turned to pants as my core clenched. I could stare at his perfect body all day and still want more. I wanted to lick the deliciously formed Vs of his stomach. I wanted to trace the shadows of muscles and press kisses on his inner thighs.

So much he denied himself by tying me up. Touch was the greatest thing a human could enjoy—it was better than sex. Touch could be anything from consoling to inspiring—to go through life without being caressed by another? My heart hurt for him.

"Do you ever let anyone touch you?" I whispered as he strapped my other wrist with a cuff, locking the bar in the center to keep it from contracting. The pressure of being spread stretched my shoulders. It felt nice, for now, but I knew it would begin to ache very quickly. He'd tightened it so there was no room to move or wriggle.

"No," he snapped. "Stop talking." He climbed off the bed and disappeared again.

The next time he returned, he held the gold tie.

He obviously wasn't going to use it to bind my wrists seeing as I was trapped. My eyes. *He wants to blindfold you.*

Panic laced my blood at the thought of being in the dark again.

"You want me to fuck you, this is how it's gonna be. You don't touch me. You don't see me. You take what I give you and don't ask for a drop more."

"I let you restrain me, but I don't want to be blindfolded."

Kill chuckled, running his rough fingers down my cheek. "Still thinking you have the power to say no." Bending over me, he whispered in my ear, "Where you're concerned, I've given the wrong impression. You don't get to ask me for things. You obey me and hope to God you please me. You're only here because I want you to be here—but under my fucking terms. Got it?"

He's lying not only to me, but himself. Yes, I was bound and about to be fucked under his rules. But only because I'd kissed him. Only because *I* wanted this.

My heart beat harder for a man so deeply entrenched in denial. Could he not even admit to himself that he'd met another woman who could affect him like his Dead Girl? So what if I looked like her? I was different from his past. Different from *my* past. What was happening between us was exactly that—between us—not between ghosts and memories.

If he needs to believe his fibs, let him.

I needed to make him keep me. I didn't mind playing his rules in order to do that.

Nodding, I whispered, "Okay. I'll do what you want."

Surprise flared his eyes, followed by smoldering lust. "Damn right you will."

In a fast move, he leaned over and pressed the tie around my vision. His fingers were soft as he secured the blindfold behind my head, blotting out the soft light of the bedroom. Instantly, my other senses went haywire. Prickling with extra sensitivity and heat.

My eyelashes crushed beneath the restriction, and I swallowed my rising panic as he secured the knot at the back of my head. I winced as he tugged accidentally on my hair.

"Why?" I panted. Without vision, my body became a focal point. My breasts were suddenly heavier, my core suddenly wetter. My heart whizzed faster while my breathing slowed with self-preservation.

"You know why."

I do know why. I just didn't think it was the reason he thought.

His fingertips trailed down my stomach, following my belly button and the dip of my muscles to my core.

I tensed against the cuffs, my toes curling against the overload of sensation. I burned where he touched; I shivered where he didn't. I wanted to be consumed.

"The darkness, the blindness. Everything is amplified. Do you feel me?" His breath skated over my skin, making me tremble as my need turned into a beast demanding more.

"Yes," I moaned as his touch followed the lace of my panties, caressing ever so lightly over my clit. I bowed off the bed as his touch turned ticklish, tracing the inside of my thigh all the way to my knee. "You're focused entirely on me. I can see how wet you are through your underwear. I can smell how much you want me."

I moaned as the bed shifted with his weight.

"Your senses overcompensate. You'll want me more. You feel everything I do to you ten times more. Do you deny it?"

I thrashed as he dragged his touch over my panties again. "No. It's true."

"Maybe it will help you remember," he murmured against my mouth. I arched up, seeking his lips. Desperation filled me for a simple mind-warping kiss.

But he was gone.

"I know how it feels to be robbed of sight. I know the panic as your senses become hyperalert." His voice was hypnotic and dangerous, drugging me, pushing me deeper into his spell. "Every smell, every motion, every sound. You can't control it."

I writhed beneath him, my fingers opening and closing over nothing, craving the ability to touch him and make him suffer as much as I did.

Everything he said was true. I could smell the muskiness of his arousal, and the salty tang of his unique ocean and leather. I could feel every motion of the bed, sense his weight like a physical force above me, and could hear the shallowness of our matching breathing, the distant tick of a clock, and the rush of my racing heartbeats.

I was happy he couldn't see into my thoughts, because he wouldn't like what else he was making me feel.

Togetherness.

By cutting off my eyes, he asked my body to reach out and connect. To form conclusions by touch and instinct alone. He forced my brain to unlock things it wasn't ready to unlock.

The sensation of *knowing* him. Of recognizing his smell and body all crashed over me until I couldn't bear it.

Licking my lips nervously, I whispered, "Please, stop torturing me."

He chuckled. "I'm not torturing you. I'm not even touching you. You're doing it to yourself. You're getting wet all on your own. You're craving something I haven't even said I'll give you."

I moaned in frustration. "Then touch me. Take me. Do something!"

"Calm your breathing. Don't strain," he murmured against my ear. My jaw gritted as his fingers hooked around my underwear and pulled them down. I shivered as he freed my legs and the bed wobbled as he fumbled with his boxers.

Somehow, I knew he was naked. Some part of me knew without the aid of sight. I also knew he hovered above me with his hot, hard cock just waiting to claim me.

"Who are you?" he demanded, shattering the rapidly winding anticipation.

The question sent me whirling back into amnesiac darkness. Instead of straining for an answer I wouldn't get, I whispered, "I might be the person you need to save your life."

Kill reared back, his lack of body heat obvious as a chill bit into my nipples. "What makes you think I need fucking saving?" His entire body vibrated with loathing, sending the bed into an anxious wobble.

Tread carefully. Don't push. Not now. Not yet.

"I don't. But you do."

I bowed off the bed as he suddenly raised my hips, positioning my strewn form over his lap. My spread legs snugged against his hips as he angled his cock to my entrance. I'd never been taken like this before.

Not that I would remember.

But the strangeness of being joined only where it was essential made me sad. I'd wanted his weight to smother me. I wanted the joy of experiencing his galloping heart as he thrust into me. But this way, all I felt was the poised invasion of his erection and the unhurried imprisonment of my hips.

I wished I could touch him. Everyone needed touching. Everyone needed a hug now and again. My arms ached to leach some of his angst away.

It wasn't fair he took so much from me all while granting me nothing. I wanted to *know*. I wanted to understand if I was insane for feeling such a connection to him or if I was truly listening to my heart.

"The flames of beasts came out to feast. No priest can save the singed deceased," his voice whispered over my skin.

My heart lurched to a stop.

"What?" I panted, craving his touch but begging to know what he'd said. It tugged at some dark recesses of my mind, rattling the door that remained stubbornly shut.

He was so close, positioning himself deeper between my spread legs. His hands captured my hips, bending over me, bringing body heat and the tickle of breath on my lower belly.

"It's inked into your side," he said quietly, as if afraid it would jar something in my mind. I'd already figured out I must've been in a fire and survived. It also made sense that I might've lost people I loved in the flames.

You littered yourself with tattoos about loss, lust, and heartbreak for a reason.

The evidence was there—just waiting for me to make the correct conclusions.

"What does it mean?" Kill asked, his tension and animosity mysteriously gone.

"I don't remember." I sucked in a breath as his fingers moved to my kneecap, his touch tracing ink after ink while his other hand trailed my scars.

I shivered.

His voice came again. "We met in a nightmare, loved in a prayer. We gave everything until both were laid bare."

I shot awake, my heart thundering with a connection.

Write it down. Quick. *I scrambled out of bed, searching for a pen to jot down the verse that'd come to me in my sleep. My notebook grew week by week as snippets fell from the vault my mind had become, raining onto dry dirt where shoots of newfound hope appeared.*

My hands shook as I scribbled.

My mind full of a soul mate I'd lost.

The profound sense of love suffocated my heart. I loved someone who wasn't real. I'd given my heart to the boy in my dreams. What did it all mean?

Was my nightmare the man between my legs who was as inept at solving my puzzle as I was? Could it be possible?

Cruel fate. Cruel love.

No matter the truth, I couldn't stop my misbehaving heart beating harder for Kill. For *Arthur*.

He sat up. His touch went to my foot, capturing it, raising it for inspection. I froze as his fingers traced the tiny proverb I'd found hidden on the side of my arch.

My lips moved with his as he said, "I loved and lost. He loved and found. But they had the greatest laugh of all."

His voice cracked. Then the peaceful curiosity twisted to anger again. He grunted, "You tattooed yourself with nonsense. Nonsense you can't even remember."

I shook my head. "It's not nonsense if one day it will lead me to the truth. It's wealth—don't you see?"

"No, I don't see. I don't understand any of it." His touch turned possessive as he positioned his cock once again by my entrance. I bit my lip as he eased forward, spreading me.

"Enough talking," he groaned as he slid his delectable length inside me, pulling me higher off the bed and onto his hips. He sank deeper and deeper until only my shoulders remained on the mattress and my hips fully straddled his.

He teased me, pulsing but not thrusting.

"I hate that you look like her," he muttered. "But I can't deny you feel fucking good."

I tried to rock, to encourage him to thrust, but the position he'd put me in was of complete control. I couldn't peek or cheat. He'd locked me in the darkness with no power.

Claustrophobia clawed a little and I squirmed for freedom.

But then he moved, driving his hips upward and all thoughts of escape exploded from my thoughts.

Pulling almost all the way out, he entered me again, groaning quietly.

My mouth parted as he stretched, then withdrew, then filled me again. Torturing me as surely as any punishment possible. I arched up, pressing my hips harder onto his. But it didn't do any good.

Despite my predicament and complete subservience to this man, I found sublime peace in having him inside me. He belonged there. I'd been made for him to fill me.

Don't be so stupid.

I waged between ridiculous notions and the starkness of my reality as he rocked with a mind-numbing rhythm.

There, in the darkness with no words or worries, he was my sanctuary.

His rock turned determined. His voice rained angry around my ears. "Give me something true. Right now."

I gulped; all hazy passion left my system. My heart filled with fear. So much truth hidden in so many secrets. "I wish I could."

I wish I could make you believe the impossible.

"Try."

I gasped as he drove deeper. "You don't want to hear what I have to say."

He cursed beneath his breath, his hands clutching my hips. "What's your name?"

My name?

That elusive silverfish that refused to be caught.

"I don't know."

"Tell me," he commanded, rocking harder, making my mouth fall open with bliss.

My eyes flew open behind my blindfold as I sucked in a breath at the blatant beg in his tone.

Need granted me recklessness. "Please, Kill…give me more. I don't know my name. Don't punish me for something I can't control. Just make me yours."

My heart seized as he jerked. His cock slid ever deeper, making us both groan. He pressed down on my belly, keeping me pinned. "You'll never be mine. I don't want you to be mine."

Pain splashed from my soul to my heart.

I don't want you.

How was this man so much more broken than me? So blinded to a life where he wasn't living, merely existing?

I waited—for what? An apology? Something to heal the agony he'd caused. But nothing came.

I resorted to living with questions.

I hoped with all my soul that I would find the truth before this nightmare was over.

I expected him to use me roughly—to take me hard. But he just kept up his mind-numbing rock while my skin itched for contact. He pushed me off him, withdrawing his hard heat.

I felt empty as he unlocked the spreader bar, allowing my arms to come together. Flipping me onto my belly, he pressed himself over me.

I sighed with relief to have his weight blanketed, then gasped in delight as he slid deep inside. His stomach pressed against my ass every time he thrust.

I wanted more. I wanted his hands on me. His lips on mine.

It was a hopeless wish.

Then a whisper-soft kiss landed on my shoulder blade—so fleeting I would've missed it if my senses weren't on overload with awareness. A single kiss planted almost fearfully on my flesh with a touch so loving, so adoring, a small sob erupted up my throat.

I didn't know why I hurt so bad. I didn't know why I wanted to cry so much. But his single act of sweetness drove me to break.

I needed to remember. I needed to remember *him*—the boy, my past and future—so agony would find someone else to torment.

His mouth settled over my spine, making my back bow, pressing my flesh into his mouth.

I moaned as he wrapped an arm under my chest, holding me tighter to his lips. His tongue swirled, tasting me with infinite gentleness.

I couldn't breathe. Tears scalded my cheeks as he trailed kisses up the length of my spine to the nape of my neck. Then the touching stopped. The only sensation of him still being there was his soft puff of breath as he leaned close, and his cock thrusting shallowly and relentlessly into me.

I wished I could see him. I wished I could read the story in his eyes as he looked at me. He touched me like a man in love. He touched me like a man who *knew* me. Who'd adored and wanted me for just as long as I'd wanted him.

It was a lie.

By blindfolding me, he kept me trapped worse than any amnesia, almost as if he wanted to indulge in his memories but not include me.

Selfish.

A flash of hatred worked its way through my soul.

I groaned as he suddenly picked up his pace. The rock disappeared under a siege of claiming.

In and out.

Deeper and harder.

My heart exploded as every sense relocated in my core. Every stroke of his cock sent an earthquake rippling through my body. His balls tightened, pressing deliciously against my clit. With my legs together and his weight above me, my orgasm built fast, finding friction against the mattress.

He reared up, impaling himself deeper. Mysteries thickened between us as our hearts raced.

"Please...tell me who you are," I moaned, tears trickling down my cheeks as my mouth opened with delirium.

He didn't reply. His touch turned angry, spreading my thighs, keeping me at his mercy.

My leg swung backward, boldly wrapping around his and connecting with hot flesh.

He froze, his cock twitching inside. "What the fuck are you doing?"

"Trying to remember," I breathed.

He paused. I waited to see if he would push me away, but slowly he thrust again, obeying the pressure of my leg around his—dictating the speed and depth.

Power shot through me as he groaned, his erection growing bigger and harder—stretching me impossibly more. The silkiness of his skin sent ripples of lust into my core.

I wanted him. So much. It wasn't enough to have him inside—I wanted his heart.

"Touch me," I begged. "Fuck me."

He sucked in a breath. Words dangled unsaid between us. I hoped against hope he'd voice them, but he didn't.

Instead, he pushed away my foot and smothered my body with his.

His cock drove into my pussy, hot and tempting. I wriggled beneath him, welcoming.

Then he did something I would never have suspected.

He fisted my hair, arching my head to kiss me.

His lips descended on mine.

Hard.

Fast.

Wet. And possessive.

I couldn't breathe or think as his tongue invaded my lips, taking so much, giving so much.

All my attention was on his kiss and I cried out as his hips thrust hard, driving his cock fast and deep inside.

Stars twinkled behind my eyes. I bucked beneath him, assaulted by sweetness and violence. Tenderness and hate. He nipped at my lips, biting me, while his cock drove deeper and deeper.

He swallowed my screams, feeding me on his groans.

Not seeing or being able to touch him made the taking so much... more. He took everything I had to give.

The orgasm started behind my memories, dark and lurking just like everything else in my life. He rode me hard, pushing my body up the bed.

"Fuck. Take it. I can't fucking—"

I had no words for him. Not this time. Not when I wanted to remain in nothing but warmth and sparkles of my building release.

"Goddammit, I can't. I... shouldn't. Fuck me... This is wrong, so... fucking wrong." He grunted with every thrust.

My ears twitched with his torment. This was wrong? What, connecting? Making each other feel incredible? I couldn't believe that. I didn't want to believe it.

Tilting my hips, I drove us to the pinnacle of no return.

"There's nothing wrong about this," I moaned as his cock stroked and detonated the fireball in my core.

I came with an explosion, squeezing along his length with ferocity that made my eyes water. He followed, his groan so loud, it set off another earthquake inside me. The release felt like a bomb, a grenade—bullets of power and rage and freedom.

He fucked me with abandon. Losing all pretenses as we came hard and long. Throwing ourselves into the grey where there were no ghosts or memories—only us and pleasure.

Chapter Eleven

She looked at me as if she understood. She saw straight into my soul and *understood.*

She'll never understand.

She twisted my mind.

I hated her for offering a second chance with every blink of her green eyes. She offered the priceless gift of forgetting and letting go.

My heart wanted to believe so fucking much.

It'd been so long since anyone cared.

But that was what made her doubly dangerous.

Emotions were the devil and I had no intention of falling for her tricks.

Seeing through bullshit was what got me through circumstances that should've killed me. I couldn't afford to listen to anything but the whispered murmurs of hate.

It was all I knew.

The only thing I understood after what'd happened.

—Kill

Three days passed.

After Kill took me, he'd left without a word, leaving me unbound and sated to do what I pleased. Half an hour after one of the best orgasms of my life, the front door slammed and the empty house settled around me like a tomb.

He'd gone.

To deal with business? To respond to the phone call? Either way, he'd gone alone, and for that I was grateful. Relief thrummed through my blood, but my nerves wound tight with what my future meant.

That first day had been awkward. I'd showered, found a spare toothbrush in his vanity, and dressed in clothes he'd bought me from the plaza. I didn't know what to do, where I could go, or what was expected of me. So I stayed in my room and asked every question I could think of to try and trick my brain into answering me.

That night, I waited up for him. I paced his home until well past midnight.

I stayed awake until two a.m. before finally succumbing to sleep, and when I woke, I found him in front of his computers, clicking madly, trading markets I would never understand.

We bumped into each other the next morning in the kitchen. I'd raided his supplies to create a breakfast of yogurt with berries that'd been delivered the day before in a weekly supply of healthy meals.

He'd frozen in the doorway and glared at me as if I were a stranger.

I hadn't said a word, hoping he would shed light on his issues. But he'd turned and left, leaving the house for the second time.

I might remain in his home for now, but I wasn't stupid to think I had unlimited time to remember. Overhearing his phone conversation confirmed that I would still be sold. Regardless if Kill was on board with that decision or not.

He was the president of Pure Corruption, but he obeyed another—the man he admitted was his boss, who was currently incarcerated at Florida State. I didn't know why Kill had stooped to such a horrible crime as trafficking, but I wasn't delusional to think I could make him care.

Not that I achieved any progress. Kill hated me—or hated the way I made him feel. Either way…I was on borrowed time.

The next day, he left again. No touching, no explanation—he acted as if I weren't there. We were ghosts in the same house, drifting past one another. There was no mention of sex, or how soon he meant to get rid of me—even his questions about my memories and tattoos never came.

He withdrew into himself, becoming pensive and quiet and so damn surly, I stopped asking him the simplest of questions and avoided him.

An unlikely routine sprang up as simplistic and easy as if we were following some carefully scripted plan.

Arthur would leave first thing in the morning. To go where—I didn't know. I would stay in bed until I was sure he'd gone, then make my way to his office and stare at the equations on the wall.

Something about them tugged my brain. Taunting me with answers I couldn't see.

I snooped in his wardrobe, looking for some treasured mementos that might show me a link to my past or his. I strolled around his home searching…searching for something, *anything*.

He didn't seem concerned about leaving me alone for so long. Was he so confident in his fucking me that I would stay? Stay for *what*? He'd given me nothing.

Minute by minute, my world shrank to the small circumference of his home. And in his home, I felt both safe and watched. Both comforted and unsettled.

I tried to use his computers, but they were password protected.

I tried to go for a walk, but the gate was code encrypted.

I tried to find a weakness in the property's exterior, but it was a fortress. Every blocked avenue made me itch for freedom and I began looking for ways to run.

At night when he returned, I stopped trying to talk to him. I ceased padding down the stairs in the middle of the night to spy on him as he furiously clicked his mouse and placed trades on the flashing graphs and foreign currency pairs.

The longer we didn't talk, the more I noticed the sharpness in his green eyes, the intelligence burning bright—the almost scary intensity that made him glow as night after night he sat at his desk and muttered the same thing over and over, while staring at an image I couldn't see.

"I will have my vengeance. I will find my peace. I will ruin those motherfuckers and hope to God I will be free."

I'd tried to find out what the picture was, but the drawer was locked with no key to be found.

The rest of his house gave no clues as to who lived behind his impenetrable green gaze, and I grew antsy as more minutes ticked past and I remained in the dark.

I need to remember.

I tried. Shit, how I tried. But all my attempts were in vain. I gave up harassing my brain for answers or clues. I became trapped and I didn't care about anything but running.

I couldn't stay any longer in the house of a biker president who no longer noticed me.

I didn't want to live in the blank world of forgotten anymore.

I have to leave.

There was nothing for me here. Arthur had made that abundantly clear—pulling away from me so his conscience would be clear when he sold me.

I didn't want a man like that—who could so easily walk away from what was between us.

You deserve more.

I agreed wholeheartedly, so why did my soul scream whenever I thought about walking out the door and never coming back?

Chapter Twelve

I was a weapon.

I'd been honed by the best, given the skills to excel and an empire to rule.

I was a warrior.

I'd been granted ultimate power, intelligence to succeed, and powerful allies to make my wishes come true.

I was a king.

And kings were never distracted by those weaker than them.

—*Kill*

"You're coming with me."

I looked up from where I sat cross-legged on the bed. The only reading materials in Kill's house were trade journals, company manifests, and a book called *So You Think You're a Genius.* It had mind puzzles, equations, and a bunch of very technical tests that proved in actual fact that no, I wasn't a genius.

Last night, when Kill didn't come home till three a.m., I found a weakness in the back fence. The stone wall was rougher there, less perfectly built, and gave just enough finger grips to climb the three-yard imprisonment.

I didn't know what existed behind the wall, and I'd have nothing to take apart from a few pieces of fruit from the kitchen to sustain myself. The catering service Kill ordered only delivered at the start of the week—frozen, calorie-counted healthiness that kept me and him alive with no mess or joy of cooking.

Unfortunately, another order wasn't due for a few days, and I wanted to leave tonight.

I couldn't stay in this house another moment.

Resting the book on my knees, I asked coldly, "To where?"

His eyes narrowed at the frost in my voice. "To Pure Corruption. Time for our weekly meet, and I need to take you in. Brothers want to discuss your future."

My throat closed. I knew this day would come—I just hoped it wouldn't interfere with my runaway plan.

My hands balled. "You said you wouldn't get rid of me till you knew—"

"Doesn't matter what I said. I'm done babysitting you and I have a lot of shit on my plate."

I'm not babysitting a traitor.

Burn, baby girl. Burn.

I shuddered as the vile voice echoed in my head. Gripping the hardcover of the book, so I wouldn't show my fear, I snapped, "What do you propose to do with me?"

He stiffened, not moving from his place by the door. "What's with the fucking attitude?"

My eyes opened wide. "Seriously? You have the balls to ask me what's with my attitude?"

He stalked forward, growing bigger and bigger as his temper seethed. "Yes. I'll ask again. What's with the fucking ice, sweetheart?"

I slammed the book closed and threw it at his head.

He ducked, spinning around to watch the heavy volume slam against the carpet. He turned to me face me with violent, incredulous eyes. "What was that for?"

"What was *that* for?" I shot up from my butt to my knees, and grabbed two handfuls of my hair. "I'll tell you what it was for. I sewed you up. You took me shopping. You made love to me three nights ago, and then you just walked out of my life! No explanation, no hint at what you mean to do with me. You're driving me insane, and I know that there's something you're not telling me—a lot of things actually. But you've driven me so far away that I'm . . . I'm—"

Kill lowered his head, looking up through thick lashes. "You're what? Spit it out."

I dropped my hands from my hair, feeling drained and no longer wanting to fight. "I'm done. I'm no closer to figuring out who I am or how I know you than I was when I was first stolen." Rolling my shoulders, I muttered, "I heard you on the phone. You're still going to sell me, so everything else . . ." I shrugged, my voice slipping into sadness. "Guess none of it matters, because when I have an owner who's beating me senseless and fucking me within an inch of my life, I'll be grateful I don't remember anything. Grateful for your coldness, that I have no link to my past, because I'll never be that person again."

The room thickened with tension.

Arthur took a step toward the bed, then another. His boots were silent on the thick carpet and he'd taken off his leather cut, so all he wore was his black T-shirt and jeans.

"Listen closely, Forgetful Girl." His nostrils flared as he said, "Three days ago I did not make love to you. I *fucked* you. I told you I wanted nothing more than a release. And that's what I got. I don't have to explain myself to you and what I do in my life is of no concern. I had things to take care of—Club business that will *never* be discussed with you or any other woman in my world."

My heart fisted and I swallowed hard.

"You always knew your future and I could punish you for eavesdropping on a personal conversation. In fact, you've pissed me off so much, I think that's exactly what I'm going to do."

I went ice-cold. "What?"

He closed the distance to the bed, pressing his knees against the mattress. In a horribly fast move, he grabbed my hips, flipped me onto my back, and wrapped his strong fingers around my ankles. In an effortless pull, he positioned my body onto the edge of the bed.

He smirked. "Wearing a skirt. That's rather convenient."

I struggled, digging my hands into the quilt, trying to get away. "Don't touch me."

His right hand disappeared up my skirt, stroking the satin between my legs.

My eyes almost rolled back at the sudden pleasure of his touch.

"You want me to touch you. Admit it."

"I want you to tell me who you are."

He shook his head, his fingers working against my clit. "I don't know you."

"Tell me how she died."

The second the words were out of my mouth, I wanted to take them back—not just for my safety but because of the brokenness inside Kill's eyes.

His fingers pinched my clit cruelly. "I told you never to talk about her."

Courage shot through me and I asked, "Did she burn? Did she die in a fire?"

Did she somehow make it out of a burning house where no one saw, and was given a new identity because she remembered nothing? Because if she did, then look at my scars!

With a vicious jerk, he ripped off my satin G-string and shoved the floaty pink skirt up around my hips. "You keep talking and you're going to get hurt."

He fumbled with his belt, ripping it open and unclasping his fly. His cock strained against the thin material of his black boxer-briefs.

I couldn't move as he pulled a condom from his pocket and shoved both boxers and jeans to his knees. Something else fell from his hand, thudding gently to the carpet.

I tried to see what it was, but Kill gave me no room to move.

He didn't care that he stood naked before me with his mermaid tattoo and her hair caressing around his cock. He didn't care that the Libra star sign tattooed in the waves seemed to glow and tease me with memories. And he didn't care that a tear—so full of confusion, need, and madness—trickled down my cheek.

His hands shook as he rolled the condom down his length, sheathing his large erection. My body warmed and melted, twisting my desire to run.

"How do you know she's gone, Killian?" I whispered. "Why are you so sure she's dead, when I know things I can't explain?"

He froze, his hand fisting the base of his cock. I didn't expect an answer. I never expected the truth, but was granted with one sentence. "She died due to complications in surgery. She never woke up. It's undisputable and true and every time I fucking look at you, you remind me of that fact. Are you happy now?"

I tilted my hips, inviting him to take me. "No, I'm not happy that you're hurting."

His gaze flashed with pain; his eyebrow rose, almost as if he was suspicious of my permission.

I nodded gently, biting my lip as he ducked his knees and positioned himself at my entrance. There was no need for foreplay; my body was drenched, wanting to connect after three days of terrible loneliness.

"What surgery?" I whispered as my mouth fell open from being filled so slowly.

He gritted his teeth, sinking completely inside me. "Enough talking."

My body tensed then relaxed as his long length stretched me. I couldn't let it go. "Did you see her at least? Please...I need to know."

His eyes glowed with agony so deep, it completely overshadowed his lust. Sighing hard, he thrust, but his heart wasn't in it—it was lost to him, ruined by a dead girl. "I saw the photos. I read the police report. I told you I stood on her fucking grave. She's gone."

My back bowed as he drove fiercely into me, embracing his anger.

My heart thudded thick and needful. I wanted to forget about the morbid conversation and embrace the sensation of him inside me, but I couldn't let it go. I had to chase. Had to hound. It was the only way I'd find the truth. "You sound as if you didn't get to say good-bye. Why did you have to read police reports? Weren't you together until the end?"

His face went black. Fingernails pierced my hips. "I was in fucking prison."

Silence filled my head. White noise and confusion. "What… what for?"

He laughed, sounding manic. His hips pistoned, driving me higher and higher toward the strangest orgasm. One entwined in finding out the truth all while our bodies devoured each other.

"I was betrayed." Bowing over me, he growled, "But it doesn't hide my sins. I was incarcerated for murder, sweetheart. How does that make you feel?" His green eyes flashed as he savagely thrust into me.

My pussy throbbed and bruised. I couldn't stop my hand rising and cupping his cheek, stroking his rough face. "You're still paying for your sins."

He slapped my hand away. "Don't touch me."

He increased his tempo, quickly leaving the realm of speech and focusing on the finale. I wasn't ready to break the link between us. Not yet.

Ask him.

Ask him the question.

Jealousy burned in my heart that this man, currently driving into me, still loved another. But hope glowed, too. I pinned all my hope from the last few days on one answer.

One answer only he could give me but I worried he never would.

Crying out as he planted his hands on either side of my body and driving fast and ruthless, I panted, "Tell me her name. What was the name of the girl you loved?"

The world ceased moving. Everything screeched to a stop.

Kill's cock twitched inside as he just stood there like an iceberg.

He grabbed my throat, hissing, "*Never* ask me that again. You're not worthy of her name."

Then his hand moved from my throat to my eyes, planting heavily over my vision. The world went dark but every instinct shot into hyperawareness.

His hips thrust harder, his cock bringing such heat and pleasure.

"I can't stand you looking at me with her eyes. I can't stand looking at you, period, while I'm fucking you." His voice broke, but he smothered his agony with a growl. His pace increased, leaving sex behind and pounding straight into punishment.

I couldn't see. His hand was hot and heavy.

I couldn't breathe. His pace was too fast and deep.

I couldn't fight. The pleasure was too intense and strong.

And I couldn't stop my response to his anger pulsing between my legs.

I came.

Hard, long—spiraling down and down, darker and darker, losing myself to the muddy, desolate world of Arthur Killian.

With a roar, he spurted inside, filling me, ruining me, taking everything that I ever was.

Time passed.

I didn't know how much—could've been five minutes or an hour—but Kill roused me from my sex-haze slumber as he tripped over the book on the carpet. He was fully dressed and in control again as he bent to pick it up.

Propping myself on my elbows, I didn't care my skirt was bunched and showing my very used and exposed pussy. All I cared about was the black-shrouded vision of the man who carried so much turmoil inside.

I'm not afraid of him.

The sudden realization that I couldn't fear someone who struggled more than me was empowering.

He turned to face me, waving the book. He cocked an eyebrow. "You were working on your IQ?"

I smiled, remembering a particularly hard mathematical question. I could've stared at it for the rest of my life, or been given the best calculator in the world, and still never understood how to solve it.

I didn't even attempt to work it out. After all, *he* wasn't there to fix my mistakes and erase my incorrect answers.

I scooted higher, tugging down my skirt. "I'm no good at math."

"The answer is nine hundred and eighty-four squared."

My mouth hung open. "You've memorized the answers?"

He scowled. "You think I cheated?"

I beckoned him to come closer, glancing at the page-long equation with font so small I practically needed a magnifying glass. "You took two seconds to figure it out." I looked up into his confident gaze. "Have you done the problem before, and either remembered it or—"

His lips twisted. "Or what? I'm a genius?" He raised an eyebrow. I couldn't sense if he was mocking me or seriously pissed off at my disbelief.

"*Are* you a genius?"

He dumped the book on the bed and crossed his arms. "There are a lot of theories on what makes a genius, but technically my IQ is one hundred and fifty-eight and a genius is anything over one hundred and sixty, so you could say…I'm close."

I nodded, thrilled that he was talking to me after three days of silence. "Fascinating. Tell me the meaning of life, oh brainy one."

His mouth twitched despite himself. "There *is* no meaning of life."

I thought back to the mantra he whispered every night in his office. Tilting my head, I murmured, "I think you have a meaning—a purpose. You're driven by it and won't rest until it's fulfilled."

He took a step backward, his face going white.

I stood upright, not wanting him to leave when I was close to bulldozing down one of his walls. Something soft and cool prodded against my toes.

I looked down.

My eyes fell on the well-handled Libra eraser.

"Homework tonight?"

I let him in, locking the door behind him. "My mom and dad are out. We have the place to ourselves." I whispered, "I need you."

The foyer of the home I shared with my parents went instantly thick with sexual tension.

His green eyes flared; he swallowed. "I—you know how much I want you, but... you're too young."

"I'm fourteen next week. And I've known you since I was born." I went to hug him, but he moved quickly out of reach. "Please, I love you. I want you to be my first."

He sighed heavily. "I will be your first. But wait a little longer. I don't want to hurt you." His hand disappeared into his pocket, pulling out the brand-new Libra eraser I'd given him last week. He'd told me to get a better eraser. And I'd wanted to remind him of all the good qualities he possessed being a Libra.

Holding it up, he muttered, "You gave me this. It's all I'm accepting from you until I'm sure I'll never lose you."

"You will never lose me."

Sadness beyond his seventeen years flickered in his gaze. "I lose you every time I go home without you. The day I make love to you is the day my life is over."

My heart squeezed. "Over?"

"It'll be over because I'll give you my soul when you give me your body, and I'll never be able to live without it again."

I crumbled to a puddle, picking up the eraser and holding it to my heart.

"I—I gave you this." I held it up, tears streaming through my eyes. "I gave you this the night I begged you to take my virginity."

Kill stumbled, his legs buckled, and for a second I thought he'd pass out. Then rage—undiluted, terrible rage—filled his body. "Shut up!" he roared. "Shut up with your mind tricks and fucking illusions!"

"It's not a trick! You have to believe me!"

He lurched forward, snatching the eraser from my fingers. His face was livid as he raised his fist as if to strike. His jaw-length hair fell forward in an unruly mess.

"Don't!" I curled into a little ball, protecting my head with my arms. "I remember you. I remember stolen kisses on a rooftop beneath the moon. I remember you helping me with my homework. I remember the days spent swimming naked at the private beach we found. I remember the love I felt for you—the love that never—"

He kicked me.

The pain in my ribs ripped through my confession, shutting me up. Heat spread through my side, licking with fire, singeing my already scarred skin.

I sucked in a ragged gasp, holding my side. My eyes turned glassy with sadness and regret.

Kill squatted over me, seething with ferocity. "I'm done with you playing on my pain. I'm done being manipulated. I told you I'd been betrayed in my past, and I won't let some whore twist my memories and make me believe a heinous lie. You're ripping my fucking heart out and I won't let you do it anymore!"

"It isn't a lie. Tell me how I know things! Tell me how I could have those memories if it wasn't the truth!"

Grabbing my hair, he jerked my eyes to look into his. "You're a liar and a con artist. They told me where they stole you from. I know who you are, and all this bullshit about loving me—it makes me want to kill you for having the *nerve* to hurt me like that."

Shoving me away, he threw the eraser on the floor and stormed toward the door. "I'm done. I never want to see you again. Spread your lies somewhere else, sweetheart. We're through."

He slammed the door.

The scrape of a key sounded in the lock.

He left me to my doom.

Chapter Thirteen

I was loved once.

I loved in return.

I gave myself completely, utterly, and with no boundaries.

And I received her love unequivocally.

Owning something so precious made me the richest man alive. But losing it made me sink into destitution so bleak and damned, I had no chance of crawling out of the darkness.

I didn't want to.

I couldn't.

There was nothing but pain left for me.

Now I loved no one.

Now I was feared.

It was time to make her fear me.

She pushed me too far and I refused to let her hurt me further.

So I'd hurt her first.

I'd hurt her to continue surviving.

—*Kill*

The door opened a few hours later.

My eyes soared up, hoping and fearing Kill had returned to hurt me worse. Not that he could. It wasn't the bruise on my ribs that hurt me every time I breathed, but the betrayal of thinking I understood him. I thought he was broken... in need of someone with the truth to glue him back together again.

But he'd shown me the stark reality.

There was no fixing someone who didn't want to see past the pain. He truly believed I wasn't her. His conviction was so absolute it robbed me of my own belief and made me apologetic for all the agony I'd caused.

I'm not her. Or am I?

The questions ran around and around inside my head.

I wanted to know how the memories of a dead girl existed in my tangled brain, and I knew the only way that would happen was if I broke through to Arthur and not Kill.

I looked up gingerly, trying to figure out what to say.

I'm sorry.

Give me a chance to explain.

Please, help me to understand.

But it wasn't Kill who'd come for me.

Standing in the doorway was a Pure Corruption brother. I stared into the blue eyes of the black-haired, mohawked biker called Grasshopper.

He looked younger in the sunlight than he did when covered in blood from battle. His lips were full and set into a gentle but firm smile, and he had a cute dimple on his right cheek. "Hi," he said.

His forehead furrowed as he stepped toward me. "Um—you okay?"

I locked my arms harder around my knees. I hadn't moved from the carpet, leaning against the bed, twirling the Libra eraser in my fingertips. Kill hadn't been thinking straight when he threw it at my feet—it was obviously a treasured belonging.

I wished it was magic: twist it one way and unlock the truth, spin it another and have everything lost be found. But no matter how much I held it, it didn't give me what I needed.

"Yes." I ran a hand through my hair, hoping I didn't look like a domestic violence case who'd been crying. I hadn't been crying—I felt...numb. Quakingly sad and confused.

Grasshopper's eyes fell to my naked leg beneath my skirt and the colorful ink of flowers, small unicorn, and petals permanently transforming my thigh, calf, and toes. "Nice piece."

I let my arms fall from my position, shooting my leg out and resting it on the carpet. "It is nice. Pity I don't remember why I had it done, or where, or even the pain."

His eyes widened as he ducked in front of me. "You don't remember the pain? What—is that like a childbirth thing where they say the girl never remembers being torn in two by a fucking spawn and then a year later does it all over again?"

I cringed, laughing uncomfortably. "Thanks for painting such a lovely image inside my head." My fingers traced a strange equation over my knee, which faded into a scripted line that I couldn't read from the angle I rested. "Not quite. I seem to have forgotten a lot of basic things."

Grasshopper sniffed, pushing upright to tower over me. Holding out his hand, he said, "Well, you're still alive, so you know how to eat, sleep, and communicate. That's something."

I eyed his open palm. Suspicion flowed swiftly in my blood. "I don't mean to be rude, but why are you here? I haven't seen any of the men from the compound since that night. Arthur said he lived alone."

Grasshopper burst into laughter, his blue eyes sparkling. "Arthur? Fuck, you call him Arthur? No wonder he's pissed off."

I didn't move. Something cold slithered down my back. As nice as Grasshopper seemed to be, I didn't like the reason why he was here—in his boss's bedroom.

"Sorry, my mistake. Kill. President Kill."

Grasshopper nodded, holding out his hand again, waggling it a little in impatience. "Yes, I know the dude. He's a good man and for him to have snapped the way he has means you're not good for his health, little lady. Come on, get up. Time to go."

I balked. "What? I don't want to go."

Grasshopper gave up the pretense of waiting for me to hand myself over to his control, and grabbed my elbow instead. Dragging me to my feet, he noticed the eraser in my clenched fingers. "Shit, where did you get that from?"

I cradled it to my chest. "I gave it to him. A long time ago."

The jovial, almost curious interaction faded from his eyes. "Ah, I get it now." His face hardened; his persona went cold. "You're playing with him. Sorry, but I don't have time for bitches trying to fuck up one of my brothers—especially my Prez."

Snatching my wrist, he forced my fingers to unclamp and tossed the eraser on the bed. The same bed where Arthur had fucked me; the same bed where I'd seen the level of his grief. "Come on. You're not going to hurt him anymore. You're done." He strode toward the door, dragging me easily.

I jammed my heels into the carpet, scratching at his hand. "No—wait. I can't go. I have to stay."

He didn't say anything, carting me out of the room and down the corridor.

"You don't understand. I know him. I might be—"

He jerked to a stop. "Did he fuck you?"

I blinked. "That's none of your bus—"

"I'll take that as a yes. Answer me three questions—if you answer them right, then I'll leave you here and tell Kill to be a man and sort it out with you face-to-face. But if you're wrong—you're coming with me. You're never seeing him again. And you better hope to God the man who has bought you has a better tolerance for liars."

Bought? I was already sold?

The world fell away. The corridor spun sickeningly. Kill told the truth when he left.

I never want to see you again. We're through.

Shit! I'd been prepared to leave because of Kill's horrible silent treatment, but that was before I'd seen the truth glowing in his eyes. He was just so used to being hurt, so used to nursing his grief and living with a broken heart. He hated me because I represented hope. That would scare anyone who loved someone as much as he did.

"I'll answer your questions, only if you answer one for me." *Please, know the answer. Please, be close enough to Kill that he told you.* "What was his dead girlfriend's name?"

Grasshopper froze, and his fingers bit into my flesh. "How do you know about her? Damn, you're good. No wonder he's been so fucking screwed up the past few days. If it were me, I would've killed you for bringing all that back."

"Bringing what back? Please—I need to know!"

He threw me away, running both hands through his hair, messing up the perfection of his mohawk. "Fine! You want to know? Kill was sentenced to life in prison—"

Life?

"I know—he told me he was in jail when she died."

He shook his head, smiling cruelly. "Not *when* she died. He was in jail *because* she died." He crowded me against the wall. "Don't you get it? He was done for murder! He killed her."

My heart didn't know if it should give up or explode. "That can't be true! He told me she died in surgery—"

"Injuries that *he* gave her."

My mind turned into a vortex, swirling faster and faster with horror.

Flames.

The smoke disorientated me, skipping my mind back to my birthday two weeks ago.

I'd turned fourteen. My parents hosted a barbeque for the entire Chapter. Men in leather jackets, women wearing their lover's patches, and children all raised in the lifestyle came to celebrate my day.

We'd been a family. A happy, tight-knit family.

But now I crawled along the carpet that was drenched in blood. I scurried from flames hotter than any barbeque and the right side of my body became as char-grilled as any hamburger.

The pain.

It was excruciating, but then... it disappeared.

Shock gave me energy to keep crawling and choking and reliving the horror of seeing who'd poured gasoline through my family's home.

I saw who struck the match.

I knew.

I had no choice but to survive so they would pay.

"Anyone in there?" The voice crackled with flames.

My throat was parched, my eyes blind from fumes. I couldn't answer.

I crawled…

I dragged my burning body…

I…crawled…

I went blank.

Grasshopper shook me. My neck bounced on my spine like a rag doll as I blinked the horrible flashback away.

"He set fire to my *house*?" I whispered, terror squeezing my lungs.

My soul fractured into a billion pieces. The boy with the green eyes tried to *murder* me?

I scrambled at Grasshopper's jacket, hating the skull and raining coins embroidered into the thick leather. Something about it looked wrong…terribly, terribly *wrong*.

"Why?" I begged. "Why did he try to kill me? We loved each other!"

Grasshopper stepped back, trying to push me off him. "Get a fucking grip, bitch. I have no idea what you're talking about."

"Yes, you do! Tell me. You *have* to tell me."

Every muscle in my body trembled, my stomach hurled, and the corridor walls closed in—faster and faster, crushing me like a tin can until the pressure in my head grew too much. Way, way too much.

I screamed, tugging on my hair, willing the memories to unlock and grant me relief. But the pressure just kept increasing, building, *building* until every hair follicle hurt my skull, until my eyes felt too big, until my tongue felt too swollen.

I couldn't see. I couldn't hear. Only the chugging crazed beat of my freaking-out heart echoed in my ears.

"Plea—" I slurred.

The crash of everything from my past consumed me and I couldn't bear it any longer.

I let go of sanity.

I succumbed to the silently screeching dark.

Fuzz and cotton wool and clouds were my welcome-back-to-life party.

I smacked my lips, grimacing at the horrible taste in my mouth. My nose was blocked and my head bellowed with pain.

I moaned as feeling came back to my body; I winced as I touched my ribs.

He kicked me.

Hot tears came to my eyes as I recalled what had happened. He'd been nasty since I'd arrived, but that kick... It spoke volumes.

I doubted he knew how much he'd shown me in that brief moment. His anger had been uncurbed, unrestrained. He'd kicked me. Not the bed or the chair. *Me.*

Because *I* was the one hurting him. *I* was the one forcing him to face things I could only guess at. He carried so much inside he looked like he was drowning every second.

The kick shocked me, not because it'd been a horrible betrayal of violence, but because it was a cry for help.

My vision flickered as my thoughts turned to the rest of the afternoon.

I recoiled, not ready to pass out again from overload of stress and secrets.

Rubbing my eyes, I sat up. My heart fell to my toes.

I was in a cell. A cube with a sink, kitchenette, toilet, and bed. There were no windows, pictures, or carpet, and only one way in and out which was undoubtedly locked.

The bright lightbulb above me was harsh and piercing and there lurked a rank scent of fear and vomit.

Where am I?

Standing unsteadily, I made my way to the heavy door and knocked. "Hello?"

I waited for a response.

I continued to wait.

I was more patient that I'd ever been.

Nothing.

Ignoring the splintering headache, I turned to investigate every inch of the small box. I looked under the bed, between the springs and the mattress, even tried the faucets to see if there was anything I could unscrew and use as a weapon.

Just like my knock.

There was nothing.

Then the lights went out, drenching me in darkness.

I stood in the middle of my prison and began to cry.

Morning.

Grasshopper woke me with the scrape of a key and the blissful opening of the door. He carried in a steaming Pop-Tart and some water.

I hadn't slept at all. My mind didn't want to fall back into the abyss of unconsciousness. Instead, I repeated everything I'd remembered so far.

Corrine.

Buttercup.

Barbeque.

Flames.

I tried to piece them together like a glow in the dark puzzle—only the pieces refused to merge and there was nothing luminescent about them.

I still wore the pink skirt that Kill had pushed up my hips to take me, and the cute grey sweater that hadn't kept me warm throughout the night. The blankets on the bed smelled of perfume, and I'd thrown up at the thought of the other women spending the night here—waiting for their new fate.

Grasshopper placed the Pop-Tart and glass on the rickety table beside the bed. "You okay?"

I snorted, rubbing my forearms and not making eye contact. "What do you think?"

He growled under his breath. "If you're hurting a smidgen of what he is, then I'd say you're hunky-fucking-dory."

I gritted my teeth and didn't say a word.

Uncomfortable silence reigned; I made no move to break it. Grasshopper bounced on the ball of his shoes. "Brought you breakfast."

"Don't want it."

"You have to eat."

"No, I don't."

He bent over and captured my chin, making me look at him. His blue eyes were strained, tiny lines feathering around them. "Stop it. Be good and you can come hang with us in the den. You've got another night with us before the handover."

I wrenched my jaw from his hold, breathing hard. "I don't want to eat. I don't want to 'hang' with trafficking bastards, and I sure as shit don't want to talk to you." Hunching my shoulders, I curled into a ball and closed my eyes. "Leave me alone."

Grasshopper stood over me. The sound of his grinding teeth was the only noise. His nostrils whistled annoyingly as he deliberated doing God knew what. "Remember those three questions I was going to ask you? Back at Kill's place?"

A stabbing pain spread through my body at his name. I didn't reply.

He huffed. "Look, give me the answers and I'll decide if there's any merit to Kill's behavior... If not... I'll speak to him."

I stiffened, opening my eyes and glaring. "You're sick, you know that?"

He scowled. "Why am I sick for trying to be nice to you? I don't have to, you know. I could leave you alone until the sale is done. Let you go fucking mad in here." He crossed his arms, blue eyes piercing mine. "Unless you're already mad, of course. Then it won't matter."

I sat up, nursing the fire in my belly. "Ask. Then leave me the hell alone."

What are you doing?

Everything inside screamed for me to clamp my lips together and not play his horrid little game, but there was a small part of me that still hoped for redemption.

Grasshopper swallowed, taking his time to form the first question. "When he took you—did he fuck you doggy-style?"

My mouth fell open. "That's the most disgusting, prying question I've ever—"

"Just fucking answer it. Did he?"

I narrowed my eyes. I refused to answer such an invasive, personal question. Didn't matter, though, because my silence gave away the answer.

He took me on all fours once. The other times had been different...

Grasshopper sighed, dragging a hand over his face. "He did. Just like he always does with Club whores or any other woman who slithers their way into his bed."

My heart twisted green with envy, rotting with jealousy for a man who I hated. Who'd *kicked* me...taken everything from me...who'd burned down my—

It wasn't him.

I slapped that thought away, but the thread of truth worked its way past my defenses and grabbed a bullhorn so I couldn't ignore it.

It wasn't him with the match. You know that.

I balled my hands. No, it hadn't been him who set my house alight.

A man with green eyes. An older man in a black leather jacket and a vicious smile.

Green eyes.

Green eyes.

Green eyes.

"Next question," Grasshopper said. "Did he tie your hands so you couldn't touch him?"

I couldn't stop the spring of tears shining my shame and answer.

Grasshopper nodded. "I take that as a yes." Lowering his voice, almost as if he felt sorry for me, he muttered, "Last question."

I already knew what it would be.

"Did he blindfold you so you couldn't look at him?"

I couldn't. I just couldn't.

I placed my palms over my eyes and turned away, hating the sobs that boiled in my chest.

A small cry spilled from my lips as Grasshopper rested a heavy, comforting hand on my back and rubbed circles. "Three yeses. That means, whatever you think you saw—whatever you thought you felt—it was all a lie."

He kept stroking me, the gentleness of his concern seeping into my weary bones.

I sucked in a breath, whispering raggedly, "Explain how I know about the eraser. That he trades the stock market. That he's the kindest, sweetest boy I've ever known? That I *loved* him?"

Silence was thick, before Grasshopper replied, "We can't explain what happens when our minds decide to go on fucking vacation. Who the hell knows how and why we create fantasy worlds. You said so yourself, you don't remember anything. You're making it up. You're creating lies that you believe so deeply that to you they're truths—but to Kill... It's fucking killing him."

He stopped stroking me and stood in creaking leather and boots. "Don't take it personally. He's an asshole to all women. I probably shouldn't tell you this, but he lost his virginity the day he got out of prison. He only did it 'cause the bastard was twenty-four, had never been in a pussy, and was the youngest president to inherit the Club. He needed to man up—and fast." A proud glint formed in his gaze. "I was the one who brought the whore to him. I was the one who was there from the beginning, helping him turn this Club around."

I bit my lip, willing my breathing to be silent—to hear every word this man might spill.

He nodded, lost in his own thoughts. "He bound her, blindfolded her, and fucked her from behind. To this day, he's never done it any differently."

He took me facing him. Twice.

My heart twisted in a weird combination of disgust and optimism.

"Why?" I breathed.

"Why?" His eyebrows rose and he chuckled. "Thought that would be obvious."

I waited, not moving.

He sighed and muttered, "Because he can't stand them to be close, because they aren't her. He can't stand for them to look at him, because he thinks they see what he did. And he can't stand to be touched any more than necessary as he can't—under any situation—be offered comfort when he's the reason why she's no longer around to be loved."

My heart shattered.

Kill confused me utterly.

But I pitied him more.

"How—how do you know all this?"

Grasshopper smiled sadly, moving toward the door. "How does anyone ever know the inner secrets of a man ridden by demons?"

I shifted onto my knees, begging him silently to finish his riddle before abandoning me to loneliness.

He cocked his head. "By watching. By listening to what they *don't* say. By riding beside them when they snap and fly from the compound to visit the grave of a corpse. By being the only one they confide in."

He opened the door, stepping through.

"Wait!" I cried.

He turned, his eyes resigned. "What?"

I wrung my fingers, wishing I had more knowledge. Wishing upon wishes that all of this made sense to my mind while it made implicit sense to my heart.

I ached for him.

"Why are you telling me? Why show me his secrets, when you just proved I'm just like all the rest? That I'm not...her?"

He took a moment to reply. "Because you'll never see him again. And hopefully, knowing what haunts him will give you the closure you need. To know that you never stood a chance." His voice lost its chivalrous edge, sliding straight into arctic. "I told you so you'll never try and ruin him again, because you're *nothing* to him. Just like all the rest."

His words tore me into pieces and there was no one who cared to sew me back together again.

He slammed the door.

He left me to bleed out with a soul that was unstitched and drifting away with endless pain.

"What's my name?"

Nothing.

"What's my name?"

Silence.

"What's my *name*?"

Blankness.

I cursed in frustration. The swear word bounced around the black box with no one but me to hear it.

Fourteen hours had passed since Grasshopper fed me breakfast and shone light on his president—a man he obviously loved. Six hours had passed since another Pure Corruption brother brought me dinner of microwaved lasagna and a soft drink.

Two hundred and seventeen times I'd asked myself the same question.

Two hundred and seventeen times I'd gotten no reply.

It was all enough to drive me into madness.

I gave up, sliding down the wall to lie on my side on the lumpy mattress. My inhale and exhale were the only noises in my silent world. It was as annoying as a tap dripping, or a clock ticking, or a fly buzzing.

There's no way I'll sleep.

I was drained but not sleepy. Teary but not hysterical. I'd made it this far without losing faith—I just had to keep going, no matter what tomorrow brought.

Balling my hands, I wedged them beneath my cheek and began all over again.

"What's my name?"

Nothing.

"What's my name?"

Silence.

"What's my *name*?"

Sarah.

I froze, turning to stone.

"What's my name?" I whispered.

Sarah.

"Sarah! Dammit, leave the poor pussy alone."

I grinned at Corrine, tucking the little black-and-white kitten into my jacket. "Pussy, huh? That's a bad joke—even for you."

She giggled, her blonde short hair ruffling in the winter wind. Living in England was a privilege, to be around monarchs and history and pedigree of families who could trace their lineage back to the Stone Age, but damn, the weather sucked.

I'd moved to England to study my degree. I'd moved from the United States. I'd moved because...

Like always the wall came up, slamming shut in my face. I sighed, so used to not remembering anything before my fourteenth birthday that I no longer cared. I had a great new life, a boyfriend who adored me, and an education that allowed me to work with animals who appreciated everything I did for them.

I was living the dream.

So why does your heart pine for something you don't recall?

The question was like a haunting—never leaving me alone.

Corrine looped her arm through mine, joining forces against the ice. We lived not far away, in a quaint studio apartment that we both could barely afford and that created multiple problems whenever one of us wanted our respective lovers to spend the night.

Living with no recollection of my past or family was hard, but somehow I'd made it. The doctors said I might remember someday. But as the years ticked past, that scenario became more and more unlikely. There was nothing they could do for complete amnesia brought on by almost dying. And I was beyond grateful that my other brain functions seemed to be normal. No one could explain the burns to my body—or how I was supposedly found in a ditch of some field.

It was all a mystery, never to be solved.

In tribute to a past I no longer knew, I'd inked the mirroring side with everything I could imagine I liked when I was a little girl. I went crazy, and paid the price in pain and needles, but every time I looked at the tattoo, I somehow felt closer to my past.

However, there was one hidden design that I knew would someday unlock my mind.

An equation.

Buried and obscured so the scrap of truth would be seen only by me. No one else would get it. No one would give me a key to solving it. It was my ultimate goal to know.

"Fancy a movie tonight?"

"Sure," I said, pressing my nose against the soft bundle of fur. I hated seeing abandoned pets. I single-handedly kept the animal shelter in business by delivering homeless creatures.

I did it because I was homeless in a way, too.

"Good. I'm thinking something sexy. Fancy watching some naked man with blue eyes ravaging the heroine?"

I laughed, squeezing her arm tight. "I'm all for that—but can my hero have green eyes instead?"

The past faded away.

A smile bloomed on my face.

"My name is Sarah, and I'm beginning to remember."

Chapter Fourteen

Work came in many forms. Many obsessions. Many goals.

Mine hadn't deviated since my life had changed forever.

I had a plan. I'd been working on it for eight long years.

Every contact, every dollar, every trade was all for one outcome.

And finally, after all this time, I could taste freedom from my quest.

I was about to become their worst fucking nightmare and they were completely oblivious.

—Kill

"Morning," Grasshopper said, sticking his head around the door.

I sat up, stretching and trying to hide my yawn. There was something different inside me—a cracking of sorts. It was as if the wall that barricaded everything wasn't as strong anymore—hairline fractures, tiny fissures had diseased the fortitude, allowing spears of light to glow.

I was told I might never remember before my fourteenth birthday. Until a week ago, I couldn't recall anything at all and lived another life that I was only just starting to remember—yet the memories that were coming fast were the ones buried so deep they were sluggish and heavy, and so unbearably precious to be viewed after all this time.

"I'm here to take you to the bathroom. You can freshen up. I have some clothes for you, and then you can come eat with the boys."

I blinked, trying to steady my world of biker lunches and showering, before being trafficked to some unknown buyer.

Ask him.

I shot to my feet, feeling gross and unwashed but more alive than ever. "Kill's dead girl. I know her name."

Please, be right. It has to be right.

Grasshopper scowled, his blue eyes darkening. "I highly doubt that."

Sucking in a breath, I said quickly, "Sarah. Her name was Sarah." *Is Sarah.* I strode forward, rushing, "I don't know my last name yet, but I remembered! Don't you see? Tell him my name and he'll understand. He'll know I'm telling the truth!"

I bubbled with excitement and a hint of fear. What would he do when he learned that everything I'd said was the truth? Would he beg forgiveness for kicking me? Would he slam to his knees and actually hug me—to allow me to hug him back for the first time since my "death"?

Grasshopper's face had gone scarily unreadable. I couldn't tell if he believed me or wanted to throttle me. Cocking his head, he said, "Get in the shower and I'll call him. I'll get him to join us for lunch before you leave."

I couldn't help it. I launched myself at his leather-jacketed frame and hugged him. "Thank you."

He stiffened. A hard hand wedged between us and drove me backward. He refused to make eye contact. "I'm not as fucked up as Kill is, but I still don't like bitches hugging me." Opening the door wider, he motioned me through. "Shower. Then you can break the news to my Prez."

Thirty minutes later, I entered the same room where Kill had made us strip and told us of our purpose. The floor had been washed of his blood and the button leather couches were pristine.

The shower had been heaven, even though the soap had been an overpowering masculine body wash with no conditioner for my hair. Grasshopper had given me an outfit of a gold bikini with diamantés and a wraparound bronze dress. It would've been perfect for a day out at the beach or pool party, but I was mildly weirded out to be wearing something so...fantastical in a biker compound.

"You sure I have to wear this?" I plucked at the material for the twentieth time. My damp red hair hung down my back, no doubt springing into humidity-induced curls.

"Yep. Prez's orders," Grasshopper said, striding across the large space and past the blown-up magazine covers on the wall. "This way."

I stopped short as I noticed Kill on one with crimson writing and the slogan, *Biker billionaire helps expose corruption in local council.*

My mouth hung open, my heart rushed hard, and my core melted at the dashing debonair appearance of Arthur Killian in a crisp sexy suit. He wore an emerald tie to bring out his eyes and they glowed like kryptonite from the glossy oversize cover.

Why is he on magazines?

I drifted to the next one.

Kill sat behind a wooden desk, his elbow resting on its surface, his pinky finger pressed against his bottom lip. The intensity in his gaze spoke of intelligence and ferocity. In the background rested his Triumph, painted a matte black, looking roguish and evil.

Goose bumps spread over my arms as I read the article description: *Arthur "Kill" Killian lives up to his name by slaughtering the foreign currency market and showing Wall Street how it's done.*

"What are you looking at?" Grasshopper stomped back toward me, impatience etching his face.

I pointed at another cover, this one with a mug shot of Kill holding a plaque with his birth date and messy long hair and a look in his eyes that said one thing—he was a boy whose soul had died and only vengeance remained. He simmered in the picture. He looked as if he would reach from the page and murder those who wronged him.

From betrayal to billions—the story of the kid and the benefactor who turned a life of crime into the purest of community service.

I swallowed hard.

"That's when they took him?" I leaned forward, drinking in the image of Kill when he was younger. His jaw was just as wide, his nose just as sharp, but there wasn't the brutal edge about him or the veneer of tolerance he used now. The mug shot was raw and visceral with hate and the burning desire for revenge.

"Yep. Seventeen, poor dude."

I shook my head. "You said he was sentenced to life imprisonment. How did he get out so soon?"

Grasshopper tapped his nose, then pretended to zip his lips. "That's for us to know and for you not to. None of your business, but it was a fucking blessed day for all when he took over the Corrupts and made us Pure Corruption."

Grabbing my elbow, he carted me away from the stunning images of the boy I loved and the man I couldn't understand and through another door.

I slammed to a halt.

The room was nothing fancy: grey walls with a ceiling fan, polished floorboards, and windows looking over the compound behind, but the large oval table that sat twelve or so guys was definitely the centerpiece of the décor.

The same abacus, skull, and waterfall of coins had been heavily engraved into the table with the motto that I was beginning to understand: PURE IN THOUGHTS AND VENGEANCE. CORRUPT IN ALL THINGS THAT MATTER.

Grasshopper pulled out a chair for me.

I inched closer, unsure.

"Guys, this is Sarah."

I trembled at the familiarity and homecoming of my name. I quickly glanced around the room, looking for *him*.

Nothing.

The men ranged from early twenties to late forties, all wearing the brown leather jacket of the Pure Corruption MC and all at ease with each other—unlike the first night I'd arrived.

"Hey," some said, while others nodded in greeting.

I clutched the front of my bronze dress, sitting awkwardly in the chair provided. "Hi," I murmured.

Sitting primly, I narrowed my eyes, inspecting each biker. Friendly hazel, blue, and green gazes met mine. Each man sat comfortably in his chair, assured of his position and right to be there. The kinship in the room didn't hide anything malevolent, and I let the tension ebb from my limbs.

Then my eyes met his.

And my world went instantly bleak.

Brown eyes, deep-set in a face that spoke of handsomeness but couldn't quite disguise the evil in his soul. Thin lips, long hair tied in a greasy ponytail, and a tattoo of an alligator on his neck peeked from the collar of his leather cut.

He nodded, his lips curling at the corners. Something flickered in his hands, drawing my attention.

A lighter.

The tension I'd released shot straight back into my muscles tenfold. Gripping the lip of the table, I never looked away as he flicked the lighter, releasing a small lick of orange flame.

My mind twisted behind the locked door, hurling itself in panic against the amnesiac barrier. My fingers went unwillingly to the fresh burn on my forearm, rubbing at the painful searing that'd sprung from nowhere.

Him.

He was the one who burned me.

That night.

The night they stole me.

Try as I might, I couldn't remember anything more or how I came to be kidnapped, but I knew with utmost conviction—he was the one to grace my body with yet another scar.

Was it the new burn that set off another episode of amnesia?

Could my brain be so traumatized by fire that the barest of flames on my skin made me turn inward and hide?

My heart raced.

Not only was I dealing with remembering *one* past but it seemed I had two to unravel. A past where my home was England and Corrine and a brown-eyed boyfriend I couldn't recall, and a lifetime before that one...a childhood of motorcycles, family, and green-eyed lovers who helped me with homework.

Will I ever know the truth?

I jumped as the sandy-blond guy, Mo, sprawled in his chair beside me. His arrival snapped the awareness between me and Lighter Boy, breaking whatever panic attack I might've had.

Mo grinned. "Been staying with the boss, huh?" He whistled. "Kinda a big honor to go home with the Prez, you know. What did you do to fuck it up?"

My nostrils flared, body stiffened, and I refused to reply. My eyes skittered back to the asshole playing with his lighter, but he dropped his attention to the table, blocking me from reading his thoughts.

Grasshopper sat on my left, scowling at Mo. "It was always only temporary, dude. She's the sixth sale—remember?"

The door opened behind me and the scents of grease, cheese, and salami filled the room. The men around the table smacked their lips, eyeing up the huge pizza boxes that were deposited onto the table by a younger member with no patch.

There weren't too many men—twelve, fifteen, and most of them seemed open and friendly. But I couldn't shed the horrible feeling of dining with the devil with Lighter Boy across from me.

How did he take me?

How did all of this happen?

And where the hell did they kidnap me from if I'd been living in England? There was no way they could've smuggled me internationally. Could they? But most of all—what was the *point*? Why me? Why the girl who couldn't remember but had some inexplicable link to their boss? The boss who slaughtered a rebellion the night I arrived.

It all felt like a chess game where everyone knew the rules but me. I was a pawn. Being slid left and right until someone smacked me from the checkered board and killed me off in a brutal checkmate.

"'Bout fucking time you got here, boy. I was wasting away I was so damn hungry," one biker growled, his goatee bristling. He reached across and flipped up a lid, stealing a piece of delicious-looking pizza.

I was suddenly thankful for staying at Kill's place. At least he ordered healthy food—even if he didn't cook. I doubted I would've enjoyed a calorie-controlled diet if I'd been a guest of the compound.

Mo stood up, leaned over his brothers to fill a paper plate with two pieces of pizza, then skidded it down the table to me.

I caught it, unable to stop the growling in my stomach. Margherita and Meat Lover's. I would've preferred Hawaiian but the flavor dancing on the air made my mouth water.

The room went quiet as the men helped themselves to pizza and someone brought in a cooler full of beer. I refused the offer and nibbled on my food while watching the rest of them.

My eyes kept returning to Lighter Boy, wishing I understood. The rest of the men looked dangerous with scars and piercings and the occasional feral glint in their eyes, but they were also...*normal.* They laughed and joked, spoke of mundane things while eating—chatting about family, grumbling about wives and household chores. I found it mildly unsettling to be around such everyday life when society had already painted them with the "outlaw rebel" brush.

"Buttercup, eat your spaghetti. The meetin's coming up and you know you can't be here."

I shoved the unwanted spaghetti around my plate, sulking. I wanted to listen in—after all, I was his only child and I needed to know how the Club was run, so I could take over when he was gone. But he never stopped reminding me that girls didn't run the Club. That girls remained on the outskirts—being protected by the men like my dad, who did naughty things to keep up our way of existence.

"But I want to listen."

He ducked to my eye level. "Go find your friend. He can help you with your homework."

"Don't wanna," I pouted. I was ten years old and it sucked that the boy I'd always looked up to suddenly wanted nothing to do with me. He said he was too cool for kids.

Bully.

My dad laughed, ruffling my unruly hair. "Ah, Buttercup, don't hate the boy. Mark my words, the minute you turn thirteen that kid will notice you again."

A small smile spread my lips. "Really?"

My father grinned, his light blue-green eyes crinkling at the corners. His auburn hair was slightly darker than mine and I'd inherited the small freckles on my nose from my mother, who was a pure redhead.

"Truly. No boy or man will be able to resist you. And that's why I'll be ready to shoot him if he tries anything."

The flashback ended, slipping me back into lunch conversation as gently as melting into a warm bath. My heart glowed with love. To remember my father—his face, his voice—it was more than I'd ever hoped for.

Unbelievably cherished.

Relief was swift and full of content. I'd finally earned a concrete puzzle piece in my hunt for answers.

"So, Sarah... what did Kill do to keep you entertained at his place?"

I took a bite of my pizza, letting the wash of conversation lap around me.

A finger poked me in the side. I narrowed my eyes. "What?"

Grasshopper frowned, pointing at a young biker with brown hair pulled back in a wet gel look. "He asked you a question."

"He did?"

The guy nodded. "Yep, used your name and everything."

The pizza slipped from my fingers. I should've jumped to his question—so in tune with the name I'd only just remembered. Shouldn't I?

Ignoring the chill trickling down my back, I asked, "What was the question? Sorry."

Mo spoke around a mouthful of pizza. "He was being an asshole."

"Oh?"

He chuckled. "He wanted to know what Kill did to keep you 'entertained.'" He waggled his eyebrows.

Two reactions rushed through me. One, to blush and look away. Two, to grin and play them at their own game. Two people lived inside me. The girl who lived abroad and studied hard, and the teenager who'd been brought up with men just like these and a confidence that only came from being around safety and family.

Keeping my eyes resolutely from Lighter Boy's I said, "If you must know, he took me shopping, brought me lunch, and respected my boundaries." I kept my face deadpan. The answer was, for all intents and purposes, true—the reply came from the mind of Sarah.

Sarah is quiet and serious.

My eyes went wide, my brain pointing out yet another twist in my journey to remember.

Then who was the vivacious girl who loved a biker's son? *Who was I when I kissed Kill so wildly in the changing room?*

Grasshopper groaned. "Boring. Tell us the juice. I already know he fucked you."

"Stop that." I turned to stare at him. A strange bond had formed between us—not friendship or understanding—just mutual…respect? Or just a truce because we both knew I'd be leaving in a few hours. "You might know but I don't want others to—"

"Ah, pumpkin." A man with a large belly laughed. "He kept you at his place. We know he fucked ya. So…dish it up."

Annoyance wrangled with mischief. The men, excluding Lighter

Boy, watched me with eager amusement and intrigue. It was so nice to be around people again. I'd forgotten the ease of being in a group, of laughing with strangers who slowly became friends.

Friends were all I could gain with my mind like a giant sieve. I had no family.

But I do.

My heart swelled like a hot air balloon. For the first time in years, I wasn't alone. I came from someone. I *belonged* to someone.

And it isn't the boy from your dreams. He didn't want me.

My spine straightened as tiredness fell over me. Kill still hadn't showed up. What did that mean? That he still despised me? Still completely in denial that the woman he'd mourned for years actually was never dead?

Was that even possible?

"Come on, Sarah. Tell us—is our Prez a good fuck?" The guy with the belly elbowed another, winking at me.

I reclined in my chair, wishing I had a napkin for my greasy fingers. I embraced the side of the girl still hidden to me. The girl called Buttercup. The girl who would've laughed and joked with men similar to these all those years ago. "Well... what do you want to know?"

The men slapped their hands on the table, their low timbre laughs reverberating around the table. "Oh, shouldn't have said that, girl."

"Tell us the kinky dirt."

"Tell us something that'll make you blush."

My back tensed but I smiled at the rough gruff men, not afraid of them as I'd been raised by a brethren similar in some other time and place. I was as much a part of this world as any other—more so in fact: the smell of gasoline and thunder of a motorcycle was the lullaby of my past.

Fear skittered quickly.

So why, if you came from this world, do you fear it so much?

My fingers ached to grab my hair and shake. The questions were piling up and I had no answers to tame them.

Calmly Lighter Boy stood up, wiped his mouth, swigged the rest of his beer, and made his way around the table to leave. His brothers didn't look up, transfixed on waiting for any gossip from me. But I couldn't look anywhere else.

Opening the door he looked back, brown eyes locking with mine. His lips spread over his teeth, sending a shiver over my scalp. His eyes shouted that he wasn't finished with me. Whatever he'd stolen me for had yet to come to pass.

Waggling his fingers condescendingly, he left the room, closing the door behind him.

My heart charged around my chest.

You need to remember. And fast.

My time had screeched to an end. I'd been sold. I would soon leave and never get a second chance. I had to fight.

Mo nudged my ankle under the table. "Tell us. It's cruel to make a man wait."

"Yeah, it's called blue balls," the prospect joked.

Masculine laughter rippled around the room.

Taking a deep breath, I asked, "You want details..."

"Hell yeah!"

Grasshopper grinned. "One tiny juicy detail. Come on, give it up."

My mind raced with everything Kill had done—the way he'd made me feel, the vulnerability and brokenness he kept hidden below surly curtness. "Okay, one detail. When he took me shopping, he pushed me against the changing room wall and kissed me so hard his teeth punctured my bottom lip."

My tummy fluttered recalling the passion, the confusion, and most of all the need.

The laughter died; men looked at each other with strange expressions on their faces.

Mo finally muttered, "As fucking if. Tell the story but don't lie about it."

Grasshopper threw me a look, stuffing his face full of pizza. I couldn't read the message in his eyes.

A lie because he kissed me? Was that so hard to believe?

Yes, if what Grasshopper said is right. Bound, blindfolded, no touching—the only way Kill would sleep with a woman.

I lost the spark to interact with them, letting my soul sink down and down into the forgetful darkness inside. It wasn't their business what their president did with me. Especially seeing as my answers unsettled them. And I wanted to hoard those precious memories—they were my only illumination in the dark.

"Try again, pumpkin. Something believable this time," the guy with the belly said, swiping his mouth free of pizza crumbs.

Balling my hands under the table, I said, "What happened at Kill's place—"

"Is none of your goddamn business." That voice. Smooth but gravelly. Deep and powerful. An earthquake invoker—his words aftershocking around the room with force.

Awareness electrified the fine hairs on the back of my neck. Every inch of my body hummed.

The room went quiet. Achingly quiet.

I spun in my chair. My heart erupted into sparks and comets.

Kill's face was closed off and angry, his hands fisted by his sides. His eyes were bloodshot and fresh bruising marked his face. Gone was the collected angry president, replaced with an exposed man searching for violence. "I trust you to do *one* thing and this is what I fucking come back to?"

Everything about him seethed with rage, his hair was tussled, and the scent of winds, salt, and leather threaded with the sharpness of alcohol.

Where had he been? *He's been fighting.*

Kill never looked at me. Instead, he directed his anger at Grasshopper. "I see you're disobeying me again and feeding the damn girl?"

My back bristled. I wanted to yell at him to talk to me, but my lips stayed firmly glued.

Grasshopper stood, wiping his hands on his faded jeans. "Hey, Prez. My bad. She's been cooped up in that room for a couple of days—felt it important to give her some fresh air, you know?"

Mo's eyes bored into the back of my head, but I never took my attention off Kill. I drank him in from his bloody knuckles to the grass stain on his jeans. My mind raced with all sorts of fabrications of what he'd been doing the last two days.

I'd *missed* him.

I wanted to tend to his new injuries just like I'd done the first night I'd arrived. I wanted to heal him—fix whatever drove him to such destructive behavior.

Maybe he wasn't fighting? Maybe it was self-defense?

My mind skipped into all new horrors thinking of him being hurt maliciously by others.

Unconsciously, I leaned forward, drawn to him as surely as a tide to the moon. "You're hurt."

His nostrils flared and the cognizant awareness between us sprang up as if we'd never touched or kissed or fucked. It was thick and rampant and bogged down with issues—but there. And strong. So damn strong.

My skin prickled with heat and my core melted beneath his scrutiny.

"Why the fuck did you call me, Hopper? You knew the plan. You knew why I wanted it this way." Kill ran a hand through his tangled hair, still refusing to look at me.

"Got something to check. To make sure once and for all—before your chance is gone—that what you believe is true."

"Fuck you, man. I told you." Kill stepped forward, the room glittering with violence. The other men stood up, the soft scrape of chairs and rush of mixed breathing setting everyone on edge.

"You can curse at me all your want, Kill, but hear her out. Last time. I fucking swear it. And then she's leaving. Gone."

Kill blanched at the term "gone." His knuckles whitened, clenching harder.

In the sudden cease-fire, Grasshopper pulled me from my chair. I stumbled upright, moving to stand before Kill. Grasshopper didn't remove his hold, his fingers burning around my elbow.

His body locked in place, preparing himself. "She remembered her name."

The wave of emotion from Kill almost drowned me. So much in one buffet of feeling—I'd never decipher it all.

Kill's eyes fell to where Grasshopper touched me. Dark possession flashed across his face. My stomach fluttered with butterflies.

I want you to touch me.

I want you to remember me.

Then Kill crossed his arms, shutting me out, just like the damn wall living in my brain. "You brought me back for more lies?" His ire fell on me, his green eyes blazing like an emerald fire. "This will be fucking interesting."

I swallowed. A whiff of alcohol once again crept over my senses. Was he drunk? Hungover?

"You're so blind."

His lips twisted into a sneer. "I'm blind because I won't fall for a scam?"

"No. You're blinded by grief and stubbornness."

Kill flinched, shifting closer so his body heat tangled with mine. "You know nothing of stubbornness."

God, he annoyed me. Without persistence I wouldn't be standing here right now. I would've already been sold because I wouldn't have offered to heal him and found a way into his life.

Words and anger frothed in my mouth, I wanted so much to let loose.

But the stiff way Kill held himself, the hunch of his shoulders and knotted muscles in his neck were signs of a man struggling—a man in bone-deep pain. I couldn't kick him when he already curled around what was left of his tattered heart. To love a ghost so strongly that the man literally killed himself with heartbreak ought to be romantic.

It wasn't.

It was just endlessly, terminally sad.

And nonsensical.

Especially because I believed I had the power to relieve his suffering.

Grasshopper shoved me forward. "You wanted to see him. I got him here for you. Best tell him your name, girl, so we can all move on."

Dread thickened my blood. Why did that sound so ominous? Shouldn't he be happy that everything I'd said was real? Kill no longer had to live with the guilt of thinking he'd murdered me. He could be happy!

"Tell him," Grasshopper prompted.

I couldn't stop looking at Kill. His green eyes were icy and full of mistrust. "Well? I'm here against my fucking wishes. Tell me, so I can leave and put this nightmare behind me."

Nightmares. Dreams. I'd found him in my dreams and awoken to him in my nightmares. Would there be a place for us in real life?

Stop stalling and tell him.

Balling my hands, I said, "I remember you from my past. I remember the fire and barbeques and Libra erasers. I remember homework and TV and stolen kisses. I remember you, Arthur Killian—I remember you when you were younger and not broken. My name is Sarah and I'm yours." My voice broke but I battled through the sickness of laying my heart at his feet. "I remember you and I need you to stop pretending before it's too late."

The room disappeared.

I forgot about the other bikers.

I ignored the entire world as Kill ever so slowly uncrossed his arms and closed the small distance between us. His face was impenetrable, eyes blank, jaw clenched.

My skin sparked, begging for his touch. My mouth ached, pleading for his lips.

"You…" His voice was a deadly hiss.

My body stiffened, fighting the urge to flee.

Mo stood up, standing on my other side, flanking me like Grasshopper.

Ironically, they were protection against the man I loved. Ready to stop me being hurt by the monster rapidly slipping into simmering rage before us.

Kill's frame trembled. He shook his head. "I have to stop *pretending*?" he whispered.

The pent-up anger in his tone terrified me.

I couldn't help it; I took a step back. "Yes. My name is Sarah. You know me!"

He mimicked my step. "Let me get this straight. *I'm* the one who needs to stop pretending?" His eye flashed and I truly feared him as his soul disappeared. He was locked and barricaded and so wrapped up in grief he couldn't see the truth.

Tears bruised my eyes. "I'm standing right in front of you. Why are you doing this?!"

Grasshopper said, "Kill, it's not the girl's fault—"

"Not her fault?" Kill roared. "Not her fucking fault that she's torn my heart out all over again and has the *nerve* to tell me to stop pretending?" He pointed a finger in my face. "I've never met someone so despicable or so clever at manipulation, and I've met a lot of fucking traitors."

Turning his full terror upon me, he snarled, "You're worse than them. At least they stabbed me in the back and left me to rot. You—you just keep stabbing me. Over and over and fucking over until I'm bleeding from every slice."

Tears welled, and, unwilling to break the seal of my eyelashes, they glassed my vision, making his anger swim and dance. "I don't know what you want me to say! You have to believe—"

"I don't have to believe a fucking word you say. You. Aren't. *Her!* You will never be her. You will never convince me of your bullshit."

My body was too heavy. I wanted to collapse, but I had to keep fighting. I couldn't give up.

"Yes. I am!" I screamed. "If you just listen to what I'm—"

"She. Is. Dead! Just like you'll be if you don't shut the fuck up!"

"Killian," Grasshopper muttered. "Dude, it's okay."

Kill turned his arctic ferocity on his second in charge. "No, it's not okay. I want her gone. Now. Immediately, before I do something stupid."

"Stupid like believe me?!" My voice seemed to cower in the face of his wrath.

Kill towered taller and taller as if he sucked the life from the room. His voice dropped to the worst hiss imaginable. "I'll never be that gullible, sweetheart. And just for fucking closure, you *aren't* her. And now I know for sure."

"How? How do you know?"

He smiled coldly, dragging out my worst fears. "You're a liar, *Sarah*. Give it up. It's done."

Tears slicked down my cheeks. "I'm *not*. You're just in denial. Complete and utter heartbreaking denial. Don't do this! Don't hurt me like this."

He laughed.

It sent shivers down my spine.

Rolling his shoulders, he muttered, "Fine. I'll give you one chance. One final chance. Tell me...are you certain your name is Sarah?"

I breathed hard, terrified of his question. Why did he want me to confirm it? It'd come to me. It fitted. I had memories of Corrine using it. It was mine.

Horror made me second-guess everything; terror made me realize how badly everything had gone so wrong.

Don't give in.

Slowly, I nodded. "Yes. I'm sure."

He grinned, eyes flat and face emotionless. "Thank you for digging your own grave and proving what a liar you are."

I curled into myself, not wanting to hear any more. Not wanting to be subjected to his cruelty another second.

"You're wrong, Sarah," Kill breathed. Quickly, he grabbed my throat, holding me tight.

My body pressed against his and for a horrid second I thought he meant to strangle me. His eyes tore into my soul and ripped it into pieces. With more pain than I'd ever seen in a man's face, he pressed his forehead bitterly against mine. "Her name wasn't Sarah." With confusing tender fingers, he cupped my chin, ensuring I never looked away as he delivered the crushing sentence.

"Her name was Cleo. And I killed her."

Chapter Fifteen

Some said sinners go to hell and saints go to heaven.

If that was the truth, then I'd lived the past eight years in brimstone and fire.

My heart burned with lies and a need so fucking deep to believe every word Sarah said. I wanted to have the strength to let go of my hate and just...give in.

But everything I did, every path I followed, and every revenge-filled purpose I followed wasn't for me but for *her.*

I owed her memory vengeance.

I owed her peace.

Because I saw how she died.

I'd witnessed the end.

And she would be screaming in purgatory until I gave her justice.

By taking the lives of those who took ours.

Everything else I wanted—it wasn't enough to make me stop.

—Kill

Cleo.

Her name was Cleo.

My name is Sarah.

Cleo.

He killed her.

The pressuring headache of believing a fabricated lie of my own creation clouded my vision. How did I have memories that I couldn't explain? How did I live a past that might not even be real?

Cleo.

It didn't ring any hopeful bells inside. It didn't tug on threads of a past I thought was true.

I retreated into myself, and didn't raise my eyes as the dining room emptied like sands through splayed fingers, leaving just Kill, Grasshopper, and me.

"I'll take her." Grasshopper reached for me. I didn't struggle as his hands landed on my shoulders, pulling me from Kill's crushing tender hold.

Everything inside that'd been so passionate and raw had mysteriously disappeared. I'd been consumed by the black hole, fallen through the crater that my nightmare earthquake had created. I'd plummeted into the amnesiac darkness completely.

I was done.

"You okay, dude?" Grasshopper asked when Kill remained silent and frozen. He barely breathed, his boots glued to the floor.

It took a minute for him to reply. Clearing his throat, Kill said, "I will be once she's gone."

I flinched, wishing I could fall to the floor and nurse my bleeding heart.

"Well... I'll get going, then. You just, um, rest up. I'll be back soon enough." Grasshopper guided me toward the door.

Back without me. Their lives would continue... without me.

I didn't look back.

I couldn't look back.

The door closed behind us and I hunched over my gnawing stomach. The pain deep inside devoured me.

"It'll be okay," Grasshopper whispered. "You'll see. It's for the best—for everyone."

I had no reply. I doubted I'd speak again. Why bother when it only brought more disaster?

We kept walking.

Past the first magazine of Kill and his mug shot.

Past the next one of him looking part businessman, part biker lord.

With each step I left pieces of myself behind, leaving a trail of crumbs for no one to follow or seek the girl lost inside me. I would leave. And never come back. My one chance was over—the life I believed was a lie.

I no longer trusted myself. I didn't trust a brain that was so adamant and fed such lifelike occurrences—staining my sanity until I knew I must be mad.

At least my imagination excelled. It would be the one place I could escape to when my future in slavery became too much.

"Wait." Kill's voice rang out.

Grasshopper stopped, his fingers tightening on my elbow to stop me, too.

I didn't turn around but my back prickled as Kill moved toward us.

"Forget something?" Grasshopper asked.

My ears strained for Kill's reply, even now wishing upon wishes that he had made a mistake and finally realized it.

"I'll take her."

What?

God, no. Please. I couldn't have him take me away and deliver me to someone else. It would be the epitome of callousness. He'd already daggered my heart, he didn't need to keep twisting it.

Grasshopper let me go, stepping aside as Kill took his place. "Are you sure? I mean—"

"I'm sure. I need to see with my own eyes that she's gone."

My nerve endings sprang to life the moment his fingers wrapped around my wrist.

Grasshopper huffed. "You don't trust me to do it?"

Kill growled. "Yes, I trust you. But I need to do this. I need to know that I'll never suffer again."

Suffer?

What a heartless bitch he made me sound. I'd meant to heal his brokenness, not make it worse. I'd offered my love, my kindness, and my friendship—how did he think my goal was to make him hurt?

"I get that," Grasshopper said. "I'll call ahead and let the buyer know you're the one coming."

"Good. Thanks."

Awkwardness settled and Kill's fingers tightened around my wrist.

"Okay, Sarah. Guess this is good-bye." Grasshopper's voice reluctantly tugged me from my sad stupor.

I swallowed, keeping my head down and eyes averted. "Thanks. For trying, at least."

Kill flinched. I hoped he heard the reprimand in my voice directed at him—for his lack of belief or decency of just *listening* to me.

Kill dragged me forward without another word.

Past the last magazine cover.

Past where I'd stood and stripped for him.

Through the compound and into the garage.

Cleo.

Her name was Cleo. It sounded right… but wrong.

Could I have remembered the wrong name?

Could all of this be undone if I just had more time to untangle my memories?

"Please, Kill. Don't do this," I whispered as he dragged me toward a black SUV.

Kill gritted his jaw but didn't reply. His hand stayed latched around my wrist, his legs chewing up the floor as if he wanted to break into a sprint and run far away from me.

My heart stuttered at the hate reverberating from him. I didn't fight—there was no point. But I wished he would just stop for one moment. Just stop and…

What? Expose himself from years' worth of denial and put himself in a place of agony to try and believe? Something like that would take more strength than anything, and as much as I hated it, I could understand his reluctance.

It was easier to continue living a lie than deal with the consequences of what it would mean if I *were* Cleo. So many questions would then exist...How were we separated? Why did he think he killed me? What really happened all those years ago?

I reached out, wrapping my fingers around his arm where he held me. He didn't stop or look down.

"I'm sorry, Arthur. I'm sorry for the pain you're going through. I'm sorry to make you confront things you obviously aren't able to. But please don't do this. Let me go. Release me. I'll never come back and you'll never have to see me again, but please. Please don't sell me."

"Don't use my name." He tugged me faster, reaching the black 4WD and opening the back door.

My heart winged frantically. "You have to know I didn't mean to hurt you! It's all true inside my mind. Everything I feel for you—everything that happened, it's all real."

How is it real?

Did my mind steal someone else's memories or was everything a story—told to keep myself from going insane with no past?

Kill refused to make eye contact. Grabbing me around my bronze-encased waist, he threw me onto the backseat of the car.

My teeth rattled as he punched the door closed, shaking the entire vehicle.

Two seconds later, he climbed behind the steering wheel and pressed the garage door opener.

Twisting the key in the ignition, the engine started with a growl, then slid seamlessly into gear and exploded from standstill to motion.

"Ah!" I slid wildly on the pristine tan leather as he floored the acceleration, shooting from the garage and into Florida sunshine. He drove like a damn lunatic, taking corners too fast, making the wheels squeal.

My stomach crashed against my insides. Nausea made me sweat as I fumbled for a seat belt.

Did he not care at all?

He's such an . . . ass. An uncommunicative ass who doesn't want to face the truth.

"Kill—"

He swiped his hand through his hair, pressing harder on the gas. "Don't."

I hugged my chest, slip-sliding even with the seat belt tight as he careened around a corner. "Please . . . you have to listen to me. I didn't do it to hurt you! I honestly believe I know you. I can't explain it—"

"You don't need to explain it. You're done here. You succeeded in seeing me again and you've made it worse for yourself."

"How?"

He clutched the steering wheel, his knuckles going white. "I told you before that you wouldn't get sweet or caring from me. I told you not to lie to me or to try and touch me. Yet, you did all of those fucking things. You dragged more emotion out of me in a few days than anyone's been able to do in years and I fucking hate you for it. Not only did you force me to come back and listen to more of your lies, you think after everything you've done that I'll just let you go?" He shook his head, chuckling sadly. "That's not how sins work, sweetheart. They demand payment. Same fucking payment that I paid."

He sped past street signs, driving like a reckless idiot.

"And vengeance? What of that?"

His head swiveled, green eyes latching onto mine before returning to the road. "You don't know a fucking thing about vengeance. Don't spin another tale. I'm done with your bullshit."

"You're right. I don't know about revenge. I have no enemies—that I can remember. But I do know what they say about it. That carrying out harm to others not only hurts your intended victims, but yourself, too. You end up being hurt. Forgiveness—"

"*Forgiveness?*" he yelled, punching the steering wheel and making the horn blare. "You *dare* talk to me about forgiveness? You have no right—none—to try and preach how I should live my life. You don't know a damn thing of what they did to me. To her. To my fucking future. They ruined me!"

The twisted agony in his tone turned my heart into a mangled, useless thing. I wanted to take his pain and cure him. I wanted him to let it go so it didn't fester and kill him. The more time I spent with him, the more I wondered what happened to the simple, kind boy from my past.

"You don't look ruined. Want to know what I see when I look at you?"

"No. Shut up."

"I see a man who's so intelligent I can imagine it's exhausting living inside your brain. You're wealthy, respected by peers and government and media. You have it all."

A vein throbbed dangerously in his neck as he shook his head, laughing under his breath. It sounded manic—like the tip of a volcano that was about to explode from the depths and rain molten lava. "Have it all? I have it *all*?" He hunched over the wheel. "You have it wrong, *Sarah*. I have nothing. Fucking nothing because they took it all."

"I know you're hurting. And I won't try and understand what you're dealing with, but you can't live your life blocked from feeling. You'll snap."

He's already done that.

I feared for his sanity. I hadn't meant to push him. But this would be my last opportunity. My farewell attempt to make him crack and listen.

He laughed coldly. "Snap? Sweetheart, I snapped years ago and don't need any woman trying to make me fucking soft. I'm done and I'm gonna make sure I never have to lay eyes on you or hear your lies ever again."

My shoulders slumped as standoffish silence filled the car. How could I make him see? He meant to sell me—get rid of me. What sort of man did that?

A broken one.

I just wanted to be freed. I would leave—I would give him my word he would never see me again. He didn't need to ruin my life just like his was. "For a genius, you don't seem to understand," I whispered.

He gritted his jaw, refusing to reply.

My mind raced with ways to get him to pay attention—something had to trigger inside him. I just had to keep pushing. "What happened in the changing room that day? Explain to me the connection. That kiss, Killian... It was more than two strangers lusting after each other. It had layers... history."

"Shut the fuck up."

"No."

His jaw tightened, the vein in his neck still throbbing crazily. "You're only making this worse."

"For you or for me? Tell me what you felt. Tell me what you were thinking when you kissed me."

He growled under his breath. "What happened is none of your—"

"Goddamn business," I finished for him. Throwing my hands up, I snarled, "I already know, genius. It's because of her. *Me!* You're so damn in love with a dead girl that you can't—just for a single moment—allow yourself to enjoy another woman. Even if that other woman is her!"

He attacked the steering wheel. Whirling it to the right, he shot from traffic and slammed to a stop in a turning lane. Spinning in his seat, he brought the wrath of hell upon me. His arm shot forward, smacking my thigh so hard my muscle smarted through the bronze dress. My skin pricked with heat from the reprimand—of being hit like a disobedient child.

"You aren't her. Why the fuck won't you get that?"

"I agree I can't remember the right name, but explain the rest. Please, I'm begging you—explain the rest, so it makes sense, because right now the only conclusion I can see is that I'm the girl you think you killed."

His face went white. Holding up a shaking finger, he hissed, "You mention her again or speak to me like that and we'll have a serious fucking problem."

Tears burned my eyes; my lip wobbled. "What *happened* to you?"

What happened to the genius boy who stole my heart and gave me his? What happened to us?

"Life happened, sweetheart. Just like it's happening to you."

I couldn't stop shaking. "You need to let someone in. You have to stop hurting!"

"There's no space for anyone but me."

"No. There's no space for anyone but her!"

He pushed me—such a juvenile thing to do but the rage in his eyes glittered dangerously.

I slid on the leather, rubbing my knee where his large fingers had touched me. "What do you feel when you look at me? Do you see the girl you loved or do you see the girl you're about to sell? Is that why you can't stand me? Because I remind you so much of a girl that you let down in your past?"

He exploded.

Tearing off his seat belt, he wrenched open the door and flew from the car. In cyclonic rage, he punched a street sign, then whirled around and kicked the SUV tire. He glowered at me through the open door. "Shut up! One more word about things you don't understand, and I'll knock you out so cold, you'll wake up belonging to someone you've never seen and I'll be long gone."

Shaking out the pain in his knuckles, he snarled, "Understand?"

"Understand, Buttercup? I expect to see you there. I don't want to be the only one telling our parents that we want to be together."

I smiled, beaming at the green-eyed boy I wanted to spend the rest of my life with. "I will. I wouldn't miss it for the world."

Jagged agony lacerated my heart as knowledge blazed bright and horrid.

I made a promise to be there. We both did. But neither of us kept that promise.

We never saw each other again.

Our love died forever two weeks after my fourteenth birthday—

six months before he turned eighteen, so close to having everything we'd ever wanted.

I crumbled in on myself. The memory came with emotions too overwhelming to process. Why had it been the last time I'd ever seen him? What *happened* to us? What horrible tragedy was my mind trying to hide?

The fire.

Blood.

Gunshots.

Screaming.

My heart tried to leap from my chest. The stench of death suffocated my lungs. The fire was lit to cover up a murder. It consumed the corpses of...

The wall grew thicker, firmer, lacing itself with padlocks and heavy chains, determined not to let me see.

Whose blood did I crawl through to safety while the flames of hell turned me to cinders? Who dropped the match that stole my life and memories?

Killian breathed hard, not offering any consolation as I came apart before him. The memory of a love so pure and unsullied buckled my lungs and I sobbed.

I thought I was done in the dining room with the cloying scent of pizza. But I wasn't. Not truly.

This was my breaking point. Right here, on the side of the road, on the way to be sold.

Wrapping my arms around my rib cage, I surrendered to the keening rage and grief inside. I allowed it to spew forth, exorcising my lackless memory and torrenting over my knees. With each sob, I curled further until my forehead touched my knees and still I kept folding. Folding in on myself, becoming a piece of origami, twisting from the girl I wished I was to nothing more than a commodity to sell.

I wasn't aware of anything as my world spiraled into grief.

I forgot about Killian and yielded to the burn of scalding tears.

I didn't see him stalk around the car.

I didn't hear him open my door.

I didn't care.

About anything anymore.

Burrowing my face into my knees, I cried harder, purging myself of everything that had happened.

A comforting pressure rested on my shoulder blades. I curled harder, my arms crushed between my stomach and legs.

The pressure moved to my biceps, forcing me upright—demanding I abandon my sanctuary and straighten.

No!

I wanted to remain cocooned and as small as possible.

I fought the pressure, but Kill gave me no choice but to ease upright, revealing my rivering eyes and blotchy cheeks.

I frowned in confusion. Kill stood with his face tight and gaze churning. He hands dropped from my body the moment I obeyed and sat up. Quickly, I looked away. I couldn't see him. Not after what he'd said and done—how remote and unfeeling he was.

My tears flowed harder as Kill unbuckled my seat belt, and without a word, tugged me into his arms.

The force of his embrace dragged me close. I crashed against his chest. His heart raged beneath my ear, chugging as fast as mine.

His scent of winds and leather wrapped around me like a soft blanket, his strong grip locking me to him so I could never escape.

It instantly felt like…home.

His smell, his warmth, his solidness. I *knew*. My body responded and another cry escaped my lips.

I didn't want to question why he'd given in. Why he'd granted me safety in his embrace. But I would take full advantage.

Wrapping my arms around him, I held him as tight as humanly possible while misery continued to crash. I didn't hold him for solace, I held him for an anchor, so I wasn't swept away by tears.

Pressing my face against his chest, I expected nothing more. The fact that he hugged me was more than I'd ever hoped.

But then his hold lashed tighter, squeezing hard and strong. He held me like a man who was eternally sorry and wanted his body to transmit the measure more surely than words. He held me like a man saying good-bye.

Snuggling into his chest, I sucked in a heavy breath.

This was where I belonged. Here. With the man from my nightmares. The boy from my dreams.

"Arthur..." I trembled.

He stiffened, pushing me away. Dropping his arms, the static heat from our embrace faded into the air. His voice bristled. "I'm sorry."

My eyes locked onto his, while I attempted to wipe away sticky tears on my cheeks.

His forehead furrowed. "I'm a bastard—I know that—but I'm not normally this nasty. I truly am sorry for what I've done—for kicking you and treating you so cruelly. You don't deserve it." His green gaze remained unreadable, locked from all emotion, arms rigid by his sides.

I nodded, swallowing back the strange feelings that were so real, yet years too late. "I understand. You can't stand to suffer what happened in the past."

He nodded. "Just..." He sighed. "Let's agree to disagree. No matter what you say or do, you'll never get me to believe you. I've lived for too long believing things others wanted me to believe, and it's brought me nothing but hardship. I know what I saw. I know what I feel. She's gone, and I won't have her memory tarnished."

His shoulders slumped. "Just...accept and let's move on. Okay? It's best for both of us."

I hung my head, not wanting to look into his familiar gaze. He wanted me to drift away—to stop reminding him of the pain inside.

He was weak.

"I'll accept that." Lowering my voice, I pleaded, "But please let me go. Drop me off at the nearest police station, and I swear on my life you'll never see me again. Just please—" My voice cracked again. "I don't want to be sold."

For the longest moment, he stared at the ground. Thoughts flashed over his face, ideas forming then discarded. Hope remained in my heart but I knew it was hopeless.

He raised his head. "If there was something I could do, I'd do it. I'd let you go, truly. But this is above my head now. Things are going on that even I'm not privy to and I can't go against orders."

"Can't or won't?"

He smiled sadly. "Won't. He's the only person that's ever been there for me. Thick and thin. He took me from my ruined beginning and gave me an empire to rule. I'll be forever grateful and won't go behind his back."

My heart panged for his loyalty, for his love. The love I wasn't worthy of.

My head hung and silence fell between us.

I didn't say a word—no acknowledgment of his decision or argument for my freedom. It was over.

After a minute, Kill nodded as if I'd accepted his skewed promise. Pressing his lips together, he closed my door and climbed back into the driver's seat.

It was done. I'd fought and lost. He'd argued and won.

Our time was over and I now had to face the future.

The next time Kill stopped the car we were at the harbor.

He parked and climbed out, coming to open my door and offer his hand. It seemed the fight in the car had given him closure and he treated me like any other girl he'd been told to sell.

Not that I knew what that was like, of course.

Taking his hand, I slid from the SUV. Squinting against the midafternoon sun, I asked, "How many?"

His eyes remained emotionless as he slammed my door and locked the car with the remote. "How many what?"

Taking my hand again, more out of imprisonment than togetherness, he led me toward the dock and the glittering teal ocean. His grip was dry and warm, encircling my fingers in a way that made my body sing with electricity. He could deny he knew me. He could yell and fight against everything I'd tried to show him, but he couldn't hide the connection between our bodies.

"How many girls have you trafficked?" Sadness sat on my chest. I hated to think that this man could be involved with something so wrong. It was worse than theft...It was tantamount to murder. Effectively cutting a woman's life span into the will of an owner who might grow bored of her within a few hours.

Not to mention the horror they would endure before their—*my*—last breath was taken.

Kill tensed, never looking at me. "You're the sixth and last. If you must know, I refuse to involve myself in crime, regardless of what you think of me."

My feet stumbled. The magazine covers and the praise of helping the community popped into my mind. Everything pointed to him behaving within the law. He'd come from crime—there was no doubt about that—but I had the feeling he'd turned his Club from the dark and into the light.

"It was a fucking blessed day for all when he took over the Corrupts and made us Pure Corruption." Grasshopper's voice echoed in my ears. If that was true—then what the hell was this about?

"What do you mean?"

His boots crunched on gravel as my jeweled flip-flops that Grasshopper had given me slapped quietly. My left leg and foot danced with color in the sunshine while my scars caught the light in a mixture of shy disfigurement.

"Stop asking questions," Kill muttered, closing the distance between us and a white speedboat. The port wasn't too busy, only a few clusters of people and vessels moored to creaking riggings.

"Why did you agree to sell me and the other women, then? If

it goes against your beliefs, it must be something big. It can't be for money—you already have more than enough from stock trading."

He gave me a sideways look, surprise flicking. "You're right—it's not for money."

A skipper with sun protection smeared thickly over his nose and a baseball cap covering his blond hair jumped from the speedboat as we slowed to a stop. "You Kill? Jared called and said there was a change of plans."

Kill tilted his chin. "Yep. You know where we're going?"

"Sure do. Not far. Fifteen minutes at the most."

Kill turned to me and pointed at the gleaming white speedboat. "Get in."

"Jared? Who's Jared?"

Kill smirked. "Grasshopper. Jared's his real name."

"Oh." For some reason, it felt odd that the man I'd grown accustomed to had such a normal name. I liked MCs for that reason. Your birth name didn't define you—your brothers did that with nicknames.

Thorn.

My eyes widened. Thorn was my father's nickname. I frowned trying to remember his birth name and why he'd earned the strange term of Thorn.

Kill grabbed my elbow, jerking me toward the boat. The sides gleamed with a motif and the name *Seahorse Symphony.* "I'll help you."

I pulled back, suffering a horrible highlight reel of what would happen if I got on that boat. I'd never see him again. Never be free. Subservient to a sadistic asshole for the rest of my life.

I can't.

My stomach twisted and I looked over my shoulder. Freedom. I wanted it. From him, my memories, everything that had happened. I wanted to go back to the simplicity of treating animals and knowing where I existed in the world.

But that was also a lie.

I didn't know where I belonged. I worried I never would.

Sarah was only part of me. Who knew what the other part was.

I squirmed in Kill's hold. Looking up into his fierce face, I begged, "Please... don't do this, Arthur."

His green eyes flashed. "Stop asking me that. I'm sick of hearing it. I've told you why this has to happen and there's nothing that will stop it." Jerking me close, he clamped his hands on my waist. "It's over, Sarah."

With powerful arms, he picked me up and swung me over the side of the boat. "And you never learn. My name is not yours to use. I'll be glad when you're gone, so I don't have to keep reminding you."

Ouch.

My heart twisted as my feet landed on the rough bottom of the vessel. The gentle bob and sway of the tide made me instantly nauseous and craving solid ground.

With my balance compromised, I gripped the side of the boat.

Glaring at me, Kill threw his leg over and jumped aboard. Planting a heavy hand on my shoulder, he marched me toward the back bench and pressed me into a sitting position.

The skipper watched us but didn't say anything. Instead, he leapt into his craft, turned the key, and pushed off from the dock.

The whirr of the motor curtailed all conversation and the whip of the wind stole tears from my eyes. Within minutes we were out of the harbor and bouncing on waves—the loud slaps of water against the hull echoed in my ears, drowning out my thoughts and rapidly building fear.

Do something.

Like what?

I had no idea how to stop this. The momentum only gathered more inertia the more I tried to prevent the inevitable from happening.

Jump overboard.

And what, suffer death by shark?

I hated that there was no way for me to run—only crystal turquoise ocean and me with no ability to walk on water.

"Where are you taking me?" I asked, loud enough for my voice to carry.

Kill didn't make eye contact, staring at the horizon. "To your new future."

A chill that had nothing to do with the whipping wind darted down my back. "I can't make you let me go? You would never have to see me again. You don't have to do this."

He shook his head. "I told you. I'm not the one doing this."

I crossed my arms as the warm Florida sun turned cool with sea breeze. "What do you mean exactly?"

When he didn't answer, I snapped, "The least you can do is give me answers. Let me understand just a little bit, before you walk away from me."

My gut rolled painfully.

I'll never see him again.

He kicked you.

He almost sold you.

He's not a good person.

So why did my soul cleave in two?

The man before me wasn't the man I'd pinned all my hopes on. He was nothing like the boy from my dreams. It shouldn't hurt so much to leave. He was a stranger who'd given me pleasure and granted me the right to heal him when he was vulnerable.

Nothing more.

Try telling that to my stupid, stupid heart.

He finally looked at me. "I've told you the most I'm ever going to say. I'm doing this because the man I'm loyal to—the man who gave me everything and understands my need for vengeance—asked me to do this for him." Running a hand through his messy long hair, he finished, "I'm loyal to those who have proven themselves. I don't need to know any more than that."

I could no longer look at him.

Silence fell and I looked to the horizon, hoping for better answers.

I stood on the deck of an impressive superyacht.

The speedboat looked tiny compared to the sleek power of the black-and-silver vessel. The same motif and name *Seahorse Symphony* emblazoned the side and the light wooden deck was gilded with gold.

"Where are we?" I whispered to Kill.

He gritted his jaw and didn't reply, his focus remaining entirely on the looming cabin in front. His legs spread against the rolling seas—the waves slower and bigger this far away from shore. *Why are we here?* To do illegal business where landlubber police couldn't reach us? Or for a fast getaway once the transaction had been completed?

Transaction.

Even I had resorted to referring to myself like merchandise. It was easier that way—helped numb any stupid idea that I was still human. I wasn't. I was a toy—had been the moment I stepped foot on this luxury floating prison.

A steward appeared from the interior, weathered and tanned from a life spent on the water. He wore a pristine white uniform with pleats and creases in all the right places. "Hello, Mr. Killian. We're honored that the president himself could join us. Must say, Mr. Steel is much obliged you've come."

Kill stiffened, his fingers locking tighter around my wrist, where he held me. Why he held me I didn't know. It wasn't like I could run anywhere. Unless I could suddenly sprout wings that I'd forgotten about, I was chained here.

"No need to kiss my ass. Change of plans. I wanted to deliver the girl myself."

To make sure Grasshopper didn't realize the awfulness of what was about to happen and free me.

"Well, it's our pleasure to receive you." The steward flashed us a smile, glowing too white and perfect. "Mr. Steel is expecting you. Please, follow me."

My stomach knotted and I wanted more than anything to throw myself overboard and swim far away.

Kill sensed my unease. His fingers switched from my wrist to my elbow, latching tight and keeping me imprisoned by his side.

Together, we followed the steward. The only sounds were the slap of my flip-flops, the screams of gulls, and the gentle kiss of water on fiberglass.

This nautical world. This foreign dimension.

It's my home now.

My hair fluttered with the wind as we traversed the pristine deck, past a spa and outdoor bar, and traded sunshine for the shade of opulent walnut and carpeted interior.

My heart thundered as Kill yanked my elbow, jerking me from my safe zone of pressing against him and into the limelight and center stage.

Tears were thick molasses in my heart, forming a ball in my throat—slowly choking me.

The dimness of the sitting room took a while to become clear after the glare of sunshine.

Kill noticed him before I did. His body hummed with aggression, tempered by civility. "Mr. Steel."

"Pleasure. Please, come in. Come in." The voice was far too posh and overly cordial. Fake. *Imposter.*

My instincts told me to bolt—that this wasn't a sumptuous vessel but a nest of vipers.

Kill carted me forward, even though I tried to lock my knees from obeying. He shot me a look, growling under his breath, "Behave."

Stumbling forward, my eyes struggled to pick out the features of the man who would become my owner. He sat with his legs stretched out, reclining on a designer chair in the middle of the gorgeous oceanic room. He held a martini glass and wore a crisp linen suit.

Kill nodded. "I'm running low on time. Let's conclude this quickly."

My already broken heart shattered further. He couldn't wait to be free of me. To never look at me or relive his sins again.

Heartless bastard.

Mr. Steel saluted us with the martini glass. "If that is the case, we shall begin momentarily. We mean to catch the tide, too, so a quick agreement would be valuable to all."

My eyes bugged. Who was this asshole who spoke as if he had descended from the queen? His pronunciation was impeccable. I studied him harder, drinking in the bleached-blond hair, trimmed goatee, and piercing black eyes. His skin glowed from sun exposure but he didn't have wrinkles. I struggled to estimate his age due to the obvious cosmetic surgery and Botox. It was impossible to truly know.

Kill strode across the thick carpet, dragging me unwillingly closer.

The closer we got, the more I sensed the sort of man the buyer was.

He had class—stinking of violence beneath the expensive aftershave.

He had suaveness—evilness hiding behind oiled perfection.

But in his prettiness lurked a disease that sent my heart burrowing in my chest. He was sin personified and I wanted nothing to do with him.

Coming to a stop before him, the buyer's eyes slithered down my body.

I fought the urge to shudder and look away.

"Fantastic first impression." His attention went first to my tattooed leg, then my burned one. Curiosity etched his face.

Kill breathed hard beside me.

The buyer sat taller in his chair, his voice dropping to a demand. "Show me more."

What?

Kill suddenly let me go, moving behind me. My stomach twisted and I gasped as his hands came around me, undoing the fastening of my dress with swift efficiency. "Kill—"

With nimble fingers, he yanked the wraparound bronze dress off my shoulders, giving me no choice but to relinquish it.

I couldn't believe he'd done that. He was so cold, so detached. He didn't believe I was the girl from his past but surely I *meant* something? We'd slept together. I'd healed him. It took a special type of person to block all that out.

Someone whose been trained to do it for years.

"Intriguing," Mr. Steel said, throwing back the rest of his martini.

I bit my lip in horror, clasping my arms over my chest, dressed only in the awful gold bikini. My scars were on display—the treasure of my tattoo visible for all to see. I *hated* him seeing me—*studying* me—making me feel cheap and nothing more than something to buy and sell.

My scars itched, almost as if new fire singed me from the buyer's horrible inspection. My tattoo was all color and shadows, coaxing his eyes away from my ugliness toward the artisan beauty I so adored.

"She's unique." He placed his empty glass on the side table, then rubbed a finger over his mouth. "Your colleague gave nothing away on the phone and I can see why." He smacked his lips together. "I like her."

Kill stiffened beside me. Every muscle locked down; he'd become a pissed-off statue. The biker lord had gone, swallowing back his given right to rule and accepting a different hierarchy.

He wasn't in charge. And he wasn't dealing well with it.

"You don't say much, do you?" Mr. Steel asked suddenly, looking at Kill.

Kill narrowed his eyes. "What's there to say? You like her. It's done. The deal was already arranged—it's a matter of a signature and it's finished." I couldn't tell if he was pleased the client approved of me or furious.

Mr. Steel chuckled. "So impatient." Looking between the two of us, he added slyly, "If I wasn't mistaken, I would say you wanted off my yacht due to this woman." His lips spread over his sharp teeth.

"What happened between you two? I'm not in the habit of accepting used stock."

My cheeks flared.

"Nothing," Kill growled. "Now, are we done or not?"

Mr. Steel chuckled. "Temper, temper."

"Finish it. I have to go." There was no emotion in Kill's voice, just indifference.

Indifference?

It was worse than hate. Worse than anger. Indifference was the blankness of all feeling—the place where people went when emotions were too much and they gave up.

My ridiculous hope that he would change his mind evaporated—wisping away with a heavy sigh.

I've been so stupid. So unbelievably idiotic to stay. I should've shot him when I had the chance.

"Fine. If you're so in a rush, let's move over to the bar and begin." The man stood, moving through the expensive world of teals and greys. The décor was stunning. Masculine but feminine, with hard lines of dark wooden furniture and graceful curves of hand-blown glass statues.

I moved without waiting for Kill to direct me. I never wanted him touching me again.

The bar was surrounded by bottles of expensive cognacs and whiskeys, all glowing amber in the sun streaming through the window.

Kill didn't want me. He was in my past. So I forced myself to forget about him seething beside me. Instead, I invested all my attention on the buyer—Mr. Steel. He was my future, my enemy, my penance for sins I couldn't remember. I had to study him and understand how to survive.

What did he keep hidden beneath his white linen suit? What secrets lurked behind his black eyes?

You don't want to know.

He was wealthy—I knew that much. There was no doubt I would live a life of luxury for however long I pleased him.

Until he throws you overboard to the sharks.

The thought came and went, sending a gust of ice down my spine.

Buying and selling women for whatever reason wasn't right. He had no ownership over me—no matter how many numbers existed in his bank account.

"Drink?" Mr. Steel asked as he pulled out a bar stool.

"No." Kill shook his head.

Mr. Steel smiled at me. "I won't offer you refreshment, my dear. I'm sure we can find something much more fitting the moment this meeting is concluded."

I wanted to be sick. I wanted to kill him.

I didn't say a word.

Kill balled his hands, his back tensing beneath his leather cut and creaking softly. "Enough. Sign over what you promised and she's yours."

Mr. Steel narrowed his eyes, dropping into negotiation and business rather than hosting. "Fine, let's talk." His eyes slithered over me again. "I want her, Killian, but your price is too high." He reclined against the bar behind him, his gaze never looking away from my chest.

I bit my lip, wishing I had the power to fly away. Be free from all of this. Fly high to find my memories.

Anger seeped through my blood like lava. I glowered at Kill. He wasn't paying attention to Mr. Steel, his gaze locked on me, his chest rising hard. His jacket tightened around his shoulders as his muscles tensed. His reaction let me glimpse into his soul, giving away how much he deplored everything going on. It gave me power. It set little flames licking my insides.

He gazed at me with vulnerability. He looked lost and desolate and angry—so damn angry.

Seconds ticked past and he didn't sever the connection between us—refused to look away.

As long as he stared at me that way, I could survive without memories, without the past or future. I could survive in his present and find a resemblance of happiness.

I'm her.

I'm not crazy.

Mr. Steel sneered, "Am I interrupting something?"

Kill snapped out of whatever held us prisoner. "You want her. There's no negotiation."

"There's always a negotiation. You need that stock. I need that girl. But you need the stock more. So I'll give you seventy-five percent, and I'm being generous."

Stock?

I knew I wasn't being traded for money—but stock? What stock? And why?

Kill crossed his arms. "No. That's a fucking rip-off. Full control or no girl."

I closed my eyes, letting the pink of my eyelids grant me a new world as the sun bounced across my face. I didn't want to watch men scrabble over me as if I weren't a living thing.

The men continued to argue but I faded them out. Kill wanted what this man had. And badly. I was his bargaining chip. My heart sank like a treasure chest into a bottomless sea. *No matter what exists between us, this will be the last time I'll see him.*

The transaction would mean I would float away like a blue-blooded princess aboard this magnificent yacht to face a future of unknown sadism and slavery. While the man I wanted sold me with no hint of a soul.

"No. Full stock or nothing—" Kill's voice shredded my fragile serenity.

"Stop. I'm done arguing. I have questions before I agree to anything. Do not rush me." Mr. Steel snapped his fingers. Silence fell while a steward appeared from nowhere, poured a finger of amber liquid into a goblet, and passed it to him. He faded from the room via a door hidden like a bookcase.

"Now, questions..." Mr. Steel's eyes flashed as he took a sip of his new beverage.

Kill's nostrils flared, drawing energy from the room just like he had back at the compound. "What do you want to know?" Grabbing my elbow, he jerked me close. We both shuddered as a crackle of electricity thrummed between us. I *hated* that he affected me. It wasn't just him who wanted to be far away. It hurt too damn much.

Breathing hard, Kill shook me for no other reason but annoyance at still wanting me. "Tell me what you want to know. That she's unique? Intelligent? Qualified in veterinary science? Or perhaps you want to know what she's like in bed? That she writhes more perfectly than any woman I've ever met? That she tastes like fucking buttercup sunshine? That despite everything that's happened to her, she's still the strongest, stubbornest thing that refuses to be broken?"

Every sentence twisted the dagger in my heart until blood rivered inside. He used it. My nickname.

Buttercup.

I wanted to slap him more than I'd wanted anything.

Bastard!

"She's one of a kind, Mr. Steel and if you don't see that, then you're a fucking idiot." His chest rose and fell, his eyes bright and glassy.

If I'm so perfect, why don't you keep me, then, you stupid wanker?

My heart twisted into a painful knot. "Fuck you, Arthur," I whispered hotly. "Fuck you. Fuck you. Fuck you!"

Kill took a step back, eyes wide.

I turned on him, ready to attack. My nails wanted to draw his blood. I wanted to make him hurt as much as I did.

But Mr. Steel's arm wrapped around my waist, dragging me backward. I cried out as his cold reptilian fingers kissed over my scarred hipbone.

I'd forgotten all I wore was a bikini. I'd forgotten everything but wanting to savage Arthur Killian.

"You're feisty." His voice threaded down my ear and into my

brain. "You're passionate—I like that. Passion is good and strength is even better."

I shivered, wriggling in his grip. "Let me go."

Instead of obeying, he spun me around in his hands, imprisoning me between his spread thighs. I curled my nose at being so close to this monster. "Let me go!"

He smiled, crinkling the tanned skin by his eyes. His teeth were slightly crooked, his jawline strong and spoke of a man used to getting his own way. "You don't tell me what to do. Ever." His nose brushed against mine in a horribly tender move. "Tell me, girl. What happened to your body?"

Kill faded into the background as I fought the urge to vomit all over Mr. Steel's white suit. The pads of his thumbs traced circles around scarred flesh and inked.

When I didn't reply, he murmured, "You're like yin and yang. Half stunning, half deformed. Tell me. I want to know how you became like this."

I locked my spine, revolting against his touch but unable to pull away. Kill moved closer. His breathing labored and bulk as terrifying as any punishment. Was he there to make sure I didn't get away, or fighting the urge to tear me from this asshole's hands?

"I don't have to tell you anything," I hissed. "Let. Me. Go."

Mr. Steel's eyes narrowed. "I see discipline will be in order." His voice lowered to a whisper. "That's perfectly fine. I enjoy a bit of *punishment* to get my point across."

"You'll never touch me."

His fingers tightened, proving that in actual fact he already was. He cocked an eyebrow, daring me to deny it.

"Fuck you." It seemed I liked that phrase currently.

Mr. Steel stiffened, then...he laughed. "I love your temper. It will make things extremely interesting."

"It's not a temper—just disgust. Stop touching me."

Amazingly, Mr. Steel obeyed. His voice was well-smoothed silk as he said, "I did as you asked. Now you give me what I asked. Tell me what happened."

I breathed hard. "No. The story is private."

Even I don't know the full tale. And every damn day I dived into the cesspool that'd become my memories only to drown in them. In fact, I wanted all my memories deleted. Every single encounter and kiss and Libra eraser recall, I wanted it all gone so I never had to see Kill's traitorous face again.

Mr. Steel smiled coldly. "Privacy is a thing of the past. You need to understand that—otherwise your new life will be immensely uncomfortable."

Kill stepped forward, his presence burning my back. Wherever he moved, his body called to mine. My flesh to his. Magnets. Worse than magnets—kismet alignment.

Yet he doesn't feel it.

Or chooses the life of misery by ignoring it.

Bastard. Asshole. Weak!

Did he not feel what happened when he hugged me in the car? I couldn't describe it. The way he held me hadn't been erotic or sexual. It'd been warm and comforting knowingness.

I'd been *home.*

His body, his heart, his screwed-up head—it was home to me, and he'd just cast me adrift without a backward glance.

"You'll never know anything about me. Privacy or not," I growled, locking eyes with the man who'd thrown away all morality and justice to purchase me.

Mr. Steel's face went red. "You—"

"She's amnesiac. She's broken in that respect. Her only flaw, I can assure you," Kill jumped in, his voice strained and empty.

Mr. Steel took a moment to absorb the verdict of my broken brain. He tilted his head. "Is she normally this difficult?" He glowered in my direction.

Difficult?

They weren't the ones being fucking sold! All of this was Kill's fault. He was the difficult one by being a jackass and unbelievably stubborn.

My back stiffened and I threw pure hatred at the man who should be saving me from this nightmare, not shoving me headfirst. "I hate you, Arthur Killian. I gave you everything. I'm yours from before and now, yet you throw me away as if I'm trash."

Mr. Steel looked at both of us, a smile plastered on his face. "Shit. It's like watching a theatre production. You weren't meant to fuck up the girl, Killian. That's the new master's job. Don't you know the rules of trafficking?"

Kill stood locked to the carpet, not saying a word. His gaze tangled with mine, hiding so much but not hiding enough. I saw the fine edge of panic, the uncertainty—the second-guessing of right and wrong.

Mr. Steel continued, "Rules. Use the women. Take what you want from them. But don't ever give them anything in return."

"He didn't," I snarled. I couldn't help myself. "Don't worry about that. He took everything and gave nothing. I'd say he was a professional at selling women into slavery."

Kill's mouth parted, agony slicing over his face.

Good. I wanted him to hurt.

Mr. Steel laughed loudly. "Shit, I'm liking you more and more every second. And in response to your previous statement about her being broken, Mr. Killian—I don't believe that's true." His smile stretched as he looked me up and down. "I wouldn't say broken. I would merely say clouded. She knows there's nothing in her past that will help her future." The smile turned frigid. "Smart, really."

He repulsed me.

He was evil.

He would die before he ruined me.

My questions from before were answered. What did he hide beneath that glittering veneer?

Darkness.

Oozing filth that I would never be free of. It would stick to me like black oil, even now smearing all over me. But I would willingly wade into his oil and use his darkness to slaughter him.

Mr. Steel lashed out, his fingers imprisoning my hipbones again. "I see what you're thinking. Might as well forget those dangerous thoughts." He dragged me closer, breathing hot on my neck. "They'll only bring you endless pain, lovely."

"Lovely, don't be late today. You know your father is putting together a surprise party. You can't miss it. It'll break his heart."

I bounced on the spot, full of life, full of hope. I was seeing him. I was celebrating my teenage beginning. My heart grew full to bursting at the thought of spending an uninterrupted hour beside him.

I was in love.

"I won't, Mom. Art won't let me be late."

The memory snapped its Pandora's lid closed, leaving me bereft. My heart filled with lead.

Truth.

I'd finally been shown the name of the green-eyed boy I loved.

Art.

Short for Arthur.

It was real—not in my head. I *knew*!

I launched myself away. Mr. Steel cried out in surprise as I stumbled backward and tripped over my own feet. Locking eyes with Kill, I shouted, "Art. I used to call you Art. You never let your mother cut your hair beyond your collar. You got your first motorbike when you were twelve. Art—you have to believe me."

Kill's face crumbled, water swam in his eyes, but *still* he didn't believe. Still he preferred grief to hope.

I screamed as Mr. Steel snatched me, spun me in his arms, and slapped me.

My head snapped sideways as stars burst behind my eyelids. I moaned in protest as his hand captured my breast, pushing aside my bikini top to reveal my tattooed nipple.

"Fuck me." He sucked in a breath. "You tattooed your nipple, too.

You must have a high pain tolerance." His eyes glinted as a Cheshire grin spread his lips.

My jaw locked as repulsion shuddered through me. I knocked his hand away. My stomach rolled. "I think the fire would've hurt more than anything a man with a needle could ever do. I'm immune to pain. And now thanks to the bastard behind me, I'm immune to emotional pain, too."

Gathering spit in my mouth, I spat it right onto Mr. Steel's chin.

Everyone froze.

Kill growled, "Fuck!"

Mr. Steel hadn't moved and I shoved him. I didn't know if it was shock or sheer disbelief that a slave girl had spat and cursed him but he didn't move.

I rounded on Kill.

He backed up, eyes wide. "Stop it. Just fucking stop it!"

"Stop it? *You* stop it!" I shoved him just like I had Mr. Steel. My fingers sparked from touching his chest, but I welcomed the fire, nursing it deep in my heart. "Stop being so fucking weak, *Art*!"

Then I was falling, spread on the plush carpet with a man above. The steward flew from nowhere, wrenching my arms behind my back, binding them with twine. A harrowing flashback of being bound at the very beginning of this mess made me snap.

"Don't touch me!" I bucked and squirmed, gaining carpet burn for my efforts.

But it was no use.

"Get off her!" Kill shouted. The weight of the steward disappeared and Killian hauled me to my feet. He breathed harder than I did, his face white and tight. Glaring at Mr. Steel, who'd climbed to his feet and now stood livid with anger, he hissed, "Do we have a fucking deal or not?"

"*What?*" I yelled. Then…I laughed. It was the only output I had left. Sheer mania. "You're insane." I laughed harder. "You're certifiably nuts. God, what the hell was I doing thinking I could convince you."

Kill didn't say anything; he just stood and watched me unravel with that bone-breaking despair in his eyes. I hated that despair. I hated that even now I wanted to fix him, save him. Even after everything he'd done and let happen.

Mr. Steel's voice cut through my crazed giggles. "You're lucky I like strong women, otherwise you'd have a bullet in your fucking brain and this meeting would be over."

I couldn't stop the silent humor still shaking my frame. I didn't know why I couldn't stop. Panic? Terror? It didn't matter because it made me feel powerful and unpredictable and above these men who drove me mad.

The twine around my wrists wasn't tied properly and I shrugged out of it, throwing the binds at Mr. Steel. "Here's what I think of you and your boat. It's not strong enough to hold me." I giggled again, tears forming in my eyes.

Don't fall. Please don't fall.

Even if it was from mirth, I didn't want tears. If they trickled down my cheeks that would be it for me. They would propel me into the deepest sadness I'd ever known.

I was so close to snapping completely. One brittle splinter from losing my mind forever.

Mr. Steel smiled. "You're different, I'll give you that." Inching forward, he whispered, "In fact, you have me so intrigued I'm willing to make you a deal. Obey my next request and I'll treat you like a queen rather than a whore. Whatever I take from you, I'll give back tenfold." His fingers kissed my cheek sending icicles to my heart. "I'll worship you all while I destroy you."

The fire that'd brutalized my skin now lived inside me. Vengeance. I never knew what it felt like before, but now I did. I wanted revenge on Arthur "Kill" Killian. I wanted to shove what he'd made me become in his face so he would never *ever* forget me.

Arching my chin, I seethed, "Fine. It's more than he ever gave me."

The sharp intake of breath and the soft clinking of a heart breaking came from behind. I didn't turn. I was done with him.

"Strip, lovely girl. Show me everything you are and I'll make you mine." Mr. Steel backed away, his touch still freezing my cheek like a permanent mark.

Tension sprang into the cabin. Billowing heat and intensity came from behind me from Kill. My eyes narrowed as the scent of lust sprang into the air.

My muscles locked.

If I did this, I would willingly hand myself over to the devil. If I did this, I would turn my back on Sarah, on Buttercup, on every single thing I'd fought so hard to remember. I would say good-bye once and for all to the boy I'd once loved in my nightmares.

I'll never wake up from this.

Balling my hands, I looked over my shoulder at Kill. He looked ruined—destroyed—a shadow of the biker lord who'd kissed me so savagely.

My heart hurt to see him in pieces. Then fortified to know I'd won.

Gritting my teeth, I slid my hands beneath my red curls and tugged at the bikini strings. The triangles of gold sprang away, dangling down my stomach as I reached behind my back and unsecured the rest.

Kill sucked in a ragged breath. "Sarah—"

I tensed, never looking at him. "My name isn't Sarah anymore."

His lips turned white and the look of absolute regret in his eyes almost undid me.

Almost.

Mr. Steel smiled wilder. "Good girl. And the rest."

My hands fell from my back, landing on the ties on my hips. A patch of sunlight drenched me in rays and warmth, spilling through the circular window.

Don't!

What are you doing?

This wasn't me. This vengeful hate. It wasn't true, barely hiding the agony and betrayal I felt beneath. But I'd gone too far. I—

"Sarah... stop—" The blatant begging in Kill's tone tore my eyes to his. The pain in his gaze shoved the dagger the final inch into my heart, killing me for eternity. He never looked at my naked chest, pouring his confusion into my soul.

Tension thickened.

Hearts raced.

Lips parted.

I waited for him to fight for me. I waited for him to apologize and admit to everything.

But the weakness inside dropped his eyes, the despair smothering him completely.

Art.

"Do it," Mr. Steel ordered, breaking our fragile trance.

My fingers looped around the bikini ties.

My fingers tugged.

My fingers shook.

But I didn't have the courage to pull them apart.

Kill's eyes came back up, his mouth twisted with sorrow. Darkness from both sides tried to devour me, but light streamed over me like a sparkling waterfall. Golden rays dappled my body as my fingers pulled... tighter and tighter... so close to untethering the final bows that hid my decency.

Then something happened.

Something I didn't understand.

Kill's eyes fell from mine, licking my body with everything he felt and couldn't say. My nipples pebbled; my core grew wet with the shameless lust on his face. But there was something more.

Something so much more.

His eyes latched onto my hipbone, directed by the spotlight of sunshine.

A look of utter horror crossed his features.

A cry fell from his lips.

His body crumbled in on itself like an earthquake-ravaged building, stumbling to one knee.

His soul fractured, glowing brokenly on his face.

Then joy.

Sheer blinding building joy.

In an instant, he pushed upright and grabbed me in his embrace. I couldn't speak or breathe or ask what the hell had happened. His body shook and rattled as he crushed me to him—giving me everything he'd kept locked away in one simple hug.

Shivers and trembles erupted over my skin. His touch was everything I'd wanted—a harbor in this sea of craziness. What did this *mean*?

Uncertainty bubbled in my chest, churning with tears.

Then he pushed me away, his large hand splaying over my sternum and bending me further into the sunlight.

His unsaid emotions waked and eddied around us as I struggled in his hold. "What—what are you doing?"

Mr. Steel ceased to exist. The yacht was no longer our location. Kill had stolen me into his own world with one possessive hold.

His breathing was ragged. Ignoring me, he fixated on my hip.

His head bowed over my body, his long hair sweeping forward and tickling my naked cleavage as his lips moved silently.

Then my world ended as his green eyes met mine, only this time there was no confusion.

No despair.

No anger.

Only belief.

Blazing belief that humbled and terrified me.

His lips parted, sucking in a tattered heavy breath. He no longer looked at me like a brutish biker but like a lover who'd found his precious ever after.

The amazed adoration glowing in his eyes brought tears spilling over my cheeks.

He believes.

He knows.

His lips crashed on mine and his tongue shot into my mouth. With his dark taste came freedom—in one move he tore the dagger free from my heart and magically twisted my hate into undying love.

Breathing against my lips, he lamented, "I'm so sorry. So unbelievably sorry."

"What the fuck is going on?" The sound of a gun clicked as Mr. Steel dispersed our reunion, dragging us back into horror.

My naked breasts suddenly felt too vulnerable. My chest open and revealing my rapidly beating heart.

Kill wrenched me behind his back, protecting me with his large frame. "I'll tell you what the fuck is going on. The deal's off."

My eyes snapped closed as a sob escaped my control.

It's true.

He understands.

What had made him realize? What had finally shown I was telling the truth?

Mr. Steel prowled over the teal carpet, brandishing his gun. "Excuse me?" His voice darkened to black granite. "I'll say if the deal's off." His finger tightened on the trigger. "Protected by Wallstreet or not, I won't hesitate to kill you. Step aside."

Kill stood to his full height, gathering furious energy. "It's over. She's not for sale."

My body wanted to give out in relief. But questions. So many questions. How had this happened? How would I forgive him for not believing me up until now?

Mr. Steel shook his head, his lips twisting into a cold smile. "That's not for you to decide, is it, you little fucker? Wallstreet's in charge here. He assured me I'd have no issues dealing with you." He dragged a hand through his bleached-blond hair. "Give her to me and I'll forget what just happened."

"Never," Kill snarled. "She's mine and she's leaving with me. Like I said. Deal's off."

Walking backward, guiding me to the exit and freedom, Kill fumbled at the small of his back. Pulling free his own gun, he muttered, "Let it go, Steel. It's over."

Mr. Steel's face went beetroot red. "Fine! Full control of the stock. Happy?" He dropped his gun in an act of kinship. "Full control—now hand over the girl."

My heart leapt into my throat. Fear shot down my spine.

Was that all this was? A negotiation tactic to get full control?

You don't believe that.

No. Not after seeing the shackles and barricades falling from Kill's soul. He'd been more honest with me in that one second than in the entire week I'd been his captive.

Kill moved, faster and faster, to the exit. His large body blocked me from potential bullets but not from the pain if he was killed.

Mr. Steel growled, "What the fuck are you doing? You know who I am. Don't be so stupid. Full control—you won! Dump the girl and I won't fucking kill you."

"Don't want your fucking stock anymore. Told you. She's not for sale." Kill's body trembled with aggression, his hand stayed up, pointing with his weapon. "We're walking. Nothing you can do about it."

My eyes shot between the two of them.

I didn't see who moved first but Kill was the fastest. The boom of a gun exploding echoed in my ears as Kill shoved me to the ground. Then he was gone, plowing into Mr. Steel and tackling him to the ground.

I scrambled to my hands and knees as Kill's fist connected wetly with Mr. Steel's nose. Blood spurted all over his linen suit.

Mr. Steel swung at Kill's head, only to lose more ground, and was subjected to a harsh volley of fists to his rib cage. The second Kill delivered the punishment, he stood up and kicked him in the side.

A horrible memory of him kicking me like that came and went, tangling with my joy of his remembering. How would I consolidate his stubbornness and the pain he'd caused with the happiness I felt that he'd finally listened? He'd treated me terribly. Did I have enough forgiveness inside to forget?

Two stewards appeared, one holding a shotgun. "Stop!"

Killian backed away, his fists covered in Mr. Steel's blood. "Let us leave, and we'll cause no more harm."

Mr. Steel coughed, sitting up gingerly. "You think this is over? That you can come onto my boat, renege on a business arrangement, and then fucking *hit* me?"

"No. I realize what I've done. But I've already given her up once. I won't do it again." Kill's eyes landed on mine, shooting fire into my heart.

"This isn't over, Killian," Mr. Steel hissed.

Kill nodded. "I know."

A never-ending second ticked past. Mr. Steel stayed on the floor, his temper howling around us. Suddenly, he slouched. "Wallstreet owes me fucking huge for this." Looking at his stewards, he ordered, "Don't fire. Let them leave. I'll deal with him later."

Kill nodded in acknowledgement of whatever deal they'd just struck and stalked toward me. Effortlessly, he lifted me into his arms and, with a quick shift, threw me over his shoulder.

"Hey!" I clutched his jacket, blood rushing instantly to my head.

"You can shout at me all you want when we get out of here. For now, shut up," he snapped, slapping me on my butt and aiming his pistol at Mr. Steel again. "Don't move."

Mr. Steel nodded, eyes narrowed. "Oh, I'll make my move. When you least expect it." Speaking to the stewards, he snarled, "Escort Mr. Killian and his whore off my yacht. Immediately."

Kill walked backward, his arm never dropping or finger relaxing on the trigger.

Mr. Steel climbed painfully to his feet, spitting a wad of blood onto the carpet. I craned my neck, catching glimpses of his rage while hanging upside down. Kill had just made a powerful enemy—all because of me.

All because Lighter Boy burned and kidnapped me when he wasn't supposed to. I needed to know what the hell was going on.

Kill never stopped inching backward. His muscles tight and bunched, his leather jacket a warm comfort beneath me. "I'll make this right. There's no reason to have bad blood between us."

Mr. Steel laughed. "Get off my fucking boat. I'll show you how much bad blood I can cause."

Kill flinched.

What did this mean for him? How would the mysterious Wallstreet take the news that Kill couldn't sell me?

It's not my problem.

I had too many of those to think about more.

Kill continued to walk backward, training his weapon on the stewards who matched us step for step. He tripped a little as the edge of his shoe caught the lip of the inner door. I grabbed hold of the door frame, steadying both of us.

Without a word, he kept moving, backing into sunshine and past the spa and bar on the *Seahorse*'s gilded deck. Each footfall took us closer to the back of the yacht and awaiting speedboat.

"The driver works for Mr. Steel," I said, pinching Kill's black denim–covered butt.

"I know. But he won't refuse to take us back. Not now. He'll mean to teach me a lesson, and that will only be possible if Wallstreet approves it."

"And will he?"

Kill shrugged, jostling me over his shoulder. "Possibly. Depends how pissed off he is." Twisting his torso, he gently placed me upright. His emerald eyes were incandescent with feeling. The tips of his fingers kissed my cheek, nudging me gently in the direction of freedom. "Get in the boat."

My mouth dried up, tongue twisting with everything I needed to say. "Just because you saved me in the end doesn't mean I forgive you. We need to talk."

He scowled. "Not here and definitely not now." Spinning around, he focused on the stewards who waited for us to leave. "Get in the fucking boat. Now."

I didn't hesitate again.

Without looking back, I climbed down the staircase at the back of the yacht and onto the landing pad, where waves lapped and drenched my flip-flops. The sunshine kissed my skin, bringing my attention to my half-nakedness.

Oh my God. I'd completely forgotten. So consumed with the standoff of trafficker and buyer and numb to anything but the confusion glowing in my heart. Slapping an arm over my chest, I awkwardly climbed into the boat. The skipper gave me a smirk, then looked away the moment Kill jumped into the vessel.

Mr. Steel appeared at the top of the yacht, looking down on us with evil stewing in his gaze. "This isn't over, Killian."

"I never expected it would be," Kill replied.

With a slight nod from Mr. Steel, the skipper teased the engine and we shot away into whitecaps and wind. I welcomed the whoosh of air as we sped away, leaving madness behind.

Narrowing my eyes, I took one last look at Mr. Steel and the life I'd narrowly missed. Then I looked at Arthur Killian, and the questions began to build. Wave after wave of them slowly rose inside my mind, damming in one churning mass thanks to the great wall protecting my memories.

One thing was for sure.

This had to end.

Tonight.

Tonight I would know who I truly was.

And Arthur would help me remember.

Chapter Sixteen

Fuck.

It was real.

She was real.

She was alive.

And I'd... I'd...

What have I done?

—Kill

Tension.

I'd felt it. I'd witnessed it. But I'd never been smothered by it.

The fifteen-minute boat ride was torture. My heart struggled to beat beneath the thick waves of anger coming from Kill.

Anger?

I couldn't understand it. Why anger?

He didn't say a word. Didn't even glance my way.

But I felt his every thought, every speculation—lashing me like a whip.

Everything had changed.

Everything was different.

I sat beside him, red hair streaming in the wind, clutching my naked chest. I wished I had the bronze dress—anything to hide what I didn't want others to see—but the dress and the bikini top were scattered on the floor of Mr. Steel's yacht. All I had was the precariously tied bikini bottom.

The wind bit into my skin as we tore faster and faster over turquoise water. The sun beat down on scars and tattoos alike.

Kill seemed to fade, turning inward to his thoughts. His dark hair tangled around his forehead, obscuring his eyes.

He remembered.

He believed.

But why?

My gaze dropped to my hip—the same place where Kill had suddenly let go of his fierce conviction of my lies and let the truth awaken him. I searched for the key that had unnerved him so much.

There was nothing.

I saw *nothing*.

No matter how long I stared, I couldn't see what he did.

I traced a strange equation hidden beneath smoke tendrils and forget-me-nots, but it didn't mean anything to me—that part of my mind had yet to unlock.

The rage, confusion, and questions were swiftly becoming a pressure cooker inside. I knew I would explode if things didn't start making sense soon.

The moment the speedboat docked, Arthur shrugged out of his leather jacket and threw it over my shoulders. The dense material weighed a ton. My eyes flared as he stole my hands, shoving them through the sleeves like I was a child.

Why had he given me his jacket now—why not at the start of the boat ride? Was he so far inside himself even basic things were taxing?

I wanted to ask him, but suddenly didn't have the strength.

Neither of us said good-bye to the skipper, and Kill took my hand once we were on dry land, leading me quickly and firmly through the busy harbor and back to the parked SUV.

Opening my door, he didn't say a word as he waited till I'd climbed in, then jumped into the driver's seat.

This was the eye of the hurricane.

The unsustainable armistice that would tear us apart the minute we confronted all that we weren't saying.

I just hoped we'd both be strong enough to survive the uprooting of our past, present, and future.

Turning the key, Kill coaxed the gas and shot into traffic.

He drove like a devil.

He drove as if he was terrified of anyone seeing me.

He drove as if he wanted to reenter the past.

Chapter Seventeen

Everything I believed had been a lie.

The people I loved had not only stolen my life, but my ability to find goodness in others—including myself.

She was right in front of me all this time.

In my bed.

In my arms.

Yet my blind hatred and absolute conviction to never be hurt or deceived again had almost cost the girl I loved her life.

What did that make me?

And how could I ever fucking deserve her after what I'd done?

—*Kill*

Strangeness.

Strangers.

Strange happenings.

The past week of my life had just been *strange*. No explanations for behavior or hints at what was hidden. The moment we arrived back at Kill's place, he left: squealed into the garage, shot from the SUV, and disappeared into the house.

A single sentence fell from his lips, garbled and nonsensical. "Give me . . . I need . . . I'll come . . . Give me time."

Without another word, he'd abandoned me. The gates were locked, the security system activated. He didn't care about leaving me alone, standing gaping and wearing his jacket in the garage. He just took off, slamming a door in the depth of the house.

Give me time.

Where had he gone?

He'd run.

I'd sat there for a time, waiting. I'd been patient, giving him time to put his thoughts in order. After all, this wasn't easy. The girl he'd loved, the girl he thought he'd murdered, the girl he'd gone to *prison* for, was back. Alive. Amnesiac, with no memory of how or where she'd been, but back and healthy and utterly ready to talk.

That was enough to make anyone run.

But love should be stronger than the uncertainty of what it all meant. Shouldn't it?

I waited for over an hour, but he never returned.

So I entered his home full of stealth and wariness, searching for the strangest man I'd ever known. For an hour I searched, but found nothing.

He'd gone.

The pain that caused me was tantamount to being worthless and sold. What had he seen that made him save me then disappear as if I were an infectious disease that needed quarantining?

Why had he kissed me and poured every inch of his heart into mine and then left?

It didn't make sense.

It doesn't need to make sense when someone's breaking.

With a heavy heart, I tended to my other needs.

Preparing a dinner of salmon penne, courtesy of the gourmet meals Kill had had delivered, I ate alone, staring into space. My ears twitched for the barest of sounds, hoping he'd join me—drawn by pesto and cream. But he'd well and truly vanished.

Afterward, I drifted to his office, where I sat in his chair staring at the equation artwork, *begging* my mind to be kind and show me what Kill had seen.

It had everything to do with math. Everything to do with homework lessons and stolen touches. But my brain ignored my prompts, refusing flashbacks and snippets of my previous world.

It wasn't until fatigue dragged me to bed that I sat on the edge of the mattress—the same mattress where Kill had taken me for the third time—and my listlessness turned to anger.

I balled my hands.

No.

I wouldn't let him play me like this. I wouldn't let him scramble my brain anymore. I was done being kept in the dark.

After the way he'd treated me. The way he was going to *sell* me?

He didn't deserve to run off. He had an obligation to face me. He had the job of listening to me while I cursed him and his broken mind—while I shouted everything that I'd kept bottled up.

It's time for the truth.

Time for him to grow some balls and talk to me instead of running. Time for me to figure out the mess inside my mind.

Wrapping my tattered courage and strength around me, I stood and beelined for the full-length mirror in his walk-in closet.

Shrugging from his jacket, I let it thud softly against the carpet. Instantly, I missed the smell of him—the soft musk of rebel winds and salt.

With my lips pressed together and my green eyes fierce in the reflection, I undid the loops on my hips and let the remainder of the gold bikini fall to the floor.

Naked.

My heart skipped a beat as I inspected every inch of my flesh. From the top of my head, to the tips of my toes, I forced myself to recognize the outlander in the mirror. Starting with my scars, I traced the puckered skin, tickling sensitive smoothness, pining for the lack of sensation in certain areas. My skin didn't tingle or react—the nerve endings burned beyond working. The blankness was eerie, and I fluttered my fingers quicker, wanting to ignore the disfigurement and touch my tattoo.

He didn't focus on my scars.

Leaning closer to the mirror, I arched my back so my inked hip-bone reflected center place. I bent forward, squinting at the black symbols forming a diamond shape.

"Not like that. God, what's in that brain of yours?"

I giggled. "Poems are in there. Words and words and words."

"Words won't get you wealth." His voice was firm but laced with a smile. I wanted to look up and see the boy I loved, but my attention remained locked on the lined graph paper of my homework.

"Words are valuable. They're the wealth of a soul."

The boy jolted beside me. He uncrossed his legs uncomfortably. "That's mighty thoughtful for a thirteen-year-old."

I shrugged. I'd been told that many times. "Age doesn't mean a thing when you just know."

I looked up into his bright green eyes. The eyes of my nightmare lover and dream stealer.

I looked up, fell in love, and knew without a doubt he was mine. I swallowed as sexual tension sprang between us. "Age doesn't mean a thing when two people want each other."

Art looked down, fumbling with the Libra eraser. "Buttercup... don't."

"Don't what? Admit that I want you or remind you that you want me, too?"

His eyes were tortured as he looked up. "Of course, I want you. So damn much. But I'm not going near you until you're at least fifteen."

That was years away. I would self-combust before then.

"I'll make you break that promise," I murmured, already swimming with ideas on how to seduce him.

He chuckled, shaking his head. "I know you have the power to make me break it, but if you care about me at all, you'll let me wait."

"That was underhanded."

He laughed. "It's the only weapon I have against you." Tugging me close, he wrapped his arms around me and whispered, "As you wish, Buttercup."

My tummy fluttered.

As you wish. The epic line from The Princess Bride. *Farm Boy would say it to Buttercup—a secret message.*

As you wish.

I love you.

I stumbled as the flashback ended as quickly as it began.

He'd loved me so much. So deeply. Despite my frustration and hurt of his treatment recently, I couldn't hate him. After all, *I* was the one who left *him*. I'd lived a new life without remembering him, while he suffered believing he killed me. Not only did he have to console a broken heart, but he also had to come to terms with murder.

Damn, we needed to talk.

Returning my attention to the equation on my skin, my eyes strained as I tried to unlock what it could mean. It looked like a pyramid of algorithms, hiding the treasure map I needed.

"Come on. Remember!" I hissed at the mirror. The rest of my tattoo came to life, showing hidden designs that didn't offer any help. A small unicorn. A fairy hidden by petals. The star sign for Sagittarius, and filigree words wrapped around intricate colors. They were beautiful but meaningless.

I hypnotized myself as I stared harder, forcing past the sluggish forming headache and hammering at the wall in my mind.

But nothing worked.

Time lost all meaning as I dove deeper into the ink. I forgot about Kill and the buyer and the mad rush to return. I forgot about finding him and screaming at him to tell me what I needed to know.

I remained alone in the walk-in closet with only my reflection for company. Kill never came to find me and no other flashbacks came to my aid.

I gave up.

Night had turned to a new dawn, and I refused to live another day not knowing. My unlocking rested with Kill.

It was time to find him.

Grabbing his leather jacket, I slipped into the comforting warmth and went in search. My nakedness beneath the supple cut teased my nipples. I inhaled deeply, drenching my lungs in his smell, invoking a twisting need that never extinguished.

My mind wanted to confront him for answers. My body wanted to confront him for a release. Yesterday was over, the future was as dark as the night-shrouded house, but here and now—it was full of possibilities and I wanted to take advantage.

The house was silent as I padded barefoot over luscious carpet and cold marble. There were no noises, no creaks or hints of life.

Peeking into his empty office, with its four computer monitors and never-turned-off analytic software, I followed the usual trail of sitting room, den, and kitchen.

Empty.

Empty.

Empty.

I moved to the huge sliding doors leading to the back garden, cupping my eyes to peer outside to the sweeping garden beyond.

The moon cast a silver glow, turning three-dimensional into two-dimensional, glittering with mystery.

Empty.

The alarm system flickered red, warning it was activated. *He didn't leave the house.*

I kept drifting, following the layout of the dwelling, leading easily from one room to the next. Abstract art of black-and-white motorbikes loomed from corridor walls. Diplomas of mathematical excellence and philanthropic donations glinted smugly as I traversed the foyer and entered a wing of the house I explored the day before he took me to the compound.

Newspaper clippings were blown up and bordered in huge glossy frames showing stock market evaluations, graphs, and candlestick charts.

Kill's house was sterile and remote, yet permitted a small glimpse into who he was beneath the violence, curses, and anger.

There was something insanely intelligent and... defenseless.

Coming to a large door at the end of the property, I pushed it open and entered a muggy, humidity-drenched world. Watery echos bounced off the glass roof above, showing nothing but velvet night sky and glittering condensation.

My skin prickled with damp heat and the sound of splashes came from around the corner. I hadn't been in here before. The door had been locked.

I inched forward, moving past a changing room and a door to a sauna.

I stopped short.

Kill was doing laps in a large oblong pool. His powerful body sliced through the water, cutting hard and swift with the crawl. His eyes were closed, hair slicked to his skull, and the huge tattoo on his back rippled beneath the water.

I couldn't move. He looked so sleek and predator-like in the water—so powerful. Water splashed the sides as he ducked and pushed off from the crimson-decorated wall. The mosaic tiles gave the impression the water was red—as if Kill swam in blood.

His arms never stopped their deadly assault, shoving liquid away as if he wanted to murder every droplet. He pushed himself to the point of exhaustion; God only knew how long he'd been in there.

Moving to the end of the pool, I stepped from the shadows and deliberately placed myself where he would see.

One stroke.

Two strokes.

Suddenly he stopped, standing up in a wash of chlorine. His chest rose and fell, his stitched wound looking better but still a little puffy. His eyes pinned me to the spot, narrowing in a mixture of disbelief and denial.

My knees locked as his heavy breathing intoxicated me, reminding me of other activities where panting was caused. Humid air clung to my skin, dousing me in perspiration and need.

Water streamed down his face, spilling into his lips as he said quietly, "What are you doing in here?" His voice licked through the space, sending delicious shock waves through my core. Just like the night when I'd awoken kidnapped, his earthquake voice split my world and fractured everything I knew. I was in tune with him—the perfect chalice for the power he conjured.

I swallowed, trying to get a grip on my thoughts. "You shouldn't be swimming with your injury."

His eyes flashed, wrenching back whatever he'd been thinking about while driving through the water. "The stitches need to come out."

I nodded. "I'll remove them for you, but they should probably stay in another few days."

He didn't say anything, merely cocked his head. His stare unnerved me—whatever he'd seen back on the yacht had given him answers and…hope.

Tearing his gaze from mine, he waded through the chest-deep water, moving toward the side of the pool. In a smooth, effortless move, he launched himself from water to tile. The way his muscles bunched and twisted as he stood from crouch to full height made my mouth water.

His back faced me, revealing the full impact of the tattooed cut—the scar tissue beneath the design raised so many questions. My eyes trailed down and down, ratcheting my heart rate until I felt it in every extremity.

Oh God.

He was slick with water.

He was beautifully built.

He was…naked.

My lips parted, tummy coiled with desire.

He turned to face me.

My cheeks heated as my eyes locked onto his cock. I couldn't look away. I was entranced, bewitched, completely focused on the mermaid's hair looping around his perfectly formed erection. It hung heavy and hard, dripping with pool water. His balls were tight and drawn close to his body, completely clean-shaven.

His quads twitched as his hands balled by his sides. The only noise was the gentle lapping of the water and the steady drip, drip, drip of his naked form as droplets rippled over his muscles.

"Like what you see?"

I jumped, tearing my eyes from him and cursing the flush heating my cheeks. I wanted to hide, or jump him. No, I would prefer to touch and kiss and suck.

Swallowing hard, I nodded. "Yes. I've enjoyed watching you since we met."

His eyes narrowed, taking a step closer. "And when exactly was that?" His voice lashed with both violence and softness, his face not giving anything away. "*When* did we meet?"

"I don't know what you want to hear," I murmured. "That I have two answers? The one where you tore my blindfold and I found you again, or—"

"Give me the truth." He prowled closer, his body taut. "Tell me what you've been trying to say. Give me that answer."

I lowered my chin, hope fluttering with feathered wings inside. "Are you prepared to listen?"

Are you prepared to stop hurting me after everything you've done?

My breath disappeared as his wet hands captured my cheeks, tilting my head up, giving me no choice but to look directly at him. "Why did you come find me?"

His gaze fell to his leather jacket engulfing my small frame—my very *naked* frame. Hints of flesh were revealed each time I breathed thanks to the open zipper. The heavy density protected me from the unreadable gleam in his eyes.

"Because we need to talk," I whispered. "Because you need to explain to me what you saw back there. Why you're angry with me. Why you ran the moment we got back."

He sucked in a breath, but kept all his emotions locked from view.

He took forever to reply. "I ran because I needed some time."

"Time for what?"

"Time to figure this out. To come to terms with what a fucking asshole I've been. To figure out if there is any fucking way you can forgive me."

My heart thundered in my ears. "We need to talk. About everything."

I need answers before I can forgive you.

"And if I said I needed more time? What would you do?" His fingers tightened on my cheeks. "If I said I wasn't ready to have my entire life be a lie, to have my world and everything I've been working toward for the last eight years be complete and utter bullshit, what would you say?" His blazing green gaze licked with rage and pain.

I second-guessed myself. *I should've waited.* Given him the space he needed. He'd been moody, violent, and up till a few hours ago, planned to sell me to the highest bidder. Why did I think miraculously he would be willing to talk?

Stupid. So stupid.

But I didn't want to wait. I had to *know.*

In that moment, I saw a different side of him—a man who controlled his world with an unyielding iron fist, with no room for surprises. A man whose world had just been ripped apart.

I trembled in his hold. "Why did you stop the sale today?"

He twitched. "I—" He squeezed his eyes, his shoulders sagging. "You know why."

"No. I don't. I need to hear it from you."

His eyes were tortured as they came up, slightly glassy, fully mistrustful. "How is this even possible—I thought—"

I begged, "Please, tell me what you know."

Kill shook his head, sending droplets flying before looking straight into my soul. "I—I need—I've done so much—" He cut himself off, glancing at the floor. "I can't do this."

Sickness rolled at the thought of him pulling away. "You *can* do this. Trust in us."

His fingers caressed my cheeks for an endless moment. "I don't—" His chest rose and fell as he sucked in a heavy breath. "Okay."

I shivered. Such a simple word but it held such a weighty promise.

"I'm ready to understand."

My heart wedged itself in my throat.

Please, let everything become clear.

"What did you see to make you believe?"

A flash of agony filled his face then was gone. His jaw clenched. "I'll give you the answers you need, but first, I need to hear it from you." Bowing his head, so his forehead brushed against mine, he whispered, "How and when did we meet? Tell me."

Ow. It hurt. So much.

My eyes filled with tears at the oozing blood and gravel on my kneecap. I couldn't stop my wobbling lip as pain lanced. The bike rested beside me, the bright pink frame dusty and scratched. Daddy would be so mad at me.

"You okay?"

I looked up, clutching my kneecap with white fingers. A boy I'd seen living across the courtyard from me smiled, squatting in front of my bike.

"Who are you?" I asked, wincing from another heat-wash of pain.

"Art. And you?"

"Hurt."

He laughed. "I saw you fall. You were going too fast."

I pouted. "No, I wasn't."

Shuffling closer, his grubby hands reached for my wound. "Better get your mom to fix you. I see germs in there already."

My mouth plopped open in horror. "Really?"

Standing, he awkwardly leaned down and grabbed my arm. Wrapping it around his bony shoulders, he smiled. "Come on. I'll take you home."

I blinked. My knee still throbbed with the phantom pain of the past. "I don't know how old I was, maybe four or five. You took me home after I scraped my knee—"

"From falling off your bike," Kill finished. His face twisted with heartbreaking amazement. "How—how is this possible?"

I placed my hands over his, still cupping my cheeks. "I don't know. I was hoping you could tell me."

His mouth remained parted, fear and shock blanching his skin. "I—the most—" He sighed and tried again. "I was told you were dead. I stood on your *grave*. I read your death certificate. I went to—"

Grasshopper's voice popped into my head. I murmured, "You served time... for what happened to me?" My heart fisted not wanting to know. "Why? What... what happened? Why were you sentenced? Who—"

He moved his hand to press against my lips. His eyes were heavy and dark with sadness. "Don't. Just—please, let me enjoy having you here. You're reincarnated. Let me adjust to that... before we drag up the past." His face implored. "Please... I can't talk about it. Not yet."

Impatience filled me like sticky syrup, but I nodded. "Okay."

Dropping his hands, Kill said, "Come. Let's go upstairs. Let's talk." Taking my fingers in his, he tugged me toward the exit and grabbed a neatly folded towel from a basket. Letting me go, he quickly wrapped it around his hips, hiding what I most wanted, and took my hand again.

We moved quickly but not too quickly. We stole glances but didn't speak. We climbed the stairs together, never looking away.

Nervousness was thick and rampant; I worried my heart would never find a normal rhythm again.

The minute we entered his bedroom, he released my hand. Without a word, he disappeared into the bathroom.

I stood for a moment in rejection. Did he need more time? Space?

No. I wouldn't let him run. Not this time.

Chasing him, I followed the trail of droplets on the carpet. The moment I entered the bathroom, the air instantly thickened with tension.

Kill's tattooed back remained unyielding and knotted. He didn't turn to face me. Instead, he kept his attention averted—deliberately cutting me off while he fumbled with whatever he dealt with.

Tearing the towel from his waist, he jumped into the shower and wrenched on the water. Forcing his head under the heavy stream, he sighed heavily. No sound escaped but I felt his confusion and anxiety right in my soul.

I stood there—a voyeur with no place. I couldn't take my eyes from his naked form. All I wanted to do was hug him, to tell him it was okay to be overwhelmed—I was, too.

Join him.

I couldn't deny I wanted to jump into the shower. I wanted to feel him close. I wanted to touch him, and find out once and for all why he lost it today.

But I couldn't.

Something held me back.

Pumping spicy body wash into his hands from a bottle, he lathered his body with clinical cleanliness before rinsing completely and stalking from the shower.

His green eyes met mine briefly as he reached for a fresh towel, rubbing his hair until it stuck out in sexy strands, then wrapped a new towel around his perfectly cut and defined body.

Without a word, he stormed to the vanity, grabbed a pair of tiny silver scissors, and disappeared into the bedroom.

At a loss of what to do, I followed him only to find him laid on the bed with his damp hair on the pillow, eyes locked on the ceiling, and the silver scissors in his open palm.

"Do it. Don't want these things in me anymore." Raising his head, he added, "Once they're out... we'll talk."

He's stalling for time.

I didn't know if I should be pleased I affected him so badly or worried.

Moving toward the bed, I climbed hesitatingly onto the mattress and shuffled closer. Kill didn't look at me; his free hand fisted by his thigh.

Taking the offered scissors, I leaned over his wound. The skin had healed enough to stay knitted together. Touching his flesh, I checked there was no infection or temperature. Satisfied it wouldn't be detrimental, I sat straight. "I need tweezers."

"Top drawer in the bathroom."

I scooted off the bed, retrieved the tweezers, and climbed back by his side. His skin was cool on the surface from his cold shower but beneath it raged a fire that burned all my thoughts to ash.

Being this close. Both of us mostly naked. In bed.

It was a dream. A nightmare. A fantasy all come true.

The jacket was cumbersome on my frame. The cuffs hanging over my hands. I wouldn't be able to do something as delicate as remove stitches while fighting the dense material. It had to come off...only, I had nothing on underneath.

It doesn't matter.

He'd seen me naked. He'd been inside me.

So why do I feel so shy and vulnerable?

Forcing myself to be brave, I shrugged out of his jacket, and placed it gently at the foot of the bed. "Thank you for letting me wear it."

Kill's nostrils flared as he forced himself to continue staring at the ceiling. I knew he'd be able to see I was naked but he nodded curtly. "Only old ladies and members ever get the privilege."

"Then why did you let me wear it?"

His head turned to face me; his eyes stayed locked above my collarbone. "Take my stitches out."

Pain lashed through my heart. The rage he constantly carried glittered in his eyes, dampening the small amount of trust we'd formed. The tiny edge of vulnerability was gone. Disappeared, or hidden.

"Kill...don't. Please don't shut me out."

He clenched his jaw. "I'm—I'm not doing it intentionally. It's just..." His gaze softened and he reached for me before dropping his hand deliberately to the covers. "Give me more time. It's not easy. I'm so used to blocking people. So used to being a bastard to protect myself." His lips twitched into an apologetic smirk. "It's not easy to break a habit." His voice trailed to a whisper. "I still can't believe this is happening. That you're—you. And here. *Alive.*"

My hands shook, holding the scissors and tweezers. Questions hurled themselves at my brain, bombarding me with eagerness.

Forcing the urgency away, I smiled softly and bent over his scar. "The minute these stitches are out, we're talking. No more excuses."

He nodded.

Praying my hands were steady enough, I carefully snipped at the twine holding his flesh together. Concentrating so hard on one thing gave me freedom from the chaos in my brain and I lost myself in the task, leaning lower, permitting myself to be quiet and not ask questions—to just…be.

It didn't take long to remove. As I snipped the last stitch, Arthur tensed. His breathing changed and I looked up.

His eyes were riveted on my inked nipple. His bottom lip clamped between his teeth and his belly rippled with tension.

My heart instantly thundered in my ears. All excuses were gone. I wanted to dance with joy. I wanted to throw up with fear.

I'm afraid of him.

Afraid of what he could do to me—not physically but emotionally. If he was the boy from my past, he already owned my heart. What would happen when he owned my memories and mind, too? How safe would I be? What did it mean for my future?

Kill groaned low in his throat. "What the fuck are you doing to me?"

His confession tilted my world. I never thought I'd hear such lostness in his voice.

I shook my head, my body heavy and throbbing. "What are *you* doing to *me*?" Tears came to my eyes. "Please…tell me. You saw something. On the yacht—you saw something to make you believe. I need to know."

He squeezed his eyes, his lips pressing tight together. "Don't. I know I said we'd talk, but—"

"No. You can't pull away again. It isn't fair to either of us."

I drowned in his green gaze as he tore his eyes open. He wedged his elbows behind him, sitting up. "You said your name is Sarah. That's a lie. How does any of that make sense?" The way he said my name was a curse. A horror-laden curse reeking of his need to find a flaw in my whole argument so he didn't have to pick up the pieces of his shattered world.

"I don't know. I thought my name was Sarah. It fits. It feels... familiar. I didn't lie about that." My eyes desperately wanted to look down where my peripheral vision teased by his thickening erection.

"I'm not saying you lied," he growled. "I'm just saying... Fuck, I don't know what I'm saying."

Suddenly, he moved, grabbing my waist and hauling me on top of him. "You're giving me a heart attack. Sitting there naked. Healing me. The girl I've loved since I was fucking eight years old. It's so hard to shed a lifetime of belief."

I had no response. Every muscle tensed, sprawled over his bulk. "You did love me, even though you were sixteen before I managed to make you kiss me."

His eyes shot wide and a strangled gasp came from his lips. "Fuck." Grabbing the nape of my neck, he kissed me hard. His tongue licked my lips, not seeking entry, just wanting to taste.

Pulling away, he said, "You remember? Those nights we spent together? The endless homework sessions?" He swallowed hard. "That night you snuck into my room and climbed into bed with me? Fucking hell, that was the hardest thing of my life turning you away."

I smiled softly, loving the animation on his face but cold inside because he described things I still couldn't recall.

His body stiffened. "You don't remember?"

I wanted to lie—to keep him happy and hope that I didn't ruin whatever was building between us. But I couldn't. "It's selective. Parts are so clear while others are lost."

"When did you first know?"

"That I knew you?"

"Yes."

I bit my lip. "Um...I can't remember my first flashback, but the second you took my blindfold off, I knew. I recognized your eyes."

His face softened. "I want you so fucking much."

The swift change of direction sent a firework of lust to my core. "Take me, then."

Pain crossed his features, a small droplet of blood from removing the stitches bright and accusing on his skin.

He waged a battle inside before finally giving in. His hips pressed upward and I gasped. I wanted him. I couldn't deny it.

"Do you want me to take you?"

"Yes."

"Are you doing this because you think you can erase what happened? Give us back what we lost? Bring back the past?"

Yes. No. I wish.

"I'm doing this to fix our future. And to figure out what happened."

His face went cold. "Some things are better left in the dark."

My heart twisted. "Things revolving around my supposed death?"

He didn't reply.

Rushing to change the subject, I said, "Whatever happened won't change how I feel about you."

Even as I said it, I didn't know if it was true. Could I still love him, like I did all those years ago, when I didn't know the man he'd become? Or the mysterious circumstances of my death? Was I in bed with my killer?

The concept of him being a devil in disguise terrified me.

"Don't say things you don't mean," he muttered.

I hung my head, unable to hide the truth.

Tucking red wind-tangled hair behind my ear, he said softly, "Talking and answers can come later. Tell me one thing truthfully now."

"Anything."

His hips tilted dangerously. "How much do you want me?"

My eyes flared and my insides melted. I would play his game.

Questions could wait. Anything that might ruin what we had could wait an eternity. "So much."

He shuddered beneath me. Chemistry sparked between us. Passion and need. The connection beyond intense, throbbing with history so much deeper than a few misunderstandings.

Before I could answer, his skin blanched and he rolled me off him. "God, this is so fucked up."

My body went instantly cold, missing his heat. Sitting upright, he cradled his head in his hands. "I can't believe—after all this time." His biceps throbbed as his fingers latched into his long hair. "It hurts to believe. It hurts my heart to think you've been alone—all this fucking time." His eyes glowed with rage. "They told me! They made me—"

I couldn't keep up with him.

My heart thundered. I scrambled to my knees. "It's okay. We'll figure it out. As long as you keep me—"

"Keep you?" His face twisted. "Fuck, I was going to *sell* you! How can you look at me? How can you sit there and still care about me when I've been nothing but a fucking asshole to you?"

"Honestly? Because something inside me knew all along. Call it kismet or some soul-deep connection. I saw past your actions and into your heart." I took a breath, trying to steady the flutter in my chest. "This entire time I've had nothing to guide me. No past lessons or memories. I had to rely on instinct, and no matter how you treated me, everything inside vibrated with knowledge that you were the one I was running to. Even when I should've been running away."

Arthur sat stunned. His lips twisted in pain. "Fuck. Do you have any idea what that does to me? To hear how damn selfless and strong you are? To believe in us so absolutely, even when I did everything in my power to destroy you? You make me feel like a fucking monster. I'll never deserve you after I stooped to *their* level. A level I vowed never to go to."

I couldn't stand to see his anguish; I shuffled closer.

He continued, "I can't understand how this happened. I believe you *are* her—but the burns... the tattoos. It's playing havoc with my mind."

He hung his head in his hands, pulling away even more. He muttered something under his breath that I couldn't hear.

He smiled sadly. "If what you say is true, then my life just got even more fucked up and the nightmare has only just begun."

I trembled with foreboding. "What nightmare?"

He stared into the distance, seeing things I never would. Shaking himself, he said, "Doesn't matter." His eyes went sharp and he tackled me to the bed. Spreading me on my back, he murmured, "Right now, I want to focus on you—us. I want to remember you."

With nimble fingers, he followed my tattoo to my hip. His gaze locked onto the design that'd snapped him from his fugue and made him believe the truth.

Finally, he looked up. "You want to know what set me off? What makes me so fucking terrified that you're telling the truth? That all of this is real, even though it's so hard to believe?"

I nodded.

I gasped as his fingers traced the pattern inked into my skin. "It's here. After all this time, I never thought—"

Tensing my stomach muscles, I tried to sit up to see what he did. But he kept a hand splayed on my rib cage, keeping me down.

Then he began to talk.

"You were thirteen. I'd been helping you with your homework every night since you flunked math. I'd always thought of you as my baby sister or an annoying tagalong, but something changed that night." His voice was wistful, full of aching longing. "You were the one who kissed me. You threw your workbook to the side and launched yourself into my arms. We fell off the couch, crashed against the coffee table, sent paper flying. Thank God your parents weren't home, because you put up a fight when I tried to stop you.

"We rolled around, you trying to kiss me, me trying to avoid it. But you won." A smile graced his face. "Nothing would stop you from getting what you wanted. And for some inexplicable reason, you wanted me."

His eyes met mine. "You tasted of cola and sugar, and you fucking drugged me that night. I wasn't supposed to want you. I was almost four years older and already had a girlfriend. Not only was I making out with my father's best friend's daughter, but cheating on the girl I'd agreed to be exclusive with."

My heart hurt. I didn't remember his girlfriend and a fire churned in my belly to think of him loving another.

He smiled, tracing the frown on my forehead. "Still jealous, after all this time." His eyes clouded, carting him back into the past. "You didn't allow our age to get between us and you didn't accept my no as an answer. You dragged me from loving you as a little sister to loving you like a man should never love a young woman. Especially you being *his* daughter."

"I made you fall in love with me?"

He chuckled. "Cleo, you made me fucking dedicate my world to you."

Cleo.

Cleo.

My world fractured and I fell through the cracks.

"Cleo, baby, we're having a dinner for the other members tonight. Go put on your best jeans and come and help with the decorations." My mother's bright red hair shone beneath the kitchen spotlights.

Memories twisted and collided.

"Ah, so you want me to call you Cleo now? What happens if I want to continue calling you Buttercup?" My father poked me in the ribs, trying to make me laugh but only annoying me further.

"I'm not a kid anymore, Dad. Call me Cleo."

I swirled deeper and deeper into my hidden past.

"Cleo Price, I love you with all my heart and soul. You're my Sagittarius

and I'll always be your Libra." Art stole my cheeks in his warm hands and kissed me with sweetness, adoration, and most of all, the soul mate kind of love that'd blossomed from a lifetime of learning about each other.

Tears trickled down my cheeks.

My name is Cleo...

I blinked, slamming back into the present. "I'm Cleo Price. My father's name was Paul 'Thorn' Price, my mother Sandra Price. I don't have any brothers or sisters. You were my entire childhood. You were my first and only crush. You were my reason for living and I've found you."

The wall barring my family broke away, washing like a broken dam through the valley of my thoughts, sweeping away the blackness.

I remember them!

I couldn't contain my shiver of happiness.

Kill sat frozen. He didn't breathe or blink.

Sitting up, I wrapped my arms around him. "Speak to me."

He took a very long minute to thaw but finally his back sagged and his arms wrapped around me in the tightest embrace. "I've lived the last eight years believing you were dead. I'm struggling to come to terms with everything I've done—how I treated you—how I fucked you with no emotion. Fuck, it's doing my head in to think how I used you. Shit!"

He trembled in my arms and I nuzzled into his neck. "You didn't know. We've both lived with enough torture. Let the past stay where it belongs."

"No, see, that's the thing. The moment I saw you, I hated you. You looked so much like her but I convinced myself it couldn't be. I couldn't see how it would be possible you were still alive after all this time. So many times in the past, I've looked at women and seen you there. Seen you hiding in their eyes. It fucking ripped my heart out every time—so to see you... looking so like—"

He grabbed his hair. "Ugh, this hurts to get straight. I'm repeating myself yet it doesn't make it any easier."

My fingers went to his nape, massaging gently.

"To love as much as I loved you—it decimated me when you'd gone. I didn't want anyone else. I didn't want anything but for you to be alive again."

My heart hurt with my next question. "Did you?"

"Did I what?"

I couldn't voice it.

Did you do what they said and kill me?

His face tightened, understanding my unsaid question.

He grabbed my hand, linking our fingers. "I swear to you on our love that I didn't. I don't know what happened." Fear filled his voice. "I didn't, Cleo. You have to believe me."

I squeezed his fingers. "I believe you."

The relief ebbing from his muscles scared me. "Why didn't you tell the police? Why did you go to prison for a crime you didn't commit?"

The room went icy as Kill sucked up everything he'd let go. Hiding. Blocking answers that I needed. "Please...It relates to the past that I can't talk about just yet." His face twisted with torture. "Give me time. That's all I ask and I'll tell you—I promise."

I sat still. Would he ever tell me? Wouldn't it be best to rip off the Band-Aid quickly and deal with the consequences now? But I couldn't do that to him. I'd already destroyed the world he knew; I couldn't demand more.

"Okay. Time."

He reached up, kissing me sweetly. "Thank you. I'll tell you everything...soon." A cloud passed over his face. "That goes for you, too. I need to know where you've been. How you lost every memory of your past and me."

Nervousness filled me at telling him everything—things I still hadn't recalled. My mind was Swiss cheese with too many holes. Deflecting a little, I smiled. "I'm hoping you can get it straight for both of us. I remember what my parents look like. I remember my bedroom with the yellow walls and my favorite quote from *The Princess*

Bride stenciled on my ceiling. But I don't remember anything else. I don't remember what happened after my fourteenth birthday, and I don't remember how I became Sarah or lived overseas or even how I became a vet."

Kill looked away anxiously. "There's so much you've forgotten. So much we don't know if you'll remember." His shoulders bunched. "Shit, Cleo. There's so much I want to tell you and so much I hope you never—" Cutting himself off, he sighed. "It all hurts too damn much. I have too much inside my head...I'm such an asshole." Pulling away, he looked deep into my eyes. "Can you ever forgive me?"

Tears tickled my spine at the thought of him being so broken. So upside down and inside out from finally *seeing* me. "I already have. I understand."

He sniffed. "I'm so damn sorry."

I wanted to stroke away his pain. My consolation wasn't enough to save him. Directing the conversation to easier topics, I asked, "What finally made you see?"

Smiling quickly, he crushed me to him. "It was the equation. *Our* equation. The stupid geek thing that you giggled over when I showed you how awesome math could be."

My mind came up blank. It was as if my family was now free from the net that captured my mind, but the rest—it was still trapped, still squirming and trying to escape.

He let me go, his large hand falling to my hip. "Look. See for yourself."

I glanced down at the pyramid of numbers inked into my skin. I remembered the night I'd woken at some ungodly hour and scribbled the equation down before it escaped from my dreams. But I still couldn't remember how I recalled it or what it meant. It tugged so hard inside with a hidden message that I'd given it to the artist to place on my skin so I would never forget.

My heart twitched as Kill traced the pattern: I <3 U

"Do you know what it means?" he murmured. "Do you remember?"

I shook my head, wishing I could. "No."

He smiled. "It's the perfect mathematical proof that love exists, written in numbers. You had your words and poems, I had this. And I finally found a way to say I love you."

I couldn't say a word.

"I've loved you for most of my life, and then you were...gone. I don't know what you've been through and I don't know the woman you've become because of it, but I do know I'll never be able to stop it. Never be able to ignore..." His face twisted and he growled, "I'm not going to fight it anymore. Too fucking long I've been fighting and I'm done."

"Fighting what?"

"Emotion. The highs and lows of life. I've lived with revenge for so long, but you brought light back into my black world."

I bit my lip, suffering an explosion of happiness in my heart.

Kill continued, "There's so much to tell you. So much you don't know. You have no fucking idea how my life was. Everything I ever wanted was torn away from me and it terrifies me to think it will happen again."

"It won't."

"You're right. It won't. Not this time. This time I'm keeping you safe and never letting you out of my sight until those motherfuckers pay."

My heart raced. My gasp was loud in the silent room.

Leaning close, he breathed, "Does that scare you?"

I shook my head. "No."

"Well, it should."

"I understand you carry things inside. Dark things—painful things. Tell me. What happened to you?"

His eyes lost the burning intensity, hazing with lust. "Later."

I swallowed as he cupped my cheek and whispered a thumb over my lips. "I'll tell you everything...but first, I need to touch you. I need to make sure this is real."

A small smile twisted my lips. "I am real. I'm yours. You're mine. Just like we said all those years ago."

He sucked in a breath, his chest rising sharply. "God, I've missed you."

His hand slipped from my cheek to the base of my skull. His eyes tore into me, welding his soul to mine. "Every night I dreamed of kissing you." His gaze dropped to my lips. I didn't have time to gasp or enjoy the blissful anticipation of being kissed before his mouth crushed against mine.

My body melted against his, becoming one with his passion and heat. His arms wrapped around me, his heart thundering. I snuggled closer.

His lips were silk and sandpaper all at once. His tongue smooth and stealing. I opened wider, deepening the kiss until staying alive meant breaking our connection and breathing, and I never wanted to do that.

Suicide by kiss—death by lover's embrace—that was my choice.

Kill never stopped kissing me, never stopped touching.

My fingers itched to trace his muscles, to stroke and calm.

I paused.

He doesn't let any woman touch him.

He sensed my trepidation, breaking our kiss to look into my eyes. "What's wrong?"

I laughed self-consciously. "Can I—um, can I touch you?"

His gaze flared and the tender look on his face undid me. "Cleo, touch me. Only you have ever had that privilege. I've been dying for so many years to have your fingers on me again." His voice thickened. "I was prepared to spend the rest of my life without touching, knowing you were dead. I was broken...a man who couldn't tolerate the touch of another." He chuckled softly. "Every time I craved companionship enough to seek out a woman, I ended up almost killing her for not being you. I was screwed up, Cleo. A fucking mess."

Oh God.

My heart burst as his mouth reclaimed mine, stealing my reply. My hands splayed on his back, caressing every inch I could reach.

He shifted, bringing me close to his body and wedging the hard heat of his cock against my exposed hipbone. He rocked once, twice, sending a delicious sensation of need through my belly to my core. My nipples tightened as his heart galloped against my side.

Every inch of me screamed for attention. Sensitivity was both a blessing and a curse as I grew wet from his kisses.

This wasn't like before. This was more. So, so much more.

His fingers fell to my breast, squeezing once before bowing his head and sucking my nipple.

My eyes closed; lust swarmed my system.

I squirmed as his hot tongue swirled with a delicious combination of sucking and teasing. He murmured against my skin, "I wanted you so much back then. I was a stupid fool to deny you."

I moaned, grabbing his hair and shivering in bliss as I sank my fingernails into the thick, long strands. "Maybe if you knew what I tasted like, you would've recognized me when you first took me."

His teeth graced my nipple, making my breath catch. "I wanted so much to be your first. For you to be mine." He suddenly stopped licking, pressing his forehead against my sternum and wrapping trembling arms around my body. "I'm so sor—"

I tugged his hair, stopping him from apologizing again. "Don't. I don't want to hear it. Now—right here, right now—*this* is our first time. No one else exists—the past, the memories, the revenge. None of it matters. Not anymore."

His forehead furrowed as he bit his lip. A delectable flop of long hair covered one of his eyes. "Fuck, it makes me hard when you control the situation. It always did. Even when you were a bossy ten-year-old."

I laughed, amazed that the intense sexual moment could have so many facets. "You fantasized about me when you were thirteen and I was ten?" I scrunched up my nose playfully. "That's just gross."

He chuckled. "You know what I mean. I didn't want you like that. I just couldn't…I couldn't understand you. I couldn't get you out of my mind—not because you were so cute with your bouncing red hair and fierce green eyes, but because of your ginormous attitude."

His hands traced down my rib cage, his thumb skirting the hollow of my belly. He kept going, ghosting over scars and colors. His eyes burned, drinking me in, and the urge for conversation quickly faded.

My back arched into his touch.

He hissed, pressing his throbbing cock against me. "I need to be inside you, Cleo."

My eyes snapped closed at the use of my name. A full-body tremble at finally knowing where my home was.

In his arms. In his heart.

"You like that?" he murmured. "You like it when I call you Cleo? My Cleo?"

I moaned as his mouth trailed over my jaw and down my throat. "Do you want to know what I'm going to do to you, Cleo? I'm going to lick every inch, inhale every part, and then I'm going to sink slowly into your heat and make you come with your legs wrapped around my ass."

My eyes were so damn heavy, I struggled to open them to look into his gaze. "You want me to wrap my legs around you?"

He nodded, his beautiful lips wet and red. "I want your chest against mine. I want your arms tight around me, and I want your breath in my mouth. I've wanted you to touch me since the last time I saw you. Give me what I've always denied myself because I couldn't stomach any other woman taking your place."

"I love you!" he called from across the compound. The sun soaked into his dark hair, the floppy silky strands mussed from our make-out session behind the garage.

"I love you, too! Don't be late tonight."

He grinned, waving once before jogging to his house.

My breath caught at the memory. Had that been the last time I'd ever seen him?

The melancholy and confusion threatened to destroy the heat in my heart. I threw my arms around his neck, pulling him close. "I want you to look into my eyes when you slide inside me. I want you to see how much having your body in mine affects my soul."

He groaned, kissing me hard. His lips were weapons, his tongue a tool, making me writhe and want.

I wanted him to make love to me.

"I want to steal your breath, so you only survive while I breathe for you." The agony in his voice hurt me deep. He had so much still hurting him.

Whispering, I said, "I want you to come inside me, so I can claim a part of you."

His eyes flared, kissing me gently. "You don't know if you're on protection."

I shook my head. I did remember. A random memory to have come clear, but there it was. "I had a coil inserted a few years ago. I can't get pregnant."

His eyes bored into mine. He didn't ask why I'd taken such serious measures to never get pregnant. He didn't ask how many lovers I'd had. He just scooped me closer and breathed, "I've never been with a woman without a condom. Never."

I held his cheeks, my fingers burning from his heat.

His lips parted and he pressed me bone-breakingly hard against him. We fell together, kissing, touching. My hand wiggled its way between our glued bodies, finding his hard length and cupping boldly.

I stroked him. Hard, possessive—*claiming*.

His mouth opened wide beneath mine, coming undone. His legs twitched and a guttural groan sounded in his chest.

My heart raced as I grew wet with power. "Do you like that? Like having my fingers around you?"

His eyes snapped tight. "You have no idea. Being touched—it feels so damn good. But knowing it's you? My Buttercup."

A cry fell from my lips.

Kill gathered me close. "I'm sorry. I didn't mean to."

"Mean to what?"

"Use that nickname. I know it belonged to your dad."

I shook my head. "Use it. It's yours as much as his."

Concern for my parents hit me quick and hard.

... it belonged *to your dad.*

What did he mean by that? Past tense because of us, or had he died?

My heart fisted at the thought of my parents gone. Then my stomach cramped at the thought of them living the past eight years believing I was rotting in the ground.

"God, my parents." I clutched Kill's shoulders. I wanted to ignore the need to know—it wasn't exactly the best time to ask—but I couldn't stop the question falling between us like a blot of ink. "Where are they?"

The heated air between us went frigid; Kill stiffened into an unyielding plank. The tightness of his muscles and unreadable look in his eyes made my heart thud. "Where are they, Kill?"

A heavy second ticked past, then another. Finally, he closed his eyes and kissed me deeply. "I'll tell you. I'll tell you everything."

His lips trailed a path of fire down my sternum as he shifted his body, flattening me below. "And please don't call me that anymore. Not when we're alone."

When will you tell me?

I wanted to push, but swallowed my impatience. Tilting my head, I focused on the easier subject. "What should I call you?"

He chuckled, sounding strained and forced against my collarbone. "What you called me all those years ago. I want to hear it."

My heart thudded for an entirely new reason. His lips kept feathering, his tongue softly licking toward my breasts.

"Art. I called you Art."

He broke his downward journey, sliding back over me to press a possessive kiss against my mouth. "Yes."

"You want me to call you it again?"

He nodded. "More than anything." Never looking away, he reached down and tapped my thigh. Unconsciously, I opened my legs wider, letting his large bulk settle directly between them.

My breathing turned shallow as he paused, hovering protectively over me on his elbows. His fingers dived into my hair, holding me steady. "There's so much still to learn. So much that's happened that you need to know. But, Cleo, not tonight."

His hard cock nudged my entrance and I moaned at the silent question. Biting my lip from the joy at having him so close, I nodded.

Gritting his jaw, he pushed in—slowly, surely, claiming me in ways he never did when we were first in love. I'd slept with Killian, but this was the first time I'd slept with Arthur. Art. My one true connection.

There was nothing between us anymore—no latex from condoms or darkness from unremembered memories. Just us.

His eyes tightened as he stretched and filled me, the invasion never stopping until he sank as deeply as he could go. His back was bow-string tight as he released a ragged groan sheathing himself completely.

I didn't want to move or dispel the aching, delectable throbbing of having him take me so thoroughly. His body was snug and warm over mine, his green eyes glowing in the dimness of the bedroom.

Our gaze never unlocked.

We didn't move. But we were joined with ravenous, rapturous oblivion.

My jaw clenched, fighting the urge to rock. I wanted to savor the silence of just *being* for another moment—to embrace the incredible-ness of finding each other after so long.

My core rippled, welcoming him deeper.

Art groaned, letting some of his weight fall on me, pressing his forehead against mine. We were both slick with sweat even though we hadn't moved. Our bodies and hearts thrumming with energy. My tattoos were bright against the bedspread and I didn't feel ugly with my scars. His gaze remained full of perfect love—despite me having changed since he'd last seen me.

His mouth searched for mine and the moment his lips connected, I snapped. The time for serenity was over. Now I wanted to be used. I wanted to know just who impaled me and how much I never wanted him to leave.

Gathering him to me, I rocked.

He gasped; his restraint snapped and he drove into me. Hard and strong. His hipbones bruised my thighs as I opened wider, welcoming his violence, his need.

There was a fine line of making love and fucking but this was love-fucking. This was cruel but sweet. Angry but happy. It was a thousand words in one timeless action—righting the wrongs of our past and hopefully repairing a future we both didn't think we'd ever find.

"God, Cleo. Fuck." He pounded harder, his grunts mixing with my cries. My fingernails clutched his hips, riding up and down with every rock.

"Yes. Art, more."

His body pistoned into mine, trying to devour me. Tears tracked down my eyes; the world swam with desire and despair at missing him so much.

"Shit, don't cry..." Art stopped, his large thumbs brushing away the salt on my cheeks.

I nipped at his touch, arching upright to pant in his ear. "Don't stop."

I couldn't stop. I never wanted to stop.

There was nothing on earth that could get me to cease the incredible assault coming from the boy I thought I'd lost.

I cried out as he grabbed my leg, bringing it up and spreading me even wider. I thought I'd never get to touch this man—hug him or stroke as he pounded into me—but all my wishes had come true. My hands landed on his ass, clutching him harder, forcing more violence, more animalistic thrusting.

"Goddammit, Cleo," he groaned as I dug my fingernails harder.

We were so close. Our skin stuck to each other; his heart interrupted the beat of mine until I swore they beat in unison. We were too close. We weren't close enough.

"Kill, you're killing me."

"Art, goddammit," he growled. His hands clutched the bedspread by my ears as he thrust harder. The need to come ached in every part. Every stroke of his large cock sent me higher and higher up a cliff. I wouldn't hold on much longer.

Wedging my knee between us, I pushed Art away and hooked it over his shoulder. In one move, I delivered the rest of my vulnerability and trust, exposing where we were joined and letting him control however he wanted to drive us over the ledge.

He didn't say a word. His eyes smoldered and his teeth landed on my leg, biting hard as he drove deliciously hard into me. His stomach clenched with every thrust, the sheen of sweat making him glow.

My breasts bounced and I knew from his vantage point he'd see everything. My scars, my ink, the love bursting in my eyes.

"Goddammit, Cleo. You have no idea what you're doing to me."

I smiled. "I do. Same thing you're doing to me."

"You're in my fucking heart."

"I've been there since we met."

He grinned crookedly, his eyes heavy with dark lust. "You have. Always been there."

His gaze fell between us, latching onto my exposed pussy. I looked to where we were joined, panting at the mind-consuming image of his large cock disappearing inside me stroke after stroke.

His jaw clenched, his fingernails digging into my leg. "I'm gonna come. I have to come."

I nodded. "Come. Take me with you."

Setting his jaw, he increased his rhythm, pounding and fucking until his cock stiffened and his forehead furrowed with pleasure.

"Christ..." His mouth fell open and his entire body shuddered, driving himself to the pinnacle.

Deep inside I felt the first ripple and splash of his release.

"Yes, Art. God, give it to me."

He angled upward, his eyes clouded as he kept coming. His fingers landed on my clit, rubbing firm and determined, ripping me from my cliff and hurling me into the stratosphere.

My back bowed, my toes curled, and my own release appeared from nowhere, spooling me high, then whirling me like a spinning top until I exploded into cosmic pieces.

I gave him everything that I was. I gave him all my troubles and dreams and flashbacks. I let him save me. And at the same time saved him.

By the time the last quiver of our orgasms faded, we were both panting and boneless.

I groaned as Arthur slid out of me, gently lowering my cramped leg from his shoulder. I winced as he massaged the seizing muscles.

Soundlessly, he flopped onto his back, gathering me close and tucking me against his body. Instead of being self-conscious with the stickiness between my thighs, I relished being cradled.

A nuclear bomb could go off and I would have no desire to move. I was exactly where I wanted to be.

Wrapping his large body around my smaller one, his hand cradled a breast. Whispering his lips over my hair, he murmured, "Go to sleep, little Buttercup."

I sighed, battling happy tears, sad tears, confused and still lost tears, but the glow in my heart lapped up the feelings knitting them into a sated, satisfied blanket.

For the first time since I'd forgotten my world and soul mate, I fell asleep with a smile on my face and the knowledge I was utterly safe.

Chapter Eighteen

I'd admitted I was a fucking mess thinking she was dead.

It was nothing compared to the jumble of thoughts I was now.

I struggled to make sense of my world.

It was no longer black and white.

I fought against the urge to hide my heart again. It was easier, less painful when feeling nothing.

But Cleo dragged me back into pain.

Pain so vibrant and intense I couldn't breathe. I couldn't think. I couldn't move.

She was *real.*

She's come back from the dead for me.

And I would do everything in my power to never let her leave me again.

—Kill

I woke to Arthur sweeping his fingers down my stomach.

My body twisted, trying to find a way free from his touch.

"You're still ticklish. Just checking," he murmured against my hair. His fingers disappeared, dragging me closer to spoon along his sleep-warmed limbs.

I wanted more of last night. I wanted to feel him inside me again.

"I loved coming inside you," he said softy, nuzzling his nose against my ear. "I've never done it bare before. Damn, Cleo—your heat—it took every ounce of self-control I had not to come the second I entered you."

I smiled, hugging his arm. "You felt amazing."

"You felt like a fucking wet dream."

I giggled as his fingers trailed up to my breast, tracing circles around my rapidly hardening nipple. "I want you so much. All I can think about is pushing your legs apart and sliding deep inside you."

He pressed his erection against my ass, grinding himself.

I wriggled, pushing my hips against him. "Do it. Take me."

His teeth nibbled on my ear. "Can't. Got things to do."

I moaned, burrowing closer, reaching behind to grab his cock.

I missed.

Chuckling, he suddenly let me go and rolled upright. I shot to my knees, trying to catch him, but was too late. With a wry smile, he jumped out of bed and stood gloriously naked and way, way too tempting. "If I give in, we'll never leave. And this can't wait."

I flopped onto my back, sighing dramatically. "What can't wait?"

Leaning down, he grabbed my ankle and jerked me to the end of the bed.

"Hey!"

Pulling me from tangled sheets, he wrapped his arms around my shoulders and legs, then picked me up as if I weighed nothing. "Come. We're going to have a shower."

I wanted to fight—to win and reward myself by never leaving the bed, but beneath his amused expression lurked anxiety and a lot of rage.

"What is it?" I murmured, cupping his cheek and drawing his eyes to mine.

He swallowed back the dark emotions swirling on his face, shaking his head. "Nothing." Stalking toward the bathroom, he kissed my forehead. "Do you know I've never touched or been close to anyone like I am with you? I've never picked up a woman or wanted her naked flesh against mine."

My heart twisted to think of him with other women, but then warmed into a smug glow. I smiled. "Is it wrong that I like you being brutal to other girls? That I'm the only one that captured this?" I traced his chest where his heart beat beneath my fingertips, eyeing up his healing wound on his mirroring pectoral.

He grinned, gaze going soft. "Nope. I'm glad you're still jealous. It makes me feel wanted."

I laughed as he placed me on the floor of the bathroom. "Oh, you're most definitely wanted."

His stance changed from happy to sexually hungry. "Stop it. I want to wash you. Not fuck you."

I blinked innocently. "You could do both."

A dark smile stretched his lips and he stepped into the large shower. Turning on the spray, he reached for me, jerking me under the raining hot water.

My hair became instantly drenched as Arthur raised his head beneath the torrent and opened his mouth to capture cascading droplets. Water rippled down his front, darting over muscles and teasing the hard piece of equipment between his legs.

I wanted him. Badly.

He opened his eyes, water glittering on his eyelashes. "Want something, Cleo?" His tone was laced with a challenge and cockiness.

Just for that, I turned my back on him. "No, not really." I hid my smile as I reached for the body wash and squirted masculine-smelling bubbles all over my body. My legs trembled as I washed away Arthur's remnants of pleasure from my inner thighs, clenching from any stimulation on such a sensitive area.

"Not really?" Arthur purred behind me. "You're saying if I pressed you against the tiles and slid my cock inside you, you wouldn't be interested?"

I shivered as his body heat moved closer, barricading me between the glass and him.

"Stop that," I ordered. "You're the one who has big plans today. I'm busy."

His hands wrapped around me, capturing my soapy wrists and

hauling them fast and hard above my head. His weight crushed mine, pinning me against slippery cold glass.

Instantly my heart rate skyrocketed, and I swallowed back a needful moan.

"You're busy?" he whispered, rocking his erection against my ass. "Too busy to pay attention to me?"

My tongue tied into lustful knots. I had no comeback.

Dropping one hand from my wrists, he splayed his fingers on my chest, tweaking my nipple and lathering the glistening bubbles. "I'm the one who gets to wash you. Not you. Only my hands are allowed here"—his soapy fingers trailed down my stomach and cupped my core—"and here."

I bit my lip as his touch turned firm, rubbing my clit with steel-minded determination.

Harder and lower, his pressure made my legs stumble; I splayed my hands on the glass for balance, my wrists still captured in his grip.

He groaned in pleasure. "God, you look good like that." His teeth bit into my shoulder. "Spread your legs."

My breathing picked up as I obeyed. I spread my legs quickly, and he angled his knee between them. I gasped as he let my wrists go, clasping my waist with both hands. Then his thumbs pressed heavenly into the base of my spine.

"Oh God." I lost the ability to stand under such glorious torture.

"He won't help you, Cleo. Might as well implore my name instead."

My lips parted as he kneaded my ass, my muscles clenching as his touch turned inward. Every gentle massage sent shock waves through me as he worked his way to my belly.

"Please, Art. Touch me."

My legs trembled as he obeyed, his strong fingers capturing my clit. His arm wrapped around me, locking our wet bodies against each other, deliberately making me aware of how damn hard he was.

"Cleo, fuck, I want you."

I thrust my pussy harder into his touch. "More—"

My eyes flared as he sank a finger inside me.

"More?" he whispered, his voice deserting him in favor of cracked lust and sinful desire. He rocked behind me. "More of what?"

My mind filled with fizzling pinwheels as he drew tingles and wetness from my core. "More of everything. You. Your touch. Your mouth. Your..." Words escaped me as he withdrew his finger and thrust two together, stretching me, deliberately reminding me I was erotically bruised from his claiming last night. "I need you, Art. So damn much."

His teeth sank deep into my neck. His arm wrapped tighter, holding me in place as he fingered me.

My legs tried to scissor together. An orgasm hovered just out of reach. I was so turned on even the glass against my nipples was bliss.

I moaned, rocking in his hold.

Suddenly, he let me go, removing his fingers and turning off the shower.

I blinked. "What—"

"Move, Cleo. My self-control is close to snapping, but there's something I want to do first." Tapping my butt, he hurried me from the shower on unsteady legs. Every movement amplified the swollen need in my pussy.

He didn't grab a towel or let me dry off. Taking my hand, he didn't say a word as we padded wet and dripping back into the bedroom.

Traversing the floor quickly, he spun me forward, using inertia to throw me backward onto the bed. I gasped as I crashed onto my spine, staring at the man who ran a motorcycle club and made a fortune trading the markets. The man who looked at me as if he wanted to eat me alive.

Grabbing my hips, he slid me to the edge of the bed, then slammed to his knees.

My heart rate exploded, every remaining sense and atom shot to my center.

Pulling my legs apart, his eyes burned with fire. "Fuck, I want to taste you."

I bowed off the bed, a loud cry wrenched from my lungs as his hot, wet mouth latched onto my pussy.

"Shit!"

His tongue came out fast and flat, licking me like a delicious predator deciding if he wanted to devour me quickly or slowly.

I couldn't stay still as his tongue slicked to my entrance, dipping once inside me. "Oh God." My back arched as every part of my body spasmed. "Arthur!"

He placed one hand on my belly, pushing me flat against the bed, the other started at my ankle, trailing quickly up my inner thigh, up and up until he touched my clit. With his tongue licking and teeth nibbling, he pushed two fingers deep. So fast. So swift.

I had no hope of remaining sane.

My hands dove into his silky long hair, clutching the shower-dampened roots. He made a noise I instantly adored: a cross between an arrogant growl and a groan of desire.

His tongue moved faster, licking me, tasting me.

With urgent hands, he draped my tattooed leg over his shoulder, dragging me closer to his eager mouth.

When he paused, breathing hard and dousing me in hot air but no tongue, I squirmed. Tilting my hips toward his lips, I moaned, "Please... Art..."

He grumbled deep and low in his chest, his large hands trembling a little on my hips. "Fuck, you're gorgeous. You're drugging me." Then his mouth captured my throbbing clit, sending me bowing off the bed.

Every muscle and sinew locked into place as his tongue drifted lower, teasing my entrance with tentative hesitation.

"Yes. Yes..." I grabbed more of his hair, tugging him, completely caught up in needing his tongue inside me.

With a sharp spear, he drove it deep. Fucking me with heat and wetness, his breath hot between my thighs.

The buildup of the shower, the animalistic way his tongue drank me, and the erotic image of his long hair obscuring his eyes as his head bowed between my legs sent me spiraling toward the stars. The band of an orgasm shattered everything left inside. It built and built and *built*. My eyes rolled and every part of my body transcended.

Arthur sucked and nipped, thrusting and stroking.

I clutched the bedspread. My vision went black as my body combusted beneath his skillful touch.

"God!" I couldn't breathe as wave after wave of mind-twisting sensation sparked through my core. He skillfully brought me to the fastest release I'd ever had.

The moment I stopped rippling around his tongue, he raised his head. The smug satisfaction in his eyes sent shy happiness skating over me.

Standing, he didn't say a word—he didn't have to. His gaze said everything he needed. Using his fingers, still wet from being inside me, he touched my hip, and coaxed me to roll from back to stomach.

The moment I pressed my cheek comfortably against the mattress, he positioned himself behind and slid, fast, hard, and entirely possessive, inside.

"Yes," he hissed, sinking deep, his cock as hard as stone.

Part of me wanted to rest; the other part wanted to drive high again and explode just as completely. Arthur captured my hips, pulling me backward to meet his thrust. "Damn, you tasted fucking good. Never tasted a woman before." His cock stretched me relentlessly.

I could barely think; talking was a mission to Mars in effort. "You've never done that?"

His cock stroked hard, setting a punishing pace. "No. Never had anyone's mouth around me either. Didn't want to. Couldn't—"

Love erupted in my heart and another orgasm caught me completely by surprise. My legs locked together, wrapping around him from behind as he fucked me hard.

He groaned, driving faster toward his release.

"Fuck, I'm gonna come," he snarled.

"Come!" I begged. "Please."

He growled as his pace increased, then his entire body stiffened as he spurted inside me. Feeling him let go—giving in to me and becoming powerless in that second—my body unraveled for a second time. Not as intense as the first, but my core gripped his cock, milking him with pleasure.

Shuddering shock waves passed from his body to mine, our hearts thrumming out of control.

I froze.

He took me from behind.

What did that mean?

Don't read into it.

I didn't want to let the fact he'd flipped me onto my stomach be anything upsetting. Just habit probably, or he'd felt too much and needed some normalcy after a night of touching, loving, and togetherness.

He slid out slowly, flopping down spent beside me. His long hair obscured one eye and his chest still glittered with droplets in a mixture of shower and sweat.

Rolling closer to him, I brushed dark strands off his forehead. "For a novice, you were amazing."

His eyes opened, glassy and lust-sated. He chuckled. "I plan on becoming an expert. Now that I've tasted you, I never want to stop."

I've never had anyone's lips around me. If that was true, he'd never had a blow job. And for the life of me I couldn't remember if I'd ever given one to the brown-eyed boy I'd lost my virginity to.

I smiled gently. "Well, it seems as though I owe you a favor."

He froze, then a satisfied grin spread his lips. "I agree. You do." His eyes locked with mine and the sharpest, keenest love whipped between us.

I sucked in a breath. "Now?"

He sat up and kissed me, brushing my nose with his. "No. We've wasted too much time already. I have to get to the Club. I want answers."

Disappointment settled in my heart, but then anticipation replaced it. I could wait to give him pleasure. After all, we had all the time in the world now. We'd found each other. Nothing could ruin that.

Nothing.

"Answers?" I stretched, my body feeling used and taken.

Arthur climbed off the bed, heading to the bathroom for a second shower. He turned by the door, saying, "Don't you find it strange that it was you who was stolen?"

I sat up, a cold draft howling down my back. "I hadn't thought about it."

Yes, I do find it very strange.

Lighter Boy came to mind and all the questions I'd been avoiding swarmed with determination.

His emerald eyes darkened to moss. "It's too much of a coincidence."

I agree. "I'm sure it's explainable."

He bared his teeth. "That's what I'm afraid of. I went eight years thinking you were dead. Then you just turn up because my Club stole you—against orders—to traffic you into slavery? It doesn't make sense."

I couldn't stop the animosity replacing our postcoital glow. *I've been thinking the same thing.* "What are you saying?"

That someone knew who I was? Before I remembered? Before all of this?

He glared across the room. "I think there's a lot more than we both know. And I mean to get answers."

"But how? What if—"

His hands balled into fists. "I'll make them talk by any means necessary, even if I have to spill blood to do it."

The compound was quiet when we arrived.

Most of the men I'd met at the pizza lunch weren't there. In fact, the whole place looked deserted.

"How many rooms are there here?" I asked, following obediently behind Arthur. My jeans and yellow T-shirt were a splash of color in the dark grey–and–wooden floor décor.

Arthur looked completely in control in his black jeans and T-shirt with his leather jacket. There wasn't a hint of the soft, vulnerable man who'd had his tongue between my legs only hours before.

He's my secret.

Kill the biker president had replaced my soul mate, Art. I just had to learn how to love both of them—despite what he'd done.

"There are ten bedrooms, three common areas, a few offices, and the garage. Why?"

"No reason. Just wondering. And you never stay here? Do the others?"

He chuckled. "I stayed when I first arrived. But that was before the renovation and cleanup—before the crew embraced what I could do for them and followed my rules."

There was so much I didn't know: What had he been up against? How had he been incarcerated? How had he found freedom?

So much to learn before we could reconcile completely. I loved a stranger. There would be nothing powerful enough to stop my love—time had tried and failed—everything else was inconsequential. Whatever existed between us was steadfast and immune, but it didn't mean I would blindly follow him if he was doing things that were morally wrong.

"And you expect your men to stay here, but you don't?"

Arthur stopped. "When did I ever say they lived here? This place belongs to everyone. At the same time it belongs to no one. It's a place of sanctuary, brotherhood, and business. Before I took over, it was a requirement for each man, including the president, to live on home turf. To put their brothers over wives and kids, to put the Club before blood. It made for an unbalanced family.

"Men need the softness they get from women—they need to be reminded of their value and rules placed on them by loved ones. Living together, taking orders, never having something of their own that wasn't already claimed by the Club made for anger, discord, and a fucking lot of fighting. Sure, they were loyal, but this way—*my* way—means they get the love of their blood and family, and their loyalty and regiment of their Club."

Love of a woman. The love he never had. He'd tried to give his men what he would never have.

My heart broke all over again.

He smiled softly. "Win-win."

I wanted to tell him I understood—that I got why he needed his men to value love above everything, but I didn't want to point out something so tender. Instead, something tugged at my brain, wanting to break free but still prisoner to my mind. "That's not how we were raised, though. Is it?"

Arthur smiled. "You remember that?"

I shook my head. "No, it's just a feeling."

He took my hand, squeezing. "You'll remember soon enough. I'm with you now. I'll piece you back together."

My heart beat hard at the adoration emanating from him. The words "thank you" rested on the tip of my tongue. I wanted to thank him for loving me, for loving me so much he'd lived a life of utter loneliness while watching his men go home to their families. Such strange things to be grateful for, but if he hadn't—

Horror lodged quickly in my throat.

If he'd laid my ghost to rest, he might've found love with another. I might've turned up to find him happily married... with kids and no feelings left for me.

Oh God.

"Hey..." Arthur cupped my chin, bringing my eyes to his. "What is it? What's wrong?"

I gave him a watery smile. "I'm being an idiot."

He pressed his lips gently against mine, stealing the horror in my heart and replacing it with love. "I agree. You're being an idiot."

My eyes flared. "Hey, you're not supposed to agree with me." Huffing, I added, "Plus, you don't even know what I was thinking about."

His face softened, his hands grabbing my waist and holding me close. "Don't I? Don't you think I've thought about it?"

"Thought about what?"

His eyes tightened. "About letting you go..."

My heart flopped in a faint. "Eight years, Art. I would've understood. The grief..."

I would never have understood. You're mine.

He kissed me again, whispering against my mouth. "No matter how much I wished I could forget, I couldn't. You stole my heart and soul, Cleo. There was nothing left to give anyone else. I gave up trying to forget you and focused on other things."

I almost crumbled to the floor in a weird combination of thankfulness and guilt.

I asked, "Things like revenge?"

His jaw tightened.

"Who are you planning on—"

"Don't. Not yet." He stepped back, letting me go with a small shove. "It's all wrapped up in the parts I can't explain." He ran an angry hand through his hair.

My palms turned sweaty with nerves. What was he hiding?

"Explain, Art. The sooner you begin, the sooner it's over."

"And the sooner you'll run because you won't understand," he growled. Shaking his head, he snapped, "No. I can't tell you—not in words. I need to show you." His temper faded and he gave me a sheepish smile. "Today. I'll show you today."

His face lost the dark shadows of vendettas. He shoved his hand into a jeans pocket. Taking my fingers, he turned my wrist until it rested upside down and placed the Libra eraser in my palm. "I've carried this with me every day since you gave it to me. I hated it for a time because it was still here and you weren't. But then I loved it."

Dragging me into another kiss, his body shook, sending desire and pain through my system. Desire for this man who never let me die. And pain for his suffering—for everything he'd had to live through.

"I want you to have it, Cleo. It brought you back—it belongs to you."

I shook my head, trying to untangle myself from his embrace. "I can't. It's yours."

"I've got something so much better."

I knew what he would say, but I smiled and asked anyway, "And what's that?"

His lips whispered over mine. "My Buttercup."

I surrendered to his taste, kissing him back. I wanted to turn around and go back home. I wanted to ignore the outside world and the endless questions for a bit longer. I was selfish—selfish for a boy who'd turned into a man without me.

His tongue tangled with mine, our bodies pressing harder and *harder* against each other—seeking release from the rapidly building lust.

Breathing hard, I ended the kiss. Something he'd said before niggled me. "You didn't have it on you every day."

He frowned, his lips wet and swollen. "What?"

"That day I arrived. It was in your room." My mind skipped back to that night—the battle, the blood, his wound that almost made him die. More fear filled my heart. "Art, if I hadn't arrived that night... you would've died."

His jaw clenched as he looked away and I saw what he didn't want me to see. He'd been reckless with his life. Reckless with safety and his health because he had nothing to live for.

I crashed against his chest, nuzzling my head into his body and wrapping my arms tight around his waist. "Please tell me you weren't that stupid—that broken—to want to die?"

"No." His baritone echoed in my ear from where I pressed against him. "I must admit some days I was weak. Some days I didn't want to get out of fucking bed at the thought of not having anyone to live for. But vengeance is a fine thing. It kept me alive when nothing else could. I wouldn't have let myself die that night. I would've stayed alive because I fucking *refuse* to die before they get what's coming to them."

I looked up, even more confusion layering my overstretched brain. "Who?"

He brushed a thumb over the apple of my cheek. "You'll find out. I promise. And when you do, you'll understand why I'm doing what I'm doing."

"Is it anything to do with the uprising—that rebellion when I arrived?"

Arthur frowned, looking over his shoulder at the empty Club room. "That wasn't related to the Club—not directly, anyway."

"If it wasn't related to Pure Corruption, what was it, then?" I couldn't understand the dynamics. Arthur had built an MC that obeyed its own laws—unlike others.

"Four years ago when I took over, I wasn't exactly a lot of members' first choice."

I moved closer, placing the Libra eraser back in his pocket. He frowned. "That's—"

"It's yours. And anyway, I don't have any pockets." Standing on my tiptoes to distract him from giving me something that meant the world to him, I said, "You'd always be my first choice."

He grinned, but it didn't reach his eyes, absorbed with the past. "I came in, changed their patch, their oath—turned them from criminal to legit. I did everything he ever asked me to do."

"He?"

His arm wrapped around my waist again. "Wallstreet. He was the reason—" Cutting himself off, he said, "He's the only man I'll ever fight for. The only man I'll stay loyal to because of what he's given me." Waving his arm around the designer room, he added, "All of this—this belonged to Wallstreet. He built this Club, he expanded to Chapters all around the USA, but then he was put away and the guy he left in charge betrayed him."

I didn't know if I liked Wallstreet. He'd been fundamental in my sale, after all. He sounded like a bastard—not that I would say that.

Understanding swooped into my brain. "He asked you to rule in his stead?"

Arthur nodded. "Most of the crew hated how the new president ruined everything Wallstreet had built. They were happy to stand behind me, even though I came from a background that made it, let's just say…difficult. But there were others still loyal to Magnet."

"The man who betrayed Wallstreet?" I tried my hardest to understand and follow his story.

"Yes. Overnight the Corrupts became Pure Corruption and the Chapters had to obey the switch or be cut. It's been a long fucking four years." He smiled tiredly. "But for the most of it, the men are decent and just want peace and a law they can follow that will protect their assets and family."

"And you gave them that."

He gathered me close. "I gave them that."

I snuggled closer, hungering for his body. All this talking and touching played havoc with my body and mind. I loved learning, peeling back the layers to find the truth, but I would've preferred to do it in bed, where I could distract him when topics got heavy. Changing the subject, I asked, "So they all have their own homes?"

Arthur nodded. "Some have a few. They're fucking rich bastards. All of them—thanks to the skills Wallstreet taught me. Wealth is shared in the Club. I ask for obedience and trust, and in return they provide for their families, spend their time how they want, and have my back if I have tasks for them."

A splash of temper filled me. "And trafficking women, was that a task?" I hadn't meant to say it, but the crushing level of guilt I felt over the five women who'd been sold weighed on my mind. "Art, those women you sold. I can't believe—I mean the boy I knew would never have done that. Is there some way to save them?"

His eyes darkened with anger. "Don't, Cleo. You don't know what the hell is going on, and I won't let you judge me. Those trades were the first and the last, but there was a reason for them. Trust me."

I hung my head. "I do trust you, but…you *sold* people. You sent them to a life of slavery. That's not exactly easy to forget or condone."

He shook his head. "I lied to you when I said they were chosen at random. They weren't. They were marked for reasons that I won't go into with you. Don't feel sorry for them. Don't think they didn't deserve what happened."

Fear skittered down my spine. "What do you mean?"

They were chosen? Does that mean I was, too?

The question came loaded with far too many repercussions to sort through.

Arthur grabbed my wrist, pulling me close. "I mean that there's so much going on that I need to explain, but first I need to get this straightened out. Then we need to see Wallstreet."

I didn't want to go see him. What would I say? How would I hide the anger I felt?

"Prez?" Grasshopper appeared from a side door that presumably led into either an office or bedroom off the main sitting area.

"Hopper." Arthur nodded. "Did you get everything I asked?"

"I tried, but I'm still confused. You need to start talking, dude."

Arthur didn't let me go, dragging me toward Grasshopper.

His blue eyes landed on mine; his mohawk bristled. "What's she doing here? I thought you took her to the buyer?"

"Nice to see you, too," I huffed.

Grasshopper cringed. "I didn't mean it like that…not exactly." A smile tugged his mouth as he looked me up and down. "I take it lies weren't lies after all?" His gaze landed on Arthur, happiness glowing for his friend.

Art said, "She's staying with me. I made a mistake. From now on you treat her with the same respect you treat me. She's mine, wears my patch, and will eventually be my old lady."

My heart smacked against my ribs. I couldn't breathe.

It seemed neither could Grasshopper. He punched himself in the chest as he coughed. "Fuck, dude! You mean she's her? *Her* her? Fuck!" He took a step toward me, energy bursting from him.

My mind skipped, overwhelmed with the declaration of being Art's, and being elevated to power in just one order.

"But your name is Sarah. That wasn't her name." His attention turned to Arthur. "Am I missing something?"

"It seems I have two names—or two identities." *Two lives?* Too many things to remember before they made sense.

Grasshopper paused, his mouth hanging open. "So...you are her? The infamous Kill has performed a miracle and brought the dead girl back to life?" He swiped a hand over his face. "Fuck, this isn't making sense."

Arthur chuckled, the respect he had for his second in charge obvious in his eyes. "Her name is Cleo, possibly Sarah, too, but we need to confirm that. I didn't bring her back to life, but she's back in my world and never leaving."

Grasshopper's gaze flew wide. "Holy fuck. This is insane." He looked between us. "But...how? I don't..."

I laughed.

His amazement was comical. Plus, I didn't doubt he felt a little self-conscious for having stepped over the line and told me things about Arthur he probably shouldn't have. "Nice to meet you, Jared. I'm Cleo." I stuck my hand out.

Grasshopper's face darkened. "Fuck, you know my name, too. Witchcraft, I tell you." Taking my hand, he shook it once, pulling me close. "I must know everything so my brain doesn't explode."

"You and me both." I laughed again.

Arthur grabbed my hips, pulling me away from Grasshopper with a stern look. "What I want to know is how Cleo came into our possession."

My laughter faded as Arthur's voice drifted into strict business. "Explain to me where she was taken, who stole her, and what the fuck was the bullshit someone told me of her being his whore?"

My head snapped up. "What?" I looked between the two men. "Whose whore? I was nobody's—"

Arthur cringed. "Nothing. I was told a lie about who you are in order for me to go ahead with the sale. I want to know who came up with it, so he can answer my goddamn questions."

Grasshopper shifted on the spot. "Bazza. He told me that he got her from the Dagger's, along with the other girls and she'd been in his bed. *His* bed, dude. I mean—it couldn't be more of a fucking slight now that we know."

Oh my God. My head. It couldn't continue on like this, with half-truths, vague recollections, and hidden agendas. "Will someone please tell me what the hell all of this means?"

Grasshopper looked to Arthur, sharing a look that spoke volumes but remaining silent with answers.

Ignoring me, Arthur balled his hands. "You do realize I will get to the bottom of this, and when I do, I hope to fuck those I trust aren't involved."

The room's oxygen was sucked into a vacuum. Grasshopper turned cold and menacing. He morphed into a biker with a vendetta—just like his president. "Someone has to have been working us from the inside. Shit." He dragged hands through his hair, messing up his mohawk till it stood up in every which way. "Fuck!"

Arthur matched his anger with his livid face and highly strung muscles. "I want to know who, Hopper. And I want to know now."

Fear charged down my back; I wanted to run from their palpable energy building like a cyclone. Lighter Boy. It was him.

Before I could announce my epiphany, Arthur muttered, "The complications and consequences of this are gonna bring everything we've been working toward an end."

Burn, baby girl. Burn.

I shivered. "What do you mean?"

It was Grasshopper who answered. His voice low and anger lacing every word. "It means those motherfuckers have used us again. First him, now you."

Arthur's fists turned white.

"Prez, didn't think I'd see you here." Mo appeared, his blond hair sticking up as if he'd just pulled his bike helmet off. His gaze fell to mine but he kept his questions hidden.

The tension that'd built in our small group faded thanks to the newcomer.

Arthur looked at him, his eyes dark and suspicious. "Are the other guys here?"

Mo shook his head. "No, just us. No trades today. No meetings. A lot of them are having a family day."

Arthur nodded. "Good. We're going on a little trip." Dragging a hand through his long hair, he said, "The four of us are going on the hunt for fucking answers."

Finally!

Arthur took my hand. "It's time to unravel this mess once and for all. And when I find out what the fuck it all means..."

Grasshopper stepped forward, his hands curling by his sides. "It means we'll finally have what we've been working toward all these years."

Goose bumps scattered down my spine.

"Vengeance," Mo muttered, his face glowing with eager pride. "Down with denial. Death to the traitors."

Arthur nodded. "It's time for war."

Chapter Nineteen

Pain came in many forms.

Loneliness.

Betrayal.

Sacrifice.

But I'd found love to be the most painful of all.

I was invincible when no other emotion controlled me. I was single-minded in my determination to deliver justice. I had a gift of blotting out the world and throwing myself into numbers, calculations, and vengeance.

But when Cleo looked into my eyes with the same soul-depth connection we'd shared all those years ago, it fucking crippled me.

I became useless. Weak. Besotted.

I wanted to forget about all my plans and run far away to keep her safe.

Yet even though she granted me happiness with her tender touches and smiles, there was a blankness inside her, too. A scary void that blocked out all we'd shared, leaving me even more alone than before.

I loved a stranger. A stranger who knew me better than I knew myself.

Who would've thought her love for me could hurt so much?

Who could've thought my heart would break all over again knowing she'd forgotten?

Forgotten everything I'd whispered to her.

Everything we'd promised.
—*Kill*

The wind whipped in my face as I clung to Arthur's waist.

It seemed life went from normal speed to hyper-overdrive. The moment he'd decided to solve the riddle that was my life, we all sprang into action. No planning, no hesitation.

A collective nod and intelligent men turned into hunting savages—focused on one goal.

I was surprised Arthur hadn't thrown me over his shoulder and tossed me onto his bike with the rage he was in. The anger he kept wrapped around himself had been refastened after our tryst; he was back in full command.

He'd captured my wrist and the four of us stormed to the garage and its awaiting steeds. Instead of velveteen horses and lances, the knights defending my honor climbed aboard their trusty Triumphs and cocked their guns, ready for battle.

I just hoped there would be no war and answers would put aside whatever feud Arthur had with people I didn't know. I wanted life to be simple again—not the messy ball of lies it had become.

I'd tried to speak to Arthur over the whipping wind as we shot down roads beneath hot sunshine, but with helmets and the insane pace he pushed his machine, my voice had no hope of being heard.

His body was tight, fists white around the handlebars. My body plastered against his in a borrowed leather jacket.

City, suburbia, then highway became my view as the rumble and thunder of three Triumphs ate tarmac with ravenous speed.

I had no idea where we were going.

Twenty minutes went by—zipping and weaving down roads and highways.

Forty minutes—my front grew sticky and hot pressed against Arthur's powerful back.

Fifty minutes—my spine tingled with foreboding the longer we traveled.

An hour.

And *still* we rode.

The roar of not just our bike but Grasshopper and Mo's too no longer lived in my ears but in my soul. My heart purred to it. My stomach churned to it.

Family sedans slowed down to let us pass. Big rigs moved off the median to let us charge in front. Was it respect or fear that gave the bikers the road? Either way, their throttles remained high and tires chewed up tarmac as cities disappeared behind us.

We finally slowed and entered a small town. We meandered down lanes and through suburban neighborhood perfection. At every corner, my heart beat harder.

I—I know this place…

My eyes fell on a park complete with faded monkey bars, seesaw, and swing.

My world disintegrated.

"Would you let me kiss you if I pushed?"

I spun around, locking eyes with the boy who, until last week, hadn't wanted anything to do with me. He'd been so mean when I'd asked him to watch TV with me while my parents were out, I'd cried myself to sleep. I couldn't understand how we'd gone from being so close and sharing our deepest secrets to being complete strangers.

My mom said Art had needs and I would understand when puberty happened to me.

I'd scoffed and said puberty sucked.

*Art had needs—*I *was his need. Stupid boy just hadn't figured it out yet.*

I scowled. "What are you doing here?" My hands tensed around the chain of my swing. I didn't want him to see the hurt in my eyes or the love in my heart. He didn't deserve me anymore—not with his horrible behavior.

Art moved in front, grabbing the chain so my swing snapped to a halt. His groin was eye level and I swallowed hard.

Bending over me, he whispered, "I've been a fucking idiot, Buttercup."

"Don't swear and don't call me Buttercup."

He smiled, but the grin didn't meet his eyes. He looked sad and lost and afraid. "Did I ruin it? Did I break what we had?"

My stomach twisted into bows.

Letting his grip trail down the chain, he captured my hands and squatted in front of me so he now looked up as if begging. "Cleo. I know I was an ass to you. But... I miss you."

A large ball wedged in my throat.

I miss you, too.

I love you.

I want you to love me the same way.

Everything I wanted to say slammed against the ball in my throat, keeping me mute.

His cool hand landed on my cheek, smelling metallic from the chain. "We promised a while ago that we'd forgive each other anything. Will you do that for me? Will you forgive me for hurting the one girl who I love more than anyone?"

I almost fell off my swing; it was only my death grip that kept me upright. Love. *He loved me. Like a sister? A friend? An annoying little tagalong?*

My voice cracked as I whispered, "What do you want from me?" The question was strangely wise and older than my thirteen years. But I knew exactly what I was asking and I knew exactly what I wanted.

His face came close, his nose skimming mine. It was the closest we'd ever been to kissing. Tickling and planting kisses on each other's laughing faces when we were younger didn't count. This... It was different. Completely different. Wild and naughty and grown-up.

"Everything, Cleo. I want everything from you."

The slowing of the motorbike and quietening of the rumbling engine tore my mind from the past. Arthur's powerful bulk rested in my arms and I squeezed him as hard as I'd squeezed the swing chain.

I couldn't breathe as emotion tsunamied over me, drowning me in love for this complicated man. I loved him the moment he carried me home after falling off my bike. The stars made me for him. I was his and it *killed* me to think I'd forgotten it.

Forgotten him. This place. Our past.

Everything.

I'd walked away and forgotten the most important piece of my life. How had I survived without him? How had I found comfort with a boy with brown eyes who I still couldn't remember? It didn't make sense that my brain had shut off someone so important.

"I'm so sorry, Art. For leaving you."

Tears trickled down my cheeks as I hugged him harder. My arms ached, my heart burst, but I couldn't get close enough.

His arms landed over mine, squeezing back. Letting me go, he yanked his helmet off and spun to face me. "You remembered?"

"Our first kiss?"

"What I said to you that night."

I nodded, my eyes dropping to his mouth. "You said you wanted everything from me."

"And did you give me everything?"

I said softly, "There was nothing to give. You owned it all already."

His lips smashed against mine, his tongue spearing into my mouth, transporting me back to our very first kiss.

His lips were warm and tasted of blueberry bubblegum.

The moment his mouth met mine, I knew.

I knew why I'd been born and what my future had mapped for me.

I would marry him.

I would be by his side until death did us part.

His hands went to my face, holding me in place as the strangest sensation of his wet, delicious tongue coaxed my lips to open.

They did.

And I shuddered in his arms.

There was nothing awkward about our kiss. Nothing experimental or uncertain. We knew each other so well, we'd mastered our souls—it was only fitting we mastered our first kiss, too.

Art pulled away, breathing hard. "Are you remembering more? Being here?"

I frowned. "I remember that evening vividly. I remember the seesaw and the tree across the park where you pushed me up against and kissed me harder than you'd ever kissed me before. But I don't remember how we got there, where we were going, or where I lived." I shook my head, my fingers tapping my temple. "It's all there, just...filed in the wrong places."

His eyes darkened. "I hope the next place I show you will bring back everything. If it doesn't, then I don't really know what will." Giving me a nervous smile, he added, "Don't worry. Regardless of old memories, we're together now and I plan on making a lifetime of new ones."

Before I could reply, he kissed me tenderly, then spun back around. Placing his helmet back on, he eased the bike into motion, quickly catching up with Mo and Grasshopper, who had gone ahead, obviously to give us some privacy.

I wished I'd asked where we were going. What did he hope would jog my memory? The more we drove these streets, the more comfort and nervousness descended. I knew this place as surely as I knew Art when I first saw him, but memories were shrouded in mist.

The afternoon sunshine had turned from a golden glow to a russet haze as time inched onward, bathing the township in new beginnings.

My inner thighs ached and my ass was flat by the time Grasshopper and Mo slowed and turned their bikes into a pretty yellow-and-white diner.

I clutched Arthur's midriff, anticipating a corner, but he only waved and increased his speed. We shot past, leaving them in our dusty wake.

Why are we going on alone?

I didn't have to wait long to ask. Arthur drove through suburbia to the other end of town, then cut the engine and rolled to a stop in a bushy alcove off a deserted road.

Kicking the stand down, he clambered off the bike, before grabbing me and helping my jelly legs unwrap from around his trusty machine.

"We're here," he said, ripping off his helmet and shoving a hand through his slightly sweaty hair. He came closer, eyes full of anticipation. His fingers went around my chin to undo my helmet.

My skin sparked beneath his touch; I swayed closer.

His lips tilted into a half smile, showing off the sharpness of his strong jaw and the sexy mess of long strands falling over his forehead. Pulling the helmet free, he whispered, "Even after a two-hour ride, you're still fucking stunning."

I smiled as he kissed me softly. "I'm glad you think so, seeing as I have no way of making myself presentable." Looking around the vacant road, I asked, "Where exactly did you bring me?"

His eyes lost their emerald glow, switching to a flat green. "Somewhere I swore I'd never go back to. The place of my fucking nightmares."

My stomach clenched at his tone.

Burn, baby girl. Burn.

I swallowed hard. "Then why bring me here?" I peered into the bushes as anxiety settled heavily in my gut.

Danger. Run.

I shouldn't be here.

He massaged the back of his neck. "Because it might remind you enough that everything else comes back. I need to know what happened. Then I can tell you what I plan to do."

"Who you plan to hurt for revenge, you mean?"

He bared his teeth, the need for vengeance bright in his gaze. "Who I mean to kill—not hurt."

"You can't be serious."

He froze, animosity settling like fog around him. "I'm deadly serious. If you knew what they did, you wouldn't be so quick to judge."

"Tell me, then, so I can make up my own mind." My heart raced. "You can't keep talking like that. What did they do? Who are they? Just tell me their names. Tell me what you did to land in prison. Tell me how you got out so soon, even when slapped with a life sentence."

His mouth fell open. "How do you know about that?"

I crossed my arms. "Grasshopper told me."

"What the fuck?" He threw his hands up. "That damn dick. Can't keep his nose out of my business."

My temper flared. "You're forgetting that you meant to sell me. He didn't think I'd ever see you again. He told me certain things so I could go to someone new without wondering if I ever stood a chance with you." My voice trailed off remembering what else he'd said. "He told me how you took women—how he could tell I meant nothing to you by the way you treated me."

Arthur suddenly grabbed my shoulders. He shook me, forcing my eyes to meet his. "Don't believe a word of bullshit he said. You mean every-goddamn-thing to me. Never doubt that. Ever."

I smiled. "I know that. Now. But you were dense, Art. You were so wrapped up in your misery that even the truth wasn't registering. On some level you believed me, yet you kept pushing me away and treating me..."

Arthur closed his eyes, agony etching his face. He pressed a fierce kiss on my forehead. "I'm sorry. So fucking sorry. I'll tell you every damn day for the rest of our lives. I'll make it up to you—I promise."

I shook my head. "I don't need apologies. I hurt you more than I can bear by forgetting everything we had. I still don't understand how my mind deleted something so fundamental—we both have faults. But there are a lot of things we need to talk about. I need to know—"

"I know all that!" Rage colored his face. "I know we need to talk, but goddammit, Cleo. Give it a rest."

I froze at his sudden anger. What the hell had made him snap? "Art, what's gotten into you? You can't explode like that without—"

His hand swiped up, cutting me off midword. "For God's sake, just wait, Cleo. Just once in your life, be *patient*."

"I am patient!"

He scowled, stealing my wrist. "You're never patient. But I'm fucking begging you. Let me tell you my way." His face fell, unsuccessfully hiding his terror beneath his blustering anger. "Don't force me to say something I don't have the courage to. Not yet."

My heart broke. I had no reply other than wanting to kiss him senseless and heal the tattered pain in his soul.

Without another word, he pulled me around his bike and into the undergrowth. Leaves and twigs reached out with sticky fingers, scratching over leather and bare legs.

I couldn't stop repeating his grumbling remark about my patience. I was a saint when it came to waiting for answers. Unable to stop myself, I muttered, "Once in *my* life I should be patient? I think the last eight years I've shown I have a high tolerance of the word."

He turned on me, his nostrils flaring in anger. "And I haven't? I didn't have to spend the last eight years loving a ghost only to find out you've been alive all this time, living it up with people who cared for you, happily building a new life without me?"

Shit.

"That was low of me, Art. I didn't mean it like that. I just meant—"

"Fuck, this is all kinds of screwed up. What the hell am I doing?" He pinched the bridge of his nose, grabbing hold of his temper and swallowing it back. "I know you didn't. It's just so fucking hard to know you've been alive all this time while I thought you were dead. If anyone deserves the award for not losing their mind and being patient, it's me."

He slammed a fist against his chest. "You don't seem to get it..." Looking away, he laughed morbidly. "And why would you—you have no idea what happened while you were gone. But take my word for it—I've been planning this for a very long fucking time. I could've had my revenge years ago. I could've just gone in there and murdered the son of a bitch in his sleep and not cared if they killed me in the process. But Wallstreet—"

That asshole again.

"Wallstreet? What does he have to do with this?"

Arthur smiled sadly. "Everything. He has everything to do with this. And you'll see why if you just follow me and let me show you."

How had this turned into an argument? Just being back here—wherever we were—made me irritable and uncomfortable. I wanted to leave. The sooner this was over, the sooner that would happen.

Forcing myself to let go of everything, I murmured, "Show me. I want to see."

His shoulders slumped. "I know this will be hard in some ways. To recognize this place but not remember."

It was my turn to smile sadly. "It's no harder than recognizing you and not recalling our life together."

He swallowed, his powerful neck clenching with the effort. "You have no idea how true that is." Shadows swarmed his eyes. "I'm not going to deny that I'm struggling. I'm struggling with every damn memory we ever made together, knowing you don't remember." He sighed, looking away. "It's like I've had every wish come true, only to find out that part of what made us so special has disappeared."

My head ached with the pressure of his pain.

I couldn't reply.

Silently, he took my hand, looped his fingers with mine, and guided me through the undergrowth.

We didn't go far off the road before Art darted behind a tree and pressed me against the bark. His heart thundered against mine as he slapped a hand over my mouth.

"Quiet," he hissed into my ear. My back locked as I listened for what had spooked him.

Only the gentle whistle through the leaves and the soft hum of insects.

My own heart matched his in rhythm, nervousness once again thickening my blood.

A minute ticked past before Arthur let me go, his warm hand falling from my lips. "Sorry, thought I heard something." His eyes fell to my mouth, hips pressing harder. "However, this position does have some advantages."

My lips twitched as his head bowed, his lips brushing ever so gently over mine.

I moaned slightly as his hardening erection nudged my lower belly.

Laughing under my breath, I pushed him away. "Stop it. If we start, we won't get this over with." *And I really want this over with so we can leave.* I was spooked for reasons I couldn't explain.

God, everything hurt. Beyond hurt—agony. No, beyond agony—excruciating torture.

My vision was black, my lungs choking on smoke, and my entire body belonged to eternal flames.

The sound of tires squealing and then the rush of footsteps echoed in my roaring ears. All I could focus on was the crackle and spit of fire. It lived inside me, turning my thoughts to ash.

"Hello. Can you hear me?"

I screamed as something touched my charred arm.

"Don't touch her. I'll call an ambulance."

My life flickered in and out, half in this world, half in the nether. All I remembered was pain, pain, and more pain.

Then bright lights and scents of antiseptic.

"We can't treat her here. We don't have the necessary equipment. We'll arrange an airlift and get her to the closest doctor who can save her."

"Will she live?"

My ears fought the whooshing sound of fire to lock onto the answer.

Will I live?

Do I want to live?

What is there to live for?

"I don't know. It's all on her. Let's just hope she has someone to pull her through. Did you find any identification? Family we can call?"

My heart picked up its sluggish beat, fighting back the crippling pain.

Family.

Yes, I had family.

Didn't I?

I screamed again as the pain began to delete everything inside. I grasped harder to each tendril as the flames turned inward, devouring my past, my sanity, my very essence of who I was until I had nothing but emptiness.

I was blank.

The flashback ended. I stumbled, even now feeling the torture of surviving the fire. For once I found my amnesia a blessing. I wished I could've continued to forget that crippling agony.

"You okay? Shit, Cleo, you're shaking." Arthur wrapped his arm around my shoulders. His body heat was comforting but too stifling after the memory of being burned alive.

I pulled away, rubbing my hands over my face. "Yes, I'm okay. Just—let's keep moving. I need…I need to keep moving." My voice was brittle and I knew if Arthur asked me one more time if I was okay, I would lose it.

At least now I knew how I'd been taken far away after crawling through the undergrowth and passing out in a ditch. All I'd known was I had to run. Had to crawl. Had to flee in any way possible.

The nice people who'd found me had probably saved my life in more ways than one—not just my immediate predicament but taking me far away, too.

Who had wanted to kill me?

What had I done to warrant it?

Arthur stood locked in place. The look in his eyes battled with questions and the need to help.

But he honored my wish. Whispering softly, he said, "This way." Taking my hand, he ran a thumb over my scarred knuckles, granting me an anchor of our love. "One glimpse, then we'll go, Cleo. I don't want you here anymore. I hate to think of you reliving things that you're afraid to tell me." His gaze dropped to my scarred leg, brimming with hate and regret and sorrow.

"Thank you," I whispered. "Thank you for understanding."

Nodding once, he guided me the remaining way. The undergrowth thinned as we moved closer to our destination.

The high wooden fence appeared as if from nowhere, dappled with late-afternoon sunshine and stencils of leaves. The top was protected by vicious curls of barbed wire.

Every paling was straight and perfect, no warped wood or rot to be seen the entire length of the perimeter.

"What is this place?"

Arthur tugged me closer, his large boots surprisingly quiet on the strewn leaf matter and twigs. My sneakers, on the other hand, seemed to find every crackle and snap available.

Not stopping until we were in touching distance of the fence, he pulled me to stand in front of him. Backing me against the wood, he splayed his hands on either side of my head.

The intense look blazing in his green eyes undid me.

My mind raced with need. My core twisted at the thought of him taking me. Here. Now. In the middle of wherever the hell we were.

I wanted sex. I wanted to affirm I was still here. Still alive. Still his—regardless that so much had happened to prevent it.

My lips parted, breathing shallow.

His eyebrow quirked, lust shadowing his face. "As much as I'd like to give in to the idea of taking you here, Buttercup, there is no way in hell I'm dropping my guard down around this place."

I knew he was right, but it didn't stop the disappointment dousing my face.

Bowing his head, he nuzzled into my throat. "Fuck, stop looking at me like that." His hips arched against mine, a soft groan falling from his lips.

My hands shot up and wrapped in his hair as his chest brushed against my nipples. "You better move, Art, otherwise I won't be focusing on anything but you."

Swallowing hard, he deliberately leaned away, keeping his hands splayed on the palings. Gritting his jaw, he ordered, "Look through the fence. Then we can leave."

"Look through the fence?"

He nodded, swirling his finger in the air, motioning me to turn around.

Carefully I spun on the spot, twisting in the barricade of his arms. A piece of wood had a natural knot, which had fallen away, leaving an eye-shaped spy hole.

"See if you remember," Arthur murmured, his breath tickling the back of my neck.

I shuddered, completely unable to concentrate. "Stop that."

He chuckled.

The heat from his body warmed me as I closed one eye and peered through the wood.

Another compound.

This one was large, more village style than the large abode of one-story living and location of Pure Corruption. It had a massive Clubhouse in the center that looked like the congregation area and town hall. Surrounding the large building were smaller ones, all nondescript but well maintained, with motorcycles resting in front of gates and in carports.

I looked further, drinking in the lifestyle below. Children's toys were strewn on yards, cars glinted in the dying sun, and more houses existed in the distance.

What is this place?

An emblem of a bloody dagger disemboweling a rose glowed in neon on the Clubhouse.

Rose...

"Thorn, take Cleo across to Diane, would you? I have to get this done for Rubix by tonight."

My father scooped me up from the porch, where I was playing with LEGOs. "Come along, Buttercup. Time to go and bug some other family."

I stared harder, willing more memories to come. The longer I looked, the more frustrated I became. I knew I knew this place, but the damn wall refused to let me see.

Arthur pressed against me. "Recognize it?" he breathed.

I shivered as his breath skated down my neck again, making me not care in the slightest about the view in front but only the man behind. "Not really. I know I should, but it's not coming."

"What's the club's name?"

I stared at the rose and dagger and went for the obvious. "Rose and Dagger?"

He twitched behind me. "Close. Dagger Rose. They're a fifty-member-strong MC. Bigger than Pure by over half. They have Chapters all around USA, but this is the main HQ."

As I kept spying, I noticed children playing in a sandpit in one of the yards and two women taking in washing from the line. Men lazed around in the typical biker attire while others did gardening chores half-naked and content in the late-afternoon sun.

It looked normal and safe.

"Hey, little Cleo."

I looked up at the man who'd been there since I was born. He always had something sweet in his leather jacket and he hung out with my dad all the time.

"Hey."

"Where's Thorn?"

I cocked my head at the Clubhouse. "With Mom. They heard of a raid. I think they're shredding a few things."

The guy scowled, darkness flickering in his eyes before disappearing just as quickly. Reaching into his pocket, he threw a small packet of licorice allsorts at me. "Thanks, princess."

I jerked back from the fence, breathing hard.

Burn, baby girl. Burn.

Him.

The match.

The fire.

The melting house all around me.

It was all because of him.

"What did you remember?" Arthur spun me around, clutching my shuddering frame. "Hey, it's okay. I've got you. No one will touch you."

That's what I thought. I thought I was safe. I was supposed to be untouchable.

Burrowing into his jacket, I inhaled his winds and salty scent. "I'm all right. Just give me a second."

Arthur stroked my hair. "You saw him. Didn't you?"

I froze.

"Fuck, you remembered." His voice turned hard and almost evil. "That fucking bastard. That lowlife fucking piece of shit."

I squirmed in his fierce embrace, looking into his eyes. "Who? What is this place?"

He paused, his body tight with anger. "I thought you just remembered?"

I bit my lip, the heavy wall inside my mind slamming resolutely closed. There was no point prying. It was locked and impenetrable. "It doesn't work like that. I remember snippets. Things come in a flash and then fade. I still don't have enough to piece together the full story."

Sighing, I asked, "I should know that place, though, shouldn't I?"

Arthur pinched the brow of his nose, striding away with frustration. "You should, yes."

"Why?"

Standing still, he dropped his hand. "Because you were born there. You were raised there. Me, too. Our entire lives, until you turned fourteen, were spent happy—down there." His tone wasn't that of a man speaking fondly of his childhood, but a prisoner who'd miraculously escaped and wanted to slaughter the men who held him captive.

My mind slithered like a hibernating snake, hissing its way to truth, strangling all other thoughts in its way. “What happened after my fourteenth birthday?” I murmured.

Arthur went ramrod straight. “You mean…you don’t remember that either?”

Horror crept over his features.

My heart seized. “Arthur…I’m asking you…what happened that night?”

He backed away from me, his hands diving into his hair. “Don’t ask me that, Cleo. You can’t ask me that.” His face turned white.

“Art, you can tell me. I need to know. It all hinges on that one night. The fire. The blood. I remember escaping, but I don’t remember how it started or why.”

Arthur shook his head, pacing like a caged animal. “I—that night.” He looked up, tortured. “I—I can’t—shit!”

I moved forward, reaching for him.

He dodged my touch, striding toward the bike. “Come. We can’t stay here. They’ll see us. I mean to start a fucking war, but on my terms, not theirs.”

War.

This means war.

He’d said something similar in the Clubhouse.

“Why? What are you keeping from me!”

Arthur spun around, grabbed my wrist, and yanked me in the direction of the bike. “I’m not going to tell you until I know what you know. I don’t want to risk putting memories in your head.”

Lies.

He’s keeping something from me.

My stomach dropped to think that the one man who I loved—the one man who was supposed to be on my side—had a hidden agenda. I was still that pawn, being shoved around an unseen chessboard.

“It will only be worse if I find out what you’re hiding and you don’t tell me," I whispered, following in his footsteps as we stomped through the forest.

He didn't reply.

He didn't need to. He knew he was in the wrong. And he was both petrified and eager for me to remember.

War was coming.

War was imminent.

It would happen between Pure Corruption and Dagger Rose.

And it would happen because of me.

Chapter Twenty

So much she didn't know.

So much I couldn't tell her.

Death on the horizon. War in the air.

I couldn't share what I meant to do until she remembered on her own. Only then could I show her why I had to murder the people closest to me. Only then would she understand.

—*Kill*

We hadn't talked.

Not one word since Arthur dragged me away from Dagger Rose and threw me on the back of his bike. The roar of the engine nullified the awkward silence between us, but only until we arrived beside Mo and Grasshopper's Triumphs at the yellow-and-white diner.

Arthur didn't make eye contact as he took my helmet and opened the door for me. Striding inside, he shrugged his jacket off, slinging it over my shoulders in a possessive alpha gesture.

I blinked.

Why the hell had he done that? Staking a claim?

The restaurant was busy with families, a few biker members with patches I didn't recognize, and solo motorists.

Mo looked up. His dirty-blond hair caught the last rays of sunshine glinting through the glass. Waving, he motioned us over to the booth.

Grabbing my hand, Arthur guided me through the diner before sliding in beside Mo.

"Sit beside me, Sarah, Cleo, whoever you are." Grasshopper waggled his eyebrows, stroking the yellow vinyl beside him.

I flashed a smile, perching beside him. "Thanks."

"No worries." Pouring a glass of water from the jug on the table, he slid it to me. "Saw the old place, huh? Home sweet home, right?" He laughed as if he'd made the best joke in the world.

Something ached inside me.

I craved answers—to know the history of Dagger Rose, to remember the large compound. Why had something so fundamental as the location of my childhood disappeared?

Something happened down there. Something so traumatic, your brain protected you.

Some protection if it now ruined my future.

I narrowed my gaze at Arthur across the table. "It was interesting," I said. Arthur refused to make eye contact.

Dammit, what was he hiding? And why was he absolutely terrified of telling me? The scent of him clouded my nose from his jacket. Was that why he made me wear it? To remind me that no matter what happened, I was under his protection? His love?

"Interesting?" Grasshopper laughed. "I'd say it was a lot more than that."

Arthur's head snapped up, glaring at Grasshopper. "Enough." Grabbing the jug of water, he poured himself a glass and threw it back. Slamming the empty on the table, he added, "He wasn't there. Not that I could see."

Who wasn't where?

My eyes flew between the men.

Mo said, "Maybe he was off the compound?"

"Maybe." Arthur raised a finger, signaling the waitress. "But I don't like the fact that the motherfucker wasn't there. If I'd had a clean shot, I could've taken him out and handicapped them before..." His eyes fell on me, lips zipping tight.

"You've had a shitload of times you could've taken him out. That wasn't how you wanted it to go down, dude." Grasshopper glanced my way. "Cleo... maybe you shouldn't—"

"What, be here? Listen to whatever you guys are planning?" I balled my hands in my lap. "No way are you keeping me in the dark anymore. Any of you." My eyes bored into Arthur's, transmitting just how close I was to losing it and screaming for truth. "Tell me. I want to hear all of it."

Grasshopper flicked a glance at Arthur, but not before I saw the look of nervousness in his gaze.

"Stop doing that," I snapped.

"Stop what?" Grasshopper blinked guiltily.

Ugh!

"You know what. All of you do." Glaring at the men, I added, "I've remembered enough to know that Arthur and I have history. I've come from the same place he has. We grew up together. Whatever you're hiding from the past affects me, too. I deserve to know what it is."

Arthur suddenly took my hand, squeezing it in full view of his brothers. "Don't be so keen to learn horrible things, Buttercup."

"Don't 'Buttercup' me. I want the truth, Art. And I want it now." When he didn't move, I lowered my voice to a plea. "Tell me everything—including why you want to start a war. What did they do to deserve it?"

Arthur's jacket made my skin prick with heat.

All three men laughed in perfect dark sync. "What didn't they do," Grasshopper said. "Seriously, if you remembered half the shit that went down, you'd be the one with the fucking gun."

I willed another flashback to come. To remember that place—to recall which house had been ours, what it looked like inside.

Nothing.

No voices, no smells, not even sensations of knowing something. It was a big black secretive void.

My eyes flared wide as a horrible thought came to mind. "If I was born there... Are my parents still there?"

The men looked anywhere but at me. Arthur glanced out the window, the same tortured terror hiding unsuccessfully in his gaze.

My stomach sank into my toes.

No, it can't be.

No matter how I avoided the answer hiding inside my head, it only grew stronger and stronger.

They're dead.

No!

I gritted my teeth, hexing any flashbacks that might choose to come and show me the horrible truth. The last time I'd seen them... they'd been alive. Hadn't they?

Hadn't they?

Arthur's green gaze glowed with love and sympathy, sending percolating fear down my back.

A waitress appeared. "Hi, all. Here are your menus. Can I interest you in the specials?"

Everyone froze, almost as if we were guilty of talking about things that should never be discussed in public.

Arthur withdrew into himself.

I *hated* her interruption.

Another moment—that was all I needed. One moment to turn the tension into a knife and slice through the lies. Arthur would've told me.

I need to know about my parents!

"No specials and no menus," Grasshopper said. "Just bring us all a round of burgers and fries."

The cavern between Arthur and I yawned wider with every passing second. Our eyes locked, never once looking away.

A tear trickled silently down my cheek as my heart broke. I didn't need words to know. His gaze spoke too loudly to be ignored.

They're dead.

It's true.

The blonde waitress nodded, her pen scratching over a notepad. "Coming right up. Burgers all around."

The thought of food repulsed me.

How could I eat when I'd just found out I was an orphan?

Arthur growled, "We're on a deadline. Speed is paramount."

The waitress nodded again. "Sure thing, dear." Tucking the unread menus under her arm, she bustled away in her white-and-yellow uniform.

"'Dear'? Don't think you've been called that before," Grasshopper said, trying to lighten the mood. Problem was the atmosphere would never lighten until the lies were aired—permitted to rain from a cloud of history and revenge.

"Art...how could you keep that from me?" I whispered, cutting straight to the crux of my pain.

"Aw, shit," Mo muttered, scooting closer to the wall and avoiding Arthur's seething bulk.

Arthur tensed. "I would've told you tonight. When we were alone and I knew how much you remembered."

"Why do you have to know what I remember? What's locked inside my head that you're so afraid of?"

He dropped his eyes to the table.

He's still *keeping something from me!*

My temper snapped. Rage hijacked my muscles until I trembled with a potent mix of grief and ferocity. "Now. Tell me everything. Now!" Running hands through my red hair, I hissed, "Everything, Art. I won't ask again."

Silence reigned for one second. I tore at his jacket, wishing I could take it off. I felt as if he consumed me—keeping me from dissolving into madness.

That's why he gave it to me. To remind me that whatever happened in the past, good or bad, he wasn't letting me go.

Anger replaced his anxiousness. "*Fine.* You want the truth? I'll give you the fucking truth."

"Oh, boy. Here we go," Grasshopper muttered.

Arthur threw him a vicious look.

"Your parents are dead. The house fire you were in was lit to cover up their bodies and destroy evidence." Breathing hard, he dragged both hands through his long hair. "They were shot to take over the Club."

Knowing it was real and hearing it were two totally different things. My mind rebelled against the truth. I couldn't stop shaking. "Who—who shot them?"

For a second everything paused, the world ceased to spin, and even the dust motes in the air refused to move. Arthur battled with the answer, his face contorting then smoothing into acceptance. He had to tell the truth—as much as it hurt.

"Your family home was burned by Scott 'Rubix' Killian."

Green eyes.

Licorice allsorts.

My unrelated uncle.

Arthur's... "Your father killed my parents and tried to murder me?" My voice barely carried across the table. My heart ached and I rubbed my chest, trying to ease the jagged agony. "But why? I remember him always being there. They were best friends."

Grasshopper inched closer, granting me comfort but not touching.

Arthur bowed his head. "He wanted what your father had. He wanted it all."

"Who are you, Daddy?" I asked, tracing the embroidery on his black leather jacket. The words of his rank were in a font I couldn't quite make out.

He plucked me from the carpet, cuddling me close. "I'm the head honcho, Buttercup. The law."

"You're the boss?" I crinkled my nose. "You're not the boss of me."

He laughed as I squirmed out of his hold and ran to hide behind the couch. Stalking me with his hands up ready to tickle, he said, "I'm the president and definitely the boss of you."

I squealed, my seven-year-old legs not fast enough to outrun him and his tickling hands.

"What does that make me, then? If you're the president, does that

mean I'm the princess?" I couldn't believe my luck. I was Princess Buttercup, just like my favorite movie.

He smiled, smoothing my tangled hair. "I suppose you are in a way. My own little princess."

"He killed them for nothing." I curled in on myself, hugging my rib cage.

Arthur's voice was strained. "I'm so sorry, Cleo. Believe me, the fucking bastard will pay. I can't change the blood flowing in my veins, but I can make it up to you by putting him in the ground."

I shook my head. Death for death wasn't justice, it was just a tragedy. But at the same time, I couldn't stomach the thought of him living and ruling a Club he'd taken by evil—a Club belonging to my father.

I can't live in a world where my attempted murderer prospers.

My soul wept. "Why me? Did he try to kill me because we were together? Because he knew how we felt about each other?"

Arthur's eyes darkened, his hands curling tight. "No. He never planned to kill you. You were at the wrong place at the wrong time." He looked away, his jaw clenched so hard he couldn't say any more.

Grasshopper jumped in. "He wanted you alive."

My eyes shot to his blue ones, begging for the riddle to end. "Why?"

Arthur finally got his rage under control, whispering harshly, "He knew what we were going to ask him that night. He knew how much I fucking loved you. But the bastard had other plans."

I didn't think it would be possible for my stomach to fall any further, but somehow it slipped through the floor and plummeted down and *down*. "What plans, Art?" I breathed, every muscle seizing against his answer.

"Sell you," Grasshopper said. "What better way to formulate loyal Chapters than selling off the daughter of the president he just killed? He planned on using you to unite another large Club out in San Diego. You were to be used like—"

"Like a pawn." Now I saw the chessboard. Now I understood the players if not the rules. My eyes met Arthur's. "He was never going to let us be together."

Arthur shook his head sadly. "I only found out a few years later that he left you inside the house to terrify you. He planned on coming to your rescue, making you believe he tried to save your parents—just like he saved you. He planned on using your gratefulness as a weapon and bribe you into paying back the debt of his kindness."

Oh God. I had evaded not only a horrible death but a horrible existence, too. "But I escaped," I whispered.

Arthur hung his head, his face white. "I still don't know how he missed you getting away, or if someone found you and took you—"

"They didn't." I sucked in a breath. "I crawled on my own. I remember. I managed to get to the road, where someone found me and took me to the hospital."

His face twisted in brutal pain. "You do remember? God, Cleo. I never wanted you to remember that fucking night. The agony you must've been in."

I shrugged, looking down at the table. "At least I know how I got away and before he found me." I'd been destined for a fate worse than the one Arthur almost sold me into.

The irony and parallel between father and son didn't escape me. Arthur was now president—just like his father. He'd been about to sell me—just like his father.

It doesn't make sense—even more so now that I know the truth.

Sitting straight, I said, "Those girls, Art. How could you sell them when you knew what he planned to do to me? You made other girls suffer. What if that had been me? What if—"

"I would've found you and saved you. Fuck, Cleo, I would've come for you and slaughtered everyone in my path."

I shook my head. "You couldn't. You were in jail—remember? I would've been swallowed by a world that takes no prisoners. Even if you did find me once you were free, I wouldn't have been the same person I was—the same girl you fell in love with."

"You disappeared for eight years, yet you're still mine. Still the redheaded girl who stole my heart." His eyes were broken—a faded muddy green.

I smiled weakly. "Living a life where I was happy, if not lost, isn't the same as being someone's slave." Sighing heavily, I said, "You have to find them. You have to save those women you sold."

Grasshopper laughed coldly. "Do you honestly think Kill would sell innocent women into a life of horror?"

My head snapped up.

Mo said, "Those women were handpicked. Not for their looks—although they were pretty hot—but for who they associated with."

My skin broke out in goose bumps.

"They were his whores, Cleo," Arthur whispered. "We took any girl who'd slept with him since my mother died a year ago."

Diane.

The softly spoken woman with dark hair so much like her son's. The scents of fresh baking would drift across the courtyard, tantalizing my taste buds and making me skip across to Art's house and plonk myself in her kitchen with my legs dangling behind the breakfast bar.

My hand slapped over my mouth in despair. "Art, I'm so sorry."

I wanted to ask how she died but Arthur struggled to remain collected. His frayed self-control was near breaking point. He didn't move or show any sign of pain, bottling it deep, where it festered just like the pain he'd felt for me. But I knew.

"We took his whores to teach him a lesson. When he finds out those same whores are now servicing other presidents of rival Clubs, he'll bring a war down on his own head."

Since when did having bad taste in lovers become a crime payable by sexual slavery?

My spine bristled with unfairness. I couldn't keep the disapproval or disgust from my voice. "And me? What stock were you trying to buy? Why was it so important?"

Arthur sighed. "That's tied up in the part that's too involved to discuss in a diner—especially with other factions in hearing distance."

I opened my mouth to argue. I wanted to know everything. Immediately.

Grasshopper put his hand on my arm, hushing my protest. "Let it rest, Cleo-Sarah. Kill's a good man who fucking adores you. He'll tell you everything." His blue eyes landed on his Prez; ice melted down my spine at the secrets passing between the two. "You'll get your revenge, dude. Your happily ever after will be complete and those who wronged you will rot in the ground."

The sentence throbbed with righteousness. Undercurrents of promises and plans I wasn't privy to thickened the air.

No one said a word.

"He'll tell you everything," Grasshopper finally repeated, glaring at Arthur. "Won't you?"

Slowly and reluctantly, Arthur nodded. "I'll tell you everything, Cleo. And I'll hope to God you'll understand."

It wasn't until afterward—after a greasy dinner of cheeseburgers and sodas—that I realized two things were missing.

My world had broadened, my horizons vast and beckoning as memories returned and secrets were revealed, but it was the answers *not* spoken that kept fear alive in my heart.

Answers that could liquidate my entire world.

The heavy warmth of Arthur's jacket kept my body from plummeting into arctic chills as shock tried to take hold, but my determination only grew stronger.

I have to uncover what he's hiding.

Tonight had swept my past upside down and twisted it inside out.

But I *still* didn't know why or how I'd been kidnapped. I'd been barefoot and blindfolded—just like the other women. I'd been burned by Lighter Boy. *How?*

My fingers involuntarily went to the singe on my forearm. It was such an odd feeling. To remember parts—to feel whole after mimicking a sieve with missing pieces for so long.

It was a tease to remember certain things and not others.

It wasn't fair.

I wanted everything.

I wanted to gaze upon the full story that was my past and present.

However, that question paled in comparison to the one echoing around my head. The one I couldn't avoid.

The one that would shed light on the horrible despicable truth.

A man who practically raised me killed my parents out of greed. He destroyed my future, turned his back on loyalty—and for what?

For a Club that meant nothing without friends to love.

No one shared my blood. My bloodline and lineage were over.

I was the last Price to ever hold the surname.

But through all the horrible revelations, one stood out that had been brushed under the rug and kept locked deep in the unmentionable cellar.

Where had Arthur been that night?

And why hadn't he been the one to save me?

Chapter Twenty-One

I'd been so afraid love would soften me. That it would halt my thirst for revenge and drive me from my coldhearted determination to make them pay.

But it didn't.

If anything, love made my determination even stronger.

I throbbed with the urge to decimate those who had done what they did.

I wanted to avenge not only myself, but Cleo, too.

It would be my gift to her.

A gift of closure from our terrible past.

—*Kill*

"Want to know my ultimate wish?" Grasshopper asked as we stepped from the diner.

The moon climbed up the sky, taking the stage now that the sun had descended. It hung like a huge silver dollar, casting everything in a metallic hue.

My arms stayed crossed around my stomach; I was cold despite the heat from Arthur's jacket.

Arthur rolled his eyes. "With your dirty mind, I can guess."

Mo laughed softly. "I'd say your wish was for a woman with skills who could give you a blow job while riding."

Grasshopper punched him in the arm, smirking. "I wouldn't say no to that shit, but that isn't it." His smirk turned into a smile as he pointed between Arthur and me. "I want that."

A meter existed between us—a boundary that Arthur and I hadn't found the nerve to cross. I wanted him to touch me, but at the same time didn't. I wanted him to whisper in my ear and tell me it would all work out, but at the same time wanted nothing from him.

His father killed my parents.

My mind had a lot to unscramble before I would be able to sleep tonight.

"Want what?" Arthur asked, his forehead furrowed.

"What you guys have."

Arthur chuckled, it sounded layered with pain and anguish. "You want a dysfunctional relationship that has more fucking issues than a TV soap?"

Okay, that kind of hurt. I knew we had things to work through, but we weren't dysfunctional. Were we?

Arthur caught my eye, looking pleadingly into mine. His body swayed subconsciously toward me, even now unable to ignore the pull between us.

"No." Grasshopper grinned, his dimple flashing. "I want what you guys have. To have a connection that never fades—even after so many years apart. I want honesty and the knowledge that I'm not alone in the world."

My knees wobbled. Such a simple sentence but it shot me in the heart and made my anger dissolve. All the pain, confused thoughts, and misery I'd felt in the diner fizzled in my blood until they completely dispersed.

Life was too short to let the past dictate our future. Especially a future that was almost robbed from us.

Arthur sucked in a breath and closed the distance between us. I melted into him as his arm wrapped around my shoulders, holding me tight. His lips pressed against the top of my head in the sweetest of kisses. "I'm sorry, Cleo. This wasn't how I wanted to tell you."

Unlocking my arms, I hugged him back, not caring that two bikers stared uncomfortably. "I'm sorry for not dealing better with it."

Arthur made a strangling sound. "You dealt with it better than I would have. The diner is still standing and the police haven't been called. I'd say that's a success."

I laughed gently. "Suppose so."

"See... that's what I'm talking about," Grasshopper said, his posture hungry for his perfect other.

Trying to keep my head straight and not be consumed by the rapidly building need between Art and me, I asked, "Do you have someone?"

Grasshopper chuckled. "You kidding? The only women I meet are the ones after me 'cause they think I'm a rule breaker or they're looking for a cushy retirement fund."

Mo sniffed. "Kill's a kick-ass Prez, but by getting us on the right side of the law and cleaning out the Club, he's fucked us."

"What the fuck?" Arthur growled.

My eyebrows rose. "Oh?"

Grasshopper laughed. "Smug bastard over there with his genius brain for numbers went and made us goddamn rich, didn't he? Not only do we now appeal to the women who want to get off on a scary biker who says fuck you to the law—not the case now but back in the day, hell yeah—but we also have to fend off the Barbie-doll princesses who've been groomed by aspiring parents for a man with money."

I shook my head, marveling at how such a conversation could take place after something so serious. "And they don't care that you're in a Club or prefer a bike over an Aston Martin?"

Grasshopper smirked. "Hell nah. It only sweetens the package. Millionaire biker on the right side of the law with the protection of a brotherhood who would do anything to shelter their own? Who doesn't want that shit?"

Mo rolled his eyes. "I'm not getting myself an old lady." Pointing a finger at himself, he added, "Lone wolf."

Arthur chuckled, holding me closer. "Well, Lone Wolf, I apologize for making you guys so damn desirable. Now fuck off. I want to ride home alone with my girl."

Grasshopper looked down the road, his face tightening. All signs of joking and banter disappeared. "You sure that's a good idea, dude? We're in their territory, after all."

Arthur's muscles bunched, sending shock waves into mine. My fingers ached to slide down his front to his cock. The sparking interest in my core promised he felt it—felt the twitching need to connect after talking about things that had the potential to tear us apart.

I needed him inside me. I needed him now.

"We're good. We're stopping on the way. But it will be in our borders." He looked at me, promises of what we would do once alone glowing in his gaze.

A warm tingle started in my heart and radiated in my belly. He did feel it.

Grasshopper came forward and slapped Arthur on the back. "All right, Kill. We'll see you back at base." Blowing me a kiss, he said, "It's kick-ass that you're part of us now, Cleo-Sarah." He frowned. "However, might have to call you CS for short.

"See ya on the flip side." Waving, he and Mo headed to their bikes, yanked their helmets on, and took off with a roar into the night.

The second they left the parking lot, the awareness between Arthur and I sprang to a fever.

I ached. I melted.

We didn't move—almost as if we had an unspoken agreement to wait. To make sure they were gone before we gave into the overwhelming pull.

Five.

Four.

Three.

The thunder of their engines faded.

Two.

One.

Arthur moved, backing me quickly and firmly up against the wall of the diner. My back collided with bricks and my lungs practically collapsed with the fierceness of his actions.

I didn't have time to protest as his lips stole mine, hot and wet and possessive.

I moaned as his hand came up, capturing my breast. His touch bordered on painful but it only fired me more.

Kissing him back, I sucked his tongue into my mouth, arching my hips into his. The groan in his chest sent love blazing through me, incinerating my heart.

Our heads danced as we both fought for control; our breathing turned ragged as the kiss deepened. In a second we evolved from kissing to dry-humping against the painted brick wall.

"Wait—Art," I panted into his mouth as his hand dropped to cup my core. All thoughts were inconsequential as his fingers pressed intoxicatingly against my clit. "Wait!"

He suddenly let me go, backing up and dragging hands over his face. His wet lips glistened in the moonlight as they spread into a crooked grin. "Fuck, I want you so much I could take you right here—damn anyone watching."

My chest rose and fell as lust spiraled in my system, burning my morals to dust. "Let's go. The sooner we're out of here the sooner we can be alone."

The desperate look in his eyes almost made me come.

Holding out his hand, he ordered, "Let's go, then. Before we're arrested for public indecency."

We hadn't gone far—maybe half an hour—when Arthur eased on the throttle of his fierce two-wheeled monster.

The township where Dagger Rose ruled had long since disappeared as we turned off the main road and followed a rabbit warren of lanes.

The bumps and dips didn't help my sore ass, and my spine screamed by the time Arthur killed the engine.

We stopped at the beginning of a track, sand covered almost everything, and there wasn't another soul around.

Thank God it was a full moon tonight, otherwise we would never have been able to see in the darkness.

Arthur climbed off, stretching.

"Where are we?" I asked, ruffling my hair.

Grabbing my waist, he pulled me effortlessly from the bike, pressing my body against this as he let me slink down his front to my feet. "Not telling," he murmured as his fingers kissed my throat, undoing my helmet before letting it drop to the sand-covered grass below.

His eyes were green beacons in the ghostly silver night and the silhouettes of trees protected us rather than haunted.

"You tell me where we are, Cleo." He ducked, nuzzling his nose behind my ear. "Tell me what I did to you here."

My core clenched as the need that had consumed us at the diner came back with vengeance.

"I—"

With a soft smile, he pulled away. With our fingers linked, he guided me forward. He didn't say a word as we made our way down an overgrown track, our shoes sinking deeper into sand the farther we walked. The balmy evening hummed with insects and the occasional slap of water.

The tide?

I narrowed my eyes, willing any memory to come as we moved into wilderness.

"Tell me," he whispered. "Don't say you've forgotten. Don't break my heart that way." His lips tilted into a lopsided grin.

Even though he meant it as a joke, it still hurt to think how hard all of this would be for him. If I was in his shoes I would be a mess thinking of all the special times we'd had together being lost. For them to mean so little they'd been forgotten.

"I would never intentionally hurt you, Art." I squeezed his fingers. "You know that, right?"

He looked away, but not before I caught the same guilt and misery that he'd worn before believing me.

"I know there's more you're not telling me. You don't have to be afraid."

He swallowed hard. "Don't push me, Cleo. Time, remember? I still need time to get used to all of this." Yanking me to a stop, he cupped my cheek. "To get used to having you back—despite everything that happened to ruin us. Let's just enjoy this." He kissed me feather-soft. "Please?"

I sighed against his mouth. "Okay." Trying my best to lighten the mood, I whispered, "So what exactly did you do to me here?"

I shuddered as he wrapped an arm around my hips, pressing me firmly against his erection. "I finally gave in to you. I broke a few laws bringing you here." He laughed at a memory still lost to me. "Goddammit, you were so young. Too young. But we both knew what we wanted. You—fuck... you never took no for an answer."

His voice dropped to a teasing murmur. "You want to know what you did to me in return that night?"

"Yes." My heart bucked as moisture built between my legs. "What did I do?"

His eyes glazed over with reminiscent lust. "You made me come. For the first time, but definitely not the last."

My heart squeezed.

Letting me go, Arthur stole my hand again, drifting forward to wherever he wanted to take me. I would follow him anywhere. My mind was consumed with images of making out with my green-eyed lover, thrilling with accomplishment at making him come undone in my hands.

Arthur whispered, "You were so wet. So fucking sweet and responsive."

My mouth went dry as my core turned deliciously damp.

"I didn't mean to go so far. I didn't mean to lose control. But you made it so damn hard to say no."

The undergrowth suddenly gave way to the most perfect white private beach. The water glittered like gemstones—sapphires, turquoise, and lapis beneath the moonlight. The tree fronds acted as sentries keeping us safe from prying eyes, while the sand was white and virgin as freshly dusted snow.

The present fell away, giving way to the past.

"You can touch me, Art. I want you to touch me."

I didn't know what'd gotten into me but the mere thought of having his fingers on me, in me—it drove me a little mad. My mother had had the sex talk with me when I started my period two years ago. She'd told me the mechanics of lovemaking—of how babies were made and how sexually transmitted infections could tear my life apart.

But she hadn't mentioned the coiling, twisting anticipation or the sparkling awareness I suffered whenever Art was close.

Everything she'd said had fascinated and terrified me, and I made a vow to never get involved with the opposite sex until I understood every complication.

But now?

Here.

With only the boy I adored and no one to tell us to stop—I couldn't give a damn about the consequences.

My lips burned for his; I wanted nothing more than to spread my legs and let him see.

See me.

See what he did to me.

See just how much I wanted him to touch me, stroke me, claim me.

Just the thought of having his eyes on that part of my body drove tingles and throbs through my belly.

Arthur shifted closer, his dark hair mingling with my red curls on the sand. The icing-sugar granules were cool on my back and soft—so soft.

I'd deliberately worn a skirt, and with my heart rehomed permanently in my lungs, I grabbed his wrist and guided his hand over my thigh and beneath the daisy-print material.

His face tightened, eyes burning feverously.

A moan fell from my lips as every emotion and hyperaware sensation of that night exploded inside me.

I launched myself at Arthur.

With a grunt, he caught me, his mouth opened in shock as my hands sank into his hair, tilting his head to the perfect angle. I stole his protests—not that he was protesting—and kissed him hard.

I wasn't aware of us moving or falling to the sand below. All I focused on was his delicious taste, intoxicating smell, and the slipperiness of his tongue as he kissed me furiously back.

"Cleo... wait."

My teeth ground in frustration; my knees trembled as he tried to tug his wrist away.

"I can't. You're too—"

"If you say I'm too young one more time, Arthur Killian, I'll punch you."

He laughed, his arm relaxing enough for me to drag his fingers closer to where I wanted him.

"You were so hesitant about touching me. So afraid," I panted between kisses.

"You were so damn forward," he groaned as my fingers gripped around his cock. His loud groan echoed over the beach. I stroked him through his jeans, needing skin, needing nothing between us.

Our lips never unfused as we kissed and fumbled and rolled around in the sand.

One moment I was on top, tugging at his buckle and zipper.

The next he was on top, undoing my jeans and wrenching them down my legs.

Then we were side by side, kissing breathlessly, legs twining together, hips pulsing—bodies possessed with consuming one another.

Underwear was our nemesis. We couldn't strip fast enough.

Sand got everywhere, but we were both past caring.

"Touch me, Art. Just once. Then I'll stop hounding you." I nipped at his bottom lip as his head flopped forward in defeat.

"Just once?"

I'd won. Happiness and a small douse of nervousness fluttered in my heart. "Just once."

I froze as his hand moved upward of its own accord. I breathed hard and harsh then cried out as he finally, finally *touched me where I'd been burning for months.*

"Shit, Cleo. Where the fuck are your panties?"

I snickered, eyes rolling into the back of my head as his fingers traced my wetness. "I don't need them around you. They just get drenched anyway."

"Fuck." His lips found mine and his precious self-control snapped.

I screamed into his mouth as his long, strong finger went where nothing had before. Pressing up inside me, stretching strangely, erotically, and so scrumptiously I would never be the same.

"Art. God, more!"

My back bowed as two fingers entered me, hooking up and stroking my G-spot. He wasn't shy like he'd been that day. He was the one in control and I unraveled under his expert touch.

The past and present flickered fast, merging into one.

My hands felt empty as Art kissed me and continued to ease his finger in and out. It felt incredible but slowly my body became unsatisfied. It wanted more. It wanted to stretch and reach for a goal I had no words for.

I wanted to feel him.

He stiffened as my fingers found the treasure of my quest. His erection burned through his jeans, leaping against the material at the faintest touch.

"Shit, Cleo. Stop." His finger froze inside me.

I moaned in frustration. "I'm not going to stop and neither are you. Stop overthinking this, Art. Age doesn't matter. Family doesn't matter. Rules don't matter. Only you and I matter. And this... It feels right. Better than right. Meant to be."

He lost the ability to retaliate as my hands cupped him harder.

The present dragged me back as Arthur spread my legs, settling his lean hips between them. My fingernails dug into his back as he slid inside me. His mouth held mine captive as he sank deeper and deeper.

The softness of the sand below cushioned every inch, while the hardness of Arthur above pebbled my nipples and scrambled my mind.

"Fuck, I've wanted to sink inside you since that day. I was such an idiot to say no. To put us through that frustration." His lips fought with mine, stealing my reply.

He let his weight smother me. His mouth hot and wet, his hands disappearing into my hair. Fisting the strands, he kept my head back and throat exposed as he thrust.

His head lowered, lips sucking hard on my neck. He grunted with every deep plunge of his cock.

I cried out as my common sense rapidly slipped into lust-hazed bliss.

His touch in my hair bruised, his teeth hurt my tender throat, and his hips drove hard and arrogantly possessive into me, but I wouldn't change a thing.

Not a single thing.

The pleasure was rapturous. A gift only given with full trust, implicit connection, and sexual electricity.

Oh God.

My mind blacked out, consumed by having him in me, above me, around me.

Our bodies couldn't get close enough. His legs tangled with mine. His stomach stuck to mine with every breath.

Kissing.

Devouring.

Fucking.

We spun our own time frame as his hands left my hair and skated down my body. Every inch of me blazed with supernovas and stardust, wanting him to abuse me with love.

He kissed me so deeply, my mind splintered into mirrored fractals granting me a new memory while sending me whirling into another.

I held him.

I held his naked cock in my hand for the very first time. I'd never felt anything like it. Silk but steel. Velvet but rock. Dry but wet at the very tip.

He fascinated me.

He lay on his back, eyes squeezed shut. His chest rose and fell as if he'd run miles.

With my tongue peeking between my lips in concentration, I stroked him.

The reaction was instantaneous.

His torso jerked off the sand and his groan made every inch of me quiver.

I stroked him again and again. Craving the way he came undone before me, giving me complete power over him.

I fell deeper into love, harder into lust. I became obsessed with making him explode.

"I loved making you come that first time," I breathed, tearing my bruised lips from his as Arthur thrust harder.

"I couldn't help it. Fuck, you drove me mad that day. I had the self-control of a saint to stop myself from rolling on top of you and taking your virginity right there."

I cried out as his hips pulsed, his cock thickening inside me at the thought. "You should've. I wanted you to."

He came.

His head snapped back and a cry tore from his lips. His entire body quaked as I stroked him up and down, up and down.

I'd never seen someone give ultimate control to another but his body surrendered everything to me in that moment—every muscle seizing with bliss, his mind utterly blank from everything but waves of pleasure.

Spurts of white ribboned onto his black T-shirt, arching through the air with every pulse of his hips into my hand.

It both scared and thrilled me. I wanted to do it again and again. To force him to relinquish control to me—to trust me completely.

Arthur dragged me back, his hand clutching my hip as his thrusts lost uniformity, driving relentlessly and punishingly. An orgasm sparked, half from him taking me now and half from us in another time.

Art's fingers felt amazing inside me, but his thumb was the magic.

My pussy rippled around his digits as the first band of whatever teased me responded to his hesitant touch. I cried out as he thrust and rubbed, the combination of the two sensations driving me up, up and up.

"I want you to let go, Cleo. You made me come. I want to do that for you." His lips landed on my cheek, then chin, then throat, spreading fire through my blood.

His finger hooked upward, pressing against a spot inside that wasn't flesh and blood but magic and love-laced.

"Oh God. Art, yes." I wanted to beg him for more, to never stop, but he knew what I wanted.

His wrist jerked up and down as he drove his finger harder and faster into me. My hips bowed up to meet him. I lost all pretense of shyness and demure young woman and gave myself in to the grip of sin.

This was where I belonged. Here. With him.

"I'm—I'm—" I didn't know what I was. Shattering perhaps? Splitting into two as my core tightened and tightened until I thought I'd combust.

"You're coming, Buttercup. Give it to me. Give me your first." Art's lips took mine, his tongue thrusting in time with his finger.

I couldn't hold on any longer and my body demolished beneath his touch, imploding on itself before shooting outward in a billion tiny rays of heaven.

"God, I'm coming..."

I couldn't help it. The memory of that time drove me to the point of detonation.

"Fuck, wait for me. Wait!" Arthur picked up his pace. Our breathing matched—tattered and broken as pleasure became too much for single cells to feel. He was the perfect maestro—giving my body no choice but to reach the pinnacle of release.

His fingers dove into my hair again, his elbows digging into the sand by my ears as he drove himself as deep as possible.

Then he came.

Shuddering and trembling, cursing and panting, he set off my own explosion.

Tiny comets shot from my core and into my heart, and every crash of pleasure gave more of my soul to him. He gave me another piece of himself, too, but stole so much more in return.

Our hearts thrummed to the same beat as we finally calmed and our lovemaking ceased to a gentle rock.

I would always keep what happened here tonight locked away inside—just like that first time. I would hoard it like a priceless gift. Arthur was mine. As much as I was his.

It was fate.

My heart fisted with pain at the thought of never experiencing our first times together. A brown-eyed boy I still couldn't remember had taken mine in awkwardness and dissatisfaction, and Arthur . . . I couldn't think about Arthur giving up something so precious to a whore.

But that was in the past. I never wanted to be with another man. Ever.

Arthur was it for me.

For life.

"Tell me about the tattoo. Apart from the equations and the poems I recognize, I don't understand it."

My eyes opened to find Arthur propped up on an elbow, his silhouette cast in silver by the moon.

We must've drifted for a while because the moon had moved from where it had been while I'd been on my back with him between my thighs.

Arthur's face filled with pain. "You lived an entire life without me. I—I want to know what you did, who you became without me by your side."

Hating myself all over again for the pain I'd caused, I murmured, "There's nothing to tell. It's a mix of everything and nothing."

He frowned. "That doesn't make sense."

"It means nothing compared—"

"It means that—"

We stopped, smiling at each other in silence. We'd always done that—jumping over each other, trying to talk at the same time. Little things like that were starting to come back.

I wanted to squeeze him in joy.

He ducked, pressing a delicate kiss to my temple. "Go on..."

I searched my body for something that made sense. The tattoo was undeniably beautiful and fantastical, but really it hadn't helped link me to a past I couldn't remember.

"I suppose I wanted something pretty to cancel out the ugliness of my scars." I shrugged. "I was told I might never remember. In a way, I hoped the pain would jog something. That each tattoo would somehow magically unlock everything hidden inside. Silly, huh?"

Arthur shook his head. "Not silly at all. I wish it had worked—then you might've come back to me sooner."

My heart squeezed at the thought.

His eyes hooded; a finger traced up the inside of my thigh, whispering over my core. A moan fell from my soul at the barely there graze.

"Tell me about your tattoo," I whispered, fighting the already building need to connect again.

He looked down, bringing his fingers up to my lower belly, following the path of burn marks. "You know what it is—allegiance to my brothers. Before I had the Dagger Rose cut on my back, then, when I inherited the Corrupts, I had the new logo tattooed over it."

Ah, that was why it seemed a little messy. One oath over another. I didn't know it was possible to... swap, as it were.

But that wasn't what I wanted to know.

I leaned up, planting a kiss on his collarbone.

He sucked in a breath as I whispered against his skin, "Not that one. The mermaid."

He relaxed, brushing his nose down my throat. "Do you really need to ask? Red hair, green tail..."

Oh my God.

"It's Ariel from *The Little Mermaid*?"

He reared back, eyes narrowed with annoyance. "No, it's not the fucking little mermaid. It's you, goddammit."

I froze. "Ah, I get it. Red hair"—I grabbed a red curl, flicking it off my shoulder—"and a green tail for green eyes." I batted my eyelashes.

He nodded. "Exactly."

"How old were you when you got it done?"

"Twenty-four. I got it the year I got out."

"And the Libra sign... That was for me, too."

"Everything is always for you, Cleo. I thought you understood that by now."

I reached up and caressed his cheek, running my fingers along his chiseled jaw, drinking in his aquiline nose and perfectly handsome face.

I had no words. None at all.

He rolled on top of me. His biceps tensing as he kept his weight from crushing me. Looking deep into my eyes, he murmured, "I missed you so fucking much."

His mouth joined with mine in the dreamiest of kisses.

Slow and gentle.

Giving and worshipping.

A gentle tide rather than a tsunami.

This kiss was different.

Before they'd been full of violence and dominance. This was sweetness and surrender. A single moment where we weren't man and woman, but two hearts reconnecting beneath the moon as our only witness.

In that bittersweet kiss, I missed the younger him—the boy I never got to see grow up. I missed his smile. His eagerness. His simplicity.

I missed my childhood.

But your future is spread before you. Don't be sad. Don't hold onto things you cannot change.

Embracing wisdom I didn't know I had, I licked his bottom lip. "I love you," I breathed.

He gathered me close, pressing his forehead against mine. "I know. You were born for me, Cleo. My Sagittarius fallen straight from the stars."

Chapter Twenty-Two

The stars had seen fit to reunite us. What did that mean? That we'd paid our dues and finally deserved our happiness? Or perhaps we were just star-crossed lovers being taunted by hope.

Either way, I would fight to keep her.

I would fight to protect my future.

I would take extra pleasure reaping my revenge.

Not only did they have my sins to pay for but also what they'd done to the woman I adored.

I would show them what a monster they'd made when they'd tried to destroy me.

I would show them who would win.

—Kill

My body was boneless as the garage door slid into place, locking out the night sky and trapping us inside Arthur's home.

The journey had been long, and I'd never been more grateful to climb off a bike and know I was only moments away from a hot shower and bed.

Glorious bed.

Arthur captured my face, pulling my helmet off before scooping me up behind my knees and cradling me to his chest.

I didn't mind being picked up—in fact, my wobbly legs were grateful. "Bed, please, kind sir," I said, smiling tiredly.

"Anything for you, my queen." Laughing quietly, he strode toward the connecting door to his home. Somehow he managed to unlock the door, without putting me down. "I'll run you a bath if you want?"

I shook my head. "No, a shower will do. I want to be horizontal as soon as humanly possible."

"I thought you were horizontal only an hour or so ago on the beach." His smirk made me giggle.

"Yes, and I'm the one who had to sit on a hot throbbing machine with stickiness between my legs. *Your* stickiness, I might add."

His face battled with smugness and happiness. "It better be mine, woman."

We laughed together as we moved down the corridor and into the foyer.

Arthur slammed to a halt.

His strong muscles gave out beneath me, plopping me roughly to my feet.

"Oh my God. What happened?!" My eyes popped wide at the mess. It looked as if a hurricane had torn through his home, decimating everything in its path.

Arthur charged into his office. "Fuck!"

I ran after him, hands slamming over my mouth at the broken computer screens, smashed glass from the large equations on the walls, and pockmarked desk. Everything was in tatters.

He shot to the wall behind the only sofa, hurling the couch away with a furious swipe. Dropping to his knees, he pressed a button and a fake wall panel slid up. I stared in amazement as he entered a long code and the safe popped open.

What in the world?

Inching closer, I caught glimpses of cash, manila folders, and a few photographs tucked against the side.

My heart raced to see the photos. Something inside *demanded* to see—they held clues—they held parts of my past that I desperately wanted to recall.

But before I could drift closer, Arthur slammed the safe and relocked it.

"They didn't find what they were looking for, at least," he growled, staring up at me from the floor. His back was bunched, face harsh and layered with darkness from the room. He looked...not so much evil but capable. A man capable of murdering anyone who trespassed on his property or tried to steal what was his.

Looking around at the mess, I asked, "What did they want?"

He climbed to his feet, shaking his head. "I don't know." His voice changed, losing the ease of togetherness, slipping back into the bomb-proof fortress he wore when I first sewed him up.

He knows.

"Don't lie to me, Art."

My heart stuttered at the deception. It hurt. To have him lie blatantly to my face—after everything we'd been through it was like a ten-ton piano crushing my heart while playing a mournful lullaby.

"I'm not lying, Cleo. I have suspicions, but until I talk to Wallstreet I won't know if they're true. I'm not going to give you things to worry about that will only clutter your brain with more nonsense."

I took a step back. "You think my amnesia is nonsense?"

He threw up his hands. "Well, it would save us a lot of fucking time if you could just remember, wouldn't it?!"

I blinked at his sudden temper. Where the hell had that come from? From rage at having strangers violate his home? Or the inability to protect his sanctity?

They weren't strangers.

Whoever had done this knew him. Knew me. Knew what they were looking for—regardless if they found it or not.

Lights suddenly came on, bathing the room in golden warmth. The mess was even more apparent, with strewn paper and a mangled letter opener that'd been used to jack open the locked drawer of his desk.

It's open.

The drawer where he kept the letter or image that he held the night I spied on him.

His vow came back, loud and clear.

"I will have my vengeance. I will find my peace. I will ruin those motherfuckers and hope to God I will be free."

Arthur saw me looking at the drawer. His face hardened as he took a step toward me. "Cleo... don't."

My eyes flashed to him then back to the drawer. I knew I should respect his privacy, but at the same time...

Screw it.

I bolted to the drawer and slid to my knees as I scooped up the jumbled papers below.

"For God's sake!" Arthur stomped closer, towering over me with his hands on his hips. "You're so fucking eager. When will you learn to be patient?"

I didn't look up, too busy rifling through the stack of files with columns and printed digits.

Where is it?

My heart raced to find it. I had a consuming need to *know*.

"Never. I don't want to be in the dark anymore."

Arthur squatted on his haunches, pushing me away a little to press a panel in the bottom of the drawer. He pulled a small note free from the hidey-hole. "Here. Is this what you want?"

I snatched it, letting the other papers cascade down my lap.

I didn't care that I was being rude. I didn't care that I acted a little crazy.

All I wanted to do was read—read something that meant the world to him.

It was a poem.

Kisses on my fingers. Touches full of lingers.
Your heart has stolen mine; two souls beating in time.
Yet you push me away—rejection a cruel slay.

I beg you to kiss me. Take me. Claim me.
Make me yours and put my fears at bay.

I couldn't tear my eyes away.

I'd always loved to write poetry. I wasn't very good, but I found vowels and consonants a lot easier to use than division and multiplication.

Art sat frozen beside me, staring blankly at the piece of paper.

Five long minutes ticked past before his beautiful face tilted to look at mine. "You wrote this?"

I nodded, biting my lip.

He exhaled in a rush, running a hand through his long hair. "What do you want from me, Cleo?" he whispered. "You're too young. I'm not good enough—"

"Don't say that. You are *good enough for me."*

He shook his head sadly. "I'm not. You don't know what I've done. What I'm destined for. Our lives aren't meant to be together."

Terrible fear crushed my heart and I grabbed his hand, pressing it hard against my chest. "Feel that?"

His eyes flared but he nodded. "Your heartbeat? Yeah, I feel it."

"You leave me and that stops."

Temper flashed in his gaze. "I won't let you play silly games with me. You'll survive without me."

My anger met his. "No. You'll see, Art. You'll see that I was right and your heart beats for me. Mine, yours—they chime to the same beat. Wherever we end up in the world, whatever you do or whoever you decide to tie your life to, we'll never be whole unless we're one."

I pressed his fingers harder against my heart. "It's not stupidity or a young crush. It's the truth. You'll die without me. You need me as much as I need you."

The flashback ended; a rogue tear dripped down my nose, staining the lopsided cursive on the note in my hands. "I was so cocky. So sure of us back then," I murmured.

Arthur caught my tear, bringing the captured salt to his mouth and licking it from his fingertip. "You were. The day I was taken to prison I remembered that note. I remembered you saying I would die without you, and I swear on my life I felt I was cursed because in that moment I *did* die. You'd gone. Everything I'd dreamed of—our future, our love, even the quietness we'd find when doing homework together—it was all gone."

He bowed his head. "I was dead, Cleo. That note was the only thing that made me feel alive. But now I don't need it, because you've brought me back to life." His strong fingers spread on my chest, half cupping my breast in ownership while absorbing my heartbeats below. "This is mine. Mine is yours. I get it now."

I shivered in his hold. "Then why are you still keeping things from me?"

His jaw clenched as his green eyes locked me out. "I swear I'll tell you. I've promised countless of times. I just need—"

"More time," I finished for him, hanging my head. Smoothing the tearstained poem, I nodded. "Okay. I'll be patient."

The part of me that had a compulsive need to tend and nurture every creature in pain sought to comfort Art. I didn't want him to suffer anymore. If it meant I had to be patient in order for him to deal with this upheaval, then so be it.

Call it selfless or stupid, I would give him the time he obviously needed.

In a way that makes me stronger than him. So it's my duty to protect him.

Tucking wayward strands behind my ear, he helped me stand. "Thank you. Now let's go to bed. I'll deal with this shit tomorrow." Grabbing my elbow, he guided me toward the door.

I dug my heels into the tiles. "Wait. I could never sleep now. Shouldn't we call the police? Gather evidence—that sort of thing?"

He grinned as if I were a silly child who didn't understand the mechanics of the world. "Police aren't welcome here, Buttercup.

Besides, there won't be any evidence that will make sense to them. I'll get Grasshopper and Mo to have a look—see what they can find. And you *will* sleep, because I'll be beside you keeping you safe."

I huffed, unsuccessfully hiding my frustration.

Art didn't say anything else, just propelled me up the staircase and down the corridor. The bedrooms looked untouched.

Thank God.

I didn't think I could sleep in a room that had been defiled by burglars.

Striding into his room, he let me go to run both hands through his hair. "Shit, I've got sand everywhere." Motioning to the bathroom, he said, "We're having a shower, then bed. I need to rest so I can figure this shit out."

Ripping his T-shirt over his head, he unbuckled his jeans and let them fall to his ankles. With another tug, his boxer-briefs were a puddle on the carpet and he strode toward me completely naked.

Damn him to hell.

My mouth went dry and all annoyance toward him evaporated.

His muscled stomach rose and fell, hypnotizing my eyes with every breath. The etched V of his torso guided my eyes to his thickening cock; wetness rushed between my legs.

I couldn't look away from the mermaid on his thigh, dancing with every movement.

Silently, Arthur grabbed the hem of my yellow T-shirt, tugging it over my head. Biting his bottom lip, which made him so damn sexy, he lowered my zipper and peeled the denim down my legs.

The whisper of his fingers over my skin sent flutters through my core.

Dropping in front of me, he removed my panties, then placed a kiss on the top of my pussy. It wasn't just sexual, it was a worship—an acknowledgment of everything we'd been through and everything still to come.

Suddenly, I couldn't stand it. I couldn't stand the distance or emotional void. Wrapping my arms around his head, I held him against my stomach.

He stiffened, then embraced my hips with a fierceness that almost toppled me over. His touch was painful but needed. It shouted just how much I meant to him.

His breath was hot as he exhaled heavily. "I'm sorry, Cleo."

I couldn't speak; tears tangled my words.

Arthur squeezed me harder, nuzzling against my flat stomach, kissing the burns and shiny scars that licked my midriff. "I'm so fucking sorry." His voice caught, his body shuddering against mine.

I hated that he kept apologizing. None of this was his fault. It didn't make sense for him to carry so much guilt over something he had no control. And to be honest, I hated his apologies. They kept all the wrongs he'd done in the forefront of our minds. I'd already forgiven him.

I want to move forward, not backward.

I wanted to fold to my knees and hug him hard. I wanted to tell him in actions rather than words that his regret and self-hatred weren't needed anymore.

But suddenly it was over.

His arms were gone.

His retreating back was a farewell as he disappeared into the bathroom.

He's still hiding so much. It's killing him inside.

Tentatively, I followed him.

I found him already standing beneath streaming water, his hands splayed on the tiled shower wall, his perfectly formed ass tense and unyielding. The muscles on either side of his spine were locked with emotions he refused to share.

Slinking into the spray, I pressed a kiss against his spine and molded my body against his. He sighed, the tension in his body dissolving droplet by droplet down the drain.

"I love you, Buttercup," he whispered.

My heart thundered.

The first time he'd said it since this mess started unwinding.

It should've been a beginning.

So why does it sound like a good-bye?

"I love you, too, Art. So much."

Silently, he turned in my arms. With green eyes blocking me from seeing his secrets, he reached for the body wash and lathered his hands. With a gentle touch, he cupped my breasts, sliding his soapy, bubbly hands down my stomach, across my hips—one scarred and one inked—and dipping to my ass.

His fingers traced my crack. A smile teased his mouth. "Better make sure there's no sand left in there."

I laughed quietly, allowing him to wash me in his hypnotic, slow way.

He never rushed, never demanded more. The unhurried tenderness turned my bones to molten and my heart wept in gratefulness.

Finally, once I was clean, he let me go. Throwing his head back into the spray, I bent forward and pumped a generous amount of body wash into my palms.

He jolted as I placed them on his strong, broad chest.

His jaw clenched as I returned the honor, sliding my hands beneath his arms, lathering bubbles in the slight happy trail leading to his cock.

I adored him just as he'd done me, never rushing, never demanding.

When I got to his crack, my fingers disappeared between strong muscles, and he froze. His cock jumped hot and hard against my thigh.

"Damn, Cleo. Stop."

I shook my head, pressing my fingers farther. I'd only meant to wash this part of him free from sand, but I was drunk on touching him. Drunk on knowing he was mine. I wanted to touch him where no one else had. I wanted to give him pleasure.

I found his weak spot.

Art, my brawny sexy broody boy, was ticklish.

"Stop that!"

"Never!" I giggled, hooking my fingers behind his knee, where I'd somehow found out he was ticklish.

"Goddammit, Cleo. Stop!"

He jerked away, bumping both of us off the couch and onto the carpet. We rolled together, his long legs bashing into the coffee table.

The smash of a glass sounded over our struggle.

"Uh-oh. Now you've done it," I said, pinning him to the floor and straddling him.

His green eyes glowed, his large hands gripping my twelve-year-old hips. "You're gonna be in serious trouble, Buttercup."

I knew then that he was mine.

I just had to grow some boobs to make him notice me.

"I'm already in serious trouble, Art."

I sighed as the memory ended.

The unlocking of my past was coming faster. More and more flashbacks, which all included him. Each memory was out of sync, the timeline all messed up, the journeys and tribulations hidden until they unlocked, but I loved them all equally.

Sure, I would've preferred them in order, but I liked it like this. A surprise—a treat.

Arthur grabbed my wrist, jerking my fingers free and pinning my hands above my head.

In a wet glide, part from the shower and part from being wet all the time around him, he nudged my knees apart and guided his erection inside me.

The joining made us both groan, our mouths opening wide as rain fell all around us.

I was bruised. I was sore.

Yet I wouldn't trade it for anything.

This wasn't sex—it was an affirmation of everything we'd found and survived.

Arthur thrust possessively, rocking deep and true.

My orgasm arrived soft as a petal and just as delicate. The gentle waves giving me a release without draining my body of its last dregs of energy.

Arthur came three thrusts later, his teeth capturing my throat as he spurted inside.

No words were exchanged as we rinsed off and stepped from the spray.

No words were needed as we dried off and left our damp towels on the floor.

Every step I took toward the bed showed me just how tired I was.

And by the time Arthur pulled back the quilt and beckoned me into its comforting embrace, my muscles decided their time of work was done and they would go no further.

I moaned as my body snuggled into the warm bed.

Arthur climbed in beside me, his bulk granting contented happiness at the thought of sleeping side by side.

I sighed with bone-deep satisfaction as a long arm snaked around my middle, pulling my damp, warm skin against his nakedness.

Locked together like perfect yin and yang, we fell asleep with our heartbeats whirring in sync.

Chapter Twenty-Three

Heaven on earth.

That was where I lived when Cleo looked at me with love.

I didn't care that her memories were gone. We could make new ones. Lots and lots of new ones.

I intended for us to never be apart again.

We would live in our heaven on earth, where no evil was permitted to touch us.

But where there was a heaven, there was a hell.

A hell lurking dark, deep, and disgusting.

A hell waiting to steal our happiness.

And it was coming for us.

—Kill

The letter seemed innocent. A simple yellow lined note handwritten by someone with fastidious penmanship.

If I had known it would end up destroying my carefully constructed world, I might not have opened it. It tore down the falseness I'd surrounded myself with and hurled me into the dark where I remained until he found me.

Dear Ms. Sarah Jones,

You don't know me, but I know you. I've known you since you were a little girl. I held you when you were born and attended your birthday every year. You were like a daughter to me and when you disappeared, my heart broke as surely as any parent's.

But my heart has now healed, because I've found you.

Finally.

After all these years.

I had to stop reading. I needed to sit down. Finally, a clue to the past I could never recall. Who had written to me? How had they found me?

Stumbling from the doorway of my apartment building, I collapsed against the steps. My hands trembled as I smoothed the letter and continued to read.

I don't know what happened to you to leave your family and those who loved you so much. You left behind a world that never healed without you in it. I didn't know if I should find you, contact you, and tell you these things, but questions need to be answered.

Did you hate us that much?

Did you decide we were no longer worthy of being your family?

I have so many more to ask you, as I'm sure you have to ask me.

I want to meet you.

If you want to meet me, and to find out the truth of who you are, come to Florida and check into the Dancing Dolphins in the Keys. Check in under your name, and I'll come for you.

I hope you come, Sarah Jones.

It's time to take your rightful place.

It's time to come home.

The memory hadn't stopped echoing in my mind ever since I woke. A recollection and the piece of the puzzle of how I came to be here. Who had written the note? It'd been unsigned and with no return address. No matter how hard I'd tried, I couldn't recognize the voice of the author.

As Arthur rushed around, calling people to come and investigate the break-in and preparing for a new day, I sat nursing the vital clue.

Bit by bit more truth came to light.

God, it was boring.

And painful and frustrating and frightening—but most of all boring.

I stared blankly at the small TV in the hospital room, not paying attention to the bright colors or noises. My whole attention was turned inward, poking at memories that'd completely disappeared.

No trace of anything.

Not even my name.

"Hello."

I blinked, bringing the newcomer into focus. His plainclothes authority sent my heart fizzing fearfully in my rib cage. "Hello."

"I'm Detective Davidson. I'm with the FBI and I've been to visit you a few times since your accident a few weeks ago. Do you remember me?"

I narrowed my eyes, looking down my bandage-covered body. This was an accident? *What stupidity had I done? Shaking my head free from cotton wool and torturing questions, I looked at Detective Davidson. "No, I don't remember you."*

He smiled softly, the pity in his blue gaze rupturing my strength and causing tears to build. "That's okay. Don't worry about it." Shuffling closer to my bed, he said, "I've been talking to your doctors, and they said you'll be ready to leave soon. They also advised me that you still can't remember your name, family, or where you came from."

I ignored the agony in my chest. I was an orphan—homeless—a stray with no family. That was worse than the constant throb of burns and healing skin grafts. There was nothing to say, so I remained quiet.

"The state has given you the name Sarah Jones until such a time as you remember." Sitting awkwardly by my bed, he patted my knee.

I hissed between my teeth. That was my right knee. My toasted knee.

"Shit, sorry!" He hunched in his chair, keeping his hands to himself.

His fear of a girl wrapped up like an Egyptian mummy made the terribleness of my situation become humorous. I laughed softly. "It's okay." Tilting my head to study him, I asked, "Why are you here? Why is an FBI agent telling me this?"

Detective Davidson swallowed nervously. "I'm no good at delivering news subtly, so I'm just going to come out and say it. We have reason to believe the accident was intentional. Some evidence has come to light that makes us suspect you were the victim of an attempted homicide and until such a time as you remember, to bring whoever did this to justice, we are placing you in protective custody. We aren't going to advertise that you're alive, or ask for people to come forward until we know who to trust."

"You're arresting me?"

A smile twitched his lips, his brown short hair military precise on his head. "No, we're giving you a new life, away from here." Leaning forward, he said, "This is an opportunity to create a life you've always wanted, live in a country you've never visited, all while being watched over by us. As you're under eighteen, you'll be placed with a foster family until you come of legal age, but you can decide where you want to go. We normally give you a plan, a name, and a job to uphold as your new identity, but in this case you can choose."

My lungs worked harder, still aching from smoke inhalation. "What—what are you saying?"

Detective Davidson patted the file on his legs. "This, Sarah Jones, is your new life."

"I don't want a new life. I want my old one."

His shoulders rolled. "The doctors said they'd talked to you. You're suffering what's known as psychogenic amnesia. It's an act of self-preservation."

Tears pressed harder at being held hostage by my own mind. "But I'm ready to remember. I'm strong enough to understand."

Detective Davidson smiled sadly. "The doctors can explain again what it means, but it doesn't work that way. These things are very rare. Your repressed memories may be recovered spontaneously, or decades later. You might smell a particular smell and a memory will come back. Or you might hear a favorite song and everything will unlock. Because it's psychological, psychogenic amnesia can sometimes be helped by therapy. But we need to plan for the worst."

"Which is?" I whispered.

"That you might never remember. Like I said, it's very rare, but a possibility. We have to move forward."

I wanted to scream. And rage. And cry.

Not only was my body damaged but my mind, too.

Clearing his throat, Detective Davidson said, "Without thinking about the answers, tell me... what would be your ultimate profession once you finish school?"

"A vet."

I blinked. That had come from nowhere. I went deathly still, hoping to God that my memory was coming back.

"And where would you live, if you had any choice?"

"England."

My mouth plopped open. Why there? The answer had come to me but no reasoning whatsoever.

Detective Davidson smiled, taking notes in his file. "In that case, Sarah Jones, we will do everything in our power to give you a new life with a family in England, and enroll you in subjects to ensure a career as a veterinary surgeon. It will take some time to iron out the details, but we'll get started on the necessary paperwork."

This was happening too fast. Too sudden.

"Paperwork?"

He grinned, showing crooked teeth. "Yes, a new passport, new social security card—a new beginning." His eyes softened. "You will rise from this and be safe in a completely new world. And then, when you're older and perhaps remember, we'll find justice for what happened to you."

It wasn't until after hundreds of questions—most of which I couldn't answer—that I was finally left alone to go over what had happened.

Whoever I'd been up until that moment was gone.

I was about to be reborn.

I was about to disappear forever.

My knees buckled a little as the memory ended. That had been the day my life as Cleo Price had ended. It'd been the worst feeling imaginable to be a prisoner inside my own mind—to be barricaded from people who could've helped me.

Then there was Corrine.

She wasn't just a friend like I'd thought.

She was my sister.

"Nice to meet you."

I looked up from lugging my bag through the terminal toward the exit. There, in front of me, was a girl with blonde short hair and vibrant blue eyes. She was alive. Where I was dead.

Behind her stood a man and woman, both smiling nervously.

"Do I know you?" The constant fear that I knew people and offended them by not remembering had become the bane of my life. I worried constantly if someone smiled my way or waved in my direction.

Did I know them?

Did I love them once?

"No, you don't. But we know about you. You're coming to live with us." Bouncing in place, she snatched my suitcase and enveloped me in a hug. "I've always wanted a sister. We're going to school together and I want to be a vet, too! How awesome is this?"

My heart died all over again. This was my foster family. An unwanted surrogate to a home I couldn't recall.

When I didn't reply, the father murmured, "Don't be afraid. Detective Davidson has cleared it all. You're already enrolled in the finest school, and we'll take you down to the station to meet your contact early next week."

I never took my eyes off my suitcase. I hated strangers touching it. Inside held nothing I remembered, only brand-new clothes purchased for

Sarah Jones, not whoever I'd been. But it was the only thing I owned. The only thing I had to be protective of.

"I don't need a new family." I needed to be left alone. Alone in the dark so my memories might find me.

Corrine looped her arm through mine. "You're right, you don't need help. 'Cause you've got me." Dragging me unwillingly from the terminal and into watery sunshine, she sighed happily. "Welcome to England, Sarah. I have a feeling we're going to get along stupendously."

She was right.

After the first few weeks of crying myself to sleep and the uncertainty of learning to live again with a blank mind, I slowly found happiness.

I was able to heal while studying biology and English.

I was able to stop obsessing over a past I might never remember and become healthier in heart and mind.

Corrine became my entire world.

My heart panged to think I'd left her behind so easily.

She'd given me back the will to live; she hugged me when I broke and celebrated with me when I excelled. Yet the moment the letter arrived hinting I might *finally*, after all this time, find the truth, I left her without a good-bye.

I ignored the voice that said it was stupid to chase after something that should remain buried.

I hadn't dared tell her why I was going—just in case she told the officers handling my file. I'd left her a cowardly note, given notice at my job at Precious Pets, withdrew my meager savings, and booked a one-way ticket to America.

But of course she'd somehow found out my plan and tracked me down at the airport.

She hadn't tried to stop me, though.

Out of everyone, she understood the most why I had to leave. Why I had to search for the green-eyed boy I'd never gotten over.

I'd jumped headfirst into danger.

"You ready?" Arthur snapped into my musing.

The residual emotions of being so alone and afraid refused to unclaw themselves from my heart. I ached with lonely emptiness that I'd lived with for eight long years. No matter how many new memories I made, no matter how many experiences I lived, I'd never shed the desolation of not having a past.

My stomach rolled at the thought of living a life without him. Eight years had been interminable—forever would've destroyed me.

His eyes blazed into mine, focused on solving the break-in and delivering justice. He was my protector, lover, and best friend. As long as I was with him, everything would work out.

"Yes, I'm ready." Smoothing down my black blouse and skinny dark jeans, I followed him to the garage and his awaiting motorcycle.

I blinked up at Florida Penitentiary for the second time.

Nerves skittered down my spine. "What are we doing back here?"

Arthur grabbed my hand. Striding toward the imposing correctional facility, he replied, "Going to see him."

"Him who?"

"You know who. The man who gave me everything when others took it all away."

My heart skipped a beat at the hatred and guilt in his tone.

I jerked on his hand, pulling him to a stop. "Tell me. Here and now. Tell me what happened to you. Why were you in prison? The truth this time."

I wished I'd had time and access to the Internet. I would've done a search—I would've looked up his criminal record to find out just what he continued to hide.

His brow tightened, shadowing his eyes. The soft pads of his fingertips kissed my cheek as he smiled sadly. "Do you trust me?"

I frowned. "As much as I can while I'm blind from things you won't tell me."

His shoulders sagged. "Do you love me?"

I didn't hesitate. "Absolutely."

"Then let that love be enough for now. Be glad that we've found each other, because there's still so much you don't understand and I don't—I can't ruin it yet."

"Why would it ruin what we have?" I looked deep into his eyes. "Tell me. You're starting to scare me, Art."

Cupping my cheek, he kissed me softly. I would've loved to see the action from an outsider's perspective. A scary-looking biker dressed in boots and leather, kissing a girl half his size outside a prison.

Breaking the kiss, he murmured, "Let's go see Wallstreet. And then... I'll do my best to explain."

Getting through security wasn't fun.

Arthur moved through the metal detectors and body checks easily enough—used to entering on a regular basis.

I didn't enjoy being touched or made to feel like I was a criminal just for visiting one. My name was triple-checked on the approved list of visitors that Art must've called ahead for and the smiles were laced with suspicion. The grudging approval for us to move forward when they found no contraband was almost comical.

"A place like this jades you," Arthur said as we were marched down the cold, nondescript corridor. Windows with mesh and locked doors were the only décor as we moved forward into the bowels of the jail.

A guard noticed Arthur and gave him a salute. "Hey, Kill. You good, bro?"

Arthur grinned, nodding. "As good as could be expected. You?"

"Can't complain. Your buddy's well and prisoners are behaving, so all good in the hood, as it were."

Arthur waved and we kept moving.

We were led into a private room with high windows, rings bolted to the floor for chains and bindings, and a metal table in the center.

The guard who'd been our guide said, "Wait here. He won't be long."

Arthur sat down, slouching in one of the metal chairs as if he was completely at home here. I supposed he was. How many years had they said he'd lived inside these walls?

The urge to know why he'd been locked up ate at my soul. I had to know. It worried me. Worried me because it was somehow intrinsically linked to my past and all the things I was trying to remember.

The clanking heavy door opened again, spewing forth a man in an orange jumpsuit. He looked like a friendly grandfather, with shrewd intelligence but a kindness in his eyes that immediately made me gravitate toward him.

His white hair glistened neatly beneath the fluorescents and his skin glowed a healthy pink.

For a prisoner, he was meticulously clean, with clipped nails, ironed collar, and pristine shoes.

Arthur stood, smiling as the old man glided forward, unbound by shackles to sit primly on the other side of the table.

"Kill, my boy. Lovely to see you." His blue eyes landed on mine. "And who do we have here?"

I froze. Those eyes... Why were they so familiar?

Arthur linked his fingers together on the tabletop, smiling in my direction. Pride and love glowed on his face. "This is Cleo Price."

The room crackled as energy swirled from the old man. "Ah... is it now?" His eyes drifted from the top of my head to my clenched hands before me. "Now I understand." His skin crinkled as he smiled. "It all suddenly makes sense."

And you don't.

I couldn't put my finger on it, but there was something about him...

Arthur locked eyes with his friend and mentor, transmitting so many things that I didn't know. These men had history, a bond that went deep—deeper than anything I'd seen in any other relationship Arthur had.

Jealousy was an odd thing to feel, but I did. I was jealous that this man knew more about Arthur than I did. I was jealous that Arthur trusted him more than he did me. And I was insanely jealous of the loyalty Arthur had toward him—even over his loyalty to me.

Eight years apart had put me second place in his life. And I *hated* it.

The old man stretched his arm across the table, bearing a welcoming hand. "I'm Wallstreet. Real name is Cyrus Connors, but it's best you call me what everyone else does."

Slowly, I placed my hand in his. My eyes widened as he squeezed back with genuine pleasure and warmth. Untangling my fingers from his, I reclined in my seat, never taking my attention off him. "Nice to meet you."

It would be nicer if I understood you.

Flicking a glance at Arthur, I tried to read the dynamic between our odd little trio. Wallstreet cared for Arthur—there was no question about that. But something deep inside me screamed that the perfectly poised older gentleman was a front. A carefully designed persona to hide the true depth of his deception.

Wallstreet mimicked me, leaning back with a grin on his lips. "I must say, it's a pleasure to finally meet you, Ms. Price. Killian didn't speak of you often, but I feel as I've known you for many years. And to see you alive—well, it's rather intriguing after believing you were dead. I want to hear everything—I've always been a lover of mysteries."

My heart picked up its tempo. "What do you mean by that?"

Did he have something to do with my demise?

He laughed, a dimple showing in his cheek. "I meant nothing. Only that you were a large part of Kill's life. You molded him into the man he became—the boy I met all those years ago. Without you, he might never have escaped the violence of such a world and focused on his raw talents."

My eyes narrowed. Wallstreet's mannerisms nudged my subconscious. There was something there—a link to someone I knew—I just couldn't unscramble it. *Yet.*

I looked to Arthur, who never stopped watching us, his head volleying with each spoken word.

"Your math. Is that what he's talking about?"

He nodded. "You know my father hated me wasting time on it. He thought all I needed to know was how to shoot a gun and hurt people." He cocked his chin at Wallstreet. "Without Cyrus, I wouldn't have the wealth I do, the Club I run, or the masterpiece of revenge currently in play."

Wallstreet sighed contentedly. "You truly were the best student I've ever taught. And loyal." He leaned forward, patting Arthur's hands on the table. "I trust you, my son. Despite the rumors I hear of you going against my orders."

I turned into a statue.

He's talking about my sale as if I were nothing more than merchandise.

"I'm sitting right here, you know." I crossed my arms. "You're seriously going to berate him for not *selling* me? For not giving me up after all the time we spent apart?"

"Cleo, cool it," Arthur muttered. "There's more to this than you know."

Oh, for God's sake. I was done.

"Yes! Apparently everything I seem to know is either wrapped up in things you won't share or you'll 'tell me later.'"

"Funny, I didn't think you would have a temper, Ms. Price." Wallstreet smiled at me. "Kill always spoke so fondly of you."

"Just because I stand up for myself, that gives a man grounds not to speak of me *fondly*?"

Who *was* this guy? After almost a decade of having no past to rely on to make judgments, I'd learned to listen to my instincts. And they bellowed at me to pay attention.

Arthur held up his hands. "Enough. Both of you."

Wallstreet smiled, completely unruffled while I breathed hard and angry. "Forgive me. We're getting off topic." Looking at Kill, effectively blocking me out, he said, "The man destined to receive the sixth sale—"

"Sixth sale being me." I glared.

Wallstreet tensed. "Fine, my dear, yes. The sixth sale—you—was meant for Mr. Steel. He was the final pin in the plan. But no matter; we have enough to proceed without it."

Damn right they did.

I tried to calm down, to stop the boiling temper in my blood. After all, this man had protected Arthur when he'd had no one. A second father to him while he rotted in jail for a crime he still wouldn't tell me.

Wallstreet was his foster parent, just like the nameless lovely people who'd taken me in.

Wallstreet looked at me again, blue eyes glittering. "You know, there's destiny and then there's inevitability. Similar concepts but completely different in execution. I believe this is a bit of both."

My mind hurt trying to figure it out. "What?"

"Huh?" Arthur asked.

"You and her. Her and you. It was inevitable you would find each other, just like I believe destiny has a part to play in all epic love stories. The question is, have you paid enough to be free from suffering?"

"Who *are* you?" I whispered. He didn't talk or act like a criminal. He sounded like a psychologist, a dreamer.

The longer I sat in his presence, the stronger I sensed him. I suspected a hidden agenda, an ulterior motive lurking beneath the fatherly pride he felt toward Arthur.

Wallstreet ran a hand through his white hair. "I'm nobody, Ms. Price. No one of relevance, anyway. Only a man with an eye for numbers and coincidences, just like your lover."

Arthur gritted his teeth. "They broke in last night."

The swift change of topic threw me for a moment; I struggled to catch up.

"Did they take it?"

"No. They didn't find what they were looking for."

Wallstreet stiffened. "Are you sure about that?"

Arthur growled, "I'm sure. What else could it be?"

Wallstreet's eyes fell on me. I shifted in my seat as a cold gust of ice shot down my spine. "Forget it," he said softly.

Looking back to Arthur, he added, "You don't want to rush this. Years you've been planning. Don't fuck it up when you're so close."

Planning? Planning *what*? I needed to *know*!

Arthur leaned over the table, lowering his voice. "I have no intention of fucking anything up. It's time for them to pay. I gave them years. I did as you asked. It's my turn—"

"You did what I asked so you could reap what is owed to you. Don't forget I taught you the art of patience as well as trading, my son."

Arthur pulled back, chastised. "I only meant that I have more than enough wealth. More than enough standing and goodwill in the local community. I have the politicians you wanted all on our side. I control the strings of everyone you ordered me to pull into our power. It's time. I need to move before they try anything else. It's war, and I want it on my terms."

The energy he gave off singed my body—prickling with ominous foreboding. Something told me that the minor rebellion I'd interrupted when I first arrived would be nothing compared to whatever Arthur had planned.

Politicians? Power? He spoke of controlling men like puppets. I didn't like this grim, cutthroat side of Arthur. I didn't like that it had formed without me.

Unthinkingly, I rubbed the mostly healed burn on my arm as Lighter Boy popped into my head.

Wallstreet followed my fingers. His eyes narrowed. "That looks like it was painful. What happened, my dear?"

If I weren't wearing jeans and a long-sleeved top, he would've seen just how painful my past had been—my scars never failed to paint a picture of horror.

I tensed.

His question held so much more than an innocuous inquiry.

What does he know?

My gaze locked with the older man, forcing past his perception. He stared right back, temper swirling below the surface.

Arthur answered for me. "It happened the night she came to me. We haven't figured out the how or why yet."

Wallstreet went deathly still. "How did you find each other again, after all this time?"

Wallstreet and I never looked away from each other; the more I stared, the more my apprehension grew.

I recognize you. But how?

Arthur shot me a look. "One of my crew picked her up. I was fed a bullshit story about where she'd been and who she was."

Ah yes. The story that I was another one of his father's mistresses—destined to pay for the sins of the man they chose to sleep with. Even though I understood Arthur's reasoning on a personal level, it still didn't make it right.

Wallstreet finally broke gaze with me, looking at his prodigal son. "So why did they deliver six instead of five?"

Arthur shrugged.

I wanted to wave. *Me... sitting right here. Number six.*

I glanced at the guard standing by the exit. It felt so wrong to be talking about trafficking in front of a man who had the law on his side.

I wasn't a criminal or a bad person. Yet I'd fallen in love with a boy who did bad things and loved a man who seemed absolutely deadly.

And now I knew how he'd formed the hard exterior—the cold-blooded drive—it'd been taught by Cyrus "Wallstreet" Connors.

Wallstreet frowned. "Why?" Frowning, he added, "What was there to gain?"

Arthur's muscles locked down. "They know."

Wallstreet scooted closer, energy crackling even louder. "How would they know? How would they have found her after all this time?"

"Who the fuck knows, but they do. It explains everything."

Wallstreet rubbed a hand over his face. "It is incredibly convenient that the sixth just happened to be from your past."

Arthur froze, his hands curling on the table.

Wallstreet dropped his voice. "I hope this isn't true, but you have a leak." Looking my way, he muttered, "She's from your past—the same past you're trying to—"

"Motherfucker," Arthur hissed.

Wallstreet nodded sanguinely. "Exactly."

My mind spun, trapped in a cyclone of never making sense.

"Can someone please explain what the hell is going on?" I asked, not that I expected to get a response.

Wallstreet ignored me. "The original Corrupt members I vouched for are trustworthy—I have absolute faith in that. Have you welcomed any new members since?"

Arthur nodded. "A couple, but only after heavy screening and a long time as a Prospect." His back bunched beneath his shirt. He'd had to leave his leather jacket in the coat check—no gang-related memorabilia allowed in the building.

"I can't believe someone would do this. And why? After the wealth I've given them, the peace I've fought so fucking hard for."

"Why?" Wallstreet chuckled. "Anyone who knows you knows your past is your driving force."

"But that? Shit!"

The guard shuffled closer, his hand closing over a baton on his hip.

Wallstreet looked over his shoulder, smiling. "All good, Mark. Just a bit of human passion, is all."

"Fair enough. Just keep it down." The guard melted against the door again. The power Wallstreet had was impressive.

I piped up. "If you're wondering who betrayed you, I know who took me."

Silence fell like thick snow.

Why oh why didn't I mention it before? *It never came up.* I'd been so enamored with reliving our love, I hadn't had time to mention the man with the lighter.

Stupid.

"*What* did you just say?" Arthur asked, his face growing black.

Shit, if my emotions weren't already stretched to capacity, I would've felt sorry for the man I was about to out.

My heart raced.

"Lighter Boy. I don't know his name, but he was at the lunch when you came back after three days away. By the way, that reminds me. What were you doing for those three days?"

Now was not the time to ask, but the question fell out unbidden. He'd been bruised and reeking of alcohol. It seemed a little out of character—I couldn't imagine him willingly becoming intoxicated; he liked control too much.

Probably because he was stripped of it when he was thrown in jail.

It was Wallstreet who replied. "He was doing what I requested. Not only has Killian taken my instruction and done more than I ever hoped, but he also runs an empire that has many facets."

My hands balled. "What facets?"

Wallstreet smiled. "You know in your heart he isn't just a biker. Sure, Pure Corruption is his family, as much as it is mine, but it's beyond that now."

Arthur grumbled. "Those three days I was socializing with a few contacts. Building friendships with men in power that will increase our reach. And, if you must know, I spent a lot of time at the beach where I took you last night…going over the past."

My arms ached to hug him, while my mind was desperate to break open his brain and see the truth.

Wallstreet nodded. "Everything I've given Arthur is nothing compared to what he's giving back. Kill is the smartest, most capable man I've ever had the pleasure to meet, Ms. Price. You should be immensely proud of all that he's achieved."

I crossed my arms, feeling possessive and pissed off. He spoke as if he owned Arthur. As if Arthur was nothing without the things he'd learned from Wallstreet. I knew differently. I'd had the pleasure of knowing the boy before he fell into Wallstreet's clutches and I couldn't separate my rage at having to share him with this man, and the common sense that Wallstreet had saved him.

"What does Lighter Boy look like?" Arthur asked, bringing the conversation back to focus.

Sighing, I said, "He plays with a lighter, has brown hair, hazel eyes, and is skinny."

Arthur's attention turned inward, figuring out which of his brothers was responsible.

I took his silence as another opportunity to trip Wallstreet up. "How long have you been in here?"

Wallstreet grinned, letting tension ebb. "Seventeen years. Been a while."

So I can't have known him from before.

"When will you get out?"

He shrugged. "That depends on God, I suppose. I have another five to serve, but I hope that will be reduced. However, I won't know until I'm walking free from those gates."

The way he moved nudged my thoughts again, begging to connect the dots.

"Alligator. Fucking Adam 'Alligator' Braxton," Arthur suddenly growled.

"Ah yes. I remember you saying he'd been voted in by the brothers but you still withheld judgment," Wallstreet muttered.

An image of the alligator tattoo on Lighter Boy's neck came back to me. "Yep, that's him."

Wallstreet grinned, doting on Arthur as if he was his favorite pupil. "I trust you to take care of it."

Arthur shuddered. "Damn right, I will. Fucking asswipe." Snatching my hand on the table, he squeezed my fingers painfully. "He's not coming near you again. I'll call Grasshopper to track him and put him on lockdown."

Wallstreet sat taller in his chair. "How is Grasshopper?"

My ears pricked.

"He's well. Setting in place the final pieces to take down Dagger Rose."

"That's good," Wallstreet said, his blue eyes bright with interest.

Then it all suddenly made sense.

The blue eyes, the dimple, the identical traits.

Oh my God.

They were related.

Grasshopper and Wallstreet are related.

My muscles trembled with the realization. I wanted to ask—to confirm my suspicions—but something held me back.

Looking at Arthur, I tried to see if he knew the correlation between his right-hand man and the benefactor who'd brought him under his wing.

Arthur was president. He was the law in his world. But really he was as much a pawn as I was. The king sat across from us smiling and waving as perfect as any sovereign, getting others to do his dirty work, all while keeping his hands clean.

"What is it, my dear?" Wallstreet leaned forward, patting my forearm. "You look as if you've tasted something rather disgusting."

I blinked, shoving away my conclusions and hoping I looked clueless. "Sorry, I was just thinking about Alligator and how he would've known I was me, even though I didn't."

Good excuse. And now I'd said it, I truly did wonder that.

God, my brain needed a rest. It was an overstretched rubber band that any moment would snap or lose all will to bounce back into normalcy.

Wallstreet nodded, understanding sharp in his gaze. "I can imagine all of this must be so hard for you. I think you ought to go, rest up so you don't damage what progress you've made."

Trailing his fingers off my forearm, he said to Arthur. "There are men and there are other men, Killian. Don't confuse the two."

What the hell did that mean? Once again my brain whirled.

I'd thought I was intelligent, but talking to this man made me feel like I'd just crawled from the first stages of evolution.

Arthur dropped his voice. "I'm paying them back for this. With or without your blessing. And I'll make it up to you about Mr. Steel. Just give me a bit of time before you agree to whatever pissed-off demands he's making."

Wallstreet grinned. "Fair enough. And I do agree that you need to pay them back. It's time. Don't you think?"

Arthur bristled. "It's been time for a while."

Wallstreet cocked his chin. "In that case, you have my approval. Finish it, Killian. Teach those who ruined you that you now rule. Their kingdom is yours. Their lives are forfeit."

A shiver disappeared my spine.

Arthur stood up. "I will."

Wallstreet stood, too. They clasped hands.

"No touching!" The guard pushed off from the wall.

The men dropped the link, sharing a cold, secretive smile. "Let me know how it goes, son. I know you'll find what you need once it's finished."

Arthur gathered me close, the first time he'd touched me with affection since we'd walked through the doors of the jail. "I already have everything I need. I'll just be happier when it's all finished."

You and me both.

Wallstreet smiled. "You've earned it. And when Dagger Rose are no more, you'll be one step closer to our ultimate goal. Don't let me down."

Arthur bristled beside me. "I'd never let you down, Cyrus. Never."

I was left with a horrible gale inside my heart, howling with uncertainty and queries.

Would Arthur be so blindly loyal if he knew he was being lied to?

And how exactly could I show him the truth without him hating me?

Chapter Twenty-Four

Was I strong enough to protect Cleo?

Was I old enough and wise enough that I wouldn't be so fucking naïve again?

I'd achieved more than I'd ever dreamed. I'd created wealth from nothing. Re-created a life from near impossible odds. And I had a wealthy, intelligent guardian angel who'd become fundamental in my plans and rehabilitation.

He was my saving grace.

He'd taught me everything I knew.

And yet when it came to Cleo, I still felt endlessly uncertain.

The same boy loving a girl who was never meant to be mine.

The same boy with the same damn insecurities.

—Kill

I looked at the clock.

2:30 a.m.

Ugh.

I rolled over and found an empty bed.

Where is he?

The sheets were thrown back and the forlornness of his empty side hurt my heart.

After we'd returned from visiting Wallstreet, Arthur had spent the afternoon on his laptop, trading the foreign currency market as if it were an addiction. He clicked and studied and made notes in his ledger, slowly unwinding the more he traded.

We hadn't spoken much as we'd had dinner and headed to bed. I couldn't shake my confusion of going to see Wallstreet. I couldn't line up his cryptic answers or make sense of anything.

And I couldn't understand why Arthur didn't realize that Grasshopper was related to Wallstreet.

To me it was so damn obvious. But to him—to a man locked in the winds of vengeance and single-minded determination—it had never registered.

Then again, maybe he does know and it's all part of the hidden agenda?

Getting back to sleep was a lost cause. I would never relax with buzzing questions or the emptiness of the mattress beside me.

Deciding to go find him, I sat up and swung my legs out of the warm cocoon. Dressed only in one of Arthur's black T-shirts, I padded down the corridor and drifted down the stairs.

No lights were on.

I wanted to keep it that way. I liked the anonymity the dark provided. I enjoyed creeping through the shadows, almost as if I crept through my own mind.

The house had been spotlessly tidy and clean when we'd arrived home. Whoever Arthur called to come take care of it had also left his home in immaculate condition.

Knowing where I'd find him, I kept ghosting silently until stopping on the outskirts of his office.

The four smashed computers had gone, replaced with unopened boxes of new gadgets and technology. The glass from the equation poster had been swept up and the desk re-buffed.

It was as if the break-in never happened.

I found Arthur on the floor by the safe behind the couch. He rested against the wall, his legs up and head bent. His eyes glued to the photos I'd seen when he'd opened the safe yesterday.

He didn't notice me and I took the opportunity to stare at the beautiful man whom I'd been privileged to watch grow from boy to teen to capable, protective adult.

His strong hands flexed with power around the delicate photographs. His tanned and kissable throat rippled as he swallowed. His entire body was sculptured and groomed into a fighting machine—every inch spoke of readiness and a ruthless temper that could kill.

I sucked in a breath at the tiniest shimmer in his green eyes.

Tears?

No, it can't possibly be.

Anger.

Glittering anger that never left him alone—no matter how gentle and loving he was with me.

Arthur's neck snapped up; he quickly slapped the photos color side up on the tiled floor. "What are you doing up?"

I didn't take my eyes from the hidden images. "I couldn't sleep. You left—I couldn't go back to sleep without seeing you. Without reminding myself that you're real and not a dream."

He sighed, opening his arms. "Come here."

Moving around the couch, I slid down the wall beside him and snuggled into his masculine warmth. He kissed the top of my head, breathing in the scent of my shampoo. "I am real. You are real. We're never losing each other again."

His voice was strained, the strange mix of hatred and guilt plaiting together to form a heavy oath.

"What are the photos of?" I murmured. I didn't want to make him uncomfortable and force him to show me things he'd rather not reveal, but at the same time, I wanted truth. I wanted to rip aside the curtain and see the secrets beyond.

"It's nothing, Cleo. You should go back to bed." His arms tightened in direct retaliation of his words. His mouth said he wanted me gone, but his actions said otherwise.

I sighed, liquefying against him. "What are you so afraid of?"

He tensed, not answering.

I waited for a few minutes, but he never slipped or admitted.

"When will you tell me?"

"Tell you what?"

"The story of how you ended up in prison? The tale of what happened while we were apart? The fable of why you were so adamant I was dead? There's so much I don't know. So much I *need* to know before giving everything that I am to you."

"You haven't given me everything?"

The darkness was a soft voyeur around us, hushing our confessions. "No. Not yet. You're keeping too many things from me."

"You're keeping things from me, too."

"Yes, but not on purpose. I remember in sporadic bursts. I can't control it."

Arthur squeezed me hard. "Is it getting easier?" Once again the fear and hope waged war in his tone.

I sighed heavily, wishing he would stop lying and tell me what he was so afraid of. Anger filled me and I stiffened in his hold. "Wallstreet means a lot to you, doesn't he?"

Arthur went deathly still. "He's the reason why I'm free and rich and in a position to take revenge on those who betrayed me. So, yes… he means a great fucking deal."

Tracing the grout between the white tiles by my toes, I whispered, "You do know he has other plans for you? The way he watches you, Art. He's hiding so much but demands everything in return."

Arthur pulled away, untangling his arm from around my shoulders. "What exactly are you saying?"

Sitting taller, I braced myself. I hadn't meant to rip open this particular festering wound, but he'd left me no choice. "Do you know what he's truly after? Do you know what he'll take as payment for everything he's given you?"

Arthur stood up in a rush, pacing in front of me. "What the fuck has gotten into you, Cleo? You can't be fucking jealous of a guy who was the only one there for me." Stopping, he growled, "I don't care what his ultimate plans are. They're in my best interests, and I could obey every request and still not give enough to repay him for what he's done."

Pushing up off the floor, I stood with my hands fisted. "What exactly did he do, Art? Please tell me, because I'm sick of living in the dark. What is he making you do? What does he want?"

Arthur dragged both hands through his jaw-length hair. His body rippled with anger, his chest rising and falling fast. "It's none of your business!"

"You're wrong." I pressed forward, deliberately taunting him to face the truth. I might be floundering in the dark with incomplete memories, but he was worse—he willfully ignored things right in front of his face. "Do you know who Grasshopper is?"

Arthur stopped, hands tangled in his hair. His green eyes popped wide. "What? What the fuck does Hopper have to do with this?"

I wanted to shake him. "Come on. You haven't noticed? In the years you've been dealing with both men, you haven't ever truly looked at them?"

Arthur froze, his eyes blazing as realization pounded into him.

Finally.

"Oh, fuck." His hands fell from his head, hanging by his sides. "You're right. They look—" He shook his head. "It can't be. Jared's last name isn't Connors. It's Shearer. They can't be..."

Closing the distance between us, I rested my fingers on his arm. "Not having the same name doesn't mean a thing these days. He could be illegitimate, having taken his mother's name. Hell, he could've changed it. Look at me. Cleo Price has a grave and a death certificate confirming my demise. In the eyes of the law I don't exist; only Sarah Jones does. Isn't it possible that everything you think you know has two meanings? Two purposes?"

He grabbed my shoulders, bringing me closer. "You've been worried about this? Why?"

"Why?" I frowned. "Because I'm protective of you. I don't like to think of others taking advantage of your intelligence or skill. What if they're not on your side?"

His fingers dug into my flesh. "I'll say this once and only once. I love you for worrying about me and I'll never dismiss your impressions or instincts, but regardless of what you think you know of Wallstreet or Grasshopper, they are good men. *Honest* men. I agree, to you it looks as if they're using me, but, Cleo, this is an instance where you have to be patient and trust me."

His hand came up to cup my cheek. "I would never let anyone else take advantage or screw me over. I'd kill them instantly. I went to prison for something that was a lie. I served time for people I thought cared about me, only for them to destroy me without a backward glance. Everything I'm doing is to ensure they never have the opportunity to screw anyone else ever again. And I will not rest until they've paid for what they've done. Do you understand?"

The ferocity in his eyes weakened my knees with sheer promise of bloodlust. "I understand."

Running his thumb over my bottom lip, he nodded. "Good. Now, no more worrying about Wallstreet and his motives. Don't look for flaws in the man who kept me alive and sane. But I can tell you that he's been on my side since the day I met him. He's put things in motion for me, given me a purpose, a plan—and a way to get even."

My eyes widened. "What does that mean?"

His jaw tightened. "It means there is so much more than you know happening in the background. So much more than Pure Corruption and Dagger Rose. Bigger than anyone knows." He went silent, almost as if wishing he hadn't hinted at the depth of what he wasn't telling me. But then he scowled and finished, "What I've been working on, Cleo, will mean my life won't have been for nothing. That living those years in prison believing you were dead weren't in vain. I'm owed this. You're owed this. And Wallstreet is making that possible."

A shiver darted down my spine. "But, Art—what are you planning—"

He pressed a finger over my lips, hushing me. Whispering softly, he said, "Let me worry about him. Trust me that it will all work out." Ducking, he pressed a small kiss where his finger had been, murmuring, "I have something for you."

The deliberate change of subject didn't go unnoticed, but I forced myself to relax and let him continue to hide for a bit longer. "Oh?"

He took my hand, guiding me back to the safe. Stepping carefully over strewn photographs, he picked up a ring box.

A ring box?

Turning back to me, he held it out. "For you, Buttercup."

My heart rate exploded. Conclusions tripped and collided. Was he going to propose all those years ago? Had he bought a ring only to think I died and held on to it all this time?

My hands shook like crazy as I took it.

Arthur chuckled. "It's not what you think." Placing his hand over mine, he added, "You gave me the Libra eraser because I told you you made more mistakes than anyone else I knew. I gave you this because I couldn't figure out a way to tell you how fucking mad I was about you. I couldn't sort out the love I had for the little girl I'd grown up with and the woman I saw you becoming. So I let something else show it instead."

Never taking his eyes from mine, he helped me open the lid.

The moment I saw what rested inside, the past stole me away.

"Sneaky, Buttercup."

I giggled as I climbed in through his bedroom window. It was past one a.m. and the compound, including our parents, was fast asleep. Arthur lay on the top of his covers in nothing but his silky boxers playing PlayStation.

My mouth went instantly dry. "I see you dressed up for me."

His eyes trailed to his groin. I waited for him to bounce up and cover himself, to prevent any chance of something other than platonic friendship from happening.

But this time was different.

He let me stare.

He let me witness the rapid hardening of the part of him I wanted to see more than anything.

The room shimmered with lust.

"You're not supposed to be here," he murmured. The tone of his voice was pure sex, sending wetness between my legs and an eternal throbbing that made me pine for his touch.

"I'm supposed to be wherever you are," I whispered, breathless.

Art suddenly sat up, swinging his legs over the edge of his bed and patting the mattress beside him. "Come here."

The command sent a delicious clench through my core. I couldn't breathe. Seriously? He was finally going to give in to us?

Sitting nervously, I struggled to keep my eyes away from the erection now straining against the silk of his boxers.

Without a word, Art reached under his pillow and drew out a ring box. Dropping it into my lap as if he didn't have the self-control to touch me, he breathed, "Here. This is for you."

I almost dropped the box, I shook so much when opening it.

Inside rested a mood ring, but not just any mood ring… a large stone encircled by the Sagittarian archer with an arrow locked in his quiver.

My head snapped up. "Art, I love it."

Plucking the ring from the box, he grabbed my hand and we both sucked in a harsh breath. Electricity and forbidden want crackled and blistered between us. I would've given up everything for him to kiss me, to press me onto my back and climb on top of me.

I whimpered as the intensity became too much.

Art shook as much as I did as he slowly slid the ring onto my middle finger. The stone immediately turned a smoldering red.

Art chuckled. "According to the chart it came with, that means you're hungry."

"Hungry?"

He dropped his eyes. "Yeah, hungry for passion, love, connection."

I couldn't. I just couldn't do this anymore.

Launching myself at him, I scrambled onto the bed, knocking him onto his back.

His mouth fell open as I pressed my lips to his, sucking in his soul, his desire, every emotion that clogged my brain whenever he was near.

My entire body shuddered, pleasure rippling in a core that suddenly knew exactly how to get relief.

Arthur groaned as I straddled his hips, rocking and pressing my night shorts against his rock-hard erection. I didn't care the dusky pink of my pajamas was drenched from being around him. I didn't care that I could smell myself—smell how much I needed this boy.

Puberty had hit and Arthur had been teasing me ever since he first kissed me in the park. It was time for him to stop teasing and deliver.

"Cleo—wait," he hissed in the darkness.

His head arched back as I pressed viciously hard, driving myself to the point of pain as I rode him.

"Shit." He snapped.

His hands came up, capturing my face, kissing me savagely.

A moan ripped from my lungs as he thrust up, hitting the perfect spot and making me melt and freeze all at the same time.

We kissed as if the world would end. We fed, we dined—we ate every inch as our mouths attacked hungrily. When his hands fell to my hips, pressing me harder onto him, the seam of my shorts rubbed in just the right way.

I cried out, flopping onto his chest.

Instantly he stopped, his heart drumming so hard against mine. "We can't. Cleo, go. Leave before—"

"Before you fuck me?" I rocked my hips.

Temper darkened the red hot heat between us. "Don't say such crass things. It's not ladylike."

Ladylike? I wasn't a girl or a biker president princess, or even a woman in that moment.

I was his. I wanted to be used, abused, taken. I wanted dirt and filth and raw primitive fucking.

"Fuck me, Arthur Killian. I'm begging you to fuck me."

He threw me off him, tearing off the bed and moving to his wardrobe. Yanking on jeans, he dragged both hands through his hair. "Shut up. They'll hear you."

I sat panting on his bed, running my finger over my new mood ring, which now glowed a horrible black. Looking for the box, I found the placard that stated what each color meant.

Black: Sadness, depression, rejection.

Yep.

Art came closer, ducking to his haunches before me. His hands landed on my knees, tracing circles that only amplified the tangled feelings inside. His eyes fell to the damp patch between my legs; his jaw clenched.

"You told me once the traits of a Libra. I did some of my own research on you. Want to know what I found?"

I shook my head, hiding myself behind a curtain of fiery red hair. I didn't want to look at him—not after he'd turned me away, like all the other times.

Brushing the thick crimson strands behind my ear, he murmured, "You're bright and inquisitive, energetic and enthusiastic, adventurous and honest." His voice slowly leveled out from desire-filled raggedness. "You're passionate to a fault and fearless." He smiled. "I can attest to that. You go after things you want with no thought to the consequences and suffer from incorrigible optimism."

I laughed softly. "I have to have optimism—especially where you're concerned. Otherwise how could I spend so much time with you, begging for you to notice me—with the amount of times you push me away?"

He sighed, ignoring that. "Even the negative traits I found adorable."

"Negative?" I tensed for the worst.

"You're restless, impatient, tactless, and overconfident."

"Ouch."

Art moved to sit back on the bed, wrapping an arm around my shoulders. "But it's those traits that make you my Buttercup. Never give up on me. Never stop being impatient or overconfident in my love for you. I'll give in one day, Cleo. Sooner than you think."

The flashback ended as Arthur placed the mood ring back on my middle finger. "How do you have it? Wasn't it on me the night I disappeared?"

Arthur gritted his jaw, anger deep in his green eyes. "I found it in the wreckage of the house. I had just enough time to put it somewhere safe before the police arrested me the following morning."

Questions lined up in chaotic fashion. I wanted to hear his story—to figure out why they arrested him and the trial he must've been subjected to.

But the flashback had drained me. I had no more tenacious drive other than to show this man what he meant to me.

I moved forward into his embrace. His arms wrapped immediately around me, squeezing hard.

A minute passed and we just hugged, drawing and giving much-needed serenity.

Finally, Art pulled back. "Let's go to bed."

I nodded.

"Just let me lock up." Moving away, he gathered the photographs and placed them back in the safe. Locking it, he turned to face me, but my eyes landed on a glossy image hidden partly by the couch.

Without a word, I ducked down and retrieved it.

My heart swooped with gossamer wings then hurtled me into hell.

Me and him.

Young, slightly sunburned, dressed in shorts and T-shirts, surrounded by a swarm of family. My mom and dad. His mom, dad, and older brother. We were the perfect postcard of togetherness.

My eyes fell on his father.

Hatred coiled in my gut, hissing and twisting, wanting to strike him down for what he did.

Tears bruised my eyes to see my parents again. A flash of a memory appeared. My mother had been called Petal—Sandra "Petal" Price. She'd been too pure and precious to die.

A single tear rolled down my cheek as I drank in the love on their doting faces, the happiness we'd had as a family. Knowing I would never see them again ripped out my heart and left it bleeding on the floor.

It hurt.

So, so much.

"Shit." Arthur plucked the image from my fingertips, taking away my home, leaving me alone once again.

In a flash, he picked me up from the tiles and carried me toward the door. "I can't stand to see you in pain."

I didn't protest as he carted me from the room.

Over his shoulder, I noticed another photograph peeking up from the floor.

A picture of me laughing in Scott "Rubix" Killian's arms. I'd loved him. I'd trusted him.

He'd been an uncle to me but destroyed my family all for greed.

Tiredness stole everything from me; I burrowed my face into the crook of Arthur's neck. No words were spoken as he carried me back to bed.

Placing me gently on the mattress, I cupped his cheek. "I've always wondered why your mom called you Arthur. Do you know?"

His face turned soft. "Yes, I know." Throwing back the covers, he climbed in beside me, pulling me into his powerful body. "She named me after Arthur Cayley. A famous mathematician who wrote a number of papers on rules we use abundantly today."

I smiled in the dark, holding his arm around my breasts. "So she's the reason why you're fascinated with numbers."

He laughed quietly. "You could say that. I suppose she jinxed me in a way."

"Or gave you a better life path than the one your father envisioned."

Somehow I remembered Arthur's childhood wasn't as happy as mine. His family home had always been fraught with danger and nervousness. I'd never come out and asked, but I had a feeling his father did more than just raise his fists to his son. I had a feeling his older brother hurt him, too.

His voice turned to a whisper. "Perhaps."

"How did she die?" I murmured, hating to think his mother had been murdered like mine. There had been too much death. Too much unnecessary waste.

Arthur flinched behind me, taking his time to reply. "Breast cancer."

I hugged his arm closer. "I'm so sorry, Art."

Holding me tight, he growled, "No more talking, go to sleep."

I wanted to offer condolences. I wanted to turn in his arms and kiss him senseless and force him to forget the pain of being locked in prison while his mother died of cancer.

Instead, I allowed him to keep me pinned and welcomed sleep to steal me.

I made a pact as silence fell thick and soothing around us that the moment we woke tomorrow, I would show Arthur how much I adored him. How precious his undying devotion was to my memory and heart.

I would wrap my lips around his cock and adore him until I drank everything he gave me.

I would show him how much I worshiped, not just his soul and mind, but his body, too.

Sleep stole its fuzzy tentacles through my mind. The only sounds were the gentle thud of our heartbeats, once again syncing into rhythm.

I let the gentle intimacy lull me closer to dreamland, but in the last moment before succumbing, I whispered, "Don't fear the truth around me, Art. Please don't be afraid."

I never expected a reply.

I never expected him to hear me.

I only wanted the vow to trickle into his subconscious and hopefully ease some of the affliction inside.

Time ticked past, sleep came for me again.

In the final second before I fell into clouds, a tortured whisper breathed in my ear, "I'm more than afraid, Buttercup. I'm absolutely fucking terrified."

The truth of his confession trickled into my mind, numbing my heart with horror. I curled tighter in his embrace. "Why?" I murmured.

He took forever to answer and when he finally did, I wished I weren't awake to hear it.

This was what I was afraid of.

This hell masquerading as heaven.

"Because when you know what I did, Cleo. When you find out what a traitor I am, you'll leave me. You'll despise me and curse me; you'll cut out my heart and disappear."

His arms clutched me, panic drenching his muscles. "You'll leave me, Buttercup, and this time, I'll truly be ruined.

"You'll destroy me forever."

Chapter Twenty-Five

Arthur

She said she knew me from her nightmares.

I never let on how fucking true that really was.

She thought I was her protector. Her confidant and soul mate.

She believed a lie worse than all the rest I'd spun.

I hated to think how I'd betrayed her. How I'd done something completely unforgivable. I never let on how far I'd fallen.

Every time I came inside her, I wanted to beg for forgiveness.

Every time she touched me or smiled, I wanted to fold to my knees and spill the truth.

I couldn't tell her what I'd done.

But I couldn't keep it a secret much longer.

It gnawed at my soul, descending me deeper into darkness. She was my light, my hope, my heart—and I'd ruined it all before I found her.

She thought she'd awoken from her nightmares. That reality would set her free and truth would dispel the evil in her past.

But she didn't know the worst of them was me.

The one demon she should've shot the moment she opened her eyes.

The charade had gone on long enough.

But I didn't have the strength to end it.

There would be no second chances. No moving past my heinous sins.

She would steal back her love and leave me destitute.

I would have only my anger.

I would have only my vengeance.

But ultimately, I would have nothing.

Eight Years Ago

Some say everything happens for a reason. That bad things happen to good people. That evil comes for the purest of us, and destinies can change in a blink.

I call bullshit.

I say we're all fucking puppets being controlled by others. There's no such thing as freedom. No such thing as fate. They're all carefully maintained illusions.

I believed the lie once. I looked forward to my future. I held hope in my heart.

Now…

My eyes are open.

And I'll never be so fucking naïve again.

"Take it, Killian."

My eyes snapped up to latch onto the convict who'd tried to ass-rape me the day I arrived at Florida State. The key word in that sentence being he *tried*.

And failed.

Painfully and miserably.

Men had jumped on me from all corners. My pants were ripped down. My body pummeled with fists.

I'd lain there—ass naked and ready to be raped—when I'd seen two roads.

So distinct and real, I'd felt the roughness of dirt beneath my fingertips and the gleam of concrete in the sun.

Two choices.

One was to give up and let my life become a series of rapings and beatings until I died from either suicide or murder.

Or...

Kill every inch of the boy left inside me who believed he might one day be free of this life. Destroy any hope of ever having a pristine office overlooking Wall Street. That dream had been stolen the moment the handcuffs sliced around my wrists.

There was no trading for criminals.

My earliest dream had become unobtainable. It was torn away, and no matter what I did I wouldn't achieve it. So my only option was to join them.

The choice had felt like it took years to make with my bare ass in the air and men fumbling with their waistbands, but in reality it only took microseconds.

I'd chosen the second path.

The one covered in dirt and filth.

The one destined to ruin me.

"Just take the fucking tray, will ya?" The jagged scar across the convict's cheek was only just fading after a year. I'd done that to him with no remorse or second thoughts. He'd attacked and I'd defended.

Needless to say, I'd been given a wide berth ever since. No one wanted to mess with a man who'd murdered not one but three lives, and all before his eighteenth birthday.

Not even the guards tormented me. They knew I was in here for the long haul—it was best to get along, seeing as they were my family now.

Taking the tray of slop, I grinned coldly. "Thanks, Bradley. Hope there's no extra in my mac and cheese. Else you and me... we're gonna have another issue to solve."

Bradley swallowed, anger glowing in his muddy eyes. "One year you've been in here, Killian. You've got your whole life in front of you. I wouldn't be so keen to make such firm enemies if I were you."

I cocked my head, grabbing a plastic knife and fork from the container. "Oh, really? So I should've let you rape me?" I sighed dramatically. "Don't see your logic, but I'm happy to teach you another lesson."

Fisting my cutlery and shitty lunch, I glowered. "See ya round, *Bradley.*"

I stalked away before he could mutter another word. My eyes scanned the dismal excuse of a cafeteria with uncomfortable bolted stools and metal tables. Everything was metal and cream or bolts and bars. It wasn't fucking inspiring—shit, it was downright "slice your jugular and just give the fuck up right now" décor.

Life.

I have life in this godforsaken place.

Not for the first time and definitely not for the last, my hands curled, almost cracking the brittle plastic of the tray.

So fucking unfair.

So fucking *painful.*

She's dead.

Don't think about it.

My mind turned to the dark cesspit of memories. Hatred that never failed to choke me with blackness cloaked over my shoulders.

The betrayal. The dishonor. The *manipulation.*

I wanted to slam my tray to the floor and let loose the rage inside.

The day I'd walked in here, I ceased to be human and lived for only one thing.

One throbbing, vicious thing.

Vengeance.

Revenge.

Every fucking word that meant getting my own back.

That was me. I ate it. I breathed it. I fucking made love to it while I jerked off in my cell. It was the only love permitted in my soul—the only substance that kept me rising from my awful cot and facing yet another day in purgatory.

The only way I could survive every day knowing Cleo was no longer in it.

"Killian. He wants to see you." A balding man in his late fifties appeared in my line of sight, barricading me from sitting at one of the identical depressing benches.

I gritted my teeth. "Get out of my way."

Prisoner #FS788791 shook his head, showing the scribbling prison tats decorating his neck. The embroidered number on his orange jumpsuit couldn't be more demeaning. We might as well be livestock ready for the slaughter.

I refuse to fucking die in here.

The oath resonated in my heart for the millionth time since the seven a.m. wake-up bell. *I won't.* I refused to die without their blood on my hands and justice being served.

"I suggest you come with me. You get one shot. He wants to see you. Don't fuck this up." He leaned forward, smelling of grease and armpit stench. "One chance, brother. You really going to throw that away?"

My heart thudded. "He doesn't have any power. Unless he can get me out of here before I'm a wrinkly old bastard who has to piss twenty times a night, then I'm not going anywhere near him."

I'd heard the tales. The shankings. The mysterious poisonings. He wasn't someone I wanted to piss off or get chummy with.

That was how enemies started. By picking sides.

I was my own fucking side.

Vengeance.

The prisoner smiled. "You have to trust someone."

"No, I don't."

Never again. I would never be that weak.

"You need a friend in here. Life imprisonment is a long time."

I rolled my eyes. "No shit, it's a long time. Lucky for me, I prefer my own company." I tried to push past, but his bony hand clutched my forearm.

"One meeting. One chance. Don't fuck it up and he might have the power to do what you need."

Our eyes locked and I wanted to beat him to a bloody pulp—the anger, hurt, and betrayal sliced my veins with every pump of my heart.

I wasn't a prisoner of this penitentiary, I was a prisoner of what they'd done to me.

One chance.

If I did this, maybe, just maybe, I might get what I needed. To make them *suffer.*

I tore my arm from his grip. "Fine." Throwing my tray and congealed mac and cheese on the closest table, I snarled, "He gets three minutes. He tries anything, and I'm not the one who pays. Got it?"

For an eighteen-, about to turn nineteen-year-old, I was grateful I'd filled out, grown to over six foot three, and my long hair came across as slightly crazy, completely delinquent. My voice was deep—my balls had dropped years ago, and I'd been raised to use my fists first and mind later.

Too bad for my father, who taught me—he never understood my brain was the biggest, baddest part of me. Another reason why people in here avoided me. No one liked a genius murderer with a high IQ.

Double threat. Triple danger.

Prisoner #FS788791 nodded. "Deal. One meeting. Then it's up to you."

Him.

The awe-inspiring, nail-biting majesty himself.

Wallstreet to his fellow inmates, even to the guards. No one used his real name. No one dared disrespect him that way—even local politicians called him Wallstreet out of respect. Respect for what he'd created, even if it wasn't exactly legal.

Wallstreet smiled, interlocking his fingers on top of the table. His usual spot was at the back of the cafeteria, wedged in the corner of the room to protect his back and side. Two men, looking like matching carrots in their orange jumpsuits, glared as I came closer.

No one could get to Wallstreet unless he wanted them to. Money bought more than respect—it brought longevity in a place where cutthroats and psychopaths wanted you dead.

His wrinkled face and greying hair were manicured and healthy. His eyes were bright and well rested, his jumpsuit ironed—fucking ironed—and dental hygiene top-notch. He was the magistrate in here. Even the prison officials let him be in charge of the criminal population.

Cigarettes? He got them.

Drugs? He got them, too.

Women? He'd hook you up, but offered no guarantee you wouldn't die of fucking syphilis.

"Hello, Arthur. Lovely of you to join me."

Prisoner #FS788791 pressed on my shoulder—or tried, seeing as he was like Pee-wee fucking Herman—coaxing me onto the bench. I shrugged him off, preferring to tower over the man at least forty years my senior.

"Name's not Arthur. It's Killian." Arthur had died the moment Cleo had. No one would ever address me that way again. It hurt too fucking much.

I crossed my arms, planting my legs wide, hoping I looked angry as hell and just as terrifying. "Why me?"

"Excuse me?" Wallstreet chuckled, reclining a little and placing his hands in his lap. There were no dirty dishes or trays—either this douche didn't eat, or his cronies had already cleaned the table.

"Why pick me? What did I do to deserve an audience with His Grace?"

He laughed again, raising an eyebrow. "Why not you?"

"No. Answer the fucking question." I unwound my arms and wagged a finger in his face. "No cryptic crap. No bullshit. No games of any kind." Slinging my leg over the metal stool, I sat and splayed my hands on the table. "I'm sitting. I'm listening. I'm giving you exactly three minutes to tell me why the fuck you wanted to see me on the anniversary of my arrival into this hellhole, and then *maybe* I'll stick around and listen to more."

Prisoner #FS788791 growled, "Respect, boy."

Wallstreet waved him away. "It's fine, Pat. He's highly strung. That's all." His eyes glinted. "And impatient."

I nodded. "Hell yes, I'm impatient. I've avoided stepping on toes or being roped into sides the full three hundred and sixty-five days I've been here. I want to stay neutral and you're wrecking that by making people think you're playing favorites with me."

Wallstreet nodded, his blue eyes bright and sharp. "Fair enough." Looking at his three stooges, he muttered, "Leave us. I want to talk to the boy alone."

Prisoner #FS788791 stepped forward. "But what about..."

Wallstreet held up his hand, shushing him in one powerful, understated move.

What I wouldn't give to have that power. That clout.

"Give us a few, Pat." When the prisoner didn't move, Wallstreet added, "I'm not asking."

The guy grumbled but moved away obediently.

I didn't say a word, just glared until the fellow convicts moved out of hearing distance. Wallstreet visibly relaxed, which didn't make sense as he'd just shooed away his bodyguards.

"Killian. Let's start with something easy. What do you know about me?"

I tensed, willing my heart rate to remain steady and nerves to die a painful death. *I'm not afraid of you. I'm not afraid of anyone anymore.*

I rolled my eyes. "What is this? A 'get to know your fellow criminal' lunch?"

Wallstreet smiled tightly. "No. This is an interview."

I coughed. "What?"

Wallstreet leaned forward, losing the pretence of conversation, getting straight to his point. "I know about you, kid. I have a one-time deal that will change your life. I can give you back your world—with more power than you could ever dream of—so stop being a little shit. Tell me what I want to know and cut the crap, because you get *one* chance. If you fuck it up, you'll die in here, and wish to God you'd stopped flashing your cock and actually listened."

He breathed hard, running a hand through his thick grey hair. "Now do I have your attention?"

My attention was riveted to his jumpsuit collar and the vein in his neck. My mind was busy picturing how badly he'd bleed if I stabbed him with the shank I kept hidden in my cuff. My brain was busy calculating how many seconds the rubber bullets and batons would take before they ripped into my body.

One point five seconds to strike.

Four seconds before anyone understood what happened.

Eight seconds for the guards to aim and fire.

Eleven point nine seconds before any chance of being hit by a rubber bullet occurred.

But if I did, I would have zero chance at getting what I wanted.

Equations.

Algorithms.

Probabilities and calculations.

Math.

Where vengeance was my life, math was my lover. Everything—regardless how senseless, surprising, and damn fucking unfair some things were, math could always find a simple answer. Provide solutions to impossible situations.

Math was ruthless.

Like me.

I nodded. "You have my attention."

"Good." Wallstreet cleared his throat. "Let's start again. How much do you know about me?"

I sighed, preparing myself for a recital. "Everything?"

He linked his fingers again, his knuckles turning white as he squeezed. "Everything."

"You were incarcerated a while back for white-collar crimes. You skimmed the books on your Fortune Five Hundred company and hid cash in offshore bank accounts. You were only caught because your whore at the time reported you to the tax office, where they audited you and found you fraudulent of not paying taxes." I took another breath, continuing, "You made your first million before you'd turned twenty-three, had a portfolio of over fifty properties including hotels and commercial investments, along with your chain of highly successful trading companies and investment firms. Not only did you get done for tax evasion, but you're currently being investigated for negligent trades on behalf of retirees rumored to be worth over eight hundred million, but I happen to know you'll never be convicted because your bookkeeping skills are impeccable. Not to mention you have politicians and a lot of contacts in your pocket that are above the law."

Wallstreet smiled broadly. "So you've followed my career."

I never took my eyes off him. "Yes. It's prudent to know my enemies."

"I'm your enemy?"

I shook my head. "No, not right now. But you never know how the future will change. Those you hold most dear are the ones who strike the hardest."

Wallstreet laughed, slapping the table. "Your father really did a number on you, didn't he, kid?"

I bristled. "I'm not a kid." The court system didn't try me as a kid—they'd given me the maximum sentence for the coldhearted crime I committed. I hadn't been a kid since I was ten years old and started receiving daily beatings and lessons from dear old Pop.

My heart hung heavy, disobeying my strict orders not to feel despair or truly think about what my future meant. There would be no twenty-first birthday celebration or finally losing my virginity to Cleo. I'd wanted to wait until I was legally an adult. I'd wanted to make sure it was truly what she wanted.

My heart fisted in agony.

I should never have waited.

Wallstreet narrowed his eyes. "What's my real name? Have you managed to work that out yet?"

I nodded. "Your power of attorney kept your name suppressed in every newspaper article. But I already knew it." I decided to share a tiny sliver of where my passions lay. "I've wanted to trade since I was nine years old. You were like a god to me."

Wallstreet's face darkened. "Were? Past tense?"

I grinned, enjoying the slight anger glowing in his eyes. He was used to maintaining respect and didn't handle my teenage look of disdain. "Past tense. You had so much. More than I ever dreamed—but you lost it all. You're as penniless as me, but I'm better off 'cause I have youth on my side."

I didn't believe my words. My age only condemned me to live longer inside these shit-stained walls.

Wallstreet's eyes narrowed. "What makes you think I lost it all?"

"The newspaper articles. Magazines."

He shook his head. "You said so yourself... my bookkeeping skills are impeccable. Don't you think I hid things? Only gave up what I could afford to lose?"

My heart slowed—it always did when something huge attracted my attention. I could sit in a room with no food or distractions for days while chewing on an elusive equation.

My voice dropped, hiding my eagerness. "Gonna share with me?"

Wallstreet leaned closer, his voice dropping. "That depends on you."

"Me?"

"I know as much about you as you do about me. I know what you want when you get out of here, and I also know you don't stand a chance unless you somehow manage to afford a lawyer who gets you a parole hearing before you're fucking seventy." He sighed. "We both know that won't happen. Not after what your father made you do. Not to mention the testimony he submitted painting you as the villain."

My hands clenched; my heart thundered in my ears.

"Yes, Officer. I saw the whole thing. He's no son of mine. I loved the Price family as if they were flesh and blood."

Handcuffs settled icy-cold and final around my wrists. My heart didn't beat and nerves didn't clog my blood. Ever since my father had dragged me into Cleo's house, I'd been dead inside. Destined to hell for what I'd done.

I'd obeyed my father because of threats he'd made toward the girl I loved with all my soul. I'd agreed to do what he wanted to protect her. To prevent her from being raped and murdered right before my eyes.

And this was how he repaid my loyalty.

"Do you have anything to say for yourself, Arthur Killian, before we take you into custody?"

I looked down at the floor, my hair reeking of smoke, my hands covered in the charred remains of Cleo's house. I'd combed through the wreckage once it had burned to the ground and cooled.

I hadn't found her body, but I'd found the ring I'd given her.

I wanted to break down and fucking cry.

My father growled, "Of course he has something to say. Don't you, Killian? Tell them. Tell them the truth."

I hunched into myself. Even now, even after he'd already destroyed my life, he was intent on hammering the nails into my coffin.

"Well, son. What do you have to tell us?" the officer asked, shaking me.

"Killian, admit to it," my father hissed. "Tell them what a fucking murderer you are."

There was nothing left to fight for.

She was dead.

I would follow her as soon as I could find a way.

"I killed them," I whispered.

"What was that?" The officer leaned closer.

Gathering every inch of betrayal and hatred from my soul, I bellowed, "I fucking killed them. I murdered Paul and Sandra Price. Are you happy? Is that what you want to hear?"

The officer shook his head sadly. "No, son, that wasn't what I wanted to hear at all."

The last thing I heard as they stuffed me into the back of a cop cruiser was my father chuckling with accomplishment.

He'd used his youngest son to dispatch the president of Dagger Rose, all so he could take it over himself.

He'd sentenced me to a life of eternal misery, all for fucking greed.

And for that I hoped the devil would tear out his heart and eat it for fucking breakfast.

I forced the memories away—to stay locked and barricaded. If I didn't, I'd go insane with anger. My eyes returned to Wallstreet's neck, starting a new calculation on how long it would take me to rip out his voice box so I didn't have to listen to him anymore.

Wallstreet looked around, dropping his voice to a murmur. "I have a proposition for you."

My eyes narrowed. Suspicion laced my blood. I didn't say a word, letting him dig the trench he obviously thought I was stupid enough to enter.

"You have a head for numbers. You graduated top of your class in both physics and university-level math. You turned a work experience week at the local stock market into a trending explosion of blue-chip stocks by going bearish on the trade. You're a natural, Arthur, and that's a rare and beautiful thing."

I rolled my eyes. "You read my résumé. How thoughtful."

He snapped, "I'm serious."

My eyes flashed. "And *I'm* serious when I said my name is Killian. Arthur died the moment he was betrayed and thrown away to rot in this godforsaken place."

"We'll come back to that." Wallstreet looked over my shoulder before glancing back at me. "It brings me to my next point. What else do you know about me?"

Ah, the darker part of his history. The part where the police tried to trip him up. The amount of warrants served to him as the president of a motorcycle crew was insane. They'd tried to bring him down again and again. But nothing ever stuck.

Not until his bitch of a Club whore got jealous and threw him to the law.

"You want me to outline it, or are you happy to take my nod that I know about the Corrupts, its perfect history, and your iron-fist control?"

He snarled, anger siphoning through him like liquid fire. "Iron-fist control, my ass. It's out of fucking control." He stopped himself, dragging a hand through his hair again. He smiled. "Sorry, that was uncalled-for. What I meant to say was, the past few years the man I left in charge has decided not to follow my explicit instructions. He's taken my vision and ruined it."

I flicked a finger at a dent in the table. "And what does that have to do with me?"

Wallstreet grinned. "Everything, my dear boy."

Something in his voice had my head snapping up. I glared. "Spill it. Your three minutes were up four minutes ago, and I'm five seconds away from throwing my fist in your face."

He laughed. "Tell me, how often do you think in equations? Do you ever stop calculating?"

I shook my head. "I've been asked that a lot and my best reply is 'fuck off.'"

His smile grew broader.

In reality, the answer to that question was that it was like I live in the fucking matrix with green code falling around me like rain, all day every day. I knew mathematical symbols better than I did the English alphabet. I could work out the hardest trig problem without a calculator. I could give answers to any problem within seconds.

Math—my ultimate love.

Apart from her, of course.

Wallstreet smiled, leaning in once again. "Perfect, I see the answer in your eyes. That's the reply I wanted—what I needed to witness. Tell me, if you get out of here, how many people do you have to ruin?"

My breath caught in my chest. Ruin? Destroy, more like.

"Three. I have three."

"And do you have a plan on how you'll do it?"

I'll walk up to them and put bullets in their brains, then watch as the life drains from their eyes.

I shook my head. Funny, that was the first time I truly let myself contemplate how I would end it. Strangely, it was...unsatisfying. Dreadfully fucking unsatisfying. They deserved to scream. They deserved to feel what I'd felt for the past year. Abandoned, deleted, *lost.*

I gritted my teeth, looking into Wallstreet's blue eyes. "I want to make them suffer. Death will be the last thing they get from me."

The old man nodded. "Another perfect answer. And if I told you I had the means to make that happen. Would you trust me? Trust a stranger who could make you wealthier than you could ever imagine and give you everything you needed to take whatever revenge you wanted?"

I stared at him. I stared hard. I searched for a lie—a trick.

There was nothing but passion in his gaze. Passion I recognized as his own revenge. He wanted to teach whoever hadn't listened a lesson.

Something shifted inside. The traitorous bitch called hope stole once again into my psyche.

Slowly, a smile spread my lips. The suspicion in my veins dissolved and I relaxed. I saw myself in him. The burning. The cursing. The unbearable need to punish and set the status quo.

"I would."

Wallstreet reached across the table, and pulled on my collar until he whispered in my ear. "I'm going to give it all to you, my boy. You obey me, you do everything I fucking tell you, and I'll get you out of this place. I'll give you the Corrupts, I'll make you president, and I'll teach you every damn thing I know about trading, skimming, and controlling not just your empire but the world."

He let me go, holding out his hand. "In return, I ask you to be my ears, eyes, and legs on the outside. To run my business as I expect it to be run. You will be my heir."

A year ago to the day, my life had ended. I would never have guessed I would get a second chance a full 8765.81 hours later.

My brain latched onto a question. "If you can get me out, why can't you work the same magic for yourself?"

Wallstreet lowered his head, his fingers digging into the table. "Because I've been fucking stitched up and have no choice but to do my time. Thirteen more years—nine if I can get out on good behavior. That's too long to wait. It will all be destroyed by then and I can't let that happen."

I whispered, "What makes you think you can get me out? You heard what I did."

The room seemed to quiet—the sounds of my fellow inmates hushing as I waited for his reply.

"Because, Killian, I know the truth. I know everything. And no one should have to live in a world where such traitors exist."

For the first time in a year, gratefulness burned in my chest. He knew. He *believed*. My decision was easy.

I didn't hesitate or think. This was my future. The only way I would get my revenge.

I held my hand out, locking eyes with the man who'd turned from disgraced god to savior.

Wallstreet clasped my grip with his.

I squeezed hard. "You have my word."

He nodded. "I thought I would. I swear on my true name, Cyrus Connors, that I will do right by you. You will never be powerless again."

I trembled, basking in his words. My muscles twitched as the foreign feeling of happiness returned to my rotten soul.

Wallstreet added, "From now on, your name isn't Arthur Killian. It's Kill. And you're the acting president of the Corrupts."

"Kill?"

He let me go, smirking. "You'll be a killer on the stock market and a killer to those who wrong you. Best be honest about who you truly are, don't you think?"

I reclined, smiling a genuine smile. "Yes, I do think. I do indeed."

We grinned.

We nodded.

And that was how Kill was born.

The lessons began immediately.

Wallstreet somehow gained permission to remove me from laundry duty and stole me away for three hours a day in the so-called library. There, he waved away his entourage, set a notepad and pencil before me, and opened my eyes to the wonderful magic of trading.

In those afternoons, with our heads bent together—dark brown to grey—I learned how young I truly was. How archaic my unruly thoughts were.

I lost my attitude the further I fell into his wondrous education. I didn't feel the need to assert my cockiness when my brain absorbed everything he wanted to teach.

Four years I spent with him.

Wallstreet became my entire world. My friend, father, teacher, brother. I loved him. I *trusted* him. And to find that I still had the capacity for either brought tears to my fucking eyes.

I thought they'd broken me, and there was no doubt if Wallstreet hadn't channeled my hatred into something productive, I would've ended up dead or in a straitjacket.

He disciplined me when I failed, he praised me when I succeeded, and most of all he filled my brain with power.

Endless power.

The stock market. Not just options, bonds, and blue-chip corporations, but the highly volatile and equally lucrative foreign currency market. He taught me algorithms and formulas he'd guarded with top secrecy since he dabbled in trading when he was in his early twenties. Foolproof ways to watch, learn, and above all, protect his investment.

He'd never married nor had children. His family was his MC, who were currently ripping his heart apart by going against his every command. He trusted no one. He'd given this legacy to no one.

Just me.

He turned me from a heartbroken betrayed teenager to an educated man with a benefactor with power stretching not just across America but Europe and Asia, too.

Not only did he give me the reins of his trading empire, but he gave me the tools I would need to take out my vengeance cleverly, secretly, and to have so much fucking cash behind me I would never be lonely again.

Four years, six months, seventeen days I served of my life sentence.

Then I got out.

Arthur was dead. Kill was born.

Freedom was granted.

Vengeance was coming.

Four Years Ago

The day I left prison was the scariest, most exciting day of my life.

I knew no one.

My world before Florida State no longer existed, and I'd made no secret that I had nothing but hatred for the ones who'd done this to me.

Wallstreet had pulled a miracle, getting my parole hearing moved up, going above everyone's heads by enlisting favors from people who had the power to undermine the entire defense. He painted me in the perfect light of a reformed underage offender who had been a puppet for others' wrongdoings.

The ironic thing was, none of that was a lie. It was the truth. And finally, the truth had set me free.

"You Kill?"

I held my hand up, shielding my eyes from the glare of the noonday sun. Thrown across my shoulder was a tattered backpack with my worldly possessions in it. The clothes I'd worn when I'd been arrested, the rolled-up math notebook where I'd been solving a supposedly unsolvable problem, and a keepsake from Cleo.

My heart hammered. Pain. Regret. Hatred. *Guilt.*

Don't think about her.

The first opportunity I had, I'd burn the lot. Including the eraser in the shape of a Libra star sign that had never been used to rub out mistakes.

I'd only ever been truly happy around her.

I'd been so fucking in love with her.

Now she was gone. And I had to carry on living without her.

I fucking hated the memories of her—they hurt like a shank to the jugular. Every time I looked at the damn eraser, it ripped out my heart. I couldn't keep it. It hurt too damn much.

Get it together, Killian. This is your new world. The old one is dead.

Striding forward, I nodded. "Yep, I'm Kill."

The guy grinned, holding out his hand. He had to be fucking melting in the black leather jacket with a fireball and some death symbol stitched into it with the words CORRUPT AS THEY COME on the shoulder blades. "I'm Grasshopper."

My eyes narrowed. "Seriously?"

He took my bag, slinging it over his shoulder and moving toward the parking lot. "Nah, my real name is Jared Shearer. But I got the nickname 'cause I like to smoke grass and I got to be VP by hopping over other fucktards." He grinned. "Get it? Grass... hopper?"

It's fucking ridiculous.

I bit my tongue. "Got it."

The last few years of my incarcerated life faded as my past came back—reality stomping rudely into my future. I wasn't surrounded by strict laws or whitewashed walls anymore.

Car horns. Smog. Heat. Children's laughter as a family wagon rolled past. Dogs barking. The loud blare of a stereo.

Complete and utter chaos.

Everything was madness out here.

You better learn quickly how to play the game again.

"Wallstreet told me he'd arranged everything. Care to tell me if that's true?"

Who the hell knew what sort of situation I was about to walk into. After all, Wallstreet had been locked up for fucking years—who was to say he still had power enough to pull off this switch?

I would be the one who would die if it didn't work out.

Grasshopper smiled, his dark mohawk stiff with gel. "Yep, all arranged, dude. He got word to me. I'm one of the few originals."

"Originals?"

"Yep. When Wallstreet was top dog, the Corrupts were a business, you know? We had regular business meetings, profit-and-loss discussions, investment research. We existed in that grey area, you get me? Part in the law, part out of the law. We didn't do harm to others, 'cause we didn't need to run drugs or guns. Wallstreet had us hiding bucketloads of cash so good old Uncle Sam didn't get his sticky fingers on it. He also didn't agree with pimping whores or cooking meth." His voice trailed off.

The loyalty and nostalgia in the guy's voice was touching. Wallstreet was missed—even after all this time. "Sounds like a good deal."

And nothing like the Club I've come from.

"It was. We were tight. Rolling in it. The brothers were the best bastards I knew. But then Wallstreet's fucking tits on the side decided to get back at him for stepping out with a Club bunny. The feds had wanted him for fucking decades, and they finally managed to slap him with white-collar bullshit."

We stopped beside a Harley and another biker dressed all in black. The stranger, with sandy-blond hair and a crooked nose, pushed off from the machine, tossing me the keys.

I caught them, tasting the animosity in the air.

Grasshopper sighed. "Don't mind Mo." Turning to me, he muttered, "Mo, real name Tristan Morgan, is just a bit pissed." Glaring at Mo, he snapped, "Get it together. You're his master-at-arms. You have to be in for reals, dude, else no room for you in this new outfit. Boss's orders."

Mo crossed his arms, his teeth grinding hard. He didn't say a word.

My fingers clenched around the keys to the whiskey-colored Harley behind him. "Having a hard time 'cause I'm a complete stranger and stepping in to be your president?"

Mo bared his teeth. "No, *newbie*. My attitude is because I preferred it when we didn't have a fucking boy who's probably jerked off more than he's ever had a pussy. You're not a man. What the fuck was Wallstreet thinking?"

I straightened my shoulders. "I may be young, but I'm smart and willing to learn."

Mo laughed. "Takes more than book smarts and a kiss-ass attitude to run a Club."

I know. I was groomed to be VP somewhere else.

My temper—the fire I'd been able to smother ever since I met Wallstreet—simmered.

"Don't let them bitch you around, Killian. You're in charge. You answer to nobody but me." Wallstreet's voice jumped into my head. All his lessons and tips—they swam in my brain, completely scrambled. As much as I hated to admit it, Mo was right. I'd gone to prison a fucking virgin. I'd been waiting.

For *her*.

How could I pretend to be a man when I had so many life experiences to catch up on?

Can't think that way.

I had to project the power that Wallstreet had instilled in me. Mo was my bitch. The Corrupts were all my bitches. They had to obey or fucking leave. Those were the choices.

Pulling my shoulders back, I whispered, "Doesn't matter what you think. It doesn't change the fact that you now belong to me."

Mo's eyes widened, his leather jacket creaking over his muscular bulk. "No one fucking owns me, asshole."

This was it—the first standoff—and I had to show my strength. I had to be dominant—to show them I deserved the right to be at the top of the pecking order.

Pulling my fist back, I smiled with grim satisfaction as it cut through the air and crunched against his nose.

The man collapsed to a knee, holding his gushing bloody face. If his crooked nose wasn't broken before, it was now. "What the fuck—"

I might not know what pussy felt like, but I'd been in more fights than I could remember. The prison boxing team had been education for my body while Wallstreet tweaked my mind.

Grasshopper stooped and grabbed the guy beneath his armpits. "Leave it, Mo. You were being a dick. Kill is our new Prez. He takes orders from Wallstreet and no one else. If you're so fucked off at having to obey a dude younger than you, pretend it's Wallstreet you're mouthing off to and we'll see how long that shit will fly."

Mo glowered, his dark eyes watering. I guessed he was in his early thirties. In my book, an IQ like mine and the body of a tried-and-true fighter would win every time.

"You've got some nerve, kid."

I inspected my knuckles, loving the slow comprehension that I was free. Really, *truly* free. My life was my own again. And today marked the first day of my retaliation program.

"Name's not Kid, it's Kill." Swiping a hand through the hair that I'd let grow in prison, I muttered, "And if you know my track record, you'll know I earned that nickname for a reason. Best listen to your mate."

Eyeing up the bike behind Mo, I said, "Do I get my own or are you riding bitch?"

Grasshopper let his brother go, punching me in the bicep. "You've got balls, Kill. I have a feeling you're going to be the iron fist the Club needs."

That's the plan.

"You make them pay for disobeying me. Clean it out. Tear off their patches. Put an end to their fucking nonsense." Wallstreet's instructions were clear. The Corrupts were done. It was time for a new name.

"What happened to the guy I'm replacing?" Wallstreet had special plans for him.

Hopper grinned. His blue eyes glinted with a hint of evil. "You don't need to worry about him, dude. I took care of it."

My stomach twisted. "That wasn't your call to make. It was my job."

"Gut him, Kill. Make a point with him—so other rejects know what happens when they mess with you."

If I didn't have anyone to maim, how would I make my point?

Mo jumped in, swiping a hand over his sandy-blond hair. "It was him or Hopper. Shit got heated. It's done. He's been dead for two days—alligator bait, and dealt with." He stepped into my space. "You got an issue with us cleaning up shop for you?" His voice lowered to a rasp. "Don't forget, *newbie*, we still only take orders from Wallstreet and he told us to ensure it was safe for you to take over. Well, we made it safe."

Rage boiled in my blood. If anyone had got as close to me in prison as Mo was, they would've been unconscious by my feet. My entire body wanted to annihilate him before he became a threat.

That's not how shit works out here.

Taking a deep breath, I dangled the keys to the bike in Mo's face. "Wallstreet has high hopes for his brothers. I'm just delivering them. Grasshopper was right to end the old Prez if it was a matter of self-perseveration, but from now on, if you don't obey me, you don't obey *him*. And if you don't obey him, I have full permission to hurt you."

Mo's eyes burned into mine, willing me to back down. "You'll hurt me, huh?"

Lowering my brow, I growled, "You don't want to know what will happen if you piss me off."

I was done being used, abused, and thrown away to rot.

The air hazed with anger. I waited for him to strike—my muscles bunched, hands clenched. But then the tension dispersed as Mo rolled his shoulders and grinned. "I like you, newbie. You got guts, and whatever life did to you to get you in the slammer—you've come out better for it." Holding his hand out, he shook my grip in welcome. "Get on the bike; we're going home."

Home.

I wouldn't let anyone stand in my way ever again.

It was time to start my new rule.

"Will she do?" Grasshopper strolled into my new quarters. I'd commandeered Wallstreet's old rooms at the compound in the Keys. It backed onto the Everglades, all one level, with barbed-wire fencing hemming us in like animals.

I knew it was to protect us from other gangs or idiot druggies, but the second I walked through the patrolled gates and into the courtyard of the run-down, paint-peeling hellhole, I wanted out.

My skin crawled. My soul screamed for freedom. I didn't walk free from prison only to chain myself back up again with a bunch of leather-wearing bikers.

The inside of the compound wasn't much better with graffiti spray-painted on the walls, cigarette-burned couches, and bedrooms that reeked of sex, pizza, and dope.

Wallstreet's room hadn't been used—so that was a fucking blessing—but it still had bars on the windows, mildew in the carpet, and an adjoining bathroom that made my metal shitter at Florida State look like a fucking suite.

I can't stay here.

Already the walls hemmed me in—my temper rising with every breath, preparing to fight for freedom.

"You won't like it when you get there. I'll hazard a guess it'll be completely run-down and like a fucking dump site by now. But no matter where you want to go, you can't leave. Not until you've got full control. Then you can live off-site if you have the men you trust acting while you're gone—but not before, Kill. You'll stay there until you've taken care of things."

At the time, it'd been no hardship to swear. I couldn't imagine anything worse than prison. So, like a fucking moron, I swore.

Now I wanted to revoke that promise. But I couldn't. I'd given my word, and Wallstreet was the only one deserving of my loyalty.

"Kill?" Grasshopper brought my attention back to him. Striding farther into the room, he dragged a blonde with him. She had a big rack and wore a skintight tiger-print dress and heels that turned her from midget to model.

She fit the seediness of the room perfectly.

She's not her.

My heart twisted and I gritted my teeth.

"She's great. Thanks."

Grasshopper grinned, shoving the girl toward the king-size black-covered bed. "Had her on standby. Know what it's like to get out of the slammer and need a welcome party." He winked. "You got the rest of the night. Go nuts, Kill."

I smiled, remaining silent until he'd closed the door.

Striding over to where he'd disappeared, I turned the dead bolt and spun to face the whore. "What's your name?"

Fuck, what am I doing?

All I could see was Cleo. All I could hear was Cleo. All I fucking wanted was Cleo.

Her eyes drifted from the top of my head, down my chest, to my cock. She licked her lips, stumbling forward in her ridiculous shoes. "You can call me whatever you want, Prez."

I held up my finger. "I'm not the president until the ceremony tomorrow. Call me Kill. And I'm going to call you..."

Buttercup's name danced on my tongue. Her smile blazed in my brain. Her laugh echoed in my ears.

Fuck.

I was so fucking horny—had been for ten years. I'd wanted to take her, to make love to the girl who'd had my heart the moment I saw her. But out of decency for our families, and our ages at the time, I'd avoided taking things too far.

I wasn't a guy who wanted to whore around. I knew how precious Cleo was. I knew that the moment I took her, she would be mine for eternity and I'd be hers. I'd wanted it to be perfect.

You were a dick for waiting.

Now, I was about to lose my virginity to a Club bunny who'd sucked more cocks and slept with more bikers than minutes I'd been alive. 12,622,776. Okay, maybe not that many, but still—a fucking lot.

"I'm not picking your name. Give me one and I'll use it."

She smiled, resting her fingertips against my chest. "Okay, call me Meadow." Her body shifted closer, pressing her large tits against me. The softness of her body sent a need so damn strong through my blood I knew I wouldn't last long.

Placing my hands on her shoulders, completely fucking dwarfing her small frame, I walked her backward till the backs of her knees hit the bed.

She fell, sprawling onto the covers, a small laugh escaping.

Meadow's laugh was nothing like Cleo's. It was all kinds of wrong and almost threatened to kill my hard-on.

My mouth ached to kiss; my tongue wanted nothing more than to taste. But not this woman. Not a whore who I didn't want. Only the girl from my past.

The first time I'd kissed Cleo—the first time I'd broken my stupid rules and let her win—I'd known. My fate was sealed to hers and she had power over me more than anyone.

She would've given me her virginity in that wonderful afternoon, but I'd stopped. I'd been a fucking idiot and thought we had forever.

Instead, here I was about to fuck a stranger just because I had to get her out of my mind once and for all. My past was dead to me.

She had to be, too.

"Do you have a condom?" My voice was rough, angry.

Meadow nodded, pulling a packet from her cleavage. I stole it from her fingers. It was warm and the rubber inside slipped like disgusting slime against the foil. Placing it on the bedspread in easy reach, I growled, "On your knees."

I couldn't do this looking into her eyes.

I swallowed hard. *Goddammit.*

I'd survived almost five years in a penitentiary without thinking of her, yet the moment I got out and saw the gift she'd given me all those years ago, I couldn't stop her invasion.

You're cheating on her.

I wasn't.

I couldn't cheat on her.

She's dead.

Meadow rolled onto her knees, wriggling her ass, hoisting her tight dress past her hips to her waist. She wasn't wearing underwear. She spread her legs for me, just like she had for the twenty members of the Corrupts.

My teeth locked at the blatant display of female body parts. I could fucking stare all day.

My cock didn't care that this woman wasn't Cleo. It didn't care that she'd been a permanent fixture serving the men who'd betrayed Wallstreet.

All it cared about was fixing a problem. Leaving boyhood for my new future.

Unbuckling my jeans, I slipped the heavy denim to my ankles. I still wasn't used to the scratch against my legs after the well-worn cotton of jumpsuits at Florida State.

I didn't bother touching her or myself.

Grabbing the condom, I tore it open, screwed my face up at how gross the fucking thing felt, and rolled it awkwardly down my length.

"Move back," I growled.

Meadow immediately obeyed, inching her ass backward, wetness glistening between her thighs. My hands landed on her hips, positioning her exactly where I wanted.

She looked over her shoulder, hazel eyes glowing with lust. "You don't want me to suck you? Don't you want to fool around a bit first?"

Hell no.

Anger popped in my blood; I couldn't help myself. Grabbing her chin, I forced her head to face the mattress. "Don't look at me."

Don't look at me with eyes that make me hate myself. Don't make me miss her any more than I already do.

I should've been gagging for this. I should've been panting and so fucking happy at having a willing woman on her knees about to take my cock, but all I could focus on was the guilt-ridden heart inside my chest.

Godddammit, stop it.

"Give me your hands."

She obeyed without question and I used my discarded belt to tie her wrists together. Now she couldn't touch me either. I might fuck her but I would never seek comfort from her. Comfort I didn't fucking deserve.

Gritting my teeth, I grabbed my cock and positioned myself at her entrance.

Her back tensed, her fingers opening and closing in the confines.

The moment stretched, anticipation sparking in my blood.

Then I slammed home.

Possibly too hard, probably too fast. I didn't know—I had no fucking experience. But Meadow didn't seem to care. Her head flew back as I pulled out and drove in again.

"Oh God," she moaned as I moved inside her, testing, learning.

Her heat was subtle, her wetness hidden from me thanks to the condom, but the action of filling a woman like I hadn't done before was enough to make me stop thinking of Cleo and throw myself into my first-ever fuck.

That night, when the compound had finally quieted, and I'd showered off the three rounds of sex I'd indulged in, I got up the guts to pull the Libra eraser from my jeans pocket.

I flopped onto my back glaring at the ceiling of my cell... I meant room. I'd only been here a few hours, but I already hated living at the Clubhouse. It was ridiculous. A bunch of grown men all living together. What happened to freedom and our own space? What happened to disinfectant and a vacuum cleaner? What happened to family and love?

The eraser was too heavy—too knowing—in my fingers. It was the sign for justice. The sign for right and wrong. And also my star sign. Go fucking figure. Hadn't known until she'd told me.

Serendipitous, really—turned out my personality matched, too. She'd told me she was a Sagittarius. That she wasn't meant to love someone who wasn't a Capricorn or an Aries. But she'd make an exception just for me.

We'd lay on the roof of the garage where a bunch of Harleys, Hondas, and Triumphs were bedded down for the night. She'd whispered the traits of a Libra.

She rolled to face me, tracing my face with her gentle fingers. "You're graceful."

I huffed. "On my bike, maybe, but nowhere else."

"Peaceful."

I laughed. "Um, biggest lie yet."

She shook her head, seriousness drenching her green eyes. "You are peaceful. You fight for what you believe in. You fight to protect what's yours, but in your heart...you're kind and gentle and not a part of this world." Her voice dropped to a whisper. "Same as me."

My heart clenched. The words I love you *weighed on my tongue. I hadn't said it yet. But, fuck, I wanted to.*

Her lips twisted into a smile. "You're also an idealist."

I nodded, pulling myself back from love and her being mine forever. "Okay, kind of agree with that one." I had hopes. I had dreams. And I wasn't settling.

"Those all sound pretty good. Any bad traits I should watch out for?"

She sighed, her eyes latching onto my lips, making me hard and dying to kiss her. "Superficial and vain."

I sighed dramatically. "Ah, so the perfection ends." Pressing my body against hers, I murmured, "Pity I agree with them the most."

She whispered, "Reliable. You're also reliable."

The traitorous word slashed through the memory, dumping me back to the present.

Reliable.

Fuck that, I wished I was the most unreliable bastard. I wished that part of the damn Libra personality had screwed up. I was the most reliable person I knew. Pity others saw that—exploited that.

Reliability was the main reason my life fell apart.

I was too damn trusting. Too damn reliable.

Too fucking *blind.*

I balanced the eraser on my knuckles, flipping it over and over from one side of my hand to the other. *Get rid of it.*

My heart hurt to think of everything I'd lost. It was time to destroy it.

Not yet.

I can't.

...not yet.

My stomach clenched thinking about tomorrow. It didn't just clench, it fucking twisted until my last prison lunch threatened to escape though my fucking nose. For the billionth time, I second-guessed myself. So much could go wrong. So much shit could hit the fan and rain all over my headless corpse.

Wallstreet had given me the key to my future. He'd given me more than anyone, but like anything, it was up to me to make it work.

I checked the small clock on the bedside table. Four hours and counting. Four hours before I would be initiated and say good-bye to my past forever.

The next day I took control of my empire.

If it went well, I'd live to see another sunrise. If it didn't...

I'm too young to die.

Should've thought about that before you agreed to this.

A thrill of excitement ran down my spine. It was a potent mix of fear, retaliation, and the knowledge my life would never be the same.

The moment I entered the disgustingly dirty common room, the large men—some bald, some with ponytails, others with more body hair than facial hair—all turned to face me.

Grasshopper appeared from the tattered boxing ring in the middle of the room, where the rigging had been draped with extra jackets of the Corrupts, along with the items I'd told him to put in place. A large bucket of water, a blowtorch, towels, and a tattoo artist with a fully equipped mobile studio.

I nodded.

He nodded in return.

I hadn't expected to find help on this side of the world, but Wallstreet had earned not just my loyalty in this Club but Grasshopper's and Mo's, too. I felt a kinship with them that I hoped wouldn't bite me in the ass in the future.

"Everyone, pay attention," Grasshopper shouted, cutting out grumbling conversation. "As you know, Kill has been hand-selected by Wallstreet. We all know his instructions, and there won't be any arguments. Got it?"

The room suddenly thickened with animosity.

Couldn't really blame them. Staring at me with my unweathered face, no calluses on my hands, and no experience other than prison.

But it wasn't up to them to decide if they liked me. It was up to them to *obey* me.

Stepping forward, I clasped a hand on Hopper's shoulder. "I'll take it from here."

A few of the older members snickered, elbowing each other with anger in their eyes. I locked them in my stare. "I know a few of you won't survive the transition. I have no doubt I'll strip a few of you from your patches. And I also have no doubt that some of you will try and end this. But I'm here to tell you that I know how your mind works. I know because mine used to work the same way. You feel betrayed by someone you trusted. Furious at change.

"All I can offer is this. Yield or suffer. There is no other way."

Stalking to the boxing ring, I swung up through the ropes, pointing at the tattoo artist. "Today, you will swear allegiance to me; there won't be a ceremony to welcome me into your Club because the Corrupts no longer exist."

Men moved forward with outrage. "What?"

"Listen here, you little pissant."

Grasshopper jumped into the ring, waving his hand at the uproar rippling around the room. He dropped his voice. "Uh, Kill? What you doing, dude?"

I'm doing what he told me.

"I'm dissolving the Corrupts. From now on we're Pure Corruption."

His blue eyes narrowed. "And he sanctioned this?"

I nodded. "He knows. It was his plan. He knew I wouldn't be able to take over as Prez and keep the name. It just wasn't going to work. So I'm starting my own crew with his men." Glaring around the room, I preached, "You follow me, I promise you everything Wallstreet ever did. I'll give you money. I'll give you power. I'll ensure you never go to jail to serve time on shithead crimes that we don't need to do. Our law will be steadfast and you'll be true brothers again."

My voice lowered. "Don't follow me and you'll be out. Your tattoo will be burned off, and you'll be gone for good."

Shrugging out of my borrowed jacket, I tore my T-shirt over my head and straddled the tattooist's chair.

The Corrupts were about to leave their dinosaur-bone-chewing carcasses behind and enter a new century.

This was no longer a crime syndicate where personal hygiene and house cleanliness didn't matter. This would be a smooth operation. A business. A brotherhood.

Mine.

My weapon against the men who owed me their screams.

"You—you can't—"

My eyes fell on a potbellied man with a thick black beard. "Let me ask you a question. When you joined the Corrupts, what drew you to it?"

The room went quiet as men recalled their pasts.

Fists were still clenched, anger ripe in the air, but slowly answers trickled to my ears.

"To obey our own rules rather than a corrupt government."

I nodded. "Good reason."

"I joined for the business side. Wallstreet made me a wealthy man."

I thumped my naked chest, vowing, "Follow me, and I will again."

"To ride and have a place to go with brothers."

I searched for the man who spoke but couldn't pick him from the twenty pairs of eyes watching me. "Would you rather those brothers had no guidance? Violence and jail time ruining your peace?"

A ripple of discontent went through the room.

"Accept me as your president, join me and become a Pure, and I swear on my life and Wallstreet's, you will have peace, you will have your wealth, you will have your brotherhood."

My voice lost its edge; I allowed a small trace of vulnerability to show. "I know I'm new, I'm young, and I'm likely to screw up as I rebuild Wallstreet's empire, but I promise I will deliver. I understand what it's like to be betrayed, and that will never happen if you follow me."

Shit, I wasn't there for blood and glory. I was there for revenge. And if they didn't fucking like it, they knew how to leave and it wasn't through the front door.

It was Mo who vouched for me. "We've talked about this at length, Corrupts. You saw what happened to Magnet when he didn't want to be part of the evolution. Now's your time to put your oath where your fucking mouth is and pledge." He looked at me, his face hard. "As much as I don't like taking orders from a newbie, he's a good kid. He's been spoken for. And...I think we should give him a go."

The room went silent.

I looked over my shoulder at the tattoo artist. "Ready?"

The bald guy nodded, already knowing the logo, the motto, and everything he'd been told to do. He had a long night ahead of him. Amending each brother's tattoo to reflect the new logo of Pure Corruption: an abacus with a skull and coins waterfalling from its mouth. And a Libra scale hidden in the design. For balance of right and wrong.

My heart skipped as her green eyes entered my mind.

And for her.

Admit it.

I wouldn't.

My heart would never forget the girl who'd died way too young. Who left me for heaven and ruined my life more surely than any prison sentence.

"What's our new motto?" A man with a greying ponytail asked.

A smile twisted my lips. " 'Pure in Thoughts and Vengeance. Corrupt in all Things that Matter.' "

It was as if the words resonated in their biker hearts. The anger switched to eagerness and fists unclenched.

My teeth gritted against the first bite of pain as the tattoo needle pierced my shoulder blades. I would be the first to don the new cut. As was my right as president.

My mind drifted as the hum of the needle melded with the rock 'n' roll radio station someone turned on. Wallstreet's planning from Florida State was impeccable, just like his bookkeeping—so far, the takeover was following the plan to perfection.

Not only had Wallstreet taught me how to control my anger, funnel my need for vengeance, and line my bank balance using the stock market, but he'd given me the numbers of safety deposit boxes and bank account details, and handed over his entire legacy.

All for one simple request: to ensure his MC returned to its former glory. And to put into action his largest plan of all: political domination. Wallstreet was no longer satisfied with controlling companies through stocks and bonds. He wanted the power to rewrite laws and create a world he believed would be better than the shit-filled one we currently inhabited.

He wanted it all.

He wanted to take on the government one decree and corrupt senator at a time.

And I was the linchpin to make it all happen.

I would make Pure Corruption shine brighter and stronger than ever before. And when they were ready, they would be my weapon.

I would become invincible.

I'd been ruined, but now I would rule.

Nine Days Ago

Fuck, I hurt.

Everywhere.

Goddamn idiots not accepting the change of ownership. I'd won. Four years ago, I'd proven my point, taken the Corrupts and turned them into Pure Corruption, and done everything Wallstreet ever wanted me to do.

I'd gained power. I'd brought the men back from the brink of ruin and created a smooth business once again.

I was rich. I was in charge. I was... if not happy, then content.

And the time had finally come to start the process I'd been waiting 86,750 hours for—ever since my past betrayed me.

The first year was rocky. Fights, retaliations, men testing my control. But in the end they'd come to the right conclusion—there was no point in arguing. It was done. Not just on home turf but in the other nine Chapters around the states.

I had the oaths to prove it.

I was the president now.

And nobody, fucking *nobody*, was allowed to say otherwise.

Which was what fucked me off about tonight.

I was the bastard to end all bastards. My word was law and I had a shitload of new ones to dish out.

"Kill—the shipment's in full view. We need to get it locked down." Hopper cocked his head.

My eyes shot up. The truck that'd arrived at the tail end of the fight rested like a fucking poster for crime beneath a streetlight of the industrial estate where our power wrestle went down.

"Why didn't they park it at the back, for Christ's sake?"

Hopper shrugged. "Because they're a bunch of fucking monkeys. Told you we should never have let them do it."

It went against every rule I'd set down when I'd taken over, but Wallstreet for some reason wanted this one shipment to be done. Five girls to be sold. Trafficking—dirty business and one I argued against until he'd let me choose the women who'd slept with the fucking devil—my father.

A wash of light-headedness crept over me. I stumbled, then blinked. *Whoa, what the fuck?* Looking down at my all-black attire, even the darkness of the night didn't hide the seriously fucked-up situation I was in.

Ah, shit.

I hadn't felt it. Hyped up on adrenaline and acting with complete recklessness, I hadn't felt a blade slice my flesh. My jacket and T-shirt were drenched in black liquid. Not that it was really black.

It was red.

And warm.

And fucking sticky.

The very stuff keeping me alive, which should be in my veins, was pouring down the front of my goddamn chest.

Hopper's eyes followed mine, narrowing in worry. "Shit, Kill. You're not looking so hot."

I growled under my breath, "Don't let them hear you. I'll get patched up when we're back. Not before. No weaknesses. Remember?"

Hopper and Mo were the only ones I trusted. The only ones I would ever say that sort of shit to.

He nodded. "All right, let's get those bitches out of sight, before the pigs get here. Then we'll get you patched."

Together, we crossed the concrete, which was now pockmarked with bullets and stained with blood. The bodies would be left. The cops would try to work out what went down, but I knew how to plant evidence. They wouldn't go against the governor of the state, who was a personal friend and on my roll call of puppets.

No one argued with me. No one argued with a guy with a high IQ, a proven track record, and an extra arsenal.

In the four years I'd been in charge, I'd amassed more wealth than I would ever be able to spend, I'd donated to charities, funded schools, paid for politician voting campaigns—all in the name of building a rock-solid persona.

All in the name of buying unlimited power.

I wasn't hated. I was *loved*. On both sides of the law. Two lives I could use, and friends in high places, who created the perfect alibi and protected my brothers.

Moving closer to the truck, I noticed the back door was open and three women lay bound in the mud. What the hell were these idiots doing?

"Get them up," I ordered.

The two prospects and three full members who'd been on the scouting mission scowled. "Where's Slice?"

I cocked my chin behind me. "Over there."

Their eyes frowned, searching the darkness for the corpse of their ex upriser—the man who thought he could steal the Pures from under my nose. The fucking idiot who'd tried to lead a rebellion against me.

No matter what I gave them, some of the men still hadn't learned. Stand against me and you would do only one thing.

Die.

"What, so you killed our nominee and now you think we're gonna follow you?"

I nodded. "'Bout the gist of it."

"You said if we ever had an issue with your leadership we could contest."

"I said you could bring it up with me and I'd do my best to fix the issue—not to plot behind my back, asshole."

The man charged forward. "We've followed you against our will for four years, Kill. When will you fucking learn we don't want you? We want true Corrupt blood, not a fucking traitor."

I stormed to meet him, fists to fists. Adrenaline was fast leaving my system, the wound making me woozy and nauseous. Someone needed to tell the world to pick a way up and stick to it. But I wouldn't back down from a fight. Ever.

"You have one choice. You wear the cut. You follow the code. You're in for life. You either accept the changes in management once and for all, or you fuck off and don't come back. One-time offer." I stood ready to beat him to a pulp.

The guy swallowed hard. "But if you cut us out we're done. We swore an oath to Magnet. Not to you or Wallstreet. He's our true leader."

"He's also dead." I shrugged. "If you decide to leave, you'll be a deserter. So you better choose wisely, or follow the same path Magnet did."

My heart suddenly lurched painfully; agony from the bloody wound shot through my system. I shivered as a chill seeped into my bones. I needed to wrap this up fast, before I passed out like a bitch.

"Make up your mind. You got ten seconds." Nodding at Grasshopper, I said, "Pick up the merchandise. Get them back in the truck. We're not leaving them at this warehouse. Not now, with this mess."

Hopper moved forward, barking orders to loyal members while others watched the guys who preferred carnage and idiocy instead of evolution.

"Your ten seconds are up. What's your decision?"

A prospect stepped to my side—no words, just a slight nod. Good enough for me.

The other prospect backed away, shaking his head. Fine, he didn't count. He hadn't sworn. He'd just go back to being unsanctioned and free to be picked up by any old fucking group.

The main man who tried to have me killed, glared. Slowly, he gritted his jaw and nodded. "Fine. I'm in. But I want a meeting. I want a democratic vote."

I laughed. "There's no such thing in our world. Don't like it, you just lost your chance to leave, so you fucking deal. You hear me?"

The guy glowered. Shit, I didn't have the strength to fight again. The earth beneath my feet had become unstable. My heart was losing a steady rhythm. My veins were probably bone-dry after pumping that shit down my front.

"Fine."

I held out my hand, shook his once, then spun toward the truck.

Striding forward, I ignored the idiots who'd fought against us, heading straight to the pile of girls cowering in the mud.

On a closer look, the closest woman wasn't cowering at all. Her long red hair stuck to her neck, her face tilted, almost as if she could see the commotion and carnage through the blindfold. Her body was elegant with a full chest and long legs. Her parted lips full and pink.

Despite my injury, my cock twitched in interest.

I squatted in front of her, removing the blindfold.

Green eyes.

I almost fucking died on the spot.

Cleo!

No. It couldn't be.

Everything I thought I knew ceased to exist. My world spun to a stop.

Her.

The woman who haunted my dreams and made me wish so much that life had turned out differently.

The girl who'd wormed her way into my adolescent heart and refused to be carved out, no matter how many women I fucked.

The dead girl.

The girl whose tombstone rested beside her parents', hidden deep in my past.

The girl who I betrayed.

"You're doing this, Arthur. Get in there. Now." My father shoved the silenced pistol into my hand. For weeks he'd been forcing me to obey. Feeding me shit about how the Club would be better for it.

I'd ignored him. I'd fought against it.

But then he'd found my ultimate weakness.

Grabbing me around the neck, he hauled me close. "If you don't do this tonight, I'm going over there and raping that fucking bitch then putting a bullet between her eyes. I'm done with you not obeying me."

Rage crippled my heart. "Don't you dare fucking touch her."

His fingers tightened, hurting. "Do what I tell you and she lives. Her fate is in your hands, son. Choose wisely."

His voice dropped to a hiss. "One last chance. Obey and I'll let her live. Don't... and I'll make you watch while I steal that virginity you want so much and kill her."

My fingers curled around the handle of the pistol. I loved Thorn and Petal Price. They'd accepted me into their family even though I wasn't good enough for their daughter. They were good people. Decent people.

Unlike the family I came from.

The atmosphere in my home was full of greed and animosity, not love and companionship. Even my own brother hated me just because I'd earned the love of someone as precious as Cleo.

"Go, Killian. Get it done."

My father shoved me out the door, where the night swallowed me up and the devil welcomed me into his clutches.

My fingers itched to pull out the Libra eraser from my pocket. The keepsake I never found the courage to chuck out. I carried it with me every day—stoking my vengeance.

That night was forever seared onto my brain. I never truly recalled the exact sequence of events. I'd disobeyed time and time again. I remembered beatings after beatings, and when threats stopped working, my father had resorted to more... drastic measures.

The nausea that always came whenever I thought about that night wrapped around my throat.

You can't change the past.

But you can mold the future.

I leaned closer, wondering if life had finally come to torment me. To scramble my mind and show me just how much I'd lost when I gave in to my father.

Suspicion blazed up my spine and straight into my motherfucking heart. I hadn't thought I had one anymore—but there it was, shaking off cobwebs and shadowy dust to beat hot and red and true.

But then I looked closer, searching for recognition of the love that once blazed on my girl's face, and saw nothing.

She stared back with trepidation and a strange curiosity, but there was nothing linking us.

She looked like my Sagittarius, but it couldn't be her.

She was a stranger.

She had no right to wear the face of my dead soul mate or look at me through the eyes of my lover.

My heart hardened like a fossilized beast.

Whoever she was, I hated her.

Hated her to the depths of hell.

I wanted her gone.

I wanted her dead.

Present

Cleo shifted beside me.

Sleep stuck to my thoughts, making everything sluggish. How

long had I been unconscious? Dreaming of the past, the horrible shit I'd done, the mess my world had been ever since my father had beaten me stupid and dragged me into her house.

My mind locked tight, refusing to think about what happened—what I'd done.

Her body snuggled closer, tucking into mine like a mirroring piece to my soul. I nuzzled into her neck, breathing in her sleep-contented scent.

Will you ever be able to forgive me?

Will I ever live in a world where I'm not shattered by my love for you, because I know one day soon you won't want it?

My questions were self-obsessed. Focused on the pain in my heart, regardless of the pain I'd caused in hers.

If she knew how grateful I was that her amnesia kept certain things from her, she'd hate me for eternity. I was petrified every time she said she remembered a sliver of her past.

She already does hate me—she just hasn't remembered why yet.

I wanted to lay my heart at her feet and beg, fucking beg for forgiveness. But that would be asking too much. She'd never be able to grant me absolution and give me back the love I used to hold so fiercely when we were younger.

I'd lost the right to be loved by her.

No amount of revenge would make her absolve my crimes.

I would never stop living with one step in hell. I had to accept that.

You won't be granted redemption.

I held her tighter, holding my brightly inked Buttercup with arms that shook with mourning.

Her warm form sent my heart hammering with both love and grief. She was still the same girl from my past, only scarred by flames and painted by ink. She'd grown even more beautiful, more unique.

And I'd never fucking deserve her.

Who knew how much longer I'd be permitted to hold her before she remembered.

And she *would* remember.

It was only a matter of time.

I swallowed hard as my worst memory took my mind hostage.

A gasp sounded behind me.

Shit!

Spinning around, I aimed the gun at the apparition in the doorway.

There was no one there.

But I'd seen her.

I'd recognized the shape of her body I fantasized about every night. I'd recognized the small sound of horror falling from her lips.

She'd seen me.

I was so consumed with memories and melancholy, I didn't hear the noise that heralded the end of my world.

Everything seemed to happen in slow motion.

I saw the shadow.

I ordered my body to move. To protect. To kill.

I raised an arm to fight.

But it was too late.

The bat whistled through the darkness, striking the side of my head before I'd untangled myself from Cleo.

My last thought as a diabolical headache shot me into unconsciousness was *Not her. Kill me but leave her the fuck alone.*

But my mouth was no longer in my control.

My eyes closed.

My world ended.

I abandoned her to monsters all over again.

Chapter Twenty-Six

Out of every scenario I could've envisioned for my future…

This was not it.

This wasn't allowed to fucking happen.

How was I supposed to stay human when they'd taken her from me, not once, but twice?

How was I supposed to stay rational and follow my plan when they'd left me destitute?

The answer was scarily simple.

I couldn't.

I *wouldn't.*

There was only one path left for me. One target. One goal.

I wanted their screams.

They would pay for their sins.

I embraced the madness and bloodlust in my soul.

It was time to end this.

Once and for fucking all.

—*Kill*

I woke up.

I went to scream.

A hand planted over my mouth.

A weapon sailed through the air, striking Arthur in the temple.

Tears burst from my eyes as he crumbled into unconsciousness beside me.

I fought. Fuck, I fought.

But it wasn't enough.

Something pricked my arm.

Ice stole through my veins.

My eyes flew wide as something foul slapped against my mouth. The painful prick spread listless lethargy through my blood.

Clouds fogged my brain.

The glint of a needle in the moonlight told me the truth even as tendrils of vapors swam faster through my veins.

They'd found me.

They knew who I was.

I looked into the gaze of Alligator/Lighter Boy—the hazel-eyed man who played with fire—the same man who'd stolen me the first time.

Now he would steal me again. Captured and taken as if I'd never existed.

I forced my heavy head to loll to the side, more tears streaking down my cheeks.

Arthur!

He was unconscious, a trickle of blood coming from his mouth. Another biker stood over him with a bat.

"No!" I screamed, but it came out as a whispered sob behind Lighter Boy's palm.

"Got a date, pretty Dagger. Got a date with fucking destiny."

I floated away, falling faster and faster into an abyss as the drugs stole my lucidity.

The last thing I remembered was his rancid lips on mine as the shutters in my head slammed closed and I disappeared into the void.

I woke up for the second time.

Pain.

Horrendous pain lived inside my head.

Smacking my lips, I tried to lubricate my dry mouth. My body was a throbbing, screaming mess, refusing to resemble the woman I'd been before.

I searched my mind for that terrifying wall locking my past away. *Please don't let my amnesia protect me again.*

I didn't care it was a self-preservation thing. I wouldn't be able to stand it if everything I'd fought so hard to remember was... gone.

Tentatively, I prodded and pushed my mind, testing the darkness—making sure it wasn't padlocked and chained.

But something was different.

Memories swarmed—recent and terrifying.

"Take her."

"I'm not taking her."

I groaned, my cheek squashed against the hotel carpet. My head rang from being cuffed and nausea took my stomach hostage, threatening to evict the room service I'd ordered only an hour before. "What—what do you want with me?" I slurred, trying uselessly to push myself upright.

The carpet was comfortable. My only friend. I would stay there for a little while.

The men stopped arguing.

One squatted beside my face, his horrible fingers brushing aside my hair. "We've found you. After all this fucking time. Didn't believe him when he said it was true. But here you are."

"Here I am?"

The man with hazel eyes chuckled. "Here you are. A girl who should've stayed away."

Why was I there? I couldn't remember. Then, in a flash of remembrance, I said, "A letter. I received a letter."

The cold chuckle came again. "Yes, a letter from him. He said you'd come. I didn't think you would. You owe me a hundred dollars for betting wrong."

With a kick to my stomach, he rolled me over so I lay staring at the light shade above. My eyes tried to focus on the two men looming above but couldn't—they were blurs.

"Take her. We'll keep her separate from the other shipment. Kill will never know."

"Why don't we just kill her? He wants to ruin him. This would do it."

The other man, in a deeper voice that rumbled with rocks and tar, said, "It's not enough. She needs to be seen. Doubt needs to be planted before we can get rid of her. Besides, I want the money that her sweet little body will bring."

A boot pressed against my breast. I cringed away.

Cold fingers wrapped around my forearm. "What's it going to be, Cleo? Fire or persuasion?"

Cleo?

My nose wrinkled. "You've got the wrong girl. My name is Sarah."

For some reason they both laughed. "This is just getting better and better."

The deep-voiced man said, "Do it. If he's right, then it will solve our issues. He's been right about everything else."

I cried out as a knife rang in the sparsely decorated Dancing Dolphins hotel room, slicing efficiently through my cardigan.

Fight filled my limbs and I lashed out. I went to scream but a large hand clamped over my mouth.

"Do it. Now."

The flick of a lighter and whiff of fire sent my heart tripping over itself in terror.

Fire.

My nemesis. The one thing I was petrified of. I couldn't light a stovetop or go near a barbeque. Fire. I hated it. Hated!

"No!" I screamed behind the hand—the sound remained muffled and useless.

Lighter Boy moved closer, waving the naked flame by my arm. "Ready, Cleo?"

My name is Sarah!

I hated that everything they did was to the wrong person. I pitied this Cleo person but I wanted her to take whatever repercussions her life had brought upon herself—not me. I wasn't her. I didn't deserve to be burned. Couldn't they see my body was full of scars? Hadn't I suffered enough?

The first singe of flame on flesh made my body snap and shudder. The man holding my mouth moved, planting his knees on my shoulders and pinning me to the floor.

I couldn't scream.

I couldn't move.

The lighter moved closer, the merrily orange flame stealing more than just my sanity and pain but the past eight years of my life, too.

I snapped out of the memory, breathing hard.

All along, I hadn't seen the truth.

I suffered two layers of amnesia—seemingly two events triggered by fire, but all along they'd been linked. All along I'd been Cleo Price *and* Sarah Jones—joined by a tragic history.

My mind had learned that protection came from forgetting and it had once again tried to save me.

I lay on a bed that was decorated with buttercups and daisies, staring at a ceiling.

A horrible blanket of terror covered me.

No... this can't be.

My eyes drank in the cursive quote from *The Princess Bride* on the ceiling.

"As You Wish."

I gasped.

This was *my* room.

My childhood room at the Dagger Rose compound. *But that can't be—it burned down.*

"Ah, you're awake, Buttercup."

I shot upright, huddling into the corner on the bed. Everywhere around me rested familiarity and home. From the frilly yellow bedside light to the macaroni-and-glue photo frame holding a photograph of Arthur and me at our favorite swimming hole.

Although... the photo that'd been in that frame before was of us baking with his mom, all covered in flour, not swimming. And the light shade had been bigger.

"Do you like it?"

Unwillingly, my attention shot to the one man who should've been there to protect me. A surrogate father, an uncle, my in-law if Arthur and I ever got married.

Wrapping my arms around my knees, I glared at Scott "Rubix" Killian. He looked similar to his youngest son, but not completely the same. Arthur had inherited his beautiful green eyes from him, but the kindness in his soul definitely hadn't come from this bastard, who'd set my house on fire and left me to burn.

"What's going on?" I asked. My voice was a wispy thread, tangled in memories and uncertainty. Clearing my throat, I tried again. "What am I doing here?"

Rubix came closer, his black leather jacket blazing with red thread of a rose being shanked by a dagger. "You're home. What more do you want to know?"

I looked around the room that at first glance looked like my childhood sanctuary. My mind was full of curses while truth slipped though my frantic heartbeats as I tried to make sense of everything. "This isn't my home."

Rubix chuckled, sitting heavily on the edge of the mattress. "You always were smart, Buttercup."

"Don't! Don't you dare use my father's nickname for me."

He held up his hands, showing a folded file in his right palm. "Touchy, touchy. No need to draw blood... yet." His green eyes glittered. "You're right, this isn't your old room, but I thought you'd recognize it just the same." Leaning forward in a cloud of mechanical grease and leather, he murmured, "Go on. Take a guess as to where you are."

"I already know I'm at the Dagger Rose compound."

He nodded. "Yes, that's obvious. But where in the compound?"

Forcing myself not to freak out, I looked harder at my surroundings. The walls had been freshly painted to mirror mine, the bedspread as close to the one I had that it was uncanny, but the space was different, the cornicing slightly odd.

My heart charged with knowledge.

No!

This was just cruel.

Rubix knew when I'd figured it out. "Do you like the improvements? After all, Arthur was never coming home. What with serving time and then leaving to betray me even further with a rival gang, I found no reason to keep his old décor."

He reached out and patted my knee.

I cringed away from his touch.

"I had my men decorate it for you. So you felt welcome with your own family once again."

"You aren't my family," I spat. "You *killed* my family."

He laughed, waving the file in his hand. "You continue believing that, princess. And while you do, how about some light reading?"

He placed it on the bedspread, his face tightening. "Inside is the truth. The complete truth. About your death, your parents' death, Arthur's trial, my testimony, and everything your fucking lover—my bastard son—has been up to the past four years."

Standing, he ran his hands angrily through his short hair. "Read it, and then judge."

"I know enough to know I hate you. You ruined my life."

He froze, energy whipping around him. "Did I, Cleo Price? Are you sure it was me who ruined you?"

Panic drenched my system. I scrambled onto my knees. "It was you who wrote the letter. You tracked me down and brought me back. For what? What do you have to gain?"

He chuckled. "Ah, patience, little princess. You'll find out what my plan is for you soon enough." Cocking his head, his eyes dropped to my bare legs. All I wore was Arthur's T-shirt, still warm from sleeping in his arms, still saturated with his scent.

Tears sprang painfully at the thought of him beaten and bleeding.

I wanted to beg Rubix to let me go—so I could make sure he was still alive.

"How did you find me?" I whispered.

Pride and black smugness filled his face. "I tracked down the FBI detective who was dealing with your case—a Mr. Davidson, I believe. He was rather tight-lipped about a burn victim who'd been amnesiac, but I got him to talk eventually."

Chills hurt worse than any fire in my chest.

The sweet man who'd given me a second chance had been hurt or killed trying to protect my identity. All this time I thought no one wanted me—only to find out I'd been hunted by the one man intent on destroying me.

"How could you? How could you laugh and love my parents and then turn around and murder them?"

A horrible smile twisted his lips. "Like I said… don't be so sure it was me who stole your precious family, Cleo." Pointing at the file, he moved toward the door. "Read it and find out."

He slammed the exit behind him. The sound of a lock twisting dispelled any hope of escape.

My head hurt, panic drenched my bloodstream at the thought of Arthur's condition, and claustrophobia itched like a terrible enemy.

Forcing myself to keep my breathing low and even, I looked at the file.

Intolerable curiosity grew in my heart. Answers. *Finally.* Answers sat within reaching distance… black and white… truth.

But is it the truth?

I'd been around Arthur enough to know his need for vengeance rested on a betrayal of huge magnifications. He wouldn't want to kill his own flesh and blood, unless they made him do something dreadful.

Something as dreadful as murder?

I sat twining and untwining my fingers.

Courage failed me as the file seemed to grow in size, throbbing with temptation. If I read it, there would be no removing the knowledge. If I read it and it destroyed me, there would be no way to piece myself back together.

Suddenly, I wanted Corrine. I wanted her easy, breezy nature, her eternal optimism and bounce. I'd been fumbling in the dark for so long I craved *light*. I craved normalcy.

None of this is normal.

Why had Rubix stolen me?

What did he have to gain after all this time? Unless... unless there was something in my mind that he wanted? Something I'd forgotten... or deliberately deleted because my brain couldn't handle it?

The mood ring Arthur had given me swirled around my sweat-dampened digits. My stomach rolled at the way I'd left him.

Please, be okay.

Tears swarmed at the thought of him waking up alone. How would he survive me being taken?

He'll come for me.

I knew that without a shred of doubt. The only horror was—what if they killed him?

I couldn't think about that.

My eyes fell begrudgingly on the file.

Answers.

Truth.

All whispering sweet nothings in my ear to read. *Read!*

Leaning forward, I grabbed it. My hands wouldn't stop quaking as I opened the folder. A gust of terror disappeared down my spine at the first document.

Completed Testimony for Scott Killian
Witnessed and Lodged by Officer Clark

Notes: this is a true statement gathered and witnessed of the events that occurred on the night in question involving the murder of Paul, Sandra, and Cleo Price along with the destruction of their household.

Transcribed and authenticated as part of trial material for triple homicide by Arthur Killian.

Please note, this testimony was used as Evidence A in the case of State versus Killian.

Witness Testimony:

Officer: Please describe the night in question.

Scott Killian: I'd just come home from dealing with business outside our normal trading hours. My oldest son, Dax, needed some help, which called me away. I look back now and think I should've done something. I should've known. Arthur had been acting strange for weeks. He'd always been ambitious, believing he was smarter than everyone else. Flashing his grades in my older son's face as if to say he was better than us. He had aspirations. That's why he spent so much time with the president's daughter, Cleo.

Officer: Your son and the deceased were in a relationship?

Scott Killian: Yes, he made that poor girl fall in love with him when she was barely out of diapers. I watched from the sidelines, believing that Paul would put an end to the obvious issue that was going on. But he never did.

Officer: What issue?

Scott Killian: Control. Arthur was only sleeping with the daughter to gain complete control. He was using her.

Officer: What brings you to believe that?

Scott Killian: A couple of weeks ago he came to me with a plan. A plan to get rid of the president so he could take over. He believed having the president's daughter, and being the son of the VP, would ensure he could take over seamlessly. Of course, I told him no. I beat that kid up for ever thinking such a thing. I know now I should've done more, but at the time I believed I'd disciplined him enough to put such a sinful idea out of his head.

Their death is on me, because I didn't know my son's true capabilities. I raised a monster. I raised a killer, and for that I will always be sorry.

Officer: Please, continue about the night of the murder.

Scott Killian: Sure. That night, like I said, I was out. But I returned just in time to see Arthur leaving our house and crossing the compound to theirs. He disappeared inside. I don't know what made me follow him—perhaps I didn't want him sleeping with Cleo anymore, or perhaps I still didn't trust him after his admission of his plans. Regardless, I followed him.

Officer: And what happened when you followed?

Scott Killian: I followed him deeper into the house. I stayed hidden as he pulled out a silenced pistol and stood over the sleeping forms of my best friend and his wife. I watched as he raised his arm and first shot Paul in the forehead and then shot Sandra. He shot people who were almost family to him in cold blood.

Officer: Then what happened?

Scott Killian: He left, but then returned with gasoline, which he poured over their corpses. I exited the house, heading past Cleo's bedroom to see if I could save her. She was lying facedown on the carpet. He probably killed her while I was out with Dax. Not wanting to touch evidence, I left quietly.

Officer: Then what happened?

Scott Killian: My son set fire to their house, probably to try and conceal what he'd done. The moment flames erupted, I called the police and the fire department.

Officer: And you're willing to repeat what you just said in a court of law? Everything you've just told me is the truth and nothing but the truth?

Scott Killian: Oh yes. Nothing but the truth. My son is a murderer and deserves the worst sentencing imaginable. I can prove it was premeditated and will stand by my testimony to honor my friend's memory. My son must pay for what he's done.

Tears streamed down my face.

Lies.

Heinous, *horrible* lies.

Arthur never slept with me out of respect. He managed to control himself, knowing that we were too young, even when we wanted to be together more than anything.

Arthur never disrespected anyone. He was a *good* person.

An *amazing* person.

This traitorous statement sent Arthur to prison for triple homicide. It slandered him as a cutthroat beast who had no soul and could shoot people who'd patched up his bruises delivered at the hands of his father. Arthur adored my mother. So many nights he'd come around, lip bleeding from discipline and shoulders slumped from unhappiness. My mother would hug him, kiss him—she loved him like a son.

He would never be able to hurt them.

Ever.

Arthur wasn't using me. He wasn't planning to murder my parents.

Was he?

I clutched my hair, tearing it at the roots, refusing to let such evil seep into my thoughts. I knew the boy who held my heart. I knew his dreams and aspirations, and I knew how tender and loving he was.

He would never kill those he cared for. Never!

As I rocked on the bed, swallowing back sobs and terror, something twitched inside my mind.

A gentle clinking as a chain loosened around the fissured wall, falling away like dead vines.

Keys suddenly fit into locks, and the wall—the horrible, frustrating, crippling wall that I'd lived with for eight long years—began to crumble.

Brick by brick. Mortar by mortar. It collapsed into a pile of earthquake-reduced rubble.

Then the pain and fogginess of being drugged intensified as every memory that had battered for freedom suddenly rushed forward unhindered.

Shards of thoughts.

Splinters of recollections.

They all flew into being, crushing me beneath the weight of knowing.

My mind!

Everything was there.

Every file in its perfect place.

Every thought where it should be.

A perfect Rolodex of childhood happiness, teenage trials, and then...

No.

Two weeks after my fourteenth birthday. The night of my parent's murder.

No. No. No.

Please no!

My hand slapped over my mouth.

My mind snapped and the wall that'd only just crumbled was suddenly reerected, blocking out the quick glimpse I'd seen.

My thoughts scrambled, wiping any evidence free from my mind. A perfect eraser for a broken brain.

That was what my amnesia was protecting me from.

The truth about what happened that night. The truth I wasn't strong enough to face.

I knew now why Arthur thought I would run when I remembered. I understood why he was petrified to tell me.

But he had it wrong.

So wrong.

I didn't hate him—I could *never* hate him.

But I *could* hate the ones who were there that night—the ones who shattered not just my world but the boy I loved to the point of no redemption.

That night was heinous. Drenched in blood, deceit, and terror.

Arthur. God—

What they did to him... It was vile.

My heart spasmed, blocking out the rest like heavy smog.

The lies made more sense than the truth, but I knew which one to believe.

The reality wasn't clear-cut or simple. It was twisted and hid so many sins.

And my mind didn't want me to remember.

It protected me for one reason alone.

One vital self-preserving reason.

The truth had the power to kill me.

The truth was despicable.

To Be Continued...

I <3 U

About the Author

Pepper Winters is a *New York Times* and *USA Today* international best-seller. She loves dark romance, star-crossed lovers, as well as the forbidden and taboo. She strives to write stories that make readers crave what they shouldn't, and delivers complex plots and unforgettable characters that keep readers talking long after the last page is turned.

On a personal note, she loves to travel, has an addiction to crème brûlée, and is married to an incredible Canadian who puts up with her endless work hours and accompanies her on signings. She's also a firm believer that the impossible can become possible.

Playlist

Hoobastank, "The Reason"
Pink, "Try"
Bush, "Glycerine"
Rihanna featuring Mikky Ekko, "Stay"
Christina Perri, "The Lonely"
Muse, "I Belong to You"
Clean Bandit, "Rather Be"
Evanescence, "Bring Me to Life"
Florence and the Machine, "Cosmic"
Cary Brothers, "Ride"
White Stripes, "Fight for My Love"
Meg Meyer, "Adelaide"
Five Seconds of Summer, "Amnesia"
Anastasia, "Journey to the Past"
Borgeous, "Wildfire"

Their journey of forbidden pleasures continues...

Please see the next page for a preview of

Sin & Suffer.

Kill

I'M A STALKER.

Shit, I even researched the definition to see if it was true. But it was. I willfully followed, watched, and coveted Cleo Price. There. I admit it. I was in love with a child. I had dirty thoughts about a girl who didn't even have boobs yet. But that didn't stop me. Shit, it made me worse. Because not only was I a stalker, but I was an addict, too. An addict for any glimpse of her, any sound of her voice, any hope that I could ever possibly deserve her.

—Arthur, aged fourteen

"WHAT THE FUCK?"

I tried to sit upright, glaring at Grasshopper and Mo. "Let me up, you assholes!"

The room refused to stay still. The edges of my vision were fuzzy and the god-awful pounding in my skull wouldn't give me a fucking break.

"What the hell do you think you're doing?" My breathing was broken and short, my eyes burning with light from the diabolical fluorescents above.

Where the fuck am I?

Where's Cleo?

Rage battered away my pain, granting me temporary power. I shoved aside arms holding me down and swung at the faces of my captors.

My knuckles met flesh.

A bellow sounded in the square, white room. "Christ, man!"

The incessant beeping sliced through my eardrums, turning my headache into a brass fucking band of horror.

I'd never been one to panic but I couldn't control the overwhelming sensation that something awful had happened.

Something I needed to fix straightaway.

The door suddenly swung open.

I paused just long enough to take in the balding man with a stethoscope around his neck and baby-blue scrubs, before struggling with renewed determination. "Damn bastards. Let me up!"

The doctor inched warily into the room. "What on earth is going on in here?"

"He's just woken up, Doc," Hopper said, trying to grab my shoulders but unwilling to risk another fist to his jaw. "Ain't got his bearings yet."

"I've got my fucking bearings, asshole. Let me up!"

"You gotta do something, before he makes it worse," Mo growled. His lip was bleeding; his nostrils flared in pain.

Did I do that?

The headache turned feral, crumpling me in its agony as if I were nothing more than a sardine can. Clutching my skull—finding bandages instead of hair—I bellowed, "What the fuck is going on? Someone tell me before my brain explodes out of my goddamn ears!"

My heartbeat clanged to one name. A single name siphoning through my blood over and over again.

Cl…eo.

Cl…eo.

"You're in the hospital, Mr. Killian. I need you to relax." The doctor used his calm-the-unhinged-patient voice as he crept closer. Grabbing the chart from the foot of the bed and scooting backward as if he would get bitten or infected by being too close to me, he flipped the pages and scanned the notes.

I couldn't breathe properly.

I couldn't see with my peripheral, and that damn fucking beeping was getting on my nerves.

"Someone shut that thing up!"

Grasshopper ignored me, coming to the side of the bed and bravely laying a hand on my chest. "Kill, you have a serious concussion. Doctors said if you move too much before the swelling goes down, you might do some serious damage."

My headache came back with a ten-ton pressure.

"Concussion? How the fuck did I get a concussion?" My eyes flew around the room.

I wasn't in my bedroom, that was for fucking sure. White morbid walls looked like a bleached coffin, while an outdated television hung like a spider just waiting for death. The entire place reeked of antiseptic and corpses.

Hospital.

I'm in a fucking hospital.

Clutching my head, I tried to gather my temper and relax. Screaming only drove pins of agony through my eyeballs and terrified answers away. "Speak. Tell me."

Mo looked at Hopper, unsuccessfully hiding the nervousness in his eyes. They waited for me to explode again. When I didn't, Mo admitted, "Eh, you were struck in the head."

My headache tripled its efforts to turn me into a vegetable almost as if on cue.

Then . . . everything came back.

Finding Cleo after all this time.

Loving Cleo after all this time.

Holding Cleo after all this fucking time.

She's not dead.

She was never dead, just missing.

They took her!

I soared out of bed. The wires, the sheets—nothing had any power to hold me in my wrath. "Where is she!?" Shoving aside Grasshopper with superhuman strength, I swallowed hard as the room spun like a funhouse. "They have her! Goddammit, they have her."

Grasshopper, Mo, and the doctor sprang on me, each grabbing an arm or a leg. I grunted, buckling beneath their weight. In ordinary circumstances, I would've let them win. I would've been rational and collected and listened to what they had to say.

But this wasn't ordinary circumstances.

This was motherfucking war!

My father and brother had broken into my house, got past security, and taken the only thing of value I had left.

They'd stolen her from me all over again.

"Shit!" I screamed. "Shit, shit, shit!"

"Kill, calm down!"

"Let us explain!"

"Get the fuck off me." No amount of arms could hold me down. Adrenaline tore through my blood, giving me a merciless edge. My vision might be faulty, my head might be broken, but I still knew how to fight.

They weren't listening to my voice. Perhaps they would listen to my fist.

With no effort at all, I punched the three men in a connecting roundhouse, and tore at the IV in the back of my hand.

I yanked it out, blood spurting over the white sheets and linoleum floor.

The stark crimson spread macabre patterns, whispering of murder and revenge. "Someone better start talking." I breathed hard. "Now. Right fucking now."

Mo and Hopper stared, transfixed, at my bleeding vein. "We should patch you up, dude."

Waving my hand, splattering the bed with more red droplets, I snarled, "Leave it. It's not important. I don't even feel it." Strangely, that was the truth. There was nothing worth feeling now that I knew they'd taken Cleo. That agony was enough to drown me. Over and fucking over again.

I groaned under my breath as scenarios and horror-filled daydreams tormented me.

Please, please, let her be okay!

My eyes flickered to the door. All I wanted to do was leave. To chase after my rotten enemies and give them what they deserved.

Suddenly, nausea raced up my gullet. I stumbled to the side. Crashing against the bed, I gritted my teeth against the swirling room.

The doctor sidestepped, avoiding me as best he could. "If you could sit down, Mr. Killian."

"Do what he says, Kill. Just behave for once in your damn life," Grasshopper growled. "Let us explain before you kill yourself, you bloody asshole!"

A wave of brutal heat tackled me to the bed. The nausea turned to sickness. My teeth chattered as the agony in my blood came back full force. Having no choice but to lean against the bed like a fucking invalid, I muttered, "Why the hell aren't you out there looking for her? She's your responsibility, too!" The light stabbed my eyeballs as I stared at my trusted friend and vice president.

Grasshopper's black mohawk hung limp, floppy without gel. His blue eyes ringed with stress lines and bruises. He swallowed hard, refusing to answer my question.

"Well?" I prompted, holding my pounding skull. "What the fuck have you been doing to get her back?"

"Kill, back up," Mo said, inching forward, wiping at the blood on his chin with the back of his hand.

Hopper never took his eyes off me. "We had to make sure you would survive. Been for a ride in an ambulance, helped dress your naked ass into a hospital gown, and stood by you while you were given scans and all that other medical bullshit to make sure you didn't croak."

Pointing at my bandaged head, he added, "You were out of it. Talking nonsense, wouldn't wake up. The doctors thought the swelling might affect your speech. What were we supposed to do? Strap you to your bike and drag you with us to kill your own flesh and blood?"

My fists clenched. Blood dripped from my torn vein, splashing faster to the floor.

I couldn't contemplate that the two brothers I trusted above anyone had let my woman get taken. And not just taken—but they hadn't gone after her the second she was stolen.

It's not their fault.

She's yours, asshole.

This is all on you.

"Fuck!" I groaned, tearing at the bandage around my head, trying to reach inside and turn off the incessant throbbing. Why was I so weak? I'd failed her *again*!

The room swam; my eyes worked like a faulty camera lens unable to focus. "You know what she means to me. You know how damn important she is." Glaring at Grasshopper, I couldn't bring myself to be grateful for his loyalty or attempts at keeping me alive. I didn't *want* to be alive if Cleo was hurt.

I deserved to rot in hell for letting her be taken again.

"We did what—"

I slashed my hand, cutting off his sentence. "No, you did what *you* wanted to do. Not what I would've done. You know damn well I would've gone after your woman—regardless if you lived or fucking died." Punching myself in the chest, I growled, "*That's* what I wanted."

"Kill, what were we supposed to do?" Hopper snapped. "We'd go to war for a girl who would hate us if she knew we did nothing while you bled to death. No point in that fight. No one wins."

I couldn't see his logic. It was flawed. Ridiculous. Cleo would understand if I died while my men rescued her. She would expect such a gallant act.

At least she would be safe.

I didn't want to listen to fucking reason.

I want blood!

I didn't care that my ass was hanging out the back of this paisley-printed apron. I didn't care blood dripped from my hand, staining my bare feet and the floor. And I definitely didn't care about the vicelike agony in my skull.

All I cared about was Cleo.

The nausea faded and I charged myself at Hopper. In a jumble of leather and hospital gown, I pinned him against the door, threading my fingers around his throat.

"Mr. Killian, unhand him!" The doctor shouted, swatting the back of my shoulders with the clipboard.

I ignored him like a lion would ignore a flea. He was nothing.

However, the rush of energy, coupled with moving reluctant legs, made me squeeze Hopper's throat more out of support rather than rage. My vision blacked out. I blinked, trying to see. "How long? How long was I out?"

Mo slapped a warning hand on my arm, tugging me away from Hopper. "Let him go, then we'll tell you."

My brain didn't feel right. The sequences of numbers I relied on all my life, the ingrained knowledge and intelligence I'd taken for granted was muted…*faded.* Missing beneath a storm of pain and swelling. My temper was fucking insane.

Grasshopper didn't try to remove my hand. Instead, he stood taller, his breathing as calm as he could with me slowly suffocating him.

"Two days."

My world fell away.

I stood on the brink of suicidal mayhem.

Don't snap. Do. Not. Snap.

My headache consumed me until I felt sure I would explode into bloody particles and consume the entire world with my fury.

Letting him go, I staggered backward. "Two days?"

Two fucking days when my father could've done anything to her.

Hopper shrank before my eyes. "Rubix took her about fifty hours ago."

I shook. Fuck, I shook.

"Fifty hours?" I couldn't do anything but repeat him. It was all I could do to force English through my lips and not revert to primitive grunts and growls.

I wasn't human. I was an animal. An animal drooling at the thought of tearing my enemies limb from limb for what they'd done.

"Why was I out for so long?"

Mo answered, "They hit you a few times over the head with a baseball bat. The scans showed—"

"The PET, MRI, and CT scans all came back conclusive," the doctor jumped in.

I'd completely forgotten he was still there.

"You have a hairline fracture in your skull and heavy swelling on the prefrontal cortex."

I turned my attention to the man severely pissing me off. I didn't want to hear what happened to me. Didn't he get it? None of that fucking mattered!

"We kept you in an induced coma for thirty-six hours, hoping the swelling would recede to acceptable levels."

"You. Did. What?" My heartbeat exploded. "You kept me fucking drugged when my woman is out there with men who won't hesitate to rape, maim, and murder her?"

I couldn't fucking believe this shit.

"You need to get back into bed, Mr. Killian. The swelling hasn't decreased as much as I'd hoped. Your rage is associated with your injury. The prefrontal cortex is in charge of abstract thinking and thought analysis. It's also responsible for regulating behavior. I don't believe—"

I laughed. "The bump on my fucking head isn't pissing me off. My woman is *missing*."

Mo placed himself in front of the doctor. "Kill, this is serious. If you don't let yourself heal, you might suffer long-term affects."

"Yes, like . . . eh . . ." The doctor scrambled. "Your normal reactions and moral judgments might be impaired. Choices between right and wrong could be compromised. You won't be as quick to predict probable outcomes. The prefrontal cortex governs social, emotional, and sexual urges."

"I don't fucking care!" I roared. "All I care about is getting her safe. Healing can come later."

"But you might not heal correctly if you damage yourself further!" The doctor yelled, finally finding some balls. "I refuse to sign you out until you are well. You're my patient. Your recovery is on my conscience!"

Putting one bare foot in front of the other, I shoved aside Mo and towered over the doctor. "Listen to me, and listen good. I was and no longer am your patient. I can take care of my fucking self and if that means I damage myself in order to save her, then so be it." Bending so our eyes were level, I glowered into his mousy brown ones. "Get it?"

He swallowed. "Fine. I'll sign you out. But don't come back to me when you're a damn vegetable." In a flurry of blue scrubs, he dumped the clipboard on my abandoned bed and shot out of the room.

"Kill, you really should stay. Everything relies on you and that genius brain of yours. How will you run the Club, the trades—shit, the whole fucking operation, if you can't—"

I snarled, "Shut it, Hopper. This is the way it has to be. I won't waste another moment arguing when Dagger Rose has my woman."

Mo sighed. "Despite what you think of us, we did send a couple of men to the compound to spy and report back. They say they've seen her. She's alive and unharmed, Kill. You could afford to heal and let us take care of this."

That didn't make me calm down. If anything, it made me worse.

I couldn't speak. I only glared. It was enough for Mo to shut his hole and nod.

My father had Cleo.

The same fucking father who'd orchestrated two murders, sent me to life imprisonment, and left my lover to burn.

I'll fucking kill him.

Screw my plans. Screw vengeance. I wanted his soul. And I wanted it *now.*

The heart monitor squealed as my pulse skyrocketed with another dose of adrenaline. Reaching down the front of my nightdress, I ripped off the sticky sensors and threw them on the floor. "Call reinforcements. The entire crew. We're going after her."